CRITICAL INSIGHTS

Neil Gaiman

CRITICAL INSIGHTS

Neil Gaiman

Editor
Joseph Michael Sommers
Central Michigan University

PR
6057
.A319
Z76
2016

SALEM PRESS
A Division of EBSCO Information Services, Inc.
Ipswich, Massachusetts

GREY HOUSE PUBLISHING

Copyright © 2016 by Grey House Publishing, Inc.

All rights reserved. No part of this work may be used or reproduced in any manner whatsoever or transmitted in any form or by any means, electronic or mechanical, including photocopy, recording, or any information storage and retrieval system, without written permission from the copyright owner. For information, contact Grey House Publishing/Salem Press, 4919 Route 22, PO Box 56, Amenia, NY 12501.

∞ The paper used in these volumes conforms to the American National Standard for Permanence of Paper for Printed Library Materials, Z39.48 1992 (R2009).

Publisher's Cataloging-In-Publication Data
(Prepared by The Donohue Group, Inc.)

Names: Sommers, Joseph Michael, 1976- editor.
Title: Neil Gaiman / editor, Joseph Michael Sommers, Central Michigan University.
Other Titles: Critical insights.
Description: [First edition]. | Ipswich, Massachusetts : Salem Press, a division of EBSCO Information Services, Inc. ; Amenia, NY : Grey House Publishing, [2016] | Includes bibliographical references and index.
Identifiers: ISBN 978-1-68217-260-5 (hardcover)
Subjects: LCSH: Gaiman, Neil--Criticism and interpretation. | English fiction--20th century--History and criticism. | English fiction--21st century--History and criticism.
Classification: LCC PR6057.A319 Z86 2016 | DDC 823/.914--dc23

First Printing

PRINTED IN THE UNITED STATES OF AMERICA

Contents

About This Volume, Joseph Michael Sommers	vii
On Matters of Dreaming, World Building, and Finding Neil Gaiman's Magic, Joseph Michael Sommers	xiv
Biographical Sketch of Neil Gaiman, Justin Wigard	xxix

Critical Contexts

"We have an obligation to imagine": A Critical Reception of the Work of Neil Gaiman, Kyle Eveleth and Justin Wigard	3
Embodied in Name Alone: Nobody Owens and the Metonymic Estrangement from the Living and the Dead in Neil Gaiman's *The Graveyard Book*, Joseph Michael Sommers	17
In the Shadow of Balder: Breaking the Cycle of Ragnarok in *American Gods*, Kristin Bovaird-Abbo	31
Opening the Door, Crossing the Wall: (Re) Mediation and Women's Roles in Neil Gaiman's *Neverwhere* and *Stardust*, Julie Perino	47

Critical Readings

Guilty Pleasures: Neil Gaiman's Books for Children for Adults, Annette Wannamaker	67
Reimagining the Cautionary Tale: Collage in Neil Gaiman and Dave McKean's *The Wolves in the Walls*, Krystal Howard	81
"What is She?": Neil Gaiman's Intertextual Conversation on Female Artistry in *Coraline* and *The Ocean at the End of the Lane*, Marlyn Thomas	96
"Of viewpoints, of images, of memories and puns and lost hopes": Polyphony and Narrative Braiding in *The Sandman: Worlds' End*, Kyle Eveleth	112
Going Postmodern Gothic: Neil Gaiman's Feminist Fairy Tales, Jill Coste	129
"Everybody's Here": Radical Reflexivity in the Metafiction of *The Sandman*, Orion Ussner Kidder	146

The Apocalypse and Other Silly Bits: *Good Omens*, Collaboration, and
   Authorial One-Upmanship, Laura Nicosia   161

Spoilers, Sweetie—a Madman and His Monsters: Neil Gaiman's
   "The Doctor's Wife," Kelly J. Murphy   178

Crafting Advocacy through Intimacy and Empathy: A Rhetorical
   Analysis of The Reading Agency Lecture, Kristin McIlhagga   195

Resources

Chronology of Neil Gaiman's Life	213
Works by Neil Gaiman	219
Bibliography	227
About the Editor	233
Contributors	235
Index	239

About this Volume

Joseph Michael Sommers

The essays contained within this volume constitute an interesting mélange of thoughts, ruminations, perspectives, and approaches that are as diverse a look at the life and work of Neil Gaiman as any in print today, to my mind at least. The contributors and I are quite proud of that. The chapters do not radiate from any central thesis, chronology (though one is presented in the Resources section of this book), or even thematic progression nearly as much as they make a vain attempt to explore as many facets of the author and the first thirty years of his career from as many different avenues as one could fit between two covers. We start as near as possible to the beginning of his career in short stories, comics, and journalism and examine works as recent as 2016's *The View from the Cheap Seats* while we await his next volume *Norse Mythology* and the televised adaptation of *American Gods*, both slated to appear in 2017. Some subjects, like Gaiman's seminal work on *The Sandman* receive greater coverage; winning over twenty-six Eisner awards garners that sort of attention. Other topics received less.

I could cajole no one to cover Gaiman's foray into the autobiographical history of *Duran Duran* no matter how hard I tried. Perhaps, next time.

So, at best and certainly at first, consider the volume before you as the lot of us making a start, to paraphrase the great American poet William Carlos William's *Patterson*, out of particulars and making them general . . . rolling up the sum by the defective means of what one book can encapsulate of one of the most prolific writers of the late-twentieth and twenty-first century. Certainly, within these fourteen essays, introduction, biographical sketch, chronology, author's bibliography, and academic bibliography, the reader will find a great many discussions and questions—so, so many questions. One of the first questions actually ponders what a Neil Gaiman is: Is he a writer of comics that elevated the discourse of the field by reinventing it through his love of the literary masters? Is he an author of fantasy and speculative fiction, or do his narratives simply chronicle reality in all its infinites so well that they heighten the reader's imaginative acuity to the extent that she (Because in this example, the reader is a young lady. Later, she'll be something else.) can see past the realities normally taken for granted into the surreal and fantastic things underpinning it, holding its shuddering entropy together like a bobby pinned shirt or a fraying hem? Does he seek to be inspirational or is that simply a matter of consequence when one gladly throws open the library's doors welcoming all the world to have access to all the possibilities contained within—to reinvent tomorrow by knowing just a bit more about yesterday or today? Does he really think that making good art can change the world or is that just the sort of subtle irony that makes Neil Gaiman such a delightful character in his own story? Who knows.

Any answers that we proffer here are meant to provoke further questions. Gaiman is an author unbridled by the shackles of boundaries. The four-year-old who once sat in a West Sussex library surrounded by the works of C. S. Lewis and J. R. R. Tolkien let those writers suffuse his burgeoning art in a manner of world-building that could only happen at this point in history right now. This volume will discuss those libraries. It will discuss manifold mythologies. It will interrogate that great American mythology of the comic book (written by a man who was born British and moved to America). It will somehow find its way into social media as, even in an unfinalizable universe, the Internet still remains that great swirling vortex into which everyone eventually is sucked. It will compel the reader to learn how to do close literary analysis from a variety of perspectives. It will even ask you to watch some television. And, with any luck, it will inspire the reader to pick up a book—possibly a comic, maybe an audio book, or just make a visit to Gaiman's blog, Twitter page, or whatever new Internet portal he will have opened up to communicate with his reading base between the time I write this and the day this book finds its way into your local library.

Certain things will have to be touched on and discovered by the next Gaiman scholar; it might be you. I hope it is. Music is as omnipresent a force in the Gaiman's life as anything, and a chapter detailing his work with song and songwriters, such as Tori Amos and his wife Amanda Palmer, would have been a very fine thing indeed. Likewise, for as many interviews as the man has given, he took even more of them in the earliest parts of his career—Neil Gaiman: the journalist who honed the tip of his quill for myriad British newspapers and publications. (I'd prefer that to be a metaphor involving a typewriter, but, to be honest, I don't know much about typewriter maintenance.) And while we discuss Gaiman's advocacy, we don't cover his omnipresence in the new media of the twenty-first century. If there's any discussion I wish we had made more time and space for, that would be the one, as I'm not sure I can recall a single other author who takes more time out of their day (For the record, that's a singular they; to write Gaiman is to acknowledge his work and concerns with gender and gender construction. We did get that chapter.) to interact with his fans online and commune with them. Gaiman shows the power that words have by using them so often and so eloquently. In many ways, his is the story of a human being trying his best to help write a future for the human race one letter, one word, one tweet, one poem, one interview, one comic, one episode of *Doctor Who*, one library pulled from the brink of closure, and one hand turning the page of something that child might like to read if only an adult would help him at a time. So, if the guiding question to this book is "Why Neil Gaiman?" Our answer is simply because it's time, and we *did* have some space.

Hopefully, I have started this conversation off on the right note, albeit a minor one. This preface, however, is merely the prelude to the introduction, in which I consider Gaiman from many of the myriad possibilities he could be considered. He has been called by critics as "one of the most important fantasists of contemporary literature" (qtd. in Krstovic, 2), and I see little reason, nor could find manor, to argue. In fact, the introduction will go to great lengths not to place Gaiman so much as to try and catalogue him, not unlike a zoologist, in his many forms and evolutions. Gaiman is not simply an author of comics and novels, or an author for adults or children, or a video game writer, or a playwright, lecturer, social advocate, husband, father, fan, etc.—he's all of these things and more. He seems to possess no end brackets and, somehow, he teaches his readers how to embrace love, fear, pain, pride, and most of the rest of the emotional spectrum with an earnest vigor, gentle humor, and honest warmth, the likes of which humble the greats in all media to which he has contributed. Unexpectedly enough, the introduction begins in Orlando, Florida, a sentence that I am pretty sure has never before been written in the annals of writing.

From this point, we shall present the Critical Contexts, from which the book shall try and view Gaiman and his work. Justin Wigard starts us off with a short biographical sketch of Gaiman that reads quite well with the Chronology of the Author's Life and the (selected, yet rather compendious) Bibliography of the Author that the reader can also find in the Resources section of this book. Likewise, pairing well with the biography is the "Critical Reception: The Major Works of Neil Gaiman" co-authored by Wigard and Kyle Eveleth. Here, the two attempt as best as possible to contextualize the academic and popular perceptions of his work in its many and multitudinous forms. In many capacities, if the first essay is a biographical sketch of the author, this chapter serves as biography or annotated bibliography of his work. I am pleased to be the author of the Critical Lens chapter in this tool kit of perception; my chapter, "Embodied in Name Alone: Nobody Owens and the Metonymic Estrangement from the Living and the Dead in Neil Gaiman's *The Graveyard Book*," approaches *The Graveyard Book*, itself an analogue of Rudyard Kipling's *The Jungle Book* from the psychoanalytic perspective of Jacques Lacan, a name one will find repeated with some frequency in this volume. That psychoanalysis and psychoanalytic readings factor into the reception of work by a man who spent a great deal of his career writing about dreams and dreaming should likely come as little surprise to anyone. Kristin Bovaird-Abbo continues that investigation in a chapter devoted to Cultural Context: that of the Norse (and United States for that matter) in her chapter, "In the Shadow of Balder: Breaking the Cycle of Ragnarok in *American Gods.*" In it, she investigates Gaiman's curious appropriation of the Norse god Balder, as opposed to, say, Thor, in *American Gods* and pins that particular appropriation on a very opportunistic moment of good old-fashioned American luck (by way of a leprechaun). Finally, Julie Perino supplies "Opening the Door, Crossing the Wall: (Re) Mediation and Women's Roles in Neil Gaiman's *Neverwhere* and *Stardust*" as our Comparative Analysis chapter; here, looking at the unusual circumstances of novelization and remediation in the adaptive process of turning Gaiman's books into films and, in the case of *Neverwhere*, vice versa. In it, she focuses on women's roles in these works as they figure so prominently in Gaiman's corpus of work across all media, yet changing that media can bring about different manners of portrayal regardless.

Moving away from our Critical Context essays into the Critical Readings section of this book, we begin by muddying the waters and asking hard questions. "Guilty Pleasures: Neil Gaiman's Books for Children for Adults" by Annette Wannamaker, brings about an interrogation of Gaiman by way of his audience—this writer of works that would be shelved, typically, along the lines of children's works, young adult works, and adult works, would likely prefer them all to simply sit together, with no discrepancy made regarding age range. With no borders between content or filters to guide the reader, what sort of problems arise, if any, and what boons are to be had by considering fiction merely as fiction with no prerequisites for age or audience? Following up on that topic, Krystal Howard, attacks those questions head-on by examining a very traditionally held children's book in "Reimagining the Cautionary Tale: Collage in Neil Gaiman and Dave McKean's *The Wolves in the Walls.*" In it, she explains how visual and verbal collage make difficult and complex subject matter accessible to children through Gaiman and McKean's collaboration; in effect, the duo approaches the problem of complicated subject matter through a construction of accessibility for the intended audience and elevating the discourse for children. Marlyn Thomas takes the discussion a step further by juxtaposing a traditionally seen young adult narrative with an 'adult' narrative and show how they speak to very similar ends and in very similar ways in "'What is She?': Neil Gaiman's Intertextual Conversation on Female Artistry in *Coraline* and *The Ocean at the End of the Lane*." Here, she uses Virginia Woolf's *A Room Of One's Own* as a through-line for reading between the age range of the two texts in an analysis of the women contained within both.

The next several chapters take great aim at examining Gaiman's more traditionally seen graphic novels. Eveleth's "'Of viewpoints, of images, of memories and puns and lost hopes': Polyphony and Narrative Braiding in *The Sandman: Worlds' End*," as the name suggests, investigates the "fable," as he calls it, of Gaiman's *Sandman,* as an interweaving series of stories attempting to both construct and unravel meaning as means to a greater end than any kind of stable answer. Jill Coste radiates from that idea to look at Gaiman's fables, *in general, in* "Going Postmodern Gothic: Neil Gaiman's Feminist Fairy Tales." As the title of that chapter suggests, Coste approaches Gaiman's work in his fairy tale revisions and finds the gothic influences he inserts to elevate the tales by feminist markers. Orion Ussner Kidder returns us, once again, to *The Sandman* to read it, in many ways, as counterpoint to Eveleth's chapter with "'Everybody's Here': Radical Reflexivity in the Metafiction of *The Sandman*." In it, Kidder views the ongoing serialized nature of *The Sandman* as part and parcel to its ability to operate as self-reflexive metafiction: fiction that can comment upon itself as it is read. Whereby, Eveleth finds the comic as a series of widening and collapsing gyres, Kidder views it more as active thought problem in conversation with itself.

The final chapters of this volume all have exactly one thing in common: collaboration. Laura Nicosia explores the brilliant friendship of Gaiman and Terry Pratchett and the book that became of it in "The Apocalypse and Other Silly Bits: *Good Omens*, Collaboration, and Authorial One-Upmanship." In it, Nicosia discovers that the genius behind one of the great comedies written in contemporary times has less to do with the idea that two authors can craft a superior piece of humor by trying to make each other laugh but that the author was actually "one two-headed person" to begin with. Speaking of such alien creatures, Kelly Murphy visits Gallifrey by way of *Doctor Who* in "'Spoilers, Sweetie'—a Madman and His Monsters: Neil Gaiman's 'The Doctor's Wife.'" Here, Murphy examines any number of collaborations: The Doctor and his companions, the writer and his work being turned into a television drama, and the marriage of the most human of aliens with the most monstrous in order to offer commentary to the audience. Finally, a close reading of one of Gaiman's more famous lectures in "Crafting Advocacy through Intimacy and Empathy: A Rhetorical Analysis of The Reading Agency Lecture," by Kristin McIlhagga, will offer the reader the opportunity to see not only what Gaiman advocates for in his work but understand the rhetorical principles behind his efforts. In the chapter, McIlhagga shows Gaiman once again widening and closing lenses in an effort to blend the personal with the public, his eyes towards the political; here, his target is in advocacy of literacy and libraries—two causes about which he could not be more passionate as he considers the past, the present, and the future that he hopes he and his readers can build together.

Works Cited

Kristovic, Jelena. "Introduction." *Children's Literature Review*. 207 (2016) 1-3. Print.

On Matters of Dreaming, World Building, and Finding Neil Gaiman's Magic

Joseph Michael Sommers

To begin, and if the reader might indulge me: a series of anecdotes, pastiches really, that form part of the mosaic by which *Critical Insights: Neil Gaiman* came to be even before such a collection was ever a thought in my head.

* * *

When I was a young man, certainly well-before I could, in any way, claim to call myself a 'man,' but certainly young, I crafted an idea for a comic book. It concerned a young boy, not too remarkably unlike myself (as young boys, in my experience, rarely possess the foresight to think too very far outside of the self), who lapsed into a coma and entered into a reality based upon archetypal reconstructions of things within his own life . . . all of which were desperately trying to help him to wake up. It was a very Freudian sort of fumbling, but I was proud of my little thought-child and the *absolute* likelihood of the success that I would find when I possessed the wherewithal to craft it into something resembling a cohesive narrative.

I had entitled my project *The Dreaming*, and I wrote that title atop a sheet of paper in thick, lush strokes. When I looked at that sheet of paper upon which I had outlined my project, I sat in admiration of my own clichéd epiphanies and carefully crafted vicissitudes completely forgetting that Neil Gaiman had constructed roughly the very same thing years prior in what became his magnum opus, *The Sandman*, starting back in 1988.

It only took only around four solid seconds before I realized that I had cribbed an approximation of a comic that I had been reading indefatigably for as long as I could remember reading comics, right down to the name of Morpheus' realm. The word "Whoops!" immediately came to mind.

Granted, observant young man that I was, had I looked no further than my ring of house keys, at the silver ankh I begged my mother to purchase for me without offering any explanation other than a promise that I was not forgoing Christianity, I might have remembered: Oh right. *The Sandman*. That book where I fell in love with a personification of *Death* who resembled my idealized fantasy of what a girl might look and sound like. I fell in love with a construct. I had forgone the place I had met her.

That ankh still resides on my keychain decades later.

* * *

When my eldest daughter was still but a baby, a baby under a year old in that precarious period of time when relatively insane first-time parents study monitors and listen with manic rapt attention to every single sound, gurgle, and cry that comes from the nursery (Also known as: the year of no sleep), I prepped for the graduate seminar I taught on Bakhtinian literary theory and comics (Don't cringe. It was a hugely popular class.) because it wasn't as if I were going to sleep anyhow. I was, in fact, waiting for my first-born, a light sleeper and brilliant cuddler, to wake up and pull me from my work while she slept upon me in the world's most expensive, uncomfortable, and god-forsaken nursery glider.

The text we happened to be covering for that class was *The Sandman*, in its entirety (because if you're going to read something, you might as well read *all* of the something), and I was very happy. I had not revisited the series since I was a young man. At the end of the first volume, *Preludes and Nocturnes*, the reader is introduced to Death, that first construction of an ideal girlfriend from my youth (and the woman I did not marry), as she takes Morpheus, her younger brother, on her daily rounds and she tries to rouse him out from being such a dour bore.

As they wander, as she escorts the newly-departed to whatever lies hereafter, there comes a page in the comic awash in black with very little blue. It's a page where the reader finds Death and Dream arriving in a nursery. The mother, unnamed, lays her child to bed with typical parental preens of "OOTCHACOOTCHACOO," and then she leaves the room, likely only for the briefest moment, to get the baby a bottle. In the next panel, the baby meets Death. In the panel following, Death takes the baby. In the panels following that, the mother is devastated beyond words. Well, except for one: "NO!"

I dropped everything in my immediate vicinity, tore myself from the bedroom, and careened, not like an elephant, into my daughter's room, terrified and very likely crying.

My daughter was sleeping peacefully.

(Which was good because, had I woken her, my wife likely would have killed me.)

When I returned, I *know* I cried because I was struck to my core by what I had read and how it affected me so differently now as an adult, as a man with family and responsibilities and a great sense of love. I wrote Gaiman on Twitter to try and put to words somehow the range of emotions I felt in that moment because I needed to tell someone who I thought might understand what anyone else might think madness.

The tweet he almost immediately returned to me gave me salve, but I still cannot return to that page without tears welling in my eyes. (And that tweet is only for me.)

* * *

Years later, I was invited to present at the annual conference for the International Association for the Fantastic in the Arts, colloquially known as ICFA. As an academic, this is part and parcel to the job. We write. We teach. We attend conferences and present our research to other academics who look at us oddly. The notable moment in this example is that, based upon two unique factors, I was asked to speak on a panel about Neil Gaiman's *The Books of Magic*. The two unique factors happened to be:

1. I had previously presented on Neil Gaiman and, most recently, I had presented at the Modern Language Association's Annual Convention.[1]

2. For a small compensation, I am always willing to speak on most anything anywhere.

In this particular case, the compensation offered to me by the good folks at ICFA was a set of all-day passes to *all* the Disney Parks in Orlando, Florida, where the conference is annually held.

Have I mentioned my daughter yet?

If there is a greater gift a father can give to his daughter besides open access to the entirety of Disney's Kingdom, I'm not sure she (or now her sister as well) will hear of it.

Needless to say, I presented on the newly re-released *The Books of Magic* in addition to the paper presentation I had already been invited to give. Or, I should say, I eventually gave that presentation; as I was walking to my panel, as cocksure and fancy-free as a man about to speak on one of his favorite authors could be, I happened to notice that the man, himself, was concluding a book-signing approximately 150 feet from where I was, in roughly two minutes, about to give a presentation on his work.

There are moments that I like to think define academics as the academics that they are or may become. One of mine is the moment where I ran into a room full of people waiting to hear a discussion of Neil Gaiman's work and politely asked them (and the rest of the panel) if they would very much mind if I ran out for a second (or ten minutes) to get an inscription from the author in *The Books of Magic*, the only book of his I happened to have on hand at the time. They readily and quickly acquiesced, which was good as Gaiman's book signing had ended five minutes earlier. Like a gentleman, or perhaps out of fear of the mad academic babbling to his handlers that the entire reason I was standing before him was due to my being allowed to speak on him, he welcomed me entirely graciously and gave me an inscription with a very personal message. This moment happened to be the first time that Gaiman, himself, had seen the reissued *Books of Magic*, and he was quite interested in the improvements. As he was thumbing through the pages, I told him how it was due to him that I was allowed to give my family a very expensive trip to the Disney parks I might otherwise not been able to afford. He smiled at that, wrote his inscription, took my hand in his and shook it before wishing me further luck.

And I presented my talk.

Mingling the Personal and Public Spheres

There's likely no less traditional introduction to anything I have ever edited than the lines that precedes these. That is, however, quite intentional. As Kyle Eveleth and Justin Wigard state later in this anthology, the overriding question of this book concerns that peculiarly idiomatic enquiry of "What makes Gaiman [so] uniquely 'Gaimany?'"[2] Various authors in this volume come to considerably different conclusions; Eveleth and Wigard believe it to be his capacity to compose stories "with notes of nostalgia, horror, melancholy, hope, laughter, and almost everything in between." Kristin McIlhagga argues that it's his unique ability to construct empathy with his audience, whether in person, online, or in print, that makes Gaiman a voice overwhelmingly distinct. Every single writer in this volume considers him irrepressibly funny and poignant, able to convey any particular emotion necessary to tell a good story. My own answer is not much different; my belief is that the power of Gaiman's prose (and, honestly, of the man himself) resides in his capacity to press the weight of his celebrity into a manifold vision of the betterment of tomorrow. Or, to put it a bit less opaquely, I honestly believe that Gaiman feels that he can write the world into a better version of itself.

In literary and social circles, there's an approach referred to as public sphere theory; derived from the German for *Öffentlichkeit* and spearheaded by the work of Jürgen Habermas, Gerard Hauser refers to the public sphere as "a discursive space in which individuals and groups associate to discuss matters of mutual interest and, where possible, to reach a common judgment about them" (*Vernacular* 61). Essentially, it is a place, real or virtual, where individuals with some common interest or concern can recognize and workshop, if you will, problems from the real, in whatever manner one considers something real. It's not a quick and dirty affair by any means. Per Hauser, it is and must be an "ongoing dialogue" between individuals, "active members of society who lack official status" (65), voicing their concerns on very "public issues" (64). And, if you're saying to yourself: 'So, social media'? In essence, yes—that's partially accurate. However, the idea extrapolates past virtual watercooler talk into real and true thoughtful capitulation by governmental bodies by the will and cajoling of the public sphere—the best governments and governing practice, that is, are guided by the public sphere and its brightest and most persuasive advocates (Behhabib 87).

The idea here is relatively simple, Habermas suggests a few things about public sphere theory in the example I'm purporting: 1. It requires a "specific means for transmitting information and influencing those who receive it" ("Public Sphere" 136). 2. In, arguably, the best case scenario, the information arises from the world of the well-read human, "in connection with literary activities, the world of letters" (*Structural* 30-31). 3. This new and, hopefully wise, "public opinion" places the "state [and state apparatuses] in touch with the needs of society," presumably those being governed by it (31). 4. Profit for all! The overriding idea here is that, for Habermas, in the "public competition of private arguments [will come a] consensus about what was practically necessary in the interest of all" (83). The leaders of this charge come from the private realm, "the conjugal family's space" (30), and press, through their voice, their writings and convictions into the public sphere. And these leaders can come from virtually any area, but, as applies to the case of Neil Gaiman, Habermas finds one of the "*intellectuals* who [has] gained, unlike advocates or moral entrepreneurs, a perceived personal reputation in some field (e.g., as writers or academics) and who engage, unlike experts and lobbyists, spontaneously in public discourse with the declared intention of promoting general interests" (416). That is to say, Neil Gaiman, well-read and concerned for the common human, has no real need to go onto his blog or Twitter and speak in advocacy of libraries, up-and-coming artists, or just everyday folks trying to make the world a little bit of a better place with no funds and a Kickstarter, but he does so anyhow in an effort to make the world we all share together a bit of a better place.

And it's not even the fact that Gaiman does this that's so impressive and blessedly important; it's how he does it. As McIlhagga will go to great lengths to show in her rhetorical analysis of Gaiman's Reading Agency Lecture, Gaiman, even before he weaponized his own journals and Twitter account in the late twenty-aughts, imbricated his own fictions with an invitation to readers into his own private sphere, the realm of his family, in an effort to give his reading public a sort of unfettered access into his life. If one looks into some of Gaiman's earliest writings, the ones he cobbled together with Kim Newman in the early freelance journalism days, one finds, amidst the dry British wit, instructions: pieces such as "How to Be a Barbarian" or "How to Spot a Psycho." They're pieces of wisdom hiding, or—perhaps better—veiled, within larger stories; things that are almost parental in construction . . . coming from a then-young man, who likely had no further insight than what he had read about or experienced just out of high school. However, as one continues through Gaiman's catalogue, one finds that this sort of parental wit and wisdom, this sort of shared knowledge on the microscale as opposed to a macro concern for the environment or literacy rates, permeates his works.

Look no further than, for example, *Instructions*. First a poem, then a book constructed with Charles Vess' illustrations, the poem masks itself as an archetypal quest motif, but just beneath the thin veneer of fantasy comes the most realistic set of advice a young human might gain from a more worldly one. "Touch the wooden gate in the wall you never/ saw before," Gaiman intones, writing as might a journalist to look beneath the substrata for the thing in its particulars, the thing taken for granted or perhaps otherwise unobserved. "Say 'please'," he writes, "before you open the latch,/ go through,/ walk down the path." There's nothing remarkably sage here; there is no mysticism or contrived philosophy. These are, as the poem lists, instructions in the manner of how one might conduct oneself. Gaiman does rely upon the mythic tropes he knows and is known for, but they are only invoked, once again, to relay things that might otherwise be seen as tired platitudes by another adult, yet someone has to teach them to the young who have otherwise never heard them before:

> If an eagle gives you a feather, keep it safe.
> Remember: that giants sleep too soundly; that
> witches are often betrayed by their appetites;
> dragons have one soft spot, somewhere, always;
> hearts can be well-hidden,
> and you betray them with your tongue.
> Do not be jealous of your sister.
> Know that diamonds and roses
> are as uncomfortable when they tumble from
> one's lips as toads and frogs:
> colder, too, and sharper, and they cut.

There is as much practical magic here as there is in Tolkein, and there's no judgment, merely advice. In fact, "If you turn around here,/" he says, "you can walk back, safely;/ you will lose no face. I will think no less of you." These are the words of a father to his daughters as much as to the youth of the world, and they give the same familial courtesy and respect. In consideration of the poem's composition, a thing done in response to the suggestion that he, in fact, might be better served to not write poetry, Gaiman did so anyhow, stating, with tongue firmly planted in cheek: "Nobody's forcing them to read them" ("Neil Gaiman Reading"). Gaiman claimed that the poem is for what one should do if one finds themselves in a fairy tale; I would contend that he sees this fairy tale as life.

It wouldn't be the first time Gaiman conflates reality and fantasy. Written in 2000 in celebration of the birth of musician and friend Tori Amos' new daughter, Tash, the poem "Blueberry Girl," also illustrated by Vess when it was published as a book in 2010, is as much a paean to the expected child as it is a prayer to her. Gaiman writes:

> Ladies of light and ladies of darkness and ladies of never you mind,
> This is a prayer for a blueberry girl.
> First, may you ladies be kind.
> Keep her from spindles and sleeps at sixteen,

> Nightmares at three or bad husbands at thirty,
> These will not trouble her eyes.
> Dull days at forty, false friends at fifteen—

Whether he invokes the fates, the Kindly Ones, or any of a numerous triad of mythic beings to watch over his goddaughter, he conflates the actuality of her existence with other famous children who were forced to endure and thrive, such as, for example, Sleeping Beauty. He asks not for an idyllic life for her, but only kindness. He understands that there will be hardships and boredom, as happens in life. But just the same, for all the good and all the bad, all Gaiman requests of beings greater than he is kindness, a first principle and possibly one of the most necessary. And when he does make greater requests, he only requests the most basic human lessons, "Teach her we're only as big as our dreams./ Show her that fortune is blind./ Truth is a thing she must find for herself, precious and rare as a pearl." Let her imagine, he asks; yet, let her be pragmatic, and let her discover that there are certain things she will only be able to find over time, such as truth. Gaiman, again, intones that wisdom can only come with time and with age and it is a thing that must not be rushed if that pearl of wisdom is to be found. He requests no largesse and begs for nothing more than the most basic human virtues, as if they are a thing he sees as being a commodity in the world around him.

These topics are highly personal to both Gaiman and his friends; they are composed in a manner one might see handwritten on the inside of a card to a dear friend. However, in publication, Gaiman constructs an opportunity to share these thoughts with a world who he feels might need them as much as he and his family. He is the crafter of the reader's avunculate, the constructed stand-in of a father figure or an uncle, the empathic construct in which dialogue between writer and reader make connection (Sommers 260). His gift—one of words and expression—is, it would appear, an opportunity for him as a learned artist to share, as Habermas suggests, "in public discourse with the declared intention of promoting general interests." It is a humble proposition: be good, to yourself and to one another, for the benefit of all. Basic humanism, as such, can hardly be clarified as a political aspiration; rather, it appears as a practical maxim of optimism, hope, and sincerity.

An Advocate for the Human Condition

Gaiman does aspire to do more than pass on axioms and maxims I can share with my children (Although I am eternally grateful for words I, myself, cannot muster.). Indeed, no matter how important, how personal and shared that empathic connection Gaiman crafts with his audience feels to his readers, that's not necessarily his intention or even his preference. In his speech celebrating his win of the Newbery Medal for *The Graveyard Book* in 2008, Gaiman recounts his discomfort with so many individuals finding so much solace in his words. While always being respectful to them, he likewise notes that:

> I did not write the stories to get people through the hard places and the difficult times. I didn't write them to make readers of nonreaders. I wrote them because I was interested in the stories, because there was a maggot in my head, a small squirming idea I needed to pin to the paper and inspect, in order to find out what I thought and felt about it. I wrote them because I wanted to find out what happened next to people I had made up. I wrote them to feed my family.

If those words cut like a dagger, take heart, as Gaiman was not quite finished:

> So I felt almost dishonorable accepting people's thanks. I had forgotten what fiction was to me as a boy, forgotten what it was like in the library: fiction was an escape from the intolerable, a doorway into impossibly hospitable worlds where things had rules and could be understood; stories had been a way of learning about life without experiencing it. . . . Sometimes fiction is a way of coping with the poison of the world in a way that lets us survive it.
>
> And I remembered. I would not be the person I am without the authors who made me what I am—the special ones, the wise ones, sometimes just the ones who got there first. It's not irrelevant, those

moments of connection, those places where fiction saves your life. It's the most important thing there is. (Gaiman, "Newbery")

When the question is asked as to what makes Gaiman and his work so crucial in his day and age, a quality that evades so many other authors within their own lifetimes, the answer is relatively simple: He gets it.

Take that 'it' howsoever you choose. (It is, truthfully, a rather opinionated little factotum from the editor.) That 'it' may be nothing more than being an earnest provider for his family or being greedily starving to know how his own characters' stories end in manners resembling the fandom of George R. R. Martin's *A Song of Ice and Fire* or it might just be a young boy sitting in a library befriended by librarians, "good librarians" who "liked books and . . . liked the books being read" (Gaiman, "Reading"). Of those librarians, Gaiman found those who understood empathy and served as models of how it needs to be done for everyone:

> [Librarians] taught me how to order books from other libraries on interlibrary loans. They had no snobbery about anything I read. They just seemed to like that there was this wide-eyed little boy who loved to read, and would talk to me about the books I was reading, they would find me other books in a series, they would help. They treated me as another reader—nothing less and more—which meant they treated me with respect. ("Reading")

For Gaiman, librarians might as well have been magicians with grimoires holding the answers to the world's problems; being given access to their *bōchōrd*,[3] the place where they held their magic, would therefore be the greatest gift of friendship one could offer to a child, an apprentice, as it were.

As Gaiman himself recalls, the authors he found in those libraries informed him and welcomed him into their worlds, which served as egress from the one he himself lived in. For Gaiman, that's what stories *can* do—they can offer refuge for the world-weary traveler and reinvigorate the soul. They contain lives, endless multitudes of lives, lives that a reader can come to know. That is an immense responsibility and one Gaiman does not take lightly. He writes:

> Remember that whatever discipline you are in, whether you are a musician or a photographer, a fine artist or a cartoonist, a writer, a dancer, a designer, whatever you do you have one thing that's unique. You have the ability to make art.
> And for me, and for so many of the people I have known, that's been a lifesaver. The ultimate lifesaver. It gets you through good times and it gets you through the other ones.
> Life is sometimes hard. Things go wrong, in life and in love and in business and in friendship and in health and in all the ways that life can go wrong. And when things get tough, this is what you should do.
> Make good art. ("Make Good Art")

There are several places where I could have abbreviated that excerpt from Gaiman's University of the Arts commencement speech, but to do so would have been to trim Samson's hair. If the corpus of Neil Gaiman's work has a central grand unifying thesis, it's simply: Make good art.

Making good art underpins everything Gaiman does whether it be writing a teleplay, crafting a song, or raising children to be kind, adults—"Make good art" is Gaiman's 'abracadadra,' his healing incantation; it's the distillation of his advocacy and larger project. It's the magic by which he builds his empathy, and the magic he gives away freely just as it was given to him in the library. A reader can find it in every single narrative Gaiman crafts, an advocacy for humanity, a tacitly-veiled message of hope, in even the most dire of circumstances.

Which is not to say that Gaiman makes that magic an easy acquisition for the reader. As Orion Ussner Kidder's chapter will show, Gaiman does demand a bit of work to realize the magic—information may be free, but you still have to earn it. One can look no further than the little bit of doggerel Mrs. Owens sings to Bod in *The Graveyard Book* to see Gaiman's playful self-reflexivity at work. To the infant child, whose family has just been slaughtered and left to the dead to be raised as a living creature, she sings, "*Sleep my little babby-oh/ Sleep until you waken/ When you're frown you'll see the world/ If I'm not mistaken. Kiss a lover,/ Dance a measure,/ Find your name/ and buried treasure. . . .*" (26), and then the poem stops, stunted by ellipses and an explanation that Mrs. Owen essentially forgot. The message isn't complete. It's as if Gaiman challenges the reader to wonder: "Where's the rest? What's to be my take-away, Neil?" Interestingly enough, there is an ending to the poem that Gaiman just happened not to include initially. He makes the reader grow up with Bod so that the lines appreciate in value as the boy ages: "Face your life/ Its pain, its pleasure,/ Leave no path untaken" (306). He might just as well have written, "There is an answer, but you need to live a life to find it."

* * *

I began this introduction with a triptych of short anecdotes about my own life with Neil Gaiman. I did not do this because I did not know how I wanted to start this chapter, but because I knew exactly how I wanted to start this chapter. As later chapters in this volume will show, I think, Gaiman's an author who makes the personal available to the public as manner of a social contract or public trust. He seems to indicate that within his writings, the reader will find lies and truths and glorious information—but it will be the reader's task to parse the one from the other and make some meaning of it. To sweeten that exercise, Gaiman makes the pledge to show how it worked for him and how it could work for you. As he said when he accepted the Newbery Medal for a book written about a boy without a name or a family or an earthly chance in the world, who found an opportunity from an *ethereal*, otherworldly opportunity:

> Reading is important.
> Books are important.
> Librarians are important. . . .
> It is a glorious and unlikely thing to be cool to your children.
> Children's fiction is the most important fiction of all.

For as much as this author is a central figure in Western letters for his ironic humor, psychological prowess, and impossibly well-read capacities, he is also inherently important simply because he does not wish to just make art; he wants to make *good* art. *Cool* art. Art that implores children to read, not just to improve upon their literacy but to implore them to dream wildly and dream in flourishes and reveries that have not yet been imagined. Neil Gaiman is more than merely an author; he is an artisan.[4]

* * *

Oh, and that inscription he left for me in *The Books of Magic?* It reads:

Dear Joe,
Abracadabra!

Notes

1. That presentation is actually reprinted in this volume with the proper emendation in order to become a chapter.
2. They take that question a step further in explanation as: "What are the qualities that make his literature, graphic narratives, films, and other stories so compelling, so readable, and so accessible by such an immense swath of readers?"
3. Book hoard, or collection of books, otherwise known as a library, in Old English. But who wouldn't want to visit the *bōchōrd* at the first chance available?
4. My greatest of thanks to my fellow author in this volume Annette Wannamaker for helping me see the intro with greater clarity and acuity.

Works Cited

Benhabib, Seyla. "Models of Public Space." *Habermas and the Public Sphere*. Ed. Craig Calhoun. Cambridge, MA: MITP, 1992. 73-98. Print.

Gaiman, Neil. *Blueberry Girl*. New York: Harper Collins, 2009. Print.

_____. *The Graveyard Book*. New York: Harper Collins, 2008. Print.

_____. *Instructions*. New York: Bloomsbury, 2010. Print.

_____. "Make Good Art." *The View from the Cheap Seats*. New York: Harper Collins, 2016. Print.

_____. "Newbery Medal Acceptance Speech: Telling Lies for a Living . . . and Why We Do It." *Children & Libraries* 2 (2009): 7-10. Print.

_____. "Neil Gaiman Lecture in Full: Reading and Obligation." *The Reading Agency*. The Reading Agency, 2013. Web. 12 Sept. 2016. <https://readingagency.org.uk/news/blog/neil-gaiman-lecture-in-full.html>.

_____. *The Sandman Volume One: Preludes and Nocturnes*. New York: DC, 1991. Print.

Habermas, Jürgen. "Political Communication in Media Society: Does Democracy Still Enjoy an Epistemic Dimension? The Impact of Normative Theory on Empirical Research." *Communication Theory* 4 (2006) 411-426. Print.

_____. "The Public Sphere: An Encyclopedia Article." *Critical Theory and Society*. Ed. Stephen E. Bronner & Douglas Kellner. New York: Routledge, 1989. 136-42. Print.

_____. *The Structural Transformation of the Public Sphere*. Cambridge, MA: MITP, 1989. 91. Print.

Hauser, Gerard. "Vernacular Dialogue and the Rhetoricality of Public Opinion." *Communication Monographs* 3 (June 1998): 83-107. Print.

_____. *Vernacular Voices: The Rhetoric of Publics and Public Spheres*. Columbia: U South Carolina P, 1999, Print.

"Neil Gaiman Reading Instructions." *YouTube*. Uploaded by Webelfneil, 27 Jan. 2007. Web. 11 Sept. 2016. <https://www.youtube.com/watch?v=5UnfyoTSZZw>.

Sommers, Joseph Michael. "*Are You There, Reader? It's Me, Margaret*: A Reconsideration of Judy Blume's Prose as Sororal Dialogism." *Children's Literature Association Quarterly* 3 (2008): 258-75. Print.

Biographical Sketch of Neil Gaiman

Justin Wigard

Neil Richard Gaiman was born to Sheila and David Bernard Gaiman on November 10, 1960 in Portchester, Hampshire, United Kingdom. Neil was the first of three siblings (followed by the births of his sisters, Claire and Lizzy). His father worked as a grocer for several years before turning to property selling, while Sheila worked as a pharmacist. The family lived in Portchester until 1965, when they moved to West Sussex. In Sussex, Gaiman first experienced libraries at the age of four and became a regular at his local library.

Gaiman has often claimed that he was a "feral child who was raised in libraries by patient librarians" (*View* 18). He discovered early on the wealth of information, stories, and shelter only a library can provide. When he was older, Gaiman would often persuade his parents to drop him off at the local library on their way to work in order to continue working his way through card catalogues and many different genres of literature, including fantasy, science fiction, detective novels, classic literature, postmodern novels, etc. Later, he learned the card catalog so he "could look up 'magic' and . . . ghosts, and look up witches, and just read every book on that subject," particularly the works of C. S. Lewis, J. R. R. Tolkien, and Lewis Carroll (29). This would become one of Gaiman's defining formative experiences, and he later advocated for libraries as safe havens for children and as bastions for knowledge, most notably in his speech for The Reading Agency, delivered on October 14, 2013 in London (15).

Gaiman's penchant for writing began when he was "probably eight going on nine," writing poetry heavily influenced by Tolkien and Lewis that featured dragons, knights, kings, and most importantly for Gaiman, story (Campbell 22). At some point, Gaiman was given a box of comic books that contained "loads of *Fantastic Fours* in it," along with comics featuring Batman, Spider-Man, Silver Surfer, and Green Lantern that would later influence his writing career (26).

Around the age of fifteen, Gaiman told his school counselor that he wanted to be a comic book writer; the counselor suggested he try being an accountant instead (Wagner, Golden, & Bissette loc. 228). Putting aside reading and writing comics per that advice, Gaiman instead started a punk band with some mates from school. In the midst of the 1970s British punk invasion, Gaiman formed a band called "The Ex-Execs" (chosen for the aural spelling of 'XXX'). Punk still remains a major influence on all he does due to punk music's ethos of discovering the fundamentals, learning through practice, and simply getting out there to "Just do it" (Campbell 31).

Proto-Writing

After leaving Whitgift School in Croydon in 1977 at seventeen, Gaiman decided against university, viewing those four years as a delay of becoming a writer. During this time, he met a woman named Mary McGrath who was studying Scientology in town, and, after some time, the two started dating. In 1983, the two had a son together, Michael; were married in 1985; and had a daughter named Holly later that same year. Finding difficulty in publishing his major manuscripts in his late teens and early twenties, Gaiman took a different trajectory for writing: journalism.

As a freelance journalist, Gaiman made connections with many well-established creators, like Bob Silverberg, Clive Barker, Arthur C. Clarke, and Terry Jones. He honed his writing craft through interviewing authors, which Gaiman claimed was one of the biggest draws of journalism (Bissette, Golden, & Wagner loc. 350). In 1984, Gaiman was contracted by Proteus Publishing Company to write a biography on Def Leppard, Barry Manilow, or Duran Duran, the last of which Gaiman ultimately chose. According to Gaiman, he "wrote the book in a frantic two weeks, handed it over [and] it came out a couple weeks later," swiftly selling out its first print run (Elder 76). The traction from Gaiman's first book allowed him to write comics for *2,000 AD* in the United Kingdom and *Borderline* in New York City, where he met artist Dave McKean. The two became fast friends and frequent collaborators, initially, on a short graphic novel called *Violent Cases* in 1987 (McCabe 22). Their creative approaches complemented one another well, as Gaiman's tonally-dark writing matched McKean's surreal, expressionistic collages. *Violent Cases'* success led to an important meeting with DC Comics shortly thereafter.

Enter *Sandman, Good Omens*, and Early Novels

The most defining element of Gaiman's early career, other than his proclivity for black t-shirts and black jeans, is his seminal comic book series, *The Sandman*, a revitalization of DC's original *Sandman* comic series from 1939. Gaiman met DC Comics Editor Karen Berger in 1986 and pitched and eventually wrote a comic series about a little-known DC character, Black Orchid. Released in 1988, the limited series of *Black Orchid* was so successful that Gaiman was allowed to re-envision a series based on any outdated DC character. His version of Sandman became a multifaceted and complex character to match the ethereal and infinite nature of dreams: a tall, pale, brooding, and dark-haired man dressed in black robes whose powers rely on dreams and, therefore, are limited only by what is possible in a dream (Campbell 103). First published on November 29, 1988, Gaiman's *Sandman #1* ended up selling "better than any commensurate DC horror title . . . eighty or ninety thousand copies" at the time, cementing Gaiman's status as a rock-star comic-book writer for years to come (Campbell 105). Shortly after *The Sandman* ended, Gaiman welcomed his third child, Madeleine "Maddy" Gaiman, to the world on August 28, 1994.

As a journalist, Gaiman had become friends with author Terry Pratchett in 1985 and, shortly thereafter, sent Pratchett "the first five-thousand-word scene" of a novel Gaiman had not yet finished, which Pratchett offered to co-author with Gaiman (BBC "Good Omens"). What followed was a sort of apprenticeship for Gaiman as "it was like going to college . . . a fifty-fifty collaboration between a journeyman and a master craftsman and that's very much how I viewed, and still view, *Good Omens*," as Gaiman learned about the construction and form of the novel while working alongside Pratchett (McCabe 9). The end result was a novel that was so closely co-written, neither Pratchett nor Gaiman could discern where each other's writing began and ended; published in 1990, the two would go on to be nominated for both the Locus and World Fantasy awards for *Good Omens* (Wagner, Golden, & Bissette 193).

On America, *American Gods*, and Writing for Children

In 1992, Gaiman moved to America to be closer to his wife's family, taking up residence near Menomonie, Wisconsin. Upon moving to America, he became heavily invested in championing the freedom of speech and began touring the US, raising funds for the Comic Book Legal Defense Fund for cases in which a comic book writer or artist's freedom of speech came under attack (Campbell 192). These efforts by Gaiman inspired him later to create his own nonprofit organization in 2012, The Gaiman Foundation, whose first project would be donating $60,000 to the CBLDF (Brownstein). Working with the CBLDF was the first seed of Gaiman's philanthropic efforts, permeating both Gaiman's career and life, especially in the late 2010s.

Prior to moving to America, Gaiman "had been coming to America on visits, and more importantly, [he] grew up watching American television and reading American books. And then [he] moved to America and found it was really weird" (Marshall, "Neil Gaiman"). The centrifugal history and nature of America had a profound effect on Gaiman; he marveled at the fact that people who once worshipped gods of Norse mythology lived alongside people who partook of Eastern religions. Gaiman became fascinated by America's comparatively young history, compared to the United Kingdom's rich cultural history dating back centuries. Taking this as inspiration and written largely at friends' houses and in isolated cabins throughout the US, *American Gods* (2001) became the first novel that Gaiman truly felt he'd written on his own. The novel developed from a question in Gaiman's mind: what happens to these old gods, such as Odin, Bast, and Anansi, when new, secular gods like Technology and Media arise?

When Holly was four, Gaiman decided to write her a story that hearkened back to his time spent in the library reading children's novels, like Lewis Carroll's *Alice's Adventures in Wonderland*.

Drawing inspiration from Lucy Clifford's 1882 short story, "The Other Mother," Gaiman infused his own tale with gothic horror elements. His project developed into a larger children's novel, prompting Gaiman to call once again on McKean for illustrations. The resulting book, *Coraline* (2002), is a dark adventure story about a girl who, upon moving to a gothic manor, finds a door leading to a dark, fantastical version of her own house. Going through the door, she meets the malevolent Other Mother and is fearless throughout. *Coraline* proved to be immensely successful, leaping to the tops of bestseller charts, spawning a comic adaptation by P. Craig Russell, a musical, and an Academy-Award-nominated feature film (Wagner, Golden, & Bissette loc. 7557).

After finishing *American Gods*, Gaiman returned to an idea for a novel nearly twenty-five years in the making. Back in 1985, when his son, Michael, was two and the Gaiman family lived in a small, cramped British apartment, Gaiman would take Michael across the street to ride his tricycle where there was space: in a cemetery (Campbell 240). Gaiman again took inspiration from his own life, not to mention Rudyard Kipling's *The Jungle Book*: instead of a child being raised by wolves, Gaiman wondered about a child, Nobody Owens, who might be raised by ghosts, and so *The Graveyard Book* was born. Gaiman would return to the novel every few years, and much had changed in Gaiman's life from the first time he set out to write it in 1985: Gaiman now had three children (Michael and Holly were adults; Maddie was still a teenager). Moreover, he had recently divorced Mary McGrath and had found international acclaim as an author due to *The Sandman, American Gods*, and *Coraline* (Gaiman, "Half a Lifetime?"). Finally published in 2008, *The Graveyard Book* became an overnight success, emboldening him to continue writing picture books and children's novels: between 2007 and 2016, Gaiman wrote ten separate children's texts. While Gaiman drew inspiration from Norse mythology for *Odd and the Frost Giants* (2008), he visited the Republic of China in 2007 for a science fiction/fantasy convention and created a picture book based on his favorite experience in China: holding a panda. This would inspire a picture book series about a sneezy panda named Chu.

Media, Multimedia, and Amanda Palmer

To both keep abreast of technological advances and stay in further contact with his avid fanbase, Gaiman joined social media site Twitter in December 2008. Gaiman began his Twitter account with a very specific tweet in 2008, "I just opened my present from McKean, *The Big Fat Duck Cookbook*. Heavy as a stone and beautiful. 'See?' he said. 'I do read your blog'," offering a real-time window into his life and his friendship with McKean. Pursuing new storytelling approaches, Neil worked together with BBC America to create a story entirely from tweets. On 13 October 2009, Gaiman tweeted the first line, "Sam was brushing her hair when the girl in the mirror put down the hairbrush, smiled & said, 'We don't love you anymore'." Over the next week and a half, nearly 10,000 tweets from 124 Twitter users were chosen to be formatted into an audiobook titled *Hearts, Keys, and Puppetry*. Beyond telling stories, Gaiman actively shares fans' charities, causes, and questions, as well as his own life events and musings, staying connected with fans throughout his career.

In the latter half of the 2000s, Gaiman met musician/artist Amanda Palmer who had, in her own way, dabbled in as many artistic modes throughout her own career as he had. The two collaborated on a book of photographs of Palmer as a companion piece to Palmer's first solo album, entitled *Who Killed Amanda Palmer?*. They announced that they were dating on June 5, 2009; were engaged on January 1, 2010; and were legally married on January 2, 2011 (Palmer, "The Wedding Blog"). This, in turn, led to further creative collaborations in an increased public sharing of intimacy in performances like *An Evening with Neil Gaiman and Amanda Palmer*, which involved songs, duets, stories, and spoken-word pieces the two delivered across America in late 2011.

While Gaiman's humanitarian efforts have existed since his early success with *The Sandman*, 2014 saw the United Nations High Commission for Refugees (UNHCR) calling on Gaiman to visit Jordan, Syria, during the Syrian Civil War to make "one or more short films, telling stories and writing articles that draw attention to what's going on in refugee camps" (Gaiman, "In Jordan"). After Gaiman visited the city of Jordan, he penned a powerful article for *The Guardian*, entitled "So Many Ways to Die in Syria Now," taken from conversations with refugees about the political climate and quality of living in Jordan (Gaiman, "So Many Ways"). In his short film with the UNHCR, he talks about his plunge "into absolute despair at the monstrous things that human beings can do to human beings," in order to tell the stories of those who could not tell their own stories, who were "living their worst nightmares" ("3 Million Reasons"). But, in typical Gaiman fashion, he wrote of hope amidst this despair, telling stories of refugees who created artwork and schools for children, finding a cause he champions to this day on Twitter and on his blog.

In early 2015, Palmer announced via Facebook that she was pregnant, and on September 16, 2015, Palmer welcomed her first, and Gaiman's fourth, child, Anthony, to the world. Most recently, *American Gods* has been adapted and will become a television series on STARZ in 2017, and a nonfiction collection of essays, *Notes from the Cheap Seats*, which includes his inspiring "Make Good Art" 2012 commencement speech, came out in 2016.

Works Cited

"3 Million Reasons Why Your Heart Will Break in One Video." *YouTube*. Uploaded by United Nations High Commission for Refugees (UNHCR), 21 Oct. 2014. Web. 7 Aug. 2016. <https://www.youtube.com/watch?v=rIolTbJ_K5U>.

British Broadcasting Corporation. "*Good Omens*: How Neil Gaiman and Terry Pratchett Wrote a Book." *BBC News*. BBC, 22 Dec. 2014. Web. 7Aug. 2016. <www.bbc.com/news/magazine-30512620>.

Brownstein, Charles. "The Gaiman Foundation Contributes $60,000 to CBLDF for Education Program." *Comic Book Legal Defense Fund*. Comic Book Legal Defense Fund, 28 Nov. 2012. Web. 13 Aug. 2016. <www.cbldf.org/2012/11/the-gaiman-foundation-contributes-60000-to-cbldf-for-education-program/>.

Campbell, Hayley. *The Art of Neil Gaiman*. New York: Harper Collins, 2014. Print.

Elder, Robert K. "Gods and Other Monsters." *The Neil Gaiman Reader*. Edited by Darrell Schweitzer. Rockville, MD: Wildside Press, 2007, 54-78. Print.

Gaiman, Neil. "Letter from Neil Gaiman." *Chicago Public Library*. Chicago Public Library, 2016. Web. Accessed 4 Aug. 2016. <http://www.chipublib.org/letter-from-neil-gaiman/>.

_____. *Neil Gaiman's Journal*. Harper Collins Publishers, 2016. Web. 14 Aug. 2016. <journal.neilgaiman.com>.

_____. "'So Many Ways to Die in Syria Now': Neil Gaiman Visits a Refugee Camp in Jordan." *The Guardian*. Guardian News and Media, Ltd. 21 May 2014. Web. 6 Aug. 2016. <https://www.theguardian.com/world/2014/may/21/many-ways-die-syria-neil-gaiman-refugee-camp-syria>.

_____. Twitter post. 26 Dec.2008. 12:48pm. <https://twitter.com/neilhimself/status/1079815290>.https://twitter.com/neilhimself/status/1079815290.

_____. *View from the Cheap Seats: Selected Nonfiction*. New York: Harper Collins, 2016. Print.

Marshall, Rick. "Neil Gaiman Reflects on *American Gods*, 10 Years Later." *MTV*. MTV, 22 Jun. 2011. Web. Accessed 7 Aug. 2016. <http://www.mtv.com/news/1666281/neil-gaiman-american-gods/>.

McCabe, Joseph. *Hanging Out with the Dream King: Conversations with Neil Gaiman and His Collaborators*. Seattle: Fantagraphic Books, 2004. Print.

Palmer, Amanda. "The Wedding Blog." *AmandaPalmer.com*. Amanda Palmer, 1 Jan. 2012. Web. 14 Aug. 2016. <http://blog.amandapalmer.net/the-wedding-blog/>.

_____. Twitter post. 1 Jan. 2010. 8:45am. <https://twitter.com/amandapalmer/status/7272917210>.https://twitter.com/amandapalmer/status/7272917210.

Wagner, Hank, Christopher Golden, & Stephen R. Bissette. *Prince of Stories: The Many Worlds of Neil Gaiman*. New York: St. Martin's Press, 2009. Kindle.

CRITICAL CONTEXTS

"We have an obligation to imagine": A Critical Reception of the Work of Neil Gaiman

Kyle Eveleth and Justin Wigard

Writing a critical reception about Neil Gaiman seems, initially at least, a foregone conclusion: What more could there possibly be to say about one of the most influential creators of children's literature, adult literature (if there's a difference), comic books, graphic novels, television episodes, science fiction, darkly humorous novels, mixed-media, adult-style picture books, video games, and genre-bending, spoken-word performances that has not been already said? In truth, if one peruses the list of major works near the end of this volume, to even name, let alone offer comment upon, even a quarter of his contributions to the literary canon since 1985 might take twice the length of the space of this chapter. As such, we have attempted to give a brief overview of the work that has been done most recently on Gaiman's body of texts, while also providing a bit more information about some of the lesser-known aspects of his career (that is, beyond *The Sandman* and his longer fiction). Finally, we give a small taste of the possibilities yet to come in studies about Gaiman's impact on the literary world and beyond.

Academic and Popular Criticism

Broadly speaking, Neil Gaiman has become one of the core, canonical authors in several fields of literary study, including, but certainly not limited to: science fiction and fantasy, comic studies, and children's literature. To wit, in *Voices of Vision* (2005), a book of interviews with contemporary fantasy and science-fiction authors, journalist and public information specialist Jayme Lynn Blaschke features Gaiman as one of the foremost creators of fantasy/sci-fi literature, alongside heavyweights like Samuel R. Delaney, blankly stating that he might be "one of the most important fantasists of contemporary literature" (127). A year later, in an interview with the *SF Site*'s Rick Klaw, Blaschke admits that Gaiman's inclusion became one of the book's largest selling points, with its cover perhaps inspired by Gaiman's then recently-published *Sandman* collection, *The Doll's House* (1). Not long after, in 2008, critics Philip Sandifer and Tof Eklund mused that "Gaiman is one of those comics creators . . . who one could assemble a special issue on without having to justify the worth of the endeavor" (1).

This litany of critical compliment is somewhat endless (to choose an apt term) and all-encompassing of Gaiman's work regardless of genre, mode, or medium. Chloé Germaine Buckley, writing in the *Children's Literature Association Quarterly*, contends that Neil Gaiman, especially with his novel *Coraline* (2002), "has rapidly achieved canonical status" (58) in the field of children's literature, a classic to be read alongside *Through the Looking-Glass* (1871) as "a rewriting . . . by way of Freud's essay 'The Uncanny'" (58). Even more recently, in volume 207 of *Children's Literature Review* (March 2016), Jelena Krstovic observes that "commentators have admired Gaiman's skill and ingenuity in creating fanciful characters, parallel worlds, and imaginative mythologies" (2). She goes on to list eight recently-published works, ranging from monographs to articles, on a variety of Gaiman texts across genres: *The Sandman*, his novel *American Gods* (2001), his graphic novelization with P. Craig Russell of children's novel *Coraline* (2008), and even his first penned episode of the hit BBC television show, *Doctor Who* (episode 216, "The Doctor's Wife," 2011).

Book-length scholarship concerning his works range from edited collections, like Tara Prescott's *Neil Gaiman in the 21st Century: Essays on the Novels, Children's Stories, Online Writings, Comics and Other Works* (McFarland, 2015); Prescott and Aaron Drucker's *Feminism in the Worlds of Neil Gaiman: Essays on the Comics, Poetry, and Prose* (McFarland, 2012); Tracy L. Bealer, Rachel Luria, and Wayne Yuen's *Neil Gaiman and Philosophy: Gods Gone Wild!* (Open Court, 2012), to more popular publications, like fan guides such as Hank Wagner, Christopher Golden, and Stephen R. Bissette's *Prince of Stories: The Many Worlds of Neil Gaiman* (St. Martin's, 2008). Also available are popular monographs, like Hayley Campbell's *The Art of Neil Gaiman* (Harper Design, 2014);

guidebook anthologies, like Joe Sanders' *The Sandman Papers* (Fantagraphics, 2006); critical sourcebooks and companions, such as Alisa Kwitney's *The Sandman: King of Dreams* (Chronicle, 2003) and Hy Bender's *Sandman Companion* (DC Comics, 1999). Scholarly paeans include Steven Rauch's *The Sandman and Joseph Campbell* (Wildside, 2003). Articles and book chapters—too numerous to list here but well catalogued in this volume's Bibliography, located in the Resources section—abound, focusing on his ability to cross genres; to redefine publishing trends; to change comics readership; and, more than anything, to write outstanding pieces of literature.

Popular Reception: Breaking Boundaries
Indeed, since completing formal academics, Gaiman has immersed himself in his career as a writer, writing his first novel, a children's book titled *My Great Aunt Ermintrude*, partly in order to prove to his children that he was, in fact, a writer (Gaiman, "Interview"). He then sent the book out to Kestrel Books, upon which he promptly received a rejection. This turned out to be a blessing in disguise, as Gaiman recalls: "The great thing about not being very good yet is I didn't know I wasn't very good yet. I thought I was brilliant. And thinking that I was brilliant gave me the confidence to keep going until I actually happened to learn my craft enough to not be crap" (Campbell 36). Failure and mistakes, he maintains elsewhere, are part of the job. He explains that the smash hit *Coraline* was so named because of a typing mistake, in which he transposed the "a" and the "o" in "Caroline" on a QWERTY keyboard, but he never changed the error because "'Coraline' almost looks like a real name" (36).

Nevertheless, failure and its companion, feeling utterly lost, have not coincidentally formed much of the fuel for Gaiman's successes. Consider, for example, one of his most famous lectures, the "Make Good Art" talk, delivered at the commencement of The University of the Arts in 2012. In part, he says:

> When you start out on a career in the arts you have no idea what you are doing. This is great. People who know what they are doing know the rules, and know what is possible and impossible. You do not. And you should not. The rules on what is possible and impossible in

the arts were made by people who had not tested the bounds of the possible by going beyond them. And you can. If you don't know it's impossible it's easier to do. And because nobody's done it before, they haven't made up rules to stop anyone doing that again, yet.

To be sure, Gaiman's illustrious career has been guided by boundary-breaking. In 1991, *The Sandman* #19, "A Midsummer Night's Dream," became the first comic book to win the World Fantasy Award (WFA) for Best Short Fiction, which caused the WFA to change the rules to exclude comics from the competition from that point thereafter (see Wilson's introduction to *The Sandman, Vol. 1: Preludes and Nocturnes*, 1991). *The Sandman* was especially noteworthy as one of the comics that revitalized DC's presence (under the Vertigo imprint) in the market, even as comic book sales elsewhere fell, because of its appeal to readers who did not fit the usual considerations of the comic book reader mold at the time. (Think "Comic Book Guy" from *The Simpsons*.) His novels *Coraline* and *The Graveyard Book*, both ostensibly seen as having been written for children or young adults, have both won numerous awards specifically for children's and adolescent literature, such as the Locus Awards in Best Young Adult Novel and Best Young Adult Book, respectively, as well as an Eisner for Best Publication for Teens/Tweens for *Coraline*'s adaptation by Gaiman and P. Craig Russell, not to mention both a Carnegie *and* Newbery Medal for *The Graveyard Book*—the *first* book ever to enjoy winning the medals simultaneously. And while noteworthy, they have both been awarded in competitions usually reserved for *adult* fiction as well, with *Coraline* winning a Hugo and a Nebula award for Best Novella and *The Graveyard Book* winning a Hugo and British Fantasy award for Best Novel.

"Make Good Art"
These award lists are not limited merely to Gaiman's novels, and their difficulty in categorization—as children's literature, as young adult literature, as adult literature (See Annette Wannamaker's chapter, "Guilty Pleasures: Neil Gaiman's Books for Children for Adults," later in this volume.)—extends to Gaiman as an author,

plain and simple. Despite the difficulty of categorization (or perhaps precisely *because* of it) Gaiman has become one of the most-lauded individual writers of the twentieth and twenty-first centuries. This is in keeping with his mantra, delivered to the students of the University of the Arts in Philadelphia, to, above all other things and in any particularized situation, "make good art":

> Make good art. I'm serious. Husband runs off with a politician? Make good art. Leg crushed and then eaten by mutated boa constrictor? Make good art. IRS on your trail? Make good art. Cat exploded? Make good art. Somebody on the Internet thinks what you do is stupid or evil or it's all been done before? Make good art. Probably things will work out somehow, and eventually time will take the sting away, but that doesn't matter. Do what only you do best. Make good art.

And good art he has made. Collectively, Gaiman has won four Bram Stoker Awards, has two Nebula Awards, and six Hugo Awards or nominations. His novels, *Good Omens* (with Terry Pratchett) and *Stardust* have each been runners-up for the Locus Awards' Best Fantasy Novel awards; *American Gods* won the award in 2002, and, in total, he has fifteen Locus Awards or nominations. He has won multiple Best Short Story awards for such tales as "A Study in Emerald," "Sunbird," and "How to Talk to Girls at Parties," in addition to multiple Shirley Jackson Awards and British Fantasy Awards. Beyond the page, Gaiman has even secured a William Shatner Golden Groundhog (for *MirrorMask*, the BBC-scripted television series and novel), a Ray Bradbury award (for "The Doctor's Wife" from the BBS television series *Doctor Who*), and a Bob Clampett Humanitarian Award. But perhaps his most-awarded work, of course, is *The Sandman*. As of this writing and counting Gaiman's original series, its spin-off comic series, novella, and collection of short stories, *The Sandman* series (including the novelizations, one-shots, and continuation into the prequel *The Sandman: Overture*) has won over twenty-six Eisner Awards, including Best Writer, Best Single Issue or Story, Best Continuing

Series, as well as the World Fantasy Award, the Hugo Award, and the Bram Stoker Award (Hahn).

IN-DEPTH: Comics, Graphic Novels, and The Sandman
Since its publication, Gaiman's reinvigoration of *The Sandman* has become one of the most critically-lauded comic book series of all time. Running for seventy-five issues (not including the aforementioned prequels and one-shots), the success of *The Sandman* spawned numerous spin-off comic series, including *Death: The High Cost of Living*, *Lucifer*, and *Dead Boy Detectives*. The depth with which Gaiman crafted each issue of *The Sandman* helped elevate comics beyond the pulp series and colorful superheroics of previous decades, infusing connections to the works of William Shakespeare, T. S. Eliot, and Greek and Norse mythology alongside references to Mary Poppins, Julius Ceasar, and Marco Polo. Further, as Kathryn Hume notes, *The Sandman* is crafted according to one of the oldest storytelling genres: the frame tale (345). Something like a modern-day *Decameron*, *One Thousand and One Nights*, or *Canterbury Tales*, Gaiman's *The Sandman* relishes in the varied experiences of storytelling: of telling, of being told to, of being told about (Hume 346). At the same time, Hume notes that the overall structure of the work reflects a deeply Romantic mythos, one that, rather than running from death, embraces it (362). Gaiman's series offered a dark fantasy tale of epic proportions about family, love, and loss amidst a time in comics dominated by hyper-muscled superheroes and realistic, gritty depictions of the world. Though Gaiman wrote and published several projects prior to this, *The Sandman* is what established Gaiman's status as a writer of critical and cultural importance. Alongside, and certainly inspired by, Alan Moore's work on *Saga of the Swamp Thing* and *Watchmen*, Gaiman's work on *Sandman* is often credited with ushering in the modern age of comics, marking the series as a watershed moment not only for his career but for the medium itself.

IN-DEPTH: Mixed Praise in Film and Television

To this day, *The Sandman* remains the most popular topic for literary criticism about Gaiman's work, closely followed by *Coraline* and *The Graveyard Book*. Entire special issues of academic journals and, indeed, whole volumes could be given over solely to *Sandman* scholarship and still not be sufficient. However, one of the relatively-unexamined and yet important aspects of Gaiman's artistry lies in his work not on the comic's or novel's page, but on the motion picture and television screen. Following his success with *The Sandman* and *Good Omens*, Gaiman was contracted by the British Broadcasting Company (BBC) to write a fantasy television show, which he titled *Neverwhere* (Wagner, Golden, & Bissette loc. 6619). The show's protagonist, Richard Mayhew, ventures from the London he knows to the London Below, a not-so-perfect mirror image of London above. Gaiman takes several cues from "a book set in Chicago called *Free, Live Free* by Gene Wolfe," in which the city of Chicago operates much like a character in the novel, inspiring Neil to do something similar with London (Gaiman, "Letter"). First debuting on September 12, 1996, *Neverwhere* consisted of six thirty-minute episodes that were unfortunately not well-received at the time, critically or otherwise. While writing for *Neverwhere*, Gaiman compromised on elements of his script, causing him to feel that he'd lost control over the project. Consequently, Gaiman wrote a novelization of the series to realize his vision of *Neverwhere*.

Unlike the television show, *Neverwhere* the novel was published to critical and commercial acclaim; however, his dissatisfaction with the television writing and production process would keep Gaiman from working with Hollywood for more than a decade on film projects (Campbell 210). His next projects in film were an adaptation of Hayao Miyazaki's *Princess Mononoke* in 1997 for Miramax, Gaiman's directorial debut in the direct-to-video project entitled *A Short Film About John Bolton* (2002), and popular underground film *MirrorMask* (2005, with Dave McKean), which enjoyed some success on the independent film circuit but was ultimately panned for its script. It was not until 2007 that Gaiman would find silver-screen success, and it was mixed at best. Gaiman wrote or produced two films that year: the adaptation of his award-winning novel *Stardust*, directed (and scripted) by Matthew Vaughn for Paramount and featuring an enormous star-studded cast, and Robert Zemeckis' *Beowulf*, which he co-wrote with Roger Avary (*Pulp Fiction*) for Paramount/Warner Brothers. Reception of the two films was relatively positive, but ultimately lukewarm, and the distinctions between them are puzzling. In terms of monetary value, *Stardust* is the clear winner, grossing $135.5 million worldwide on an $88.5 million budget—a net gain of $47 million before considering Hollywood mathematics. Conversely, *Beowulf* had an operating budget of $150 million, considerably more than *Stardust*, yet *Beowulf* grossed only $196.4 million, $46.4 million over its budget. Though they both earned nearly the same amount, neither could be deemed an outright success, considering *Stardust*'s profits were more than half its operating budget, while *Beowulf*'s profits are not even a third of its operating budget. Stunningly, critics like Roger Ebert gave the more successful movie the lower rating: *Stardust* earned two and a half out of four stars, while *Beowulf* garnered three out of four. And much of the critical appreciation, was entirely for the film's technological prowess and its use of 3-D technology: Peter Travers of *Rolling Stone* writes that he had "never seen a 3-D movie pop with this kind of clarity and oomph." While *Empire*'s Tom Ambrose explains that *Beowulf* is "the finest example to date of the capabilities of this new technique."

Gaiman's adaptations would, however, ultimately seize the day. The film adaptation of *Coraline*, released in 2009 and produced by Laika for Focus Films was an instant success, grossing over $123 million worldwide by November 2009 on a budget of a mere $60 million. *Coraline* was beloved by critics as well: it was nominated for award by the Academy Awards, the Broadcast Film Critics Association, the BAFTAs, the Golden Globes, and People's Choice Awards in 2009. It won awards from the San Francisco Film Critics, Alliance of Women Film Journalists, BAFTA Children's Awards, Annecy International Film Festival, and the American Film Institute. In addition, *Coraline* won two Cinema Audio Society Awards (Lifetime Achievement for Henry Selick and Career Achievement for Randy Thom) and three Annie Awards (Best Music in an Animated Feature for Bruno Coulais, Best Character Design for Shane Prigmore and Shannon Tindle, and Best Production Design for Christopher Appelhaus and Tadahiro Uesugi). Again, fewer awards for the film's content as opposed to its plot, but it's important to note that Gaiman neither wrote nor produced *Coraline*.

Even these successes, however, did not persuade Gaiman to go back to television in any capacity beyond that of writer and sometimes actor. A brief stint writing a single episode of *Babylon 5* in 1997 comprised his television writing credits until after the releases of *Beowulf* and *Coraline*. Granted, it is noteworthy that Gaiman is the only other writer for the series (after the second season) other than J. Michael Staczynski. After writing for *10 Minute Tales* in 2009 and appearing as himself in *Arthur* in 2010, Gaiman was invited to fulfill a childhood dream: writing for *Doctor Who* (current edition 2006–present). As a young child, he became enamored of the fantastic travels of the Doctor and his companions, watching and reading everything he could get his hands on. Gaiman was contacted to write a script for a *Doctor Who* episode, which he announced on February 7, 2010. He continued to update his progress on the episode through his blog, giving fans insight into his creative process. Drawing on his considerable knowledge of the show, Gaiman drew up something nobody had depicted yet—a humanized incarnation of the TARDIS, the Doctor's vessel for travelling through time and space. The episode he wrote, "The Doctor's Wife," was released on May 14, 2011, drawing instantaneous and immense positive reactions from *Doctor Who* fans the world over, earned Gaiman a Hugo Award on September 2, 2012. His momentum from *Doctor Who* propelled him to guest appear on *The Simpsons* in 2011, playing himself in the November 20, 2011 episode "The Book Job," an episode that focused on Lisa's discovery that nearly all young-adult authors write through ghostwriters. To combat this, Lisa decides to write a novel of her own, which ultimately sells well. Much to her chagrin (and in a moment of self-conscious mockery), it is revealed that Neil Gaiman stole the writing credits for the book, switching out the flash drive on which the tale was told for one featuring him as the author. He thus heists his way to the top of the bestsellers list despite being revealed as fundamentally illiterate. Perhaps bolstered by these victories with major television series, Gaiman recently made a return to broadcast television, starting with his role as executive producer of *Neil Gaiman's Likely Stories*, a short-run series based on four of his short stories. His most anticipated television project, the STARZ-exclusive adaptation of *American Gods*, for which he is again an executive producer, is slated for release in 2017.

IN-DEPTH: A Middling Foray into Video Games
Continuing his expansion into different manners of storytelling, Gaiman signed on to write a video game entitled *Wayward Manor* with independent developer The Odd Gentlemen. In theory, the recipe seemed destined for success: Gaiman, as one of the most celebrated storytellers of the twenty-first century, was pairing up with an up-and-coming indie game developing company to create a macabre game set in a gothic, haunted house in which the player must take on the role of a ghost to cheekily scare squatters out of the eponymously-named manor house. Like Gaiman's first, much-maligned foray into television writing, *Wayward Manor* was strangely universally panned by video game critics, holding a 41/100 on rating aggregate *Metacritic*. A combination of graphical glitching, unresponsive mechanics, and sometimes overly-simplistic puzzles left critics puzzled, as Christopher Livingston writes in *PC Gamer* that *Wayward Manor* "becomes an exercise in trial-and-error instead of strategy." Zack Kotzer, writing for *Motherboard*, argues that *Wayward Manor* fails to capture the "creepy, clever, uncanny contemporary fantasies" for which Gaiman is known, instead watering it down into "family-friendly frights" that are "nowhere near as scary or creatively brilliant as his past work." Writing for *Kill Screen*, Lindsey Joyce laments that "*Wayward Manor* lacks any true Gaiman aesthetic [. . .] unfortunately, every bit of Gaiman's aesthetic that is present in the game is not playable, and what is playable lacks any of Gaiman's flair." Joyce chalks this up to Gaiman's veritable unfamiliarity with writing for the medium. After all, part of what makes Gaiman such a powerful presence in writing

graphic narratives, theater, films, and music is his deep respect, appreciation, and experience with those storytelling mediums. On the other hand, Gaiman writes in his journal, dated January 6, 2009 and entitled "The Awful Truth," that his only experience with a gaming console is "using the Wii as an exercisey fitness thingummy." Truly profound gaming narratives require the same nativity and love of the medium as any other, and Joyce remarks that "it seems, perhaps, that Gaiman's desire to make a video game was not coupled with a passion for the medium itself." Ultimately, *Wayward Manor* stands as a testament to a brand overshadowing an idea; Gaiman is known for the long percolating time on his projects, which often grow over years of rumination, and *Wayward Manor* screams "unfinished" in both concept and execution. As original as the story is—and the story itself *is* good—the game fails to take advantage of the hallmarks of Gaiman's dry, dark wit in ways it might not have, had The Odd Gentlemen given it further time in development. As if proof of the concerns, Joyce and others have voiced in their reviews, Gaiman has not made apparent any further plans to work in video game storytelling any time soon.

LOOKING FORWARD: The Critical Future of Neil Gaiman Studies

We have spent considerable time laying yet more praise on Neil Gaiman and his expansive *oeuvre*, but we must concede that, for an author so widely read, beloved, and recognized, there yet remains a dearth of scholarship on a significant portion of his literary corpus. For example, Gaiman's writing roots extend deeply into journalism and nonfiction, and to this day, some of his most respected writings are not "made up things," as he calls his fiction, but his observations on the real world. In 2016, readers were finally treated to an expansive collection of Gaiman's finest nonfiction writing, *The View from the Cheap Seats* (Harper-Collins). Junot Díaz's glowing remarks on the book call it "a glorious love-letter to reading, to writing, to dreaming, to an entire genre." This is high praise for any living author, but Díaz joins a host of other writers respected for their own contributions, such as Stephen King, in heaping praise upon Gaiman's influence on the contemporary written word. Our own studies in the academy should take note and do the same. It is always difficult to foresee the shifting of trends in criticism, literary analysis, rhetoric and composition studies, media studies, cultural studies, and children's literature, but we hope to offer a small selection of topics ripe for examination in the near future. In addition to his nonfiction, Gaiman's status as a cult-figure-cum-icon leaves ample room for application of star studies and brand studies, analyzing Gaiman's "authorial self" against his various personae: his online presence, Twitter user, writing commentator, and patron of the arts. More textual critiques of Gaiman's unique style of gallows humor, especially his common play with what literary critics label as the carnivalesque, is a sorely needed topic of discussion, particularly as an avenue to reconciling the split between ostensibly 'adult' fiction and so-called 'kiddie lit.' Stepping away from his purely written fiction, a closer look at Gaiman's 'lost' texts, such as *Lady Justice, Mr. Hero,* and *Teknophage,* merits a closer look, especially in counterpoint to the outstanding successes of *The Sandman.* Along those lines, further inquiry into co-authorship, co-ownership, and collaborative creation would serve as a way to discuss Gaiman's unique approach to storytelling, which is more often than not in collaboration with another artist.

There is one overarching goal for these examinations—to understand Gaiman by the criteria he uses to define himself and his works: as a *storyteller*. Gaiman is more than simply an author of fantasy, or children's literature, or ironic humor, or British understatement, or adaptation, or a ridiculously well-read writer. The critic's task, we suspect, is to suss out what makes Gaiman so uniquely 'Gaimany' within his own idiom. What are the qualities that make his literature, graphic narratives, films, and other stories so compelling, so readable, and so accessible by such an immense swath of readers? Certainly, what makes a Gaiman story precisely that is encapsulated with notes of nostalgia, horror, melancholy, hope, laughter, and almost everything in between. All of these notes are connected through Gaiman's stories and in the man himself: in his Twitter presence, his openness to interview, even in his speeches:

he weaponizes stories to make larger cultural points. Truth be told, something of what makes Gaiman so interesting is, perhaps, that we feel like we are watching yet another of his incredible—uncategorizable, unyielding, unforgettable—stories unfold before us. In many ways, we close recognizing how privileged we are to be alive *now*, as part of his audience, while his stories continue to unfold within all our lifetimes.

Works Cited

Ambrose, Tom. "Beowulf Review." *Empire*. Empire, 26 Jan. 2016. Web. 14 Sept. 2016. <http://www.empireonline.com/movies/beowulf/review/>.

Blaschke, Jayme Lynn. *Voices of Vision: Creators of Science Fiction and Fantasy Speak*. Lincoln: U of Nebraska P, 2005. Print.

Buckley, Chloé Germaine. "Psychoanalysis, 'Gothic' Children's Literature, and the Canonization of *Coraline*." *Children's Literature Association Quarterly* 40.1 (Spring 2015): 58-79. Print.

Campbell, Hayley. *The Art of Neil Gaiman*. New York: Harper Collins, 2014. Print.

Gaiman, Madeleine. "Maddy Gaiman Interviews Her Dad." *Neil Gaiman's Journal*. Harper Collins Publishers, 15 Jun., 2004. Web. 6 Aug. 2016. <www.neilgaiman.com/mediafiles/exclusive/Audio/Maddy.mp3>.

Gaiman, Neil. "The Awful Truth." *Journal: Neil Gaiman.com*. Harper Collins Publishers, 6 Jan 2009. Web. 9 Sep. 2016. <http://journal.neilgaiman.com/2009/01/awful-truth.html>.

———. "Letter from Neil Gaiman." *Chicago Public Library*. Chicago Public Library, 2016. Web. 4 Aug 2016. <http://www.chipublib.org/letter-from-neil-gaiman/>.

———. "Keynote Address 2012." *The University of the Arts*. Philadelphia, PA, 17 May 2012. Web. 8 Sept. 2016. <http://www.uarts.edu/neil-gaiman-keynote-address-2012>.

Hahn, Joel. "Will Eisner Comic Industry Award: Summary of Winners," *Comic Book Awards Almanac*. Joel Hahn, 2006. Web. 7 Aug 2016. <www.hahnlibrary.net/comics/awards/eisner.php>.

Hume, Kathryn. "Neil Gaiman's *Sandman* as Mythic Romance." *Genre* 46.3 (2013): 345-365. Print.

Joyce, Lindsey. "How Does *Wayward Manor* Fit into Neil Gaiman's Oeuvre? It Doesn't." *Kill Screen*. Kill Screen Media, Inc., 13 Aug 2014. Web. 9 Sept. 2016. <https://killscreen.com/articles/how-does-wayward-manor-fit-neil-gaimans-ouevre-it-doesnt>.

Klaw, Rick. "Like a Virgin: A Conversation with Jayme Lynn Blaschke." *SF Site Interview*. SF Site, February 2006. Web. 7 Sept. 2016. <https://www.sfsite.com/03b/jba220.htm>.

Kotzer, Zack. "Neil Gaiman's New Video Game Isn't Nearly Scary Enough." *Motherboard*. Vice Media LLC, 5 Aug. 2014. Web. 9 Sep. 2016. <http://motherboard.vice.com/read/neil-gaimans-new-video-game-isnt-nearly-scary-enough>.

Krstovic, Jelena. "Critical Reception: Neil Gaiman." *The Children's Literature Review* 207 (March 2016): 2-3. Detroit: Gale Publishing. Print.

Livingston, Christopher. "Wayward Manor Review." *PC Gamer*. PC Gamer, 16 Jul. 2014. Web. 14 Sept. 2016. <http://www.pcgamer.com/wayward-manor-review/>.

Sandifer, Philip & Tof Eklund. "Introduction." *ImageTexT: Interdisciplinary Comics Studies* 4.1 (2008). Dept. of English, University of Florida. Web. 5 Sep 2016. <http://www.english.ufl.edu/imagetext/archives/v4_1/introduction.shtml>.

Travers, Peter. "Beowulf." *Rolling Stone*. Rolling Stone, 15 Nov. 2007. Web. 14 Sept. 2016. <http://www.rollingstone.com/movies/reviews/beowulf-20071115>.

Wagner, Hank, Christopher Golden, & Stephen R. Bissette. *Prince of Stories: The Many Worlds of Neil Gaiman*. New York: St. Martin's Press. 2009. Kindle.

Embodied in Name Alone: Nobody Owens and the Metonymic Estrangement from the Living and the Dead in Neil Gaiman's *The Graveyard Book*

Joseph Michael Sommers

Any reader even remotely familiar with the prose work of Neil Gaiman can attest to his love of allegory, metaphor, and metonymy. From his early forays into journalism back in the 1980s; through his numerous short stories and related ephemera; into what many hold as their first real exposure to the writer; DC Comics' Vertigo Imprint of *The Sandman* (covered, at length, in several other chapters); and, later, a ridiculously-successful string of novels and short story collections, Gaiman has a tenacious knack for loading his characters with a seemingly thinly-layered wordplay that is highly self-reflexive of a larger metaphor inherent to the plot's development. Whether the reader is reconsidering the interplay of Death, Destiny, Destruction, Despair, Desire, Delirium, and, of course, Dream, better known as the embodied concepts or "repeating motifs" (*Brief Lives,* Gaiman # 48) of nature known as the Endless in *The Sandman*, or his and Terry Pratchett's minor alteration to the gathering of the Four Horseman of the Apocalypse in *Good Omens* (1990), in which he substituted Pollution for Pestilence (Pesty retired in 1936 due to the discovery of penicillin [249].), to the naming of "Victoria" as a distillation of the Victorian Age (Gooding 218) for Tristram's affections in his fairy story, *Stardust* (1998). In each of these instances, among so many others, Gaiman seems to sample literary riffs in an effort to embody his characters with some larger thematic conceit that services his original narrative. Upon examining *The Graveyard Book* (2008), one might suspect nothing different; it is, after all, a cleverly constructed analogue to Rudyard Kipling's *The Jungle Book* (1894). It just so happens to be set in a graveyard replete with vampires, werewolves, and an Assyrian mummy holding a small pig (239). Nevertheless, while *The Graveyard Book* is far less allegorical in its construct than analogical to the Kipling work, where it ceases to be indebted to its predecessor in most terms other than in construction and overarching scaffolding, it becomes far more indebted to exploring Gaiman's nuanced subjugation of his characters into the servitude of large metonymic bodies of reference to his main project in each narrative.

In this instance, Gaiman's construction of Bod Owens—a boy who is a body named "Nobody," a child raised in and by both the worlds of the living and of the dead—creates a complex metaphor for the insider/outsider identity Gaiman has identified in the young boy's maturation. This chapter seeks to locate Bod as literally lost and disembodied within Gaiman's construction of his own unique ontology. Bod, himself, is ostensibly caught between the living and the dead, as he does not associate well or successfully with either even though he seeks refuge and comfort from both to little avail. Yet, the Graveyard's conditional acceptance of Bod as their ward means that he must be granted the "Freedom of the Graveyard," (Gaiman, *Graveyard Book* 23) a peculiar condition that affords him many of the abilities of both human and apparition alike while really not being *entirely* either. It's difficult to consider Bod, very-much a metonymical construct of '*Nobody's child*', a human in any traditional sense as he is left orphaned from his slaughtered human family and adopted, raised, and taught of the living from an almost-entirely dead, undead, and largely non-corporeal cast of surrogates. This unusual metonymic condition leaves him in a state of development that, while not entirely arrested, seems focused not on the life ahead of him but on the lives of those who have passed that raise him. Bod approaches youth in much the same manner that the elderly might approach death, reflective and somewhat distant, even though it is his own life, and he has barely lived much in it. Gaiman constructs a sort of literal and self-reflexive *Bildungsroman*, a novel of formation (Millard), literally trying to give a corporeal form to an entity who, by his circumstantial design, tries to divest himself of a corporeal form (as convenient), in order to craft a form that he will eventually become. In other words, this coming-of-age story actually leaves Bod in the bizarre position of being entirely uncomfortable, estranged if you will, from both the living and the dead as he approaches the point in his adolescence where he must leave the Graveyard and begin his 'life' after already metonymically experiencing his death.

Critical commentary on Gaiman is a simple enough matter . . . as long as one subscribes, as Philip Sandifer and Tof Eklund rightly point out, primarily to psychoanalytic or archetypal readings of his work. Go figure that a writer most fondly considered for his work on *The Sandman* has a considerable amount of his criticism tied up with and, as they claim, "overworked" in one particular theoretical approach. Interestingly enough, both overwrought approaches tie up nicely into a metonymical reading, and I will try to escape such psychoanalysis, but, to work with identity and metonymy is to work with Jacques Lacan and his contemporaries. As such, I will fail to avoid Sandifer and Eklund's theory-bound traps. However, while I will escape them; in order to proceed with my own analysis, I must acquiesce to Lacan's. Yet, Lacanian theory allows a reading that demonstrates Gaiman's use of self-reflexive metonymy in an effort to craft a *Bildungsroman* for the reader that predates life, itself, and quite literally allows Bod to come of age from an arrested state of ageless moral growth and disembodiment. Gaiman simply teaches Nobody how to live by letting him learn, first-hand, of the manners in which humans die.

Identifying Metonymy within Gaiman

Acquiring, challenging, and potentially losing one's identity is a topic that Gaiman has worked with before in texts such as *Coraline*. Elizabeth Parson et al. has noted how that title character seems to be at odds with her own identity as she is constantly mistaken, in name, for "the more common [. . .] Caroline" (377). As such, Coraline "must resolve a sense of self" lest she continue to look into the mirror and see her parents, let alone become one of the Other Mother's victims: non-corporeal ghost children who have lost any sense of identity, their souls discarded after the Other Mother feasted upon their bodies (Gaiman 84). The body, for both Gaiman's protagonists, and, of course, Lacan, is rather important in identification. As one critic states, paraphrasing Lacan, "the mediatization of one's subjecthood [comes] through a 'body'" (Reed); what happens then when that body flickers between corporeality and transparency, as the ghost children illustrate, is another problem all together. But it is that particular blurry state of the (textually) constructed body that makes Bod's situation in *TGB* all the more interesting for me more than Gaiman's prior narratives, graphic or otherwise. Gaiman's choice of "words," says Jon Saklofske, can "simultaneously inform and deform the human body and the human being through self-reflexive elements of form and content." Somewhat cheekily naming the central protagonist "Nobody" seems to toe that line.

But, for this essay's purposes, perhaps I should clear up the central term: What is metonymy? I prefer Don Callen's *admittedly-Lacanian* definition: "Metonymy is a figurative use of signifiers [that rearranges] the purposive relationships, the teleological shape, of things.... What one sees as contiguous and as parts, the way in which they relate to the whole, must be rearranged"[1]; by Callen's definition, metonymy provides authority. "A name for a part or contiguous object is made to re-present the whole," he says; "*not just stand for the whole but in some way to refigure the whole.*" In regards to majority of Gaiman's work, the purposeful function of using metonymic constructs is to create both an intertexuality and a somewhat "paratextuality" as a result of the "incorporation of the bodies of other works within the body of his work(s)" (Smith). Clay Smith expands on that idea when he says that:

> Gaiman utilizes a constant rhetorical strategy that explicitly and implicitly cites/sites citationality within his works not as textual free play but as textual foreclosure. Most often these references appear in the form of direct and indirect quotes embedded within the body of his work, but they also assume other forms of reference.... Despite its presence in seemingly different formats . . . this referentiality (re) articulates the same message: Gaiman is the vortex.

Prior to *The Graveyard Book*, I would concur. It is with the construct of Nobody Owens, however, where Gaiman's use of metonymy becomes less incorporative and more authoritative and displacing along the routes recommended here. Nobody Owens, Gaiman's boy who (un)becomes being a boy in order to grow into manhood, illustrates a radical slip into the desire to identify with humanity. When he does, however, humanity slips from him entirely.

Psychoanalyzing Metonym and Deconstructing Textual Humanity

Humanity, however, for Bod must come at a very textually-constructed, if not heavily-indebted, price. Gaiman's obvious wordplay in the boy's name insists upon an opportunity for pedantry on the human condition (particularly when counter-pointed against so many of his custodians who exist under the condition of no longer being *living* humans) whether the character under construction cares for the imposition of self-reflexivity or not. And, if such lessons seem to be fraught with a somewhat unnecessarily heavy freight, well, one must consider Lacan's own views on metonymy; in "The Instance of the Letter in the Unconscious, or Reason Since Freud," Lacan states quite clearly at onset that to understand his concept of metonym, a concept of "text" must be considered that leaves "the reader with no other way out than the way in, which I *prefer* to be difficult" (421, emphasis mine). I shall endeavor to resist his preference myself. Regardless of either inclination, the fact remains that Gaiman constructs Bod as a characterization trapped within a *Bildungsroman* in an effort to teach the reader something of the protagonist's moral and psychical development by articulating his struggle for the audience to associate with. In other words, Bod's hopes for eventual corporeality, his humanity, is very much trapped within the cellblock of Gaiman's language and the rules of the *Bildungsroman* itself, which make a compact with the reader that growth will occur and all will be made clear by story's close. Lacan frankly disagrees with this concept. He says that "language is not to be confused with the various psychical . . . functions that serve it in the speaking subject" (413). He adds that "the subject, while he may appear to be the slave of language, is still more the slave of discourse in the universal movement of which his place is already inscribed at his birth, if only in the form of his proper name" (414). This concept is particularly touchy when your name is Nobody, that name comes by a sort of inverse rebirth out of formally-regarded state of living, and the discourse conventions you operate within actually would prefer you to become a somebody through the acquisition of *any* body by whatever means.

However, this idea simply brings the reader back to metonymy, a trope for Lacan that, while packed with all the significance and grandeur mentioned above (and quite a bit more actually), breaks down to a simple *"word-to-word"* nature of connection (421). For my purposes, while Lacan still sees metonym as many do, a part illustrating a whole, he also utilizes the definition of that very loose bond to unpack metonym of greater interpretive possibilities and valances; yes, Gaiman borrowed very loosely a title and structure from Kipling's *The Jungle Book* for his *The Graveyard Book*, but, ultimately, what more does the one inform the reader about the other in terms of the greater significance of the connection between the two? Ultimately, I would suggest nothing (while acknowledging that the feral Mowgli is, just the same, a boy without language, testing the boundaries of the constructs of what might be considered 'humanity' or, at least, 'personhood'). Likewise, Gaiman names his protagonist "Nobody Owens," who, he will show, is quite a very prominent somebody to virtually *everybody* connected within the interlocking stories of *The Graveyard Book*; in other words, to connect and exhort the connection between the insubstantial with the corporeal and, when one factors the reader into this equation, the consubstantial, is to simultaneously concoct what psychoanalysts would likely find Bod to be as both, but not simultaneously, a "true self" and a "false self" in terms of his identity (Winnicott 140). In other words, the connections between the signifiers, corporeality/humanity and the written Bod, are clear enough, but, not unlike any other set of signifiers, they can be determined and interpreted in many different ways by a reader as the weak bond of metonymy makes little remark about what is true or false regarding identity formation without the interlocution of the reader to impose order and humanity upon nothing more than weak associations. Or, as Lacan says, "metonymic structure . . . allows for the elision by which the signifier instates lack of being in the object-relation. [It uses] signification's referral value to invest it with the desire aiming at the lack that it supports" (428). All of this goes to suggest that the aforementioned mediatization of one's subjecthood through a "body," and the understanding that the body as perceived through a mirror's reflection in a whole and ideal form is separate from (and thus fragments one's perception of) the self, are heretofore unreflected; the reflection is a representation of self just as all other bodies one perceives are merely representations of others' selves, connected to but semiotically distinct from the "I" (Reed). Lacan recognizes that this central act of identification manifests both in the real actions of individual development and metaphorically in the "ontological structure of the human world" (Reed).

As a point of clarification, Lacan never uses the terms "true self" and "false self"; although he makes similar associations, he calls them true and false "identity[ies]" (413). The ideas actually derive from Donald Winnicott.[2] Without overburdening the definitions too much, for Winnicott, the true self is the "creative" and "real" aspects of life and being alive—there is a difference between them—based upon actual experiences, while the false self is more artifice, "futility," and a sham of the true self used primarily for defensive measures of protecting the true self during the development of the person (148, 142). Why is this construction relevant to this discussion? Winnicott's concept allows Gaiman's seemingly self-reflexive paradox of Bod's non-corporeality in the *Bildungsroman* to be realized by way of crafting his metonymity as part and parcel to his development. When Bod is denatured by the abandonment of his living family and conditional acceptance by the Graveyard (conditional in that he must exist in a state of fluctuating existence between the living and the dead), he is inscribed by Silas, acting as Gaiman's textual proxy, as Nobody: "'Then Nobody it is,' said Silas," (Gaiman 25); yet, he is recognized by virtually everyone else as "Bod" illustrating his corporeality, his literal eventual embodiment in reality, as something by which he will achieve as he ages and matures. When Silas is asked why he would name a child so queerly, he responds that it's "a good name" and "it will help to keep him safe" (25). The reasons behind this curious response are actually quite simple: "Nobody" is a good name because it is an appropriate name. Nobody articulates the concept of the child's necessary disassociation with the living mortal world by way of the murder of his family and, more importantly, it should keep him safe in its anonymity from the members of the living world that would seek to kill him permanently. The name "Nobody" is a metonymical false self crafted by Gaiman to both protect the gestating, primordial "Bod," the true self, who will have to find, age, and experience real life, the creative and actual, as best he can in his present circumstances, in an effort to become human while avoiding those who would extinguish Bod's chances at life. Nobody is a sham to the Graveyard, and an eye-roller to the audience, though they all love him as best they can; he is an outsider there, not to mention textually, with no real place in its world of the dead. However, within the cosmology of Gaiman's greater corpus of characters, Nobody/Bod is demonstrative in his assertions towards becoming a living textual reality as opposed to a dead signifier. Yet, fortunately or not, death rather becomes Nobody as he becomes Bod. Or, more pointedly, as Bod encounters and learns of death, he gains humanity at the expense of those who are already living.

Corporeality as the Ultimate *Bildungsroman*: To Acquire Life by Way of Death

The reader learns of Bod as the reader learns of death. Death comes in many forms in *The Graveyard Book*. From the slaughter of Bod's family by the Man Jack's knife, to the inhabitants of the Graveyard who heed to the cry of an amorphous grey blob that used to be Bod's mother begging them to care for her toddler, to a Grey Lady riding a horse who convince the graveyard that "the dead should have charity," and adopt him (30); the reader, quite literally, knows death in Bod's life before they know him, and the dead take him in as one of their own. It turns out that those who seek to kill him, the Jacks of All Trades, a sort of fraternal society of philanthropic knaves and rogues, have known about Bod, solely for the intents of killing him as well. They are a powerful secret organization of necromancers, deriving magic from death (270). However, as pertains to Bod, they specifically seek him out as he is, to them, a sort of anti-messiah; Gaiman's Jack Dandy tells of a prophecy that calls for "a child born who would walk the borderland between the living and the dead. [Further,] if this child grew to adulthood [,] it would mean the end of [the] order" (271). Two interesting points arrive from this prophecy: 1.) If true, Bod was literally brought into this world to, essentially-speaking, be brought out of it . . . or at least walk a very thin line between it and what lies beyond. 2.) There is a threshold to be crossed at adulthood for Bod. Now, the idea of a threshold separating adolescence and adulthood is hardly a new innovation. However, as the Jacks (particularly Frost, the Man Jack) mean to kill Bod, Bod's ultimate solution regarding his state of affairs is that he will kill Frost both in revenge for the murder of his family and to fulfill his destiny and achieve adulthood (181).

This potentially disturbing conclusion is established in the dark little chapter entitled "Nobody Owens School Days." A quick note on that, *The Graveyard Book* is divided into eight vignettes, metonyms in their own right, detailing small moments in the (un)life, or passage into maturity, of Nobody Owens from roughly eighteen months and onward separated by, again roughly, two years at a time. The chapters are bracketed by two larger stories, "How Nobody Came to the Graveyard" and "Every Man Jack," along with a short coda following where Bod, having reached adulthood, or, at least, some form of maturity, leaves the Graveyard, a fulfilled and embodied human at the robust age of seventeen. In "Nobody Owens School Days," Silas, Bod's guardian vampire, tells a now eleven-year-old Bod the story of how he came to live in a graveyard: that his parents and sister were killed and that he was adopted by the Owenses, with the grace of Death herself, as long as Silas would be his guardian. In the intervening narratives, Bod found himself largely confined to the Graveyard and its spectral inhabitants, largely in fear of The Man Jack who "still intends to kill [him]" (179). Bod's response is either odd given the information he just received or possibly psychopathic; he says: "So? . . . It's only death. I mean, all of my best friends are dead" (179). When Silas reminds Bod that he is, in fact, to most extents or another, alive, he also prevaricates; he says: "You're *alive*, Bod. You can do anything, make anything, dream anything. If you change the world, the world will change" (179).

There are a variety of falsehoods in that statement. 1.) Bod is somewhat alive and somewhat between life and death. Given the gift of the Freedom of the Graveyard, he possesses abilities in his youth that are paranormal in nature: he can fade into shadows, see in absolute darkness, influence the dreams and fears of the living, and even pass through solid objects. That humanity is relatively dependent upon being a social creature with *other* living humans seems to have escaped Silas' notice. Mind you, he has been undead for a very long time. 2.) Bod, by no means at this point in his existence, can do anything he wants. To this point, he has been confined to the Graveyard for his safety from the Jacks and has socialized almost entirely with those who are dead. Interestingly enough, the dead are in a permanent state of arrested development; their presences after death are exactly as they were at the moment of death. Thus, those who died in their more august years become confidants and educators to Bod, while those who died in youth become his comrades and playmates. This is the "world and domain" (229) as Bod knows it. He ages while everyone else stays exactly the same.

This becomes painfully evident towards the end as Bod reaches the end of his parallel existence; friends both alive and dead begin to shun him: the fox he had known his entire time in the Graveyard flees from him (Gaiman, *Graveyard Book* 295), "the little children [he] had played with when he was small were still little" (229), and his ghostly powers begin to fade. Nobody Owens' entire existence has been the best efforts of those trying to protect him by trying to preserve him in his current state. Ideally, to us, that would mean alive against those who would kill him; to the Graveyard, that means he would remain exactly as he was when they obtained him. Even Silas cannot offer comfort as his vampiric state has left him never-changing, not unlike the dead. Gaiman textually constructs Nobody/Bod as a sliding state between two points, life and death, unusual to the *Bildungsroman* because he grows physically, but his cognitive, emotional, and social development is being stunted in order for him to survive. . . . Whatever survival is to someone who lives under Death's blessing. His entire existence has been more of a metonym for life trying to assimilate to a people and a world more dead than alive. There are stern ramifications for this. Returning to our conversation, rejoining Silas' earlier remarks, Bod tells him that t'were he to go into the outside world, he would likely kill the Man Jack for his transgressions against him. Or, rather, Bod *wants* to kill the Man Jack. And, as Lacan states, "desire is a metonymy" (439). In this particular case, the desire to kill the killer of his family would allow Nobody Owens to become someone again. And this is exactly what will come to pass.

Prior to this, Bod does make a lone connection to a living, breathing young lady named Scarlett. She actually first met Bod when they were both roughly only four years old and was rightly confused by a seemingly sweet young boy trolling about a graveyard . . . introducing her to ghosts she could not see; her parents and, eventually, she too, suspected that Bod was probably just an "imaginary" friend (Gaiman 43, 60). A decade plus later, Scarlett and Bod are reunited as the Jacks have come to finish the job the Man Jack left otherwise unfulfilled, tying up any loose ends in the process. While Bod dispatches the other Jacks in non-lethal ways, he lures Jack Frost into the home of the Sleer, an ancient tentacled-entity that seeks a master. As Frost threatens Scarlett's life, Bod decides that he will act in a way he perceives to be heroic and permanently remove the Man Jack from both of their lives. As he is about to kill Bod, Jack says: "Good-Bye, boy" and is rejoined by "Bod, [. . .] Not Boy. Bod" (284). Bod then tricks Frost into convincing the Sleer that he is its Master, who the Sleer have been awaiting for thousands of years. As such, the Sleer take their new master before he can kill either child and pulls him "into the rock, [. . .] swallowed up by it" (285). Bod has fulfilled the prophecy. In sentencing the last remaining Jack to death, he has relinquished his status as a boy and become entirely substantial as Bod, an adolescent with a body . . . who kills people. In essence, he exchanges the Man Jack's life for one of his own, his own borrowed humanity. However, his humanity comes from a growth amongst the dead and the ethics, the *Bildungsroman* of the dead, if you will, that accompany it. Scarlett is literally repulsed by her hero. She cannot look at him as she is afraid of what he has become, a killer of men; in her eyes, he's no better than the man she just escaped (288). This leaves a now fully-realized Bod estranged from the living, again, as much as he is becoming estranged from the dead. His desires, once again, slide away. Toward the end of that penultimate chapter, Bod proclaims that he is now grown. Silas, disagrees. "Not yet," he says (291). It's only when Bod steps alone through the Graveyard's gates one final time before the last, that he realizes that ahead of him, "there was life" (307); life, to a now fully-living Bod is simply a continuation of the metonym that was his time before life.

In *Coming of Age in Contemporary American Fiction*, Kenneth Milliard claims that, "The contemporary adolescent . . . has no moral agency and has succumbed to 'the politics of despair'" (11) or what appears to be a "nihilistic futility" (12). I cannot look at *The Graveyard Book* and necessarily argue that point, but I can rejoin it with Gaiman's words that "Bod walked into [life] with his eyes and his heart wide open" (307). Whatever Bod has now become, certainly human, but human by way of an act that might otherwise be deemed as monstrous. The reader likely does not feel that monstrosity in the same manner as Scarlett; she is crafted textually within a book that does not allow her the reader's capacity to contextualize Bod amongst his peers, other monsters: vampires, ghosts, werewolves, etc. Scarlett sees him as what someone at that moment might: less human, more terrifying. His true self to her is the false self he has spent the entire book trying to escape. It brings to mind, after a fashion, a thought as to who or what Gaiman's *Bildungsroman* serves. Whoever Nobody Owens once was, he died and killed in order to live again. It would seem that he was brought back into life by way of estrangement from it. Mind you, like all real lives, it's not that simple; the book actually ends with a visual of the Lady on the Grey bidding both Bod and the reader goodbye. If only for now.[3]

Notes

1. Interestingly enough, Lacan's definition is entirely more succinct; when one parses the essay, in "The Instance of the Letter in the Unconscious, or Reason Since Freud," Lacan constructs metonymy as simply as a dictionary entry: "the part taken for the whole" (421). Granted, in typical Lacanian fashion, he undercuts the simplicity of that construct by indicating that this definition "leaves us with hardly any idea what we are to conclude about the size the fleet [of ships] these thirty sails are nevertheless supposed to gauge; for a ship to have but one sail is very rare indeed" (421).
2. By way of connection to a mother (or, for my purposes, the one who creates life in these stories: Neil Gaiman) with regards to infants and children—as Winnicott notes, the terms, like most concepts in psychoanalysis, derive from Sigmund Freud (74, 140).
3. Every writer needs an editor; editors need them on occasion as well—I'd like to thank Kenneth Kidd for his assistance with my work here.

Works Cited

Banks, Amanda & Elizabeth Wein. "Folklore and the Comic Book: The Traditional Meets the Popular." *New Directions in Folklore* 2 (1998). Web. 10 May 2011.

Brown, Paula. "*Stardust* as Allegorical *Bildungsroman*: An Apology for Platonic Idealism." *Extrapolation: A Journal of Science Fiction and Fantasy* 51.2 (2010): 216-34. Web. 10 May 2011.

Callen, Don. "Notes on Metaphor and Metonymy." *Reading Lacan.* Bowling Green State University, 23 May 2012. Web. 10 May 2011. <http://personal.bgsu.edu/~dcallen/metaphor.html>.

Gaiman, Neil. *Coraline.* New York: Harper, 2002. Print.

———. *The Graveyard Book.* New York: Harper, 2008. Print.

———. *The Sandman: Brief Lives.* DC: New York, 1994. Print.

Gooding, Richard. "'Something Very Old and Very Slow': *Coraline,* Uncanniness, and Narrative Form." *Children's Literature Association Quarterly* 33 (2008): 390-407. Print.

Lacan, Jacques. "The Instance of the Letter in the Unconscious, or Reason Since Freud." *Ecrits.* New York: W. W. Norton & Co., 2007. Print.

Millard, Kenneth. *Coming of Age in Contemporary American Fiction.* Edinburgh, UK: Edinburgh UP, 2007. Print.

Reed, S. Alexander. "Through Every Mirror in the World: Lacan's Mirror Stage as Mutual Reference in the Works of Neil Gaiman and Tori Amos." *ImageTexT: Interdisciplinary Comics Studies*. 4.1 (2008). Dept of English, University of Florida, 23 May 2012. Web. 22 Oct. 2016.

Rudd, David. "An Eye for an I: Neil Gaiman's Coraline and Questions of Identity." *Children's Literature in Education: An International Quarterly* 39 (2008): 159-68. 10 May 2011. Web. 22 Oct. 2016.

Parsons, Elizabeth, Naarah Sawers, & Kate McInally. "The Other Mother: Neil Gaiman's Postfeminist Fairytales." *Children's Literature in Education: An International Quarterly* 33 (2008): 371-389. Print.

Pratchett, Terry and Neil Gaiman. *Good Omens*. New York: William Morrow, 1990. Print.

Saklofske, Jon. "'Tales Worked in Blood and Bone': Words and Images as Scalpel and Suture in Graphic Narratives." *ImageTexT: Interdisciplinary Comics Studies*. 4.1 (2008). Dept of English, University of Florida. 23 May 2012. Web. 22 Oct. 2016.

Sandifer, Philip & Tof Eklund. "Introduction." *ImageTexT: Interdisciplinary Comics Studies*. 4.1 (2008). Dept of English, University of Florida. 23 May 2012. Web. 22 Oct. 2016.

Smith, Clay. "Get Gaiman?: PolyMorpheus Perversity in Works by and about Neil Gaiman." *ImageTexT: Interdisciplinary Comics Studies*. 4.1 (2008). Dept of English, University of Florida. 23 May 2012. Web. 22 Oct. 2016.

Winnicott, Donald. *The Maturational Processes and the Facilitating Environment*. New York: International UP, 1965. Print.

In the Shadow of Balder: Breaking the Cycle of Ragnarok in *American Gods*

Kristin Bovaird-Abbo

As evidenced by his earlier novels *American Gods* (2001) and *Anansi Boys* (2005), Neil Gaiman is no stranger to world mythologies. Both novels make abundant use of Slavonic, Egyptian, and African myths and legends, just to name a handful. Norse mythology especially inspires his writings; recently, Gaiman remarked, "Those Norse tales have accompanied me through pretty much everything I've done," he said. "They ran like a vein of silver through *Sandman*, they were the bedrock of *American Gods*" (Alter). Gaiman's love of Norse mythology stemmed from a childhood fascination, and Gaiman once noted on his copy of Roger Lancelyn Green's 1960 translation of *Tales of the Norsemen*: "This was the one I read as a child, read it until the spine gave way" ("*American Gods*"). As such, it's not surprising that several Norse gods feature prominently in *American Gods*, sharing many similarities with their mythological antecedents. Mr. Wednesday signals his identity as Odin when he proclaims that Wednesday "certainly is my day" (22). He ultimately reveals himself fully to Shadow during their time at the House on the Rock, proclaiming, "I am called Glad-of-War, Grim, Raider, and Third. I am One-eyed. I am called Highest, and True-Guesser. I am Grimnir, and I am the Hooded One. I am All-Father" (119). Another major figure, Loki (first introduced as Low Key Lyesmith) appears briefly at the onset of the novel as Shadow's cellmate, only to re-emerge as Mr. World in his known and noteworthy role of creating mischief and chaos.

One of the more crucial appropriations of Norse mythology in *American Gods* centers on its protagonist Shadow Moon. Although Shadow's true identity as Balder is not made *explicitly* clear until Gaiman's 2004 novella "The Monarch of The Glen," sufficient clues remain within *American Gods* to connect Shadow to Balder. Yet, of all the Norse characters available to Gaiman, why does he choose the son of Odin whose death serves as a catalyst for the Norse apocalypse known as Ragnarok? And why, by the novel's close, does Shadow claim that he has lost his name? As he evokes Balder's gentle nature, Shadow is able to unify the gods, even across multiple mythologies, gaining mentors and guardians who help him on his journey of self-realization. At the same time, Shadow is blessed with a certain amount of luck, particularly when he accidentally reanimates his dead wife, Laura. (As can happen in the works of Neil Gaiman.) In particular, Shadow's love for and desire to protect Laura leads her to do everything within her power after death to protect Shadow, inadvertently setting Shadow on the path to break away from the cyclical nature of his mythic destiny. The combination of Shadow's ability to unify and his providence in finding luck allows him to not only break up Wednesday's rigged game, thus averting Ragnarok; he also breaks out of centuries' worth of repeated patterns of behavior paving the way for other gods to follow his example.

Recrafting the Twilight of the Gods in Shadow

The world of *American Gods* is one where immigrants to America bring their gods with them. Once ashore, these gods manifest as human-like beings who walk amongst humanity, seeking worship but often resorting to mundane jobs, ranging from prostitute to conman, in order to survive. When *American Gods* takes place, the older gods have been largely replaced by newer gods, such as Media and Technical Boy, which reflect contemporary American passions. As a result, conflict arises between the premodern and modern gods. The novel opens as Shadow loses his wife, Laura, in a car accident days before his release from prison. As he travels home to her funeral, Shadow is hired by the mysterious Mr. Wednesday to act as his errand boy and bodyguard as the latter attempts to recruit the older gods to fight against the newer ones. As the novel progresses, however, it becomes clear that the conflict between the gods has been engineered by Wednesday and Low-Key in order to create a cataclysmic glut of chaos and death upon which they will subsequently feed. Thus, Shadow is thrust into a world where gods are real, dreams foreshadow the future, and his deceased wife is reanimated through a happy accident with a magical coin.

Wednesday's choice of Shadow rather than one of his many other sons signals Wednesday's true motive to trigger Ragnarok. When Low Key and Mr. Wednesday reveal their plan to feast upon the death and chaos created by the war between the gods, they note that they need a son of Odin. In Norse mythology, the most well-known of Odin's sons is Thor. Given that Wednesday spends much of *American Gods* claiming to fight for the old gods, Thor would appear to be a natural choice to recruit gods, demi-gods, and associates, particularly since Thor is the god most focused on maintaining the delicate balance between the gods and the giants who perpetually threaten to infringe upon Asgard. As John Aberth notes, "It was Thor who in Viking mythology was the god most devoted to combating the deadly chaos of giants, serpents, and other monsters that threatened to engulf Midgard" (25). In fact, Thor is briefly mentioned in *American Gods*; during Shadow's final conversation with Wednesday before the latter is killed by the modern gods, Wednesday mourns the loss of his thunderous son: "Big guy, like you. Good hearted. Not bright, but he'd give you the goddamned shirt of his back if you asked him. And he killed himself. He put a gun in his mouth and blew his head off in Philadelphia in 1932" (341). In his introduction to his collection *Norse Myths*, Crossley-Holland notes of Thor that he was the "most loved and respected of the gods" and that he "represented order" (xxvi). Given that many of the gods with whom Wednesday meets are content, or at least tolerant, of the status quo, Thor seems a natural choice to help recruit old gods to his ranks, thus lending Odin more credibility. Yet, we must remember that order and stability is actually the last thing that the Wednesday desires. Rather, it is Balder's association with apocalypse that draws Wednesday's attention. When Shadow comments, "You needed a son," Wednesday replies, "I needed *you*, my boy" (473, emphasis original). Not just any offspring of Odin will do.

Although Odin has many sons, Balder is perhaps the most loved among the gods. The main role that Balder plays in the larger narrative of Norse mythology, however, is as a catalyst for Ragnarok, described by Crossley-Holland as "[t]he apocalyptic final battle between the gods and giants, involving all creation, in which virtually all life is destroyed" (249). Because Balder is so treasured, Odin and Frigg take steps to ensure his safety: Odin seeks to learn more about Balder's impending death in hopes of being able to avert it (and thus prevent, or at least delay, Ragnarok), and Frigg secures promises from all of creation to not harm her son. Yet a fateful mistletoe plant escapes Frigg's notice, and Loki, jealous of Balder's immunity to injury, fashions a dart of mistletoe to kill Balder.

Gaiman retains most of these defining traits of Balder in his depiction of Shadow. In the Norse myth now known as *Balder's Dreams*, Balder is described by the other gods as "the most merciful, the most gentle and loved of them all" (147), and throughout *American Gods*, Shadow develops strong bonds with the people he meets—from his deceased wife, Laura, who repeatedly protects him, to Samantha Black Crow, who does not hesitate to lie to protect Shadow from Mr. Town and Mr. Road as they investigate the deaths of their associates. Given that the narrative opens with Shadow in jail for aggravated assault and battery, we might expect Shadow to be a man of brute force; however, the opposite is the truth, for as he reflects later, Shadow's actions were driven by a sense of justice: The men he assaulted "shouldn't have tried to rip him and Laura off like that. He was only the driver, but he had done his part, done everything that she had asked of him" (421). Even his appearance contradicts his nature, for Shadow's large size is usually the first thing that people notice when they first meet him. Sam comments, upon seeing Shadow stand up for the first time, "Whoa. You're pretty big" (145), and gods respond in similar fashion; upon first meeting Shadow, Zorya Vechernyaya asks Wednesday, "Who is the big man?" (68). Yet his gentle nature quickly overshadows his immense size, and when he does fight, it is only after he has been goaded into it, as we see when Mad Sweeney offers to fight Shadow in exchange for the secret of the coin trick (37).

Gaiman does alter one aspect of Balder's traditional depiction, and that is his great beauty. In fact, when the giantess Skadi arrives in Asgard seeking vengeance for the death of her father, she is persuaded to take one of the gods as her husband instead; she is required to choose her future spouse only by looking at the feet (Crossley-Holland 45). She selects the most finely-shaped pair of feet in the belief that they must belong to Balder (but she ends up marrying Njord). Shadow in *American Gods* is not described as being particularly beautiful; as Laura tells, him, "You're like this big, solid, man-shaped hole in the world" (326), recounting the numerous times that she has found him in a room by himself doing nothing. If he has no one with him to shape his behavior, she implies, he does not truly live. Even Gaiman himself has commented on Shadow's apparent lack of personality; Gaiman once remarked that "one of the strangest things I found when writing Shadow is that he has no personality unless he's with somebody. At which point he will adopt a personality, or occasionally mirror them" (White).

A Balder by any Other Name

As noted above, Shadow does not immediately resemble Balder on anything but a superficial level, but Gaiman develops a number of subtle parallels between the two. In a Lacanian sense, a theoretical perspective often used in conjunction with the work of Gaiman, this ability to mirror others means that Shadow has a figurative beauty similar to Balder's literal beauty. People are attracted to Shadow because when they look at him, they see a reflection of themselves, often as they wish to be seen. As Jacques Lacan notes, this is a narcissistic type of love, in which Shadow is substituted for the beloved who "reflects the ego's magnitude and value, without herself [or in this case, Shadow] being the centre of focus" (Grosz 130). Because of the positive image that Wednesday reflects back to everyone he encounters, he allows those around him to "[affirm their] own position of mastery, control, activity" (Grosz 130). Wednesday may express bafflement, telling the mystery god in Las Vegas, "*Everyone's got a hard-on for the kid I hired to run errands* [sic]" (253), but Shadow's attraction for other people is a combination of his gentle demeanor and his ability to reflect people's preferred view of themselves.

For someone like Sam, who professes her ability to "believe things that are true and . . . things that aren't true and . . . things where nobody knows if they're true or not" (348), Shadow's ability to see her truly is shocking; as they drive to El Paso, Shadow guesses what she studies: "'. . . you are undoubtedly studying art history, women's studies, and probably casting your own bronzes. And you probably work in a coffee house to help cover the rent.' She put down her fork, nostrils flaring, eyes wide. 'How the fuck did you do that?'" (149). Others are flattered by Shadow's perception of them; in Lakeside, Hinzelmann appreciates Shadow as a receptive audience, and the sensual goddess Easter is delighted at Shadow's bashful reaction: "He . . . felt a hot flush suffuse his face. The woman laughed delightedly. 'He's *blushing*! Wednesday my sweet, you brought me a *blusher*. How perfectly wonderful of you'" (271). In a world where gods seek adoration, Shadow's innocent and natural response—unlike the practiced charm of Wednesday or the blind indifference of others on the street—is a type of veneration. Because both Shadow and Balder are so beloved by the gods, they alone can unify the gods in the fight between the giants of Norse mythology and the modern gods.

A further aspect of Balder's personality that Gaiman leaves unchanged is his merciful nature. The mythological Balder sires Forseti, the god of justice, and although Shadow does not have any biological children within *American Gods*, he echoes his mythological counterpart by ironically becoming a sort of god of justice himself when he concludes that Wednesday's need for death does not justify the destruction of the world. As noted earlier, Shadow's imprisonment was a consequence of his strong sense of justice, albeit one that conflicted with society's laws. When he is first released from prison, Shadow still has a sense of morality, but it is now one with limits. After all, one cannot become a god of justice without fully experiencing all aspects of justice, ranging from passive observant to active participant, and his time in jail allows him much needed retrospection. As he tells Wednesday, "I'll hurt people if they're trying to hurt you. But I don't hurt people for fun or for profit" (35). As the novel progresses, Shadow's sense of justice evolves, and he moves from being an agent of destruction, as evidenced by his assault on his fellow robbers, to one who preserves order and who seeks to protect others. Shadow demonstrates this change when he accompanies Wednesday to the meeting at the House on the Rock: "Shadow was puzzled to realize that he was far more concerned with breaking the rules by climbing onto the Carousel than he had been aiding and abetting this afternoon's bank robbery" (115). However, it is not until later in the novel that Shadow's evolving morality begins to direct his actions; at the House on the Rock, he is largely a passive observer, but as he becomes more immersed in the world of the gods, he learns how to act positively on his sense of justice. The first time when Shadow observes Wednesday shortchange someone financially, at a gas station on the way to Laura's funeral, Shadow comments only after the fact: "The way I saw it in there, you never paid for the gas" (42). When Wednesday tries a similar trick in a coffeehouse after meeting Easter, Shadow acts to ensure that the waitress receives the correct amount: "As she walked away, Shadow said, 'Ma'am? Excuse me? I think you dropped this.' He picked up a ten-dollar bill from the floor" (276). When Wednesday chides him for interfering, Shadow proclaims the justice of his actions: "'You stiffed that girl for ten bucks, I slipped her ten bucks,' said Shadow doggedly. 'It was the right thing to do, and I did it'" (277).

Shadow's responses to his dreams are another factor that simultaneously connects him to his mythological counterpart while demonstrating his development as a figure of justice, a necessary step which will later allow him to prevent Wednesday's instigation of Ragnarok. In Norse mythology, Balder's impending death causes him to suffer from dreams which cause him to feel "fearful and exposed and doomed" (Crossley-Holland 147), and Gaiman gives similar dreams to Shadow. When he stays the night at Zorya Vechernyaya's apartment, Shadow dreams of driving through a minefield (79), and Zorya Polunochnaya tells him, "You were crying out, and moaning" (80). Just as Balder felt exposed by his dreams, so too does Shadow; within the dream, "Someone was shooting at him. A bullet punctured his lung, a bullet shattered his spine, another hit his shoulder. He felt each bullet strike" (79-80). Balder's dreams cause others to act; for example, Odin travels to Hel in order to find out the meaning of Balder's dreams and Frigg begins her journey to extract promises of safekeeping from all of creation (Crossley-Holland 147-49, 150). Shadow's dreams, on the other hand, serve to guide him, as seen in his conversations with the buffalo man and other figures from Native American and Hindu mythologies, thus allowing him to not only recognize Wednesday's con for what it is but to also know how to derail it.

As he moves among more gods and learns of their nature while developing his sense of justice, Shadow learns to view his dreams not as sources of anxiety and fear, but rather as guides of what is to come. Shadow's vigil for Wednesday on the world tree reveals this when he has a "dark dream in which dead children rose and came to him, their eyes peeling, swollen pearls, and they reproached him for failing them and it pulled him from another dream, in which he was staring up at a mammoth, hairy and dark, as it lumbered toward him from the mist" (409). Although it takes some time for Shadow to realize the significance of this dream—the children are those gone missing from Lakeside and the mammoth is a manifestation of the Hindu god Ganesh, come to tell Shadow to look in the trunks of the klunkers parked in the lake—following his resurrection, Shadow finally remembers and more importantly, interprets the true meaning of what he has seen and, therein, brings an end to the kobold's murders.

Lucky Coins and the Catalyst of Change
In Norse mythology, two events precede the apocalypse once Balder's dreams begin: wars among mortals and a winter that surpasses all winters. Gaiman incorporates both into his *American Gods*. The traditional story emphasizes the collapse of familial relationships (Crossley-Holland 173), and Gaiman's reimagining conveys a similar sense of chaos. Falling girders impede traffic, while killing pedestrians, graves are defiled, and mysterious murders are committed (328). As the narrator remarks, "The war had begun and nobody saw it. The storm was lowering and nobody knew it" (328). The world threatens to tear itself apart, as Sam Fetisher warns

Shadow before the latter is released from jail: "Tectonic places. It's like when they go riding, when North America goes skidding into South America, you don't want to be in the middle" (10). More important, though, is the natural imagery that Gaiman borrows from Norse mythology: "Fimbulvetr, the winter of winters, will grip and throttle Midgard. Driving snow clouds will converge from north and south and east and west. There will be bitter frosts, biting winds; the shining sun will be helpless . . . . so the end will begin" (Crossley-Holland 173). Because Wednesday needs to give the appearance of an impending Ragnarok in order to help recruit the various premodern gods to his side, he instigates the cold weather that continues for most of *American Gods*, telling Shadow to "[t]hink snow" (97). By the time that Shadow prepares to travel to Lakeside, the weather has changed drastically: "Shadow found it hard to believe how much colder it had gotten in the last few hours. It felt too cold to snow, now. Aggressively cold. This was a bad winter" (215-16). When he arrives in Lakeside, the winter has progressed beyond all known reality: "He was too cold to shiver. His eyes hurt. This was not simply cold: this was science fiction" (233).

At the same time, the approach of Ragnarok is an event that traditionally Odin desires to avoid because it means an end to his existence. Odin's travels to learn the meaning behind Balder's troubling dreams indicate that Odin desires to change, or at least delay, the future with this knowledge. Frigg's subsequent action of gathering promises from all creation supports this idea, for Odin "best understood that this was the greatest evil ever sustained by gods and men, and foresaw what loss and sorrow would follow in the wake of his son's death" (Crossley-Holland 154). Within *American Gods*, Wednesday exploits that knowledge to benefit from the carnage bound to result, but at the same time, Wednesday must be careful to delay Shadow's death until it is convenient for his hidden purposes. That Wednesday describes the actions of the gods as occurring "behind the scenes. Like in a theatre or something . . . now we're walking about backstage" suggests that there is a script or pattern that must be followed (306), and his familiarity with the "backstage" posits him not as an actor but rather as a director.

Despite Wednesday's best efforts, though, a rogue actor appears in the cast. Shadow's actions cause Laura to be reanimated, with the result that the script that Wednesday has so carefully orchestrated has been altered. We see early signs of Wednesday's attempts to control the events leading up to the war when he arranges to have Mad Sweeney slip the golden coin into Shadow's pocket without Shadow's realization during their first meeting (40). When Shadow loses it, having tossed it onto Laura's grave with no knowledge of its protective qualities (46), Wednesday brings Shadow to meet Zorya Polunochnaya and to receive another coin. She tells him, "'You were given protection once, but you lost it already. You gave it away. You had the sun in your hand. And that is life itself. All I can give you is much weaker protection'" (83). The timing of certain events suggests that Wednesday has arranged for Shadow to receive these coins. When Mad Sweeney finds Shadow in Lakeside, the leprechaun is terrified (193). It is important to note that Laura has just interfered with Wednesday's plan by saving Shadow from Misters Town and Stone. As Low Key later tells Shadow, "'If she'd had—the grace—to stay dead . . . Wood and Stone—were good men. You were going—to be allowed to escape—when the train crossed the Dakotas'" (475). Wednesday and Low Key have spent decades, if not longer, planning to pit the premodern gods against the modern so that they can feast on the resultant death and chaos, and so they would naturally attempt to account for all possibilities. Shadow's transference of the golden coin to Laura which then reanimates her is an act which they do not anticipate and which they cannot control. Thus, Mad Sweeney's erratic and frantic behavior just prior to his suicide makes sense if we infer that Wednesday has demanded that Mad Sweeney retrieve the coin back from Shadow (and thus from Laura) to prevent any further surprises.

Shadow's unscripted actions allow him to prevent Wednesday from launching the war of the gods and, more importantly, to truly prevent Ragnarok from occurring. Much of this is due not to anything that Shadow does himself, but rather what he inspires others to do. When Shadow first meets Zorya Polunochnaya, she warns him as they observe the stars:

> Odin's Wain, they call it.... Where we come from, we believe that is a, a thing, a, not a god but like a god, a bad thing, chained up in those stars. If it escapes, it will eat the whole of everything. And there are three sisters who must watch the sky, all the day, all the night. If he escapes, the thing in the stars, the world is over. (82)

Shadow does not yet understand that she describes reality, but her description of the chained thing evokes the Norse Loki. Following the death of Balder, the Norse gods imprison Loki until Ragnarok, when he is freed (Crossley-Holland 173). As Mr. World, one of Low Key's aliases, reveals to the Technical Boy, the battle will yield "[p]ower . . . and food. A combination of the two. You see, the outcome of the battle is unimportant. What matters is the chaos, and the slaughter" (450). As Crossley-Holland notes, "Balder's dreams are the beginning of the end . . . . and Balder's death reveals Loki as no longer equivocal but truly evil, and cruelly exposes the ultimate limitations and mortality of the gods" (224). Loki/Low Key is the thing in the stars, and Wednesday, desperate for blood, is on the verge of releasing Low Key into the world.

Interestingly, Zorya Polunochnaya mentions that three sisters guard the sky. Of the three sisters in the Slavic apartment, she is the only one that we see actually performing this duty. Zorya Vechernyaya does the shopping and the cooking, and Zorya Utrennyaya cleans. Thus another possibility is that the "three sisters" refers rather to the two other goddesses who interact with Shadow: Bast and Easter. Bast, the Egyptian goddess who spends most of her time as a cat, keeps a perpetual eye on Shadow through her folk (355, 424). More importantly, though, Bast helps guide Shadow following the death of his body on the world tree. Easter is the one who brings Shadow back to the world after he chooses the path of oblivion.

These powerful women help Shadow transition into his role of preservation of life rather than serve as the catalyst bringing death and destruction. They are attracted to Shadow because they sense his innate sense of justice and nurture it. In addition, they guide Shadow through some of the pivotal crossroads that Shadow encounters, particularly following the death of his physical body during his vigil. Zorya Polunochnaya shows Shadow the path of truth (420), and Bast keeps Shadow informed of the status of the gods assembling at Lookout Mountain, urging him to hurry along his journey (425).

Breaking the Pattern

More importantly, though, both Zorya Polunochnaya and Bast help Shadow to understand the mythological cycles, guiding him to a position where he can break his own pattern. Wednesday comments on the unending repetition: "We may not die easy and we sure as hell don't die well, but we can die. If we're still loved and remembered, something else a whole lot like us comes along and takes our place and the whole damn thing starts all over again. And if we're forgotten, we're done" (341). Low Key echoes this idea when he tells Laura, who has just brought him the bough of mistletoe, "It's never a matter of old and new. It's only about patterns" (468). When he dreams of the thunderbirds, Shadow finds himself "*tumbling down the tower of skulls*" (269, emphasis original), and when asked to recall the dream by Easter, he responds that a voice in his dream "said they were mine. Old skulls of mine. Thousands and thousands of them" (276). The significance of this dream is not made clear until after his heart is weighed following his death: "'So that's that,' said Bast, wistfully. 'Just another skull for the pile. It's a pity. I had hoped that you would do some good, in the current troubles'" (431). When Shadow returns to the living, he now knows that all of the skulls represent earlier manifestations of Balder. Their positioning in a large pile suggests that each previous life has followed the mythological script in which Balder is killed, Ragnarok occurs, and the earth has been reborn. Yet in Gaiman's reimagining of Balder's story, Shadow returns to the world that he knows, thus disrupting the centuries of previous performances. Easter's revival of Shadow is accompanied by a reversal and even an erasure of the events: "The clouds began to thin and to evaporate, creating a patch of blue sky through which the sun glared. . . . Soon the morning sun was blazing down on that meadow like a summer sun at noon, burning the water vapor from the morning's rain into mists and burning the mist off into nothing at all" (459). Ragnarok cannot occur without Balder's permanent death. Gaiman rewrites the traditional Norse mythology, where the gods are unable to persuade all living things to weep for Balder, to allow gods from other mythologies to allow him to return to life. The end result is a different ending for his Balder figure.

* * * * *

But perhaps more important than the manner and timing of Shadow's return is what has been gained: his deeper understanding of the true nature of mortals and gods. After his physical body dies during the vigil on the world tree, Zorya Polunochnaya comes to Shadow to retrieve the coin and to offer Shadow truth. The only price is his real name:

> She reached a perfect hand toward his head. He felt her fingers brush his skin, then he felt them penetrate his skin, his skull, felt them push deep into his head. Something tickled, in his skull and all down his spine. She pulled her hand out of his head. A flame, like a candle-flame but burning with a clear magnesium-white luminance, was flickering on the tip of her forefinger.
> 'Is that my name?' he asked.
> She closed her hand, and the light was gone. 'It was,' she said. (420)

Shadow chooses to exchange his name for the truth, with the result that he has destroyed the script that has previously dictated his path. Ironically, Low Key believes that Shadow is no longer a player in the game, telling Laura, "that's the good thing about having him dead on his tree. I know where he is at all times, now. He's off the board" (467). Yet Shadow's presence off the board makes Shadow more dangerous to Low Key and Wednesday's plan, for by relinquishing his name in exchange for truth, he is no longer predictable. In fact, Gaiman foreshadows this shift much earlier in *American Gods* in a chess match: "It occurred to Shadow that Czernobog was going to try to play the same game again, the one that he had just won, that this would be his limitation. This time Shadow played recklessly. He snatched tiny opportunities, moved without thinking, without a pause to consider" (76-77). By the close of the novel, Shadow has grasped this truth—that he can move independently—and applies it to a much larger board: the battlefield upon which the gods, premodern and modern, now stand as a result of Wednesday's machinations.

At last, Shadow understands what it means to be a god. Much earlier in his journey, while waiting at the center of America to retrieve Wednesday's body, Low Key reveals to Shadow the secret behind the divinity of the gods:

> You got to understand the god thing. It's not magic. Not exactly. It's about focus.
> It's about being you, but the *you* that people believe in. It's about being the concentrated, magnified essence of you . . . You take all the belief, all the prayers, and they become a king of certainty, something that lets you become bigger, cooler, more than human. You crystallize. (395)

This is exactly what Shadow does when he arrives at the battlefield: he becomes fixed—not as Balder, trapped in an endless cycle of death and renewal, but rather as himself—no longer a shadow of other people, but as himself, Shadow with a capital "S." As he tells himself when he arrives backstage at the battle: "It is that belief, that rock-solid belief, that makes things happen" (477). While so many of the gods throughout the novel strive to increase their followers, fearing the consequences of being forgotten, Shadow realizes that "We don't need anyone to believe in us. We just keep going anyhow. It's what we do" (480). Of course, Shadow believes at this point that he speaks only of humanity, but at the same time, Low Key's earlier comments reveals that the boundary between humanity and the divine is merely one of perspective. Shadow offers a new definition of being for the gods in attendance, one that relieves gods of the burden of external sources of belief. Shadow believes in himself; that is all he needs, and soon, the other gods follow suit.

And just as the Chicago apartment of the Slavic gods has changed, so too has Czernobog, who tells Shadow, "Because of you, things are changing. This is spring time. The true spring" (517). Prior to Shadow's actions on the battlefield, Czernobog has, like all of the gods, premodern and modern alike, been locked in a mythic cycle. He has known nothing but death and, as a result, has yearned only for what he has known. Yet now, when given the opportunity to kill Shadow, Czernobog makes a choice not to follow his mythic past.

In the traditional accounts of the events following Ragnarok in Norse mythology, the land is reborn following a period of raging fire and subsequent darkness: "The earth will rise again out of the water, fair and green. The eagle will fly over cataracts, swoop into the thunder and catch fish under crags. Corn will ripen in fields that were never sown" (Crossley-Holland 175). Some of the gods will survive the flames, and Balder will return from the world of the dead. Together they will reminisce as they encounter relics of a past world, and life will begin again. Yet in *American Gods*, the world is not destroyed as a result of Shadow's choice to discard his mythic script. Gaiman closes his novel with a coin toss, but unlike Shadow's earlier toss, which determined his future working for Wednesday, a mythic script one does not control this final coin. Instead, "it glittered and glinted and hung there in the mid-summer sky as if it was never going to come down" (522). Before, a coin toss resulted in only two options and, as Wednesday shows, coin tosses can be rigged. Shadow has moved beyond such limiting options, choosing instead to walk away without a backward glance; he is no longer controlled by coins or by gods. Winter has come and passed, giving way to spring and an evolution of beliefs, of new and varied paradigms.

Works Cited

Aberth, John. *An Environmental History of the Middle Ages: The Crucible of Nature*. London: Routledge, 2013. Print.

Alter, Alexandra. "Neil Gaiman Delves Deep Into Norse Myths for New Book." *New York Times*. The New York Times Company, 29 June 2016. Web. 22 Aug. 2016. <http://www.nytimes.com/2016/06/30/books/neil-gaiman-delves-deep-into-norse-myths-for-new-book.html?_r=1>.

Crossley-Holland, Kevin, trans. and ed. *The Norse Myths*. New York: Pantheon Books, 1980. Print.

Gaiman, Neil. *American Gods Author's Preferred Edition*. New York: HarperCollins, 2013. Print.

_____. "*American Gods*: An Astonishingly Incomplete Bibliography." *Neil Gaiman Blog*. Harper Collins, 11 Jan. 2016. Web. 22 Oct. 2016. <http://www.neilgaiman.com/works/Books/American+Gods/in/183/>.

Grosz, Elizabeth. *Jacques Lacan: A Feminist Introduction*. London: Routledge, 1990. Print.

White, Claire E. "Interview With Neil Gaiman." *Writers Write*. Writers Write, Inc., July 2001. Web. 05 Sept. 2016. <http://www.writerswrite.com/journal/jul01/interview-with-neil-gaiman-7011>.

Opening the Door, Crossing the Wall: (Re) Mediation and Women's Roles in Neil Gaiman's *Neverwhere* and *Stardust*

Julie Perino

Neil Gaiman's books, *Neverwhere* and *Stardust*, share a unique relationship among his romantic fantasy novels in that both books center on a male protagonist completing the hero's journey in order to help a unique, powerful woman in distress. Beyond sharing similar narrative structures, the two works have also undergone multiple textual and generic remediations. *Neverwhere* began as a BBC miniseries (1996) accompanied by an authorized novelization and comic adaptation (2005). *Stardust* began as a novel with illustrations (1997), was reprinted as a novel (1998), and was later made into a major motion picture (2007). Through these remediations, the general nature of the plots of the two texts remains the same, even as the representations of female characters change in often ambiguous ways. As the two stories are similar in their general plots and the ways in which women are represented, both are discussed. However, as *Stardust* has garnered far more scholarly attention than *Neverwhere*, much of the analytical focus of this chapter resides there. This chapter provides contrastive analysis of these varied works to demonstrate the ways women's roles as damsel, treasure, hunter, murderer, cannibal, and witch-queen change with each iteration and remediation.

In the conclusion of his article, "Neil Gaiman's Irony, Liminal Fantasies, and Fairy Tale Adaptations," Sándor Klapcsik argues, "Gaiman's ironic stories illustrate the all-encompassing influence of postmodern parody and hypertextuality in popular genres, and demonstrate the contemporary urge to rewrite fairy tales from a feminist perspective" (330). Klapcsik is not alone in noting Gaiman's tendency to write ironic, postmodern fairy tales, as Paula Brown notes that Gaiman himself defined *Stardust* "as a fairy tale and fantasy" (216), a generic definition that applies to both texts. In both, Gaiman interweaves features of fairy tales with his ironic, postmodern perspective. For modern audiences, Gaiman's embedding different elements from a range of fairy tales serves as a semiotic sign post. Gaiman's allusions to Snow White in the relationship between the witch-queen and the star in *Stardust* (Cahill 58) and to clever-child quest narratives like Jack and the Beanstalk in *Neverwhere* work as an authorial shorthand, invoking expectations in his audience in regards to the kind of story he is telling and how his characters should be interpreted, particularly in regards to the gender roles they portray.

For the women in the two texts, such shorthand in combination with Gaiman's use of irony allows for narrative and social development, giving the characters opportunities to move past the diminished framework that more recent interpretations, such as those presented by the Disney corporation, of such characters have allowed (Zipes qtd. in Greenhill and Matrix 7-8). Despite the fact that *Neverwhere* and *Stardust* are male-dominated, androcentric texts, Gaiman's stories do present far wider representations of women and female archetypes in fantasy and fairy-tale films than their audiences have become accustomed. For instance, the two texts pass the so-called Bechdel-Wallace test, which "is a litmus test for the presence of female characters in a piece of media. In order to pass, a film, TV show, or other form of media must include 1. at least two named female characters, 2. who talk to each other, 3. about something other than a man or men" (Garber). From a feminist perspective, the Bechdel-Wallace test is a low, but important, bar that indicates the subversion of some patriarchal values in a given piece of media.

Despite Gaiman's success in writing deep, interesting female characters whose lives don't always revolve around the protagonist or other male characters, the idea that Gaiman writes from a "feminist perspective" in *Neverwhere* and *Stardust* contradicts the ways in which Gaiman uses fairy-tale narrative structures in his novels to objectify women as subjects within his protagonists' coming-of-age quests; to perpetuate fairy-tale archetypes of women as sexualized and therefore dangerous beings; and to vilify the women of the real world while denying his fairy women access to the comforts of that world. This chapter will begin by analyzing the ways framing creates subjectification of the women in the miniseries *Neverwhere* and continue by discussing the way language is used to objectify women in both *Neverwhere* and *Stardust*. Through this analysis, it becomes clear that remediation, as it applies to the different adaptations of *Stardust* and *Neverwhere*, alters the visual and narrative cues associated with subjectification and objectification in the varied versions of these texts, which allows the adaptations of the source material to complicate women's roles in the two texts.

Fighting for Perspective: Women, the Male Gaze, and Visual Framing in *Neverwhere*

Throughout the adaptations of the text, the plot of *Neverwhere* functions in an episodic, ensemble cast fashion, which emphasizes the main perspective—that of the protagonist, Richard Mayhew—but also demonstrates the important roles played by other characters, like Door, Croupe and Vandemar, the Marquis de Carabas, and even Old Bailey. Moreover, regardless of Richard's position as the protagonist going through the hero's journey, the central problem of Richard's character is that he has been swept up by Door's life, taken hostage by her problems. In this respect, Door and Richard are the main characters of the story as solving their life or death problems serves as the focus of the narrative. However, the way perspective functions for Door and the other women in the miniseries emphasizes the way Richard and the other men view these characters, making them literal subjects to the male gaze. For the BBC miniseries, *Neverwhere*, these issues of gaze and female subjectivity are reinforced by the kinds of camera shots that the director, Dewi Humphreys, employs and by Gaiman's dialogue.

In an effort to demonstrate the importance of the multicast narrative while helping the audience understand who the central character is, *Neverwhere* begins with an introductory interview scene of the protagonist, Richard Mayhew (played by Gary Bakewell). This introductory scene uses close up shots, mid-frame shots, and dialogue to emphasize the fact that Richard is the focus of the interview and, therefore, the focus of the story. Beginning with a close shot of Richard that moves to a mid-shot when his girlfriend, Jessica (Elizabeth Marmur) comes into the frame allows Humphreys to emphasize Richard's role in the film. Every time Richard speaks, the camera zooms in, cutting Jessica out of the frame. This demonstrates the complicated nature of the two's relationship; the camera moves back to mid-shots that include both characters whenever Jessica speaks during the interview, something that only happens twice, and then, only briefly.

During this introduction, Jessica speaks momentarily, interrupting Richard and trying to control him, saying, "Richard, please," when Richard confesses that he collects troll dolls. For the moments when Jessica speaks, the camera jerkily moves between the close up on Richard to the mid-shot of the two of them together, and Richard's dominance in the plot is emphasized by his directly gazing at the camera, while Jessica leans against him, looking modestly down and away from the camera's gaze or intently up at Richard while he speaks. When Richard regains control of the dialogue, the camera moves back in again, cutting Jessica out of the frame more or less completely—emphasizing her peripheral role to the plot and the dominance of Richard's point of view in the film. This use of what is called rack focus, "when the focus is quickly changed, or pulled from one figure or object to another within the main shot" isn't common in most modern films because it creates a jerky movement and can be jarring to watch (Corrigan 60). By employing rack focus to move in and out between shots, Humphreys emphasizes Richard's centrality to the narrative while simultaneously visually representing the problems between the two characters: Jessica wants Richard to live up to his potential as an adult and act like a grown-up, and Richard passively resists her efforts, wanting to spend time with her socially and sexually, but not wanting to limit himself to the kind of adult life she represents.

In regards to narrative structure, Jessica functions as a modern, fairy-tale stepmother, regardless to the form of media in which *Neverwhere* is represented. On the one hand, the use of real people as actors in the miniseries increases the depth allowed for this character, despite the fact that she is mainly shown telling

Richard what to do, forgetting who Richard is, or attempting to win Richard back at the end of the series. Of these actions associated with Jessica in the miniseries, the most compelling scene between her and Richard emphasizes the ways in which her character is associated with sex, and Gaiman makes this association clear through Richard's dialogue during the episode "Earls Court to Islington." At this point in the narrative, Richard has adjusted to some of the rules of London Below while not fully accepting the reality of being unable to return to his world. He and Door (Laura Fraser) are exploring the British Museum, trying to find the Angelus in order to get to the Angel Islington and end up in the exhibition that Jessica has curated, "Angels over London." In this scene, which remains the same between the miniseries and the novel (though not in the graphic novel), Gaiman has Richard confront Jessica, who has forgotten who he is as a result of his becoming part of London Below. Richard and Jessica are face to face, staring at one another and Richard is upset, while Jessica is confused.

This confusion is portrayed by a mid-shot of the two characters staring at each other in stunned silence. Then, the camera moves back and over Richard's shoulder so that the audience can see Jessica from his perspective and witness her reaction when he confronts her and reveals his very personal knowledge of her, saying, "You're Jessica Bartam. You're a marketing executive at Stockton's. You're 26; your birthday is April 23; and in the throes of extreme passion, you have this disconcerting tendency of humming the Monkey's song, 'I'm a Believer.'" During this dialogue, Richard and the camera slowly shift closer and closer to Jessica, moving into a close-up of her face over his shoulder before the camera switches perspective to show Richard's face when he says, "I'm a Believer," and moving back to gaze at Jessica's to show her reaction to this statement.

The significance of this scene for Jessica as a character is two-fold. First, this episode represents the one in which she has the most freedom of movement and where she acts as a central figure of the narrative because she organizes the exhibit and runs the gala for it. This means that the visual frame Humphreys crafts for her in this section is largely of her own making and demonstrates her authority in this context. On the other hand, Richard overtly sexualizes Jessica in this scene through his revelation of her bedroom habits. This sexualization works in combination with the ways Jessica functions as a domesticator who wants to marry Richard, a mother-figure who wants him to grow-up, and a social climber who wants Richard to make good impressions on important people to deliberately undermine these roles for women in contemporary society just as the traditional role of folk tale stepmothers and evil queens served to warn against women having power.

Regarding such displays of female power in patriarchal texts, Sandra M. Gilbert and Susan Gubar note that "for every glowing portrait of submissive women enshrined in domesticity, there exists an equally important negative image that embodies the sacrilegious fiendishness of what William Blake called the 'Female Will'" (28). By defining Jessica through her relationship with Richard and by depicting that relationship as controlling and sexual by turns, Gaiman and Humphreys demonstrate some lingering discomfort with female empowerment. In many ways, Jessica as stepmother does not change the ways that role is presented in existing fairy-tale texts except in two ways: her control is not deadly or violent, and she is not fated to die based on her social and sexual empowerment. As a reflection of adaptations of folk and fairy-tale genres, particularly as changes put forth in contrast to the Grimm and Disney presentations of these texts, this represents a very strong narrative development indeed.

Similar to Richard, the main, female character of the *Neverwhere* series is introduced in the first episode, "Door," though her name and identity remain a mystery for the first twelve minutes of the episode, when the audience discovers that her name, Door, is the eponymous title of the episode. Door's first appearance in the episode begins directly after the opening credits, where Dewey combines longshots and visual frames to ensure that the majority of her introduction is shown through the perspective of the men chasing her. The effect of this is two-fold: the men who chase her quickly become identified as villains because the viewer finds Door apparently scared, exhausted, and physically weak. More than this, the male characters, Croupe

(Hywell Bennet) and Vandemar (Clive Russell) take on the role of the typical horror villains who walk slowly behind their intended victim, while she runs frantically. Villain and victim, then, are clearly introduced through this broken chase sequence.

This introductory sequence hints at the largest plot problem in *Neverwhere*: who wants Door dead, and why did they kill her family? The sequence that introduces these characters begins with a long shot of a lamp that is out of focus, moving quickly toward the camera with the sound of footprints in the background to indicate that whoever is holding the lamp is running. Then, the shot changes to another long shot—the zooming-in movement of the camera, indicating that we're behind the first lamp. This shot stays long and shows two florescent lights moving slowly toward the camera in a strange, floating motion. As these shots progress, the lights being carried come closer and closer to being in focus until the camera cuts to a mid-shot of Croupe, scurrying while holding one of the fluorescent lights. Following this, the camera moves to a long shot of the first lamp, still running quickly, followed by a cut to a mid-shot of Vandemar that moves into a close-up. Next, the camera returns to the long shot of the first lamp, followed by a cut to a close up of Ross. At this point, the camera transitions to a close-up of the first lamp that finally, and slowly zooms in on Door's face. This close-up quickly transitions to a well-lit long shot of Door running through an industrial area before cutting to a mid-shot of the three men watching in the background as Door runs past them as she rounds a corner. The sequence ends with a mid-shot of the three men together before transitioning to Richard's office workspace.

The framing of this sequence creates visual tension. By introducing the men before introducing Door, Dewey creates the feeling of the hunters versus the hunted, and he reinforces the dangers of the men by having Vandemar pause to throw a knife at a rat and then bite off its head and eat it in a close-up shot. Beyond the sequencing establishing who is villain and who is victim, it also creates a precedent for Door and the other lost girls of the miniseries (namely, the rat-speaker girl Anaesthesia) by which they are framed in some way: either by the gaze of male characters, indicated through camera movements, or by the men themselves whose bodies create a visual frame around these characters that signifies the visual and physical domination that the male perspective has for both the scene and the narrative. For Door, this kind of framing continues throughout the first episode, where even her killing Ross by "opening" his chest is shown from his perspective with his body physically blocking her actions and point of view from the camera. The camera only moves to indicate Door's point of view after she has killed him, but this shot takes on a more voyeuristic nature, showing Door's face to the audience to reveal her fear and horror at what she has done. Even when she is the center of the frame, the external gaze requires that the audience look *at* her rather than seeing from her perspective.

Despite Door's super powers, her "talent" for opening doors, any connection to tropes of female empowerment or "girl power" suggested by her abilities is undermined by visual and narrative frames. As Christy Williams notes in her feminist deconstruction of *Ever After*, fairy-tale films that employ the 1990s "girl power" trope walk a strangely individualistic line in their representation of feminism and female empowerment. In explaining these limitations, Williams argues:

> *Ever After* assumes a feminist stance but offers a mass-mediated idea of feminism where individual women can be strong and achieve equality through personal actions that do not, however, challenge or change the underlying patriarchal structure of society. . . . The problems identified by second-wave feminism are simplified, emptied of their radical critiques of systemic gender inequality, and marketed to young women. This limited perspective, which draws on girl power and liberal feminism, reinforces patriarchal authority by emphasizing individual achievements and isolating one woman, the heroine, as an exception to standard feminine behavior. (101)

Door, then, stands out because of her ability and because she is the only surviving member of her family who has that ability, making her unique and undermining the ideals of social equality for which modern versions of feminism advocate. Further, Door's powers are often tied to male authority, as she is frequently identified as "Lord

Portico's daughter," her powers are an inherited family trait, and as she uses her ability most frequently to open doors for men like Richard, the Marquis de Carabas (Paterson Joseph), and the Angel Islington, who is technically without gender, but is definitively male as portrayed by actor Peter Capaldi. This problem of representing a uniquely strong or uniquely empowered female lead is not unique to the miniseries or even to *Neverwhere* as the longevity of the star in *Stardust* sets her apart from the other women in that narrative as well. For Door, the filming and framing of her perspective undermines not only the notion that her point of view is *her* point of view, but also that her abilities empower her in any way that connects to larger ideals of women as socially empowered or equal to men.

Girls, Women, and Nouns: Objectification through Word Choice in the (Illustrated) Novels *Stardust* and *Neverwhere*

As coming-of-age narratives, *Neverwhere* and *Stardust* have quests for particular objects at the heart of their narratives. For *Stardust*, the majority of the characters (Dunstan, Tristran, the witch-queen, Primus, and Septimus) quest for their heart's desire, which can range from a desire to go home, find love, become king, or acquire eternal life and youth. In *Neverwhere*, similar quests are at work, with Richard wishing to return to London Above, Door attempting to gain revenge on her family's murderers, and Hunter wanting to kill the Great Beast of London Below. From a narrative perspective, the significance of the quest aspect of these stories is that only the characters in the fairy lands have quests that they wish to accomplish, which, from a gendered perspective, disconnects the women of Victorian society in *Stardust* and the *Neverwhere* women of London Above from the ideas of happiness usually associated with the happy ending at the end of the fairy tale. While denying these women the agency of having a quest or purpose other than marriage, Gaiman further complicates the gender portrayals in the two texts by having the women of the real world be women who are clearly named and are only objectified in the normal sexual and social manner one expects in a patriarchal society.

By contrast, through his portrayals of the women of faerie and London Below, Gaiman engages in a literary endeavor in which he uses language to objectify and diminish women in very literal ways. In the two works, the women of fairy, either faerie (*Stardust* the novel and illustrated novel) or London Below (all versions of *Neverwhere*) respectively, are frequently turned into objects through Gaiman's naming of and descriptions of them. However, this use of language and objectification of women is consistent through both written texts. In *Stardust* and *Neverwhere*, Gaiman occasionally endows the female characters of faerie and London Below with humanity by referring to them by gendered nouns, but he further subdivides these characters into sexual categories by describing them as either girls or women—a categorization based on sexual desirability more than by age or any other factor. The use of these descriptors is telling because this technique of referring to a character consistently by a gendered noun instead of by name does not happen to the men in either text. In particular, Gaiman objectifies and diminishes Door, Yvaine, Anaesthesia, Hunter, the witch-queen, and Tristran's mother through the nouns he chooses to use in place of their names and through his tendency to change those nouns and descriptions when the character is involved or associated with sexual situations. Given the limitations of a single chapter, I will focus my discussion on the ways Door and Yvaine are objectified and diminished and contrast that discussion with the ways other remediations of the text alter these representations. Still, it is important to note that across both written texts, the only women described as women are those in whom the male protagonist has a sexual interest or whom he perceives as old.

For *Neverwhere*, which was adapted *from* the miniseries into a sort of companion novel, Gaiman limits his naming of the main characters of London Below to names that are also commonplace nouns, effectively giving them names that reflect their narrative purpose and conflate their identity and genders with objects. For Door, having a name that represents a commonplace object is connected to her family's talent. Each member of the family of openers has a name that reflects his or her skill at opening doors, from her father, Lord Portico; to her mother, Lady Portia; her sister,

Ingress; and her brother, Arch (Gaiman, *Neverwhere* 80-9). Not only does Door's name tie to her talent, it relates directly to her role in the text in regard to Richard. Door is Richard's literal door into London Below. In many ways, his quest narrative functions so that he can become someone with the opener's power that she has. Through his quest, he becomes master of the key to all reality, which allows him to travel between those realities—to effectively open any door (341).

Beyond being a commonplace noun and the door through which Richard enters London Below, Gaiman's diminishes Door by referring to her only by diminutive gender nouns and pronouns. Although Door's point of view is introduced early in the novel (Gaiman 6), she isn't named or identified. This contrasts with Richard, Croupe, Vandemar, and other males in the text who are all immediately introduced by name within portions of the text written from their perspective. When Gaiman returns to Door's perspective for the second time (16), it takes him over six sentences to name her. As he doesn't refer to her by name, calling her by the indirect noun of "girl" seems logical, especially as Richard finds her age indefinable—she is "fifteen? Sixteen? Older? He couldn't tell" (53). However, the contrast between the gender and naming conventions for women and men demonstrates that being referred to as a gendered noun or pronoun makes that character a subject in someone else's text. In this case, being a girl isn't a descriptor defining a child of the female sex. Being a girl means being someone who is considered as a girl, specifically from the perspective of the men in the text.

Further complicating the ways in which the novel uses language to objectify Door, the graphic novel recognizes and complicates Door's subject role within the remediations of *Neverwhere* because instead of using language to objectify Door, Mike Carey and Glenn Fabry use the artistic conventions of graphic novels to portray Door as a fully adult, full-figured woman. More tellingly, they explicitly acknowledge the objectification of Door that occurs in the source text by having Richard hallucinate Door during his ordeal—a scene that doesn't occur in any of the other remediations of the text. Door appears to Richard, bending over so he and the reader have a clear view of her cleavage, and says, "I'm not real either, Richard . . . I'm probably a sexual fantasy of some kind, wouldn't you say? 'The Opener.' It's a bit blatant, really" (authors' emphasis). Within the fairy-tale framework of *Neverwhere*, then, there is as Cristina Bacchilega notes of the genre, a "normative function, which capitalizes on the comforts of consensus" (8). Thus, the subjective frame surrounding Door, created by deliberate and consistent word choice, reinforces our society's patriarchal norms, which dictate that women *must* occupy such subject positions within androcentric texts.

Stardust, the second solo novel of Gaiman's career and the first one following *Neverwhere*, continues in the deliberative use of language to create objectification and subjectification of its female characters. The star, often referred to as a common-place noun, or as an "it"—unnamed and ungendered until page 153—is so firmly entrenched within a barren patriarchal fantasy that her sexual nature is divorced from all domestic comforts of life. In *Stardust*, the King of Stormhold knocks the star, Yvaine, out of the sky, injuring her (Gaiman, *Stardust* 59). She is found by Tristran Thorne, who kidnaps her and forces her to travel with him toward his home village of Wall (99). Over the course of their journey, the star becomes indebted to Tristran (152), and the two eventually fall in love (201). Tristran and the star marry, and eventually, he becomes King of Stormhold. When Tristran dies, the star rules on in his stead as an immortal, childless queen of Stormhold (212). In a move counter to many Victorian fairy tales, Gaiman's narrative denies the star access to the world of the domestic; she cannot return home (160), eat food (124), or have children (201). Mary-Anne Potter and Deirdre Byrne argue that these aspects of the story counter the didactic formula of such tales, which dictated that a "female character journey away from a familiar place and time, guiding her towards an experience of discomfort . . . and creating a need . . . to return . . . 'home' . . . [which is] defined and delineated as the predictable and safe space of the domestic" (84). While the idea of the star escaping the confinement of the Victorian home aligns with modern perspectives of women's place in society as moving both in and out of the domestic sphere, the fact that the star's home isn't a domestic space complicates Potter and Byrne's argument as well as Gaiman's text. The ways Gaiman divorces the star's sexual nature from the comforts of life serves as a seemingly feminist move that attempts to avoid patriarchal perspectives of domestication while unintentionally reinforcing them by confining the star's sexuality and choices to those which most please Tristran, who apparently achieves his heart's desire by marrying such a woman. As Brown argues, the star's conversion from an "it" to a "she" serves as a demonstration of Tristran finding a "higher truth of the spirit because understanding Yvaine's nature is part of Tristran's *Bildung* (journey from youth to manhood)" (222). The fact that the star doesn't acquire gender or name until Tristran recognizes her as a person demonstrates the ways in which he has viewed her as an object; furthermore, the fact that her transition into gendered personhood is inconsistent, with Gaiman referring to her as "the star" off and on even after she is named demonstrates the continued project of objectification at work within the novel.

Film adaptation has a tendency to reconsider and discard aspects of the original text that movie-goers might find troubling, and so the 2007 film *Stardust* erases some of the objectification at work in Gaiman's original novel by immediately naming all of the female characters and allowing their names to be the main referent. As Susan Cahill contends, the film version of *Stardust* further complicates Yvaine's function as an object (62-3). As with the other forms of the narrative, Yvaine exists as an object to be loved by, the now more sensibly named, Tristan and to be hunted by Lamia (the witch-queen) and others. However, as Potter and Byrne argue, the director of the 2007 film, Matthew Vaughn, gives Yvaine (Claire Danes) some personhood, allowing her to use her "undomesticated" power and nature as a star to destroy Lamia through the power of "shining" (87). Yet, even Yvaine's star power depends on the Disney-like notion of "true love" that requires Yvaine to rely on Tristan to be able to shine.

Moreover, the film's ending for the confrontation between Lamia and Yvaine differs greatly from the ending for the witch-queen and the star. While the witch-queen/Lamia obsesses over gaining youth and beauty through the destruction of a younger woman in a way reminiscent of the Evil Queen in "Snow White," the written text portrays her as giving up on this quest and has the star forgive her for trying to kill her. By contrast, the film ends the relationship with the two in a life-and-death battle, which Yvaine eventually wins. Through its narrative connection to "Snow White," then, *Stardust* connects to larger fairy-tale frameworks that connect women's beauty and age to their self-worth in a patriarchal society (Bacchilega 34). By making the witch-queen quest for the heart of a star in order to gain youth and beauty, Gaiman's narrative repeats the "intergenerational female conflict" that Cahill views as "endemic to fairy tales" (59). From the physical descriptions of the two characters, to their actions in the varied texts, Gaiman's *Stardust* fits Gilbert and Gubar's description of the Grimm version of Snow White, as in Gaiman's text "the central action of the tale . . . arises from the relationship between these two women: the one fair, young, pale, the other just as fair, but older, fiercer. . . the one a sort of angel, the other an undeniable witch" (36). In regards to the star and the witch-queen in the novels, Gaiman's portrayal allows for an odd, yet peaceable resolution to this gendered conflict, more or less ameliorating the notion that older women must destroy younger women to gain the beauty that guarantees them a place in society. The film, however, explosively undoes this amelioration, "[which] points to particular unease concerning, among other things, the maintenance of beauty through artificial means and the position of the older women within such a beauty economy" (Cahill 59). Heightening the conflict between the two women in the film's conclusion increases the story's connection to that of the original narrative while visibly demonstrating that our society's discomfort with older women in power continues. This undermines the notion that the film's representations of Yvaine are empowering, as she is a beautiful woman who can never grow old and who only uses her magical abilities to destroy a powerful, old woman.

Still, Yvaine's metaphysical empowerment reverberates with ideas of girl power as described by Williams, which, though complicated from a feminist perspective, demonstrate one way of portraying strong, female characters in film. On the other hand, as Cahill notes regarding this final scene, "[t]hat Stardust stages the final battle as one that takes place between an evil queen and younger heroine serves to emphasize this unease surrounding the older, more powerful woman who must be replaced by youth, innocence, [and] passivity" (65). Tellingly, such discomfort with older, strong women continues in modern society—not only in films and novels that replicate fairy tale tropes, but also in national conversations about women in positions of power. Thus, not only do the plot and language of Gaiman's novel and Vaughn's adaptation of the script objectify Yvaine as a character, they also replicate and recreate "the patriarchal symbolical order based on rigid notions of sexuality and gender" that have dominated modern iterations of folk tales since the Grimms collected and revised them (Zipes qtd. in Brown 74).

Happy Endings? Conclusions on Fairy Tales, Subversion, and Gender

When describing and complicating Zipes' work on fairy tales and folklores, Bacchilega contends, "[i]n the middle ages, folk tales served *more* of an emancipatory function because they expressed the problems and desires of the underprivileged; in modern times, the fairy tale has more often than not been 'instrumentalized' to support bourgeois and/or conservative interests" (7). Unsurprisingly, given the end of the two multifariously-constructed texts, Gaiman's *Neverwhere* and *Stardust* subvert this role of fairy tale as both works end with the hero abandoning bourgeois society and values and living a life that is undomesticated. For the women of these works, this subversion of bourgeois interests is less dramatic, as the characters end the texts closer to living a domesticated life at the end than they had in the beginning, with Yvaine as queen of Stormhold and Door as the leader of her house. However, demonstrating that "we use the classical fairy tales in mutated forms through new technologies to discuss and debate urgent issues that concern our social lives and the very survival of the human species" as Zipes contends, notions of gender continue to be complicated across the remediated forms of these texts as do aspects of the patriarchal nature of our society (qtd. in Cahill 58). Clearly, the female characters in all forms of *Neverwhere* and *Stardust* are complex in their individual goals and, despite their referential connection to fairy tale characters, these women manage to break away from some of the traditional, patriarchal endings implicated by those narratives. Still, the very fact that such subversion fails to move the female characters past the role of subject of the male gaze or object of a man's desire demonstrates that remediation has its limits—as does the idea of happily ever after.

Works Cited

Bacchilega, Cristina. *Post-Modern Fairy Tales: Gender and Narrative Strategies*. Philadelphia: U of Pennsylvania P, 1997. *Print*.

Brown, Paula. "*Stardust* as Allegorical *Bildungsroman*: An Apology for Platonic Idealism." *Extrapolation* 51.2 (2010): 216-34. Web. *ProQuest: Literature Online* 31 Jul. 2016.

Cahill, Susan. "Through the Looking Glass: Fairy Tale Cinema and the Spectacle of Femininity in *Stardust* and *The Brother's Grimm*." *Marvels and Tales: Journal of Fairy-Tales Studies* 24.1 (2010): 57-67. Web. *ProQuest: Literature Online* 1 Jul. 2016.

Carey, Mike, writer. *Neil Gaiman's Neverwhere*. Art by Glenn Fabry. New York: Vertigo-D.C. Comics, 2007. Print.

Corrigan, Timothy J. *A Short Guide to Writing about Film*, 6th edition. New York: Pearson Longman, 2007. Print.

Gaiman, Neil. *Neverwhere*, 4th ed. New York: Harper Torch, 2001. Print.

_____. *Stardust: Being a Romance within the Realms of Faerie*. Art by Charles Vess. New York: Vertigo-DC Comics, 1998. Print.

_____. *Stardust*, 6th edition. New York: Harper, 2007. Print.

Garber, Megan. "Call It the 'Bechdel-Wallace Test'." *The Atlantic*. The Atlantic Monthly Group, 25 Aug. 2015. Web. 17 Aug. 2016.

Gilbert, Sandra M., and Susan Gubar. "The Queen's Looking Glass: Female Creativity, Male Images of Women, and the Metaphor of Literary Paternity." *Madwomen in the Attic: The Woman Writer and the Nineteenth Century Literary Imagination*. 2nd Ed., New Haven: Yale UP, 2000.

Klapcsik, Sándor. "Neil Gaiman's Irony, Liminal Fantasies, and Fairy Tale Adaptations." *Hungarian Journal of English and American Studies* 14.2 (2008): 317-34. *JSTOR*. Web. 1 Jul. 2016.

Neverwhere. Dir. Dewey Humphreys. Perf. Gary Bakewell, Laura Fraser, Hywel Bennett, and Peter Capaldi. 1996. BBC Worldwide Americas, Inc., 2011. DVD.

"Neverwhere (1996 TV Miniseries) Full Cast & Crew." *IMDb*. IMDb.com, n.d. Web. 19 Aug. 2016.

Potter, Mary-Anne and Deirdre Byrne. "Falling Down in Order to Grow Up: Two Women's Journeys from Un-domestication to Domestication in Fantasy Fiction." *Mousaion* 33.2 (2015): 73-91. *Project Muse*. Web. 1 Aug. 2016.

Stardust. Dir. Matthew Vaughn. Perf. Claire Danes, Charlie Cox, Michelle Pfeifer, and Robert DeNiro. Paramount Pictures, 2007. Film.

Williams, Christy. "The Shoe Still Fits: *Everafter* and the Pursuit of a Feminist Cinderella." *Fairy Tale Films: Visions of Ambiguity*. Eds. Pauline Greenhill and Sidney Eve Matrix. Logan, UT: Utah State UP, 2010. Print. 99-115.

CRITICAL READINGS

Guilty Pleasures: Neil Gaiman's Books for Children for Adults

Annette Wannamaker

In a speech he delivered at the Chicago Public Library in 2012 titled "What the (Very Bad Swearword) is a Children's Book Anyway?" Neil Gaiman explained that he wrote the adorable picture book *Chu's Day* because he, for lack of a better phrase, wanted to mess with people, specifically adult readers of children's books:

> [The book] exists because none of my children's picture books have ever been published in mainland China. They have been published in Hong Kong and in Taiwan, but there has never been a Neil Gaiman-written picture book in China because, I was told, in my books the children do not respect their parents enough, and they do bad things without getting properly punished, and there is anarchy and destruction and insufficient respect for authority. So it became a goal of mine to create a picture book that would contain all of these things and also be published in mainland China. ("What")

Gaiman, that moppy-headed rock star of children's literature, adult literature, comics, picture books, poetry, television series, radio shows, and just about every other genre, medium, and category of story imaginable, is a trickster of a writer who enjoys challenging himself and his readers. He manages, again and again, to discomfort us, to unsettle us, not only by writing strange and frightening works of horror, science fiction, and fantasy but also by nudging at boundaries of literary categories in ways that destabilize our readerly selves in both distressing and pleasurable ways. In this chapter, I will focus very specifically on one precise, and treacherous, textual boundary that Gaiman challenges in his works, the divide between literature for children and literature for adults. First, though, I need to briefly cover some history that explains why this particular boundary is one that makes us particularly edgy, and why the act of crossing it is so fraught with anxiety, guilt, and self-consciousness.

Treacherous Textual Boundaries: The Borders between Adult and Children's Literature

The line between what counts as a work for adults and what counts as a work for children has always been amorphous, but that hasn't stopped people from attempting to vehemently police this imaginary border. From the well-meaning adult who says, with great certainty, "that book is not appropriate for children," to the literary snob who won't read comics because "they are juvenile," folks seem intent not only on maintaining a firm separation between literature for children and adults but also on perpetuating moral judgments about reading practices that challenge these imaginary boundaries. In her book, cheekily titled *The Solitary Vice: Against Reading*, Mikita Brottman analyzes historical and cultural attitudes about reading and the ways in which these attitudes often reflect larger anxieties about societal change. Well into the twentieth century, she explains, moralists cautioned against reading novels, which they worried encouraged "unrestrained self-absorption" (Brottman 10), and intellectuals fretted about the negative effect that mass-produced "penny dreadfuls" would have upon "barely literate" (12) working class readers and child readers. Similarly, literary historian Teresa Michals connects past fears about the lower classes reading the "wrong" books to current fears about children reading the "wrong" books, explaining that, "At that time (in the eighteenth century) women and servants of all ages were routinely lumped together with children as the ideal—or the nightmare—reader of popular vernacular print," and that most novels of the time were written for a "mixed-age audience of women, children, and servants" (2). The worry that the more weak-minded members of the population (women, children, servants) needed to be protected by adult men from indelicate ideas, combined with the fact that reading is mostly a solitary (and therefore unsupervised) activity, created a large market for all-ages books that could safely be "read aloud in the family circle" (Clark 16) without fear of embarrassment or offense.

It is only recently (over the past century or so) that there has been such a distinct line established solely to separate literature for children from literature for adults. Beverly Lyon Clark explains:

> Literature for children wasn't always separated from literature for adults. Early literature in the West—mystery plays, ballads, folk tales, sermons—embraced children as part of its audience. Even later, literature for children long overlapped with that for the laboring and later working classes: children often read chapbooks, evangelical tracts, and dime novels. (16)

Clark argues that in the US the line between children's and adult literature became solidified in the early twentieth century, when literary critics began to distinguish between literature written specifically by and for adult men—"great" literature, like Herman Melville's *Moby-Dick*—and works that were "inferior," and which just happened to be written for women or the working classes or for children. While these formalist literary critics claimed to be objective in their evaluations, their assessments about which works had literary merit and which didn't were clearly based in cultural biases against women, minorities, the working classes, and children.

This old-fashioned attitude still persists today and is the main reason so many adults feel they should not be reading books that are marketed toward children or young adults and should instead be reading 'real' literature. Indeed, this enduring attitude is also the reason so many literary gatekeepers feel justified in shaming adult readers of children's books. British novelist A.S. Byatt downright mourns for the suffocated souls of adult Harry Potter fans who are, according to her, "an adult generation that hasn't known, and doesn't care about, mystery. They are inhabitants of urban jungles, not of the real wild. They don't have the skills to tell ersatz magic from the real thing" (Byatt). Professional literary curmudgeon Harold Bloom, who famously argued that the popularity of the Harry Potter books among adult readers was most surely a symptom of the "dumbing down" of American literary taste, culture, and society, said of the Harry Potter series, "Why read it? Presumably, if you cannot be persuaded to read anything better, Rowling will have to do.... Why read, if what you read will not enrich mind or spirit or personality?" (Bloom). Both authors wrote their critiques taking for granted that we all agree with their assumption that, of course, children's books are simple and shallow, while books for adults are complex and enriching.

As young adult and children's literature has continued to grow in popularity in the first part of the twenty-first century, other critics have joined this public chorus of shaming, telling those of us who read and enjoy children's books—not because we are reading them on behalf of a child, but because we find our own meanings and pleasures in these texts—that we should be very ashamed of ourselves; for example Georgina Howlett wrote in the *Guardian* that: "Once upon a time it would have been shameful for adults to read books written for teenagers, never mind admitting that publicly." In a *Slate* article, Ruth Graham wrote that, "Adults should feel embarrassed about reading literature written for children" because "the enjoyment of reading this stuff has to do with escapism, instant gratification, and nostalgia." Or, to phrase it simply, if readers (heaven forbid!) enjoy a book, it must be an inferior book and adults who read literature for children must be inferior readers. Scholars of children's literature and adult fans of children's and young adult literature have argued for decades that literature for younger readers can be as serious, complex, dense, thoughtful, and as literary as literature written solely for adults—often, even more so—but they still find themselves having to defend and justify their reading habits.

Neil Gaiman's work is solidly in the midst of these ongoing debates about what counts as literature and what doesn't because, throughout his career, he has written books for all ages and has had fans of all ages. For instance, in the 2012 speech about children's books referenced at the start of this chapter, he said:

> I've been a professional writer, earning my living through my words, for thirty years now. I have written books for adults and I have written books for children. I have written several books for adults that were awarded the Alex Award by YALSA for being books for adults that younger readers enjoyed. I have written books for children that were later republished in respectable editions that adults could buy and read in public without fear of being thought childish. So, it is embarrassing to admit that, as I write this, as I read it, and for most of the last [few] months, I have been trying to work out what a

children's book is, and what an adult book is, and which one I was writing, and why. (Gaiman, "What")

Although Gaiman humbly and coyly feigns ignorance about his writing (as many authors do), I think he knows exactly what he is doing: He has managed to tap into and capitalize upon our border-crossing anxieties by addressing both child readers who know they shouldn't be reading a book about adult things and adult readers who know they shouldn't find so very much pleasure in a children's book. And, the knowing is key. He is winking at us in the spaces between words, as if to say: "I know that you know that you shouldn't be reading this but, don't worry, it's our little secret."

While Gaiman is an especially tricky writer, there are a lot of other writers who also play in this murky space between children's and adult literature, mostly for laughs. Books like *Go the F**k to Sleep*, *If You Give Mommy a Glass of Wine*, and *All My Friends Are Dead* are funny because they are made to resemble children's picture books but are actually very inappropriate for younger children and are instead meant to be parodies aimed solidly at adults readers. All writers of children's and young adult fiction understand they must address a multi-aged audience. As one critic has argued, "children's literature has at least a double address: the children who are the ostensible audience and the adults whose decision makes it available" (Clark 15). Almost all children's books are written by adults, edited and published by adults working in the publishing industry, distributed and sold by adults, and bought for children by adult teachers, librarians, parents, grandparents, and caregivers. Children's literature scholars call this attention to the adult reader of children's books dual address because the writer has to write a book that will appeal to both the child reader and to the various adults reading on behalf of the child. Gaiman's work, though, moves beyond this usual dual address in the ways he writes books that are purposefully vague about their intended audiences. Are his recent picture book adaptations of "Sleeping Beauty" and "Hansel and Gretel," for instance, meant for children or adults or both at once? It's hard to tell.

Reading Shame, Guilt, and Pleasure

A category of readership that may apply to Gaiman's work is one that some scholars refer to as "crossover" writing. A crossover book is one that transcends age categories and appeals to a broad range of readers. Sandra Beckett explains that crossover fiction is nothing new because humans have been telling all-ages stories, like folk tales and legends, as long as there have been stories: "What's new about crossover literature" she writes "is the hype and the media attention that it has been receiving in recent years" (14). She argues that the success of the books in the Harry Potter series, initially marketed toward children but quickly adopted by adult readers as well, called attention—both negative (like Bloom and Byatt) and positive—to adult fans of children's literature. She explains that, viewed in a positive light, "Crossover fiction acknowledges that different generations share experiences, knowledge, desires, and concerns. [. . .] There is a move away from the polarization of children and adults toward a recognition of the continuity that connects readers of all ages" (Beckett 268). But—and this is key to this particular reading of Gaiman's works—a lot of the media attention crossover fiction has received has not been positive. Some writers use different names when publishing for children so as not to harm their reputation, and some children's books are published in versions with adult covers so that readers won't be ashamed to be seen reading a book for children. Adults who read children's books are thought to be "childish" and "uncultured" and are even called names like "kidult" and "adultescent" (Beckett 256). This has led many adult fans of children's and young adult literature to feel self-conscious, even ashamed, about their reading habits. Rachel Falconer writes that, "While many writers and publishers have been keen to claim that their books are suitable for readers of all ages, I would argue that cross-readers, like other cultural migrants, are often highly conscious of having crossed a border" (Falconer 3). To be an adult reading a book that is clearly marked as a book for children, or even one marked as being for "all ages," comes with a sense of embarrassment and shame, an uneasy feeling that one should be reading something else, something more refined, something "better."

This private, shameful pleasure we take from enjoying something we are not supposed to enjoy is often called "guilty pleasure." Mark Dery describes the phrase "guilty pleasure" as asscovering irony that masks class insecurities, a sort of "disapproving voice of the societal superego, internalized" (Dery). The concept of taking "guilty pleasure" in reading (or viewing or listening to) texts that our culture tells us we shouldn't is especially fascinating when examined in connection with the recent trend of adults reading children's and young adult literature. Apparently, the phrase "guilty pleasure" only recently became a regular part of popular American vernacular: "According to the online *Times* archives, 'guilty pleasure' shows up [in the *New York Times*] approximately twelve hundred and sixty times—twelve hundred and forty-seven of those since 1996" (Szalai). While "guilty pleasures" are often associated with pop culture phenomena—a secret love of ABBA, surreptitiously watching episodes of "Survivor," or reading Harlequin romances—it seems serendipitous that the phrase came into common usage in the US at just the exact same time that works of children's and young adult literature were becoming increasingly popular with a lot of adult readers: Philip Pullman's *The Golden Compass* was published in 1995, J.K. Rowling's *Harry Potter and the Sorcerer's Stone* in 1997, Gaiman's *Coraline* in 2002, Stephenie Meyer's *Twilight* in 2005, Suzanne Collins' *The Hunger Games* in 2008, Gaiman's *The Graveyard Book* in 2008, and John Green's *The Fault in Our Stars* in 2012, just to list a few books for younger readers that have also been extremely popular with adult readers.

Gaiman is acutely aware that many of his works fall into the category of "guilty pleasures," not only because they cross categories of age but also because he works in genres often considered to be "low-brow": horror, fantasy, science fiction, and those guiltiest of pleasures, the comic book and the television series. He has played with and challenged the arbitrary borders between popular and elite culture throughout his career by combining references to Shakespeare's works with references to pop songs, by creating comics dense with literary allusion, by writing frightening horror stories for children, and by writing picture books for adults. It is this category-defying slipperiness that makes his work so complex, so tricky, and so much fun to read. Roland Barthes, in his seminal work, *The Pleasure of the Text*, distinguishes between works that comfort us by meeting our expectations, "the text that contents, fills, grants euphoria, the text that comes from culture and does not break with it," and works that create discomfort by challenging the status quo, "the text that discomforts [. . .] unsettles the reader's historical, cultural, psychological assumptions, the consistency of his tastes, values, memories, brings to a crisis his relation with language" (Barthes 14). Pushing at and stretching the boundaries of genre is one way that Gaiman manages to create works of literature that make us feel uneasy; that frighten and unsettle us; and that, at their best, make us rethink ourselves and our place in the world. Horror fiction often highlights our terror at borders—that line between life and death, the thin distinction between human and animal, the tenuous difference between self and other, between what is me and what is not me. Some of his more recent works expand upon these tropes in the ways they also overtly challenge, and downright dismantle, the socially constructed border between adult and child.

Gaiman's Books for Children for Adults

William Alexander notices this characteristic in his review of Gaiman's 2013 novel, *The Ocean at the End of the Lane*, when he writes that, "If you take a step back from the plot and squint a bit, the novel is about children who cross boundaries between worlds and confront monsters, grownups and blends between the two." He goes on to explain that while *Ocean* is "heralded as Gaiman's first novel for adults in eight years. It isn't. Not exactly. It is narrated by an adult, and it is addressed to adult readers, but the book is actually for the children those adults used to be. This is what makes it remarkable" (Alexander). Even the author himself is unsure as to whether the novel is about or for adults or children. He said, "[*The Ocean at the End of the Lane*] has everything in it I would have loved as a boy. . . . And I don't think it's for kids. . . . But I'm not sure" (Gaiman, "What"). Significantly, Gaiman was writing *Ocean* at the same time he was writing the 2012 Chicago speech, which is quoted earlier in this chapter and which is focused on attempting to define (and failing to define) what exactly makes a work of literature a children's book or a book for adults. Gaiman said of *Ocean* that, "I reached the end of the book and realized that I was as clueless as when I began. Was it a children's book? an adult book? a young adult book? a crossover book? A . . . book?" ("What"). These questions about categories of writing and reading are central to the novel, which is, in many ways, a story about stories, a narrative about the ways we use narrative to shape, to understand, and to remember who we are and why we are who we are.

Gaiman begins *Ocean* with a famous quote from picture book artist and children's author Maurice Sendak: "I remember my own childhood vividly . . . I knew terrible things. But I knew I mustn't let adults know I knew. It would scare them." It is an epigraph about the complex and often dishonest relationship between adults and children, and it perfectly sets the tone for a scary story told by an adult narrator reluctantly remembering terrifying childhood experiences with treacherous adults. When he was asked about the Sendak quote, Gaiman said, "It's not there ironically; it's not there as a clever commentary. It's the idea that kids really do know things that would terrify adults. I think it's only a certain amount of amnesia that allows adults to function" (qtd. in Filgate). Because many adults like to imagine that childhood is a safe, innocent, protected space (it is for some children, but not for many), Gaiman's books for children have often been criticized for being too frightening: The monstrous Other Mother threatens to consume Coraline in the book of the same name and to replace her eyes with buttons; in one picture book by Gaiman, wolves hide in the walls, then chase a family out of their home; and a 2010 alphabet book, titled *The Dangerous Alphabet*, uses mummies, ghouls, witches, and vampires to teach a macabre version of the alphabet. It is no wonder that Gaiman has spent much of his career explaining to worried adults why child readers might not be so fragile as some adults imagine, why children appreciate and even need frightening books, and why adult readers might sometimes make false assumptions on the behalf of child readers.

For instance, in the "About the Book" section included at the end of my paperback edition of *Coraline*, Gaiman explains that *Coraline* is a novel "that children experienced as an adventure, but which gave adults nightmares" (169). This isn't the only place he makes this curious distinction that inverts a major cultural assumption about childhood, that children are fearful and adults are brave. In *The Tragical Comedy or Comical Tragedy of Mr. Punch*, the adult narrator remembers a time when he was eight years old and explains, "When I was four I believed everything, accepted everything, and was scared of nothing. Now I was eight, and I believed in what I could see and was scared of anything I couldn't." *Mr. Punch* is a comic book/picture book that, like so many of Gaiman's works, is very difficult to classify. While tiny lettering just above the ISBN mark on the back of the book reads "suggested for mature readers," the book is the size, weight, and shape of a picture book, features a sleeping boy on the back cover, and has a colorful (albeit, creepy) image on the front cover of a red-nosed Punch puppet, so that it physically resembles a book meant for child readers. The main character is a child and the main topic is children's entertainment, the traveling Punch and Judy puppet shows that were once popular in England and mainland Europe. The narrator is an adult who has an ambivalent relationship with Punch and Judy. He attends a Punch and Judy show as an adult—"the only unaccompanied adult on the tent floor, surrounded by children"—and realizes the show is grimmer and darker than he initially remembered: "Punch, of course, killed Judy. That was something I had forgotten." He describes a scene where the Punch puppet throws Judy's baby out of a window, and Judy asks the children in the audience what happened: "You wicked evil Mister Punch. It's not asleep. It's dead. He killed my baby, didn't he boys and girls?" The next frame depicts smiling and laughing children responding "yes!" and the rest of the two-page spread narrates Punch's comic murder of Judy. While the children laugh, the narrator gets up to leave: "I felt ill, and made my way out of the tent, stumbling my way through the sitting children, pursued into the daylight by Mister Punch's shrill inhuman voice as he beat the policeman to death." In this text, and in quite a few others, Gaiman challenges the assumption that when we move from childhood to adulthood, we progress from ignorance to wisdom, from fear to security, or from protected to protector. He depicts adult characters still inhabited by their childhood selves as well as children who are often expected to behave in adult-like ways.

Likewise, *The Ocean at the End of the Lane* is also a frightening book about childlike adults and children in adult situations. Indeed, the narrator introduces himself, in the "prologue," explaining that he is wearing a black suit to attend a funeral, an outfit that would normally make him feel as if he is "only pretending to be an adult" (Gaiman, *Ocean* 3). This is an apt detail for readers of Gaiman's fiction, those adults who devour his books for children, who might feel a guilty, sneaky pleasure about it, and who perhaps worry they are only pretending to be adults. It's also a link connecting the adult narrator to childhood memories and a childhood self that have been repressed. The story centers on a seven-year-old boy surrounded by dangerous adults and/as monsters who are more powerful than he is, which isn't all that different from books like *Coraline* and *The Graveyard Book*. What distinguishes *Ocean* from these books, which were marketed as works for children, even though they were read by many adults as well, is that it is told from the point of view of an adult looking back on events from his childhood, it features one scene where the child protagonist witnesses two adults having sex, and, in one deeply disturbing scene, the boy's father tries to drown him in the bathtub.

These bits, though, don't necessarily limit the book to adult readers, and the book is filled with characteristics that typically mark children's books: there is magic, there are elements from folklore and myth, and there's a child protagonist fighting to save his oblivious parents from a danger they are too dim to notice. In her book on crossover fiction, Beckett notes that, "One of the oldest and most universal forms of crossover literature is folk and fairy tales, which are part of what Stuart Hannabuss refers to as 'the common cultural pool'" (4). This is the deep cultural pool that has inspired many of Gaiman's works: *American Gods*, *Anansi Boys*, his *Sandman* comics, *The Graveyard Book*, and *Coraline* all also draw heavily on ancient stories that were once told to multigenerational audiences. The seven-year-old protagonist of *Ocean*, who is a voracious reader, describes reading a book about Egyptian mythology, saying, "I liked myths. They weren't adult stories and they weren't children's stories. They were better than that. They just *were*." (53). It's a highly self-conscious moment that is aimed directly at Gaiman's loyal, border-crossing readers.

A key moment in the novel comes during a conversation the protagonist has with Lettie Hemstock, a magical and ancient being who appears to be an eleven-year-old girl but who is something much older and powerful. The narrator says to her that "grown-ups and monsters aren't scared of things," but Lettie corrects him, explaining that "grown-ups don't look like grown-ups on the inside" (Gaiman, *Ocean* 112). She continues, saying, "I'm going to tell you something important. . . . The truth is, there aren't any grown-ups. Not one, in the whole wide world" (112). He thinks about this possibility: "I wondered if that was true; if they were all really children wrapped in adult bodies, like children's books hidden in the middle of dull, long adult books, the kind with no pictures or conversations" (Gaiman, *Ocean* 113). In addition to being a direct reference to Lewis Carroll's *Alice's Adventures in Wonderland*—another children's book read by adults, another book with childish, yet powerful, adult characters who threaten the child protagonist—this moment creates a metafictional link between identity (both child and adult) and storytelling. It describes the novel precisely and Gaiman's readers, too: those children who don't quite feel at home in children's books and those adults who worry they are only children in disguise.

In a speech he delivered to the London-based organization The Reading Agency in 2013, Gaiman focused on writing for children and on the importance of creating books that engage child readers:

> And while we must tell our readers true things and give them weapons and give them armour and pass on whatever wisdom we have gleaned from our short stay on this green world, we have an obligation not to preach, not to lecture, not to force predigested morals and messages down our readers' throats like adult birds feeding their babies pre-

masticated maggots; and we have an obligation never, ever, under any circumstances, to write anything for children to read that we would not want to read ourselves. ("Why")

While many children's books address a dual audience of a child and an adult reader looking over that child's shoulder, who might be censoring or selecting books on behalf of that child or who might be moral-hunting to make sure that a book is suitably educational, Gaiman addresses a different sort of adult reader of children's literature, that adult who is reading and enjoying books on her or his own behalf. A curious side effect of this strategy may, ironically, be the way in which Gaiman's children's books (and some of his adult books as well) are also loved by children.

Works Cited

Alexander, William. "Review: *The Ocean at the End of the Lane*, by Neil Gaiman." *Star Tribune*. Star Tribune, 19 June 2013. Web. Accessed 25 June 2016.

Barthes, Roland. *The Pleasure of the Text*. Trans. Richard Miller. New York: Hill and Wang, 1975. Print.

Beckett, Sandra L. *Crossover Fiction: Global and Historical Perspectives*. New York: Routledge, 2009. Print.

Bloom, Harold. "Can 35 Million Book Buyers Be Wrong? Yes." *Wall Street Journal*. Dow Jones & Company, Inc., 11 Jul. 2000. Web. 10 May 2015.

Brottman, Mikita. *The Solitary Vice: Against Reading*. Berkeley, CA: Counterpoint, 2008. Print.

Byatt, A. S. "Harry Potter and the Childish Adult." *The New York Times*. The New York Times Company, Inc., 7 Jul. 2003. Web. 10 May 2015.

Clark, Beverly Lyon. "Audience." *Keywords for Children's Literature*. Ed. Philip Nel & Lissa Paul. New York: NYU Press, 2011. 14-17. Print.

Dery, Mark. "Let's put the guilt back in guilty pleasures." *BoingBoing. net*. BoingBoing, 2 February 2015. Web. 19 May 2015. <http://boingboing.net/2015/02/02/lets-put-the-guilt-back-in-g.html>.

Falconer, Rachel. *The Crossover Novel: Contemporary Children's Fiction and Its Adult Readership*. New York: Routledge, 2009. Print.

Filgate, Michele. "Locked in the Sweetshop: Seven Questions for Neil Gaiman." *Poets and Writers Magazine*. Poets & Writers, 19 June 2013. Web. 8 Jul. 2016.

Gaiman, Neil. *Coraline*. New York: Harper Perennial, 2006. Print.

_____. *The Ocean at the End of the Lane*. New York: Harper Collins Publishers, 2013. Print.

_____. *The Tragical Comedy or Comical Tragedy of Mr. Punch*. Illus. Dave McKean. New York: Vertigo, 1995. Print.

_____. "What the (Very Bad Swearword) is a Children's Book Anyway?" *The Horn Book Magazine*. Media Source, 6 Nov. 2012. Web. 22 Apr. 2015. <http://www.hbook.com/2012/11/choosing-books/horn-book-magazine/what-the-very-bad-swearword-is-a-childrens-book-anyway/#>.

_____. "Why Our Future Depends on Libraries, Reading and Daydreaming." *Guardian*. Guardian News and Media Ltd., 15 Oct. 2013. Web. 8 Jul. 2016. <https://www.theguardian.com/books/2013/oct/15/neil-gaiman-future-libraries-reading-daydreaming>.

Graham, Ruth. "Against YA." *Slate Magazine*. The Slate Group, 5 Jun. 2014. Web. 10 May 2015.

Howlett, Georgina. "Why are so many adults reading YA and teen fiction?" *Guardian*. Guardian News and Media Limited, 24 Feb. 2015. Web. 10 May 2015.

Michals, Theresa. *Books for Children, Books for Adults: Age and the Novel from Defoe to James*. Cambridge, UK: Cambridge UP, 2014.

Szalai, Jennifer. "Against 'Guilty Pleasure." *The New Yorker*. Condé Nast, 3 Dec. 2013. Web. 19 May 2015.

Reimagining the Cautionary Tale: Collage in Neil Gaiman and Dave McKean's *The Wolves in the Walls*

Krystal Howard

Within the field of children's literature, considerations of the characteristics of the postmodern picturebook have always included notions of collage. As Sylvia Pantaleo and Lawrence R. Sipe note in the introduction to their *Postmodern Picturebooks: Play, Parody, and Self-Referentiality*, postmodern picturebooks often include fragmentation, intertextuality, layering/blending of texts from multiple sources, blurring boundaries, playfulness, and genre eclecticism, among others (2–3). While the term collage may initially bring to mind strictly the visual, it is a multifaceted term that can also be applied to the way in which authors assemble narratives. In her study *Collage in Twentieth-Century Art, Literature, and Culture*, Rona Cran argues for a "more flexible definition" of collage that encompasses "the workings of collage across the disciplines, navigating a path through plastic art, prose, and poetry, and exploring collage's viability as both a physical practice and a theoretical principle" (3). Likewise, Eddie Wolfram characterizes collage in art as the "sticking together [of] bits and pieces of random and miscellaneous bric-a-brac" and emphasizes that collage is intimately connected to the impulse to communicate narrative (7). Wolfram further notes that "there is nothing new about the essential idea of collage, of bringing into association unrelated images and objects to form a different expressive identity" (14). Just as Wolfram and Cran draw connections between the creation of art and narrative, Pantaleo and Sipe also suggest that many of the characteristics of postmodern picturebooks involve elements of collage aesthetics, both visual and textual.

In this chapter, I argue that in Neil Gaiman and Dave McKean's work, collage has emerged as a multidisciplinary visual, textual, and theoretical practice. Gaiman and McKean use both pictorial and written collage in their postmodern picturebook *The Wolves in the Walls* (2003); this collage aesthetic manifests itself in the pictorial art and the textual narrative. Collage within *The Wolves in the Walls* involves a combination of the traditional visual collage that McKean employs as illustrator by mixing various artistic mediums and layering styles, as well as the textual collage created through the echoing and reimagining of the wolf narrative within children's literature. It is not just that Gaiman and McKean's work employs these elements (that it uses collage illustration and intertextuality), it is the way in which these elements work together, are layered on top of, and butt up against one another that distinguishes *The Wolves in the Walls* as creating a collage effect. Young readers are asked to interpret collaged representations in the illustrations and recall and respond to a narrative that speaks of a well-known predatory villain from previous stories. Through their emphasis on collage techniques, Gaiman and McKean destabilize narrative and encourage an intimacy between young readers and their protagonist, Lucy. Additionally, they posit creative work as a way in which Lucy (and, by extension, a young reader) might understand and move beyond the individual and cultural traumas she experiences. Thus, the collage effect present in *The Wolves in the Walls* also takes on a metaphorical meaning; beyond the visual and textual aspects of collage lies the reader's role as collagist. The reader as co-creator is constantly piecing together and pulling apart the fragments of the work in order to make sense of the conflicting emotional registers (danger, trauma, and terror all saturated in a sense of play and silliness) evoked by the narrative. It is in these various ways that *The Wolves in the Walls* employs collage in order to raise questions about the connection between creation and experience and the role of voice and participation in the postmodern picturebook.

Visually, collage aesthetics are apparent throughout the picturebook as McKean uses a variety of visual media (painted images, photographs, and ink drawings) in order to juxtapose elements of fiction and reality. While collage has its roots in visual culture, Marjorie Perloff points out "the process of pasting is only the beginning of collage" (6), and Rona Cran further notes that

"Collage *is* about sticking string and scraps of ephemera to paper. It is also about an intellectual and emotional relationship with a given aesthetic environment. . . . Collage is about encounters. It is about bringing ideas into conversation with one another" (3–4). Collage is also present at the textual and narrative level in *The Wolves in the Walls*; Gaiman utilizes intertextuality to echo and reimagine a variety of other source materials including traditional fairy tales (such as "Little Red Riding Hood") and well-known contemporary picturebooks (Jon Scieszka and Lane Smith's *The Stinky Cheese Man*) that feature wolves.

Collage and Illustration: Dave McKean's Art Work

Dave McKean's collage artwork has perhaps been the most discussed element in scholarly studies on *The Wolves in the Walls*. Numerous scholars, including Jack Zipes, Karen Coats, Christine Wilkie-Stibbs, and Kimberly Reynolds, among others, have noted the unique way in which McKean injects elements of collage throughout *The Wolves in the Walls*, and many have argued that this use of collage aesthetics creates an opening for young readers to engage in participatory interaction with the picturebook. Zipes describes the assemblage and miscellany of McKean's illustrations, detailing how they "make use of puppets, photographs, maps, ink drawings, different shades of color as the settings change, and diverse fonts for the typography" (85). Echoing this sentiment, Petros Panaou and Frixos Michaelides describe McKean's techniques of using "mixed media and the blending of genres" as taking "the reader on a journey between imagination and reality: drawings and paintings (fictional part), photos (the real part), collages and graphics (somewhere in-between)" (65), suggesting that "these 'hybrids'. . . also imply a reader who, being a child of the postmodern era, accepts and celebrates flexibility, fluidity, and transmutation" (66). Similarly, Renata Lucena Dalmaso observes: "McKean's complex artistic style is characterized by a juxtaposition of collages, photographs, digital images, drawings, and paintings that result in a unique, postmodern, quasi-Gothic style," noting the variation in style across the work as "shifting form more traditional pen and ink drawings to Photoshopped collages, depending on the tone . . . the unity in McKean's illustration is often its consistent disunity and surprise" (31). While the images and their composition have been a point of connection for many scholars, few have also examined the way in which McKean and Gaiman work together through both visual and textual art in order to produce a variety of levels of pictorial and textual collage throughout their picturebook. Additionally, many scholars have hinted at, but not fully explored, what this use of layering and juxtaposition might do for the reader.

Karen Coats opens a discussion of the way in which McKean's art works to add depth to Gaiman's narrative when she notes, "Dave McKean, for instance, in his illustrations for Neil Gaiman's *The Wolves in the Walls*, melds the organic, the inorganic, and the digital into a masterful visual expression of the book's textual themes" ("Postmodern" 79). McKean himself notes on the frequently asked questions page of his personal website that the artistic materials he uses vary depending upon the project. He explains, "If the story needs close storytelling and a light, simple style of narrative, then probably pen and ink, or brushpen, or pencil would be best. If the story needs a more symbolic approach then maybe collage, or paint, or digital. It all comes down to the emotion and atmosphere you want to convey" (McKean). This blending of artistic medium is evident not only in the paratextual material (the front and back covers, the dedication page, and the title page), but also within the first two pages of the narrative.

Collage in Gaiman and McKean's *The Wolves in the Walls* begins before the reader even opens the book with the cover, which depicts at its center the hand of a child holding a pencil. The child protagonist pictured is Lucy, whose figure is painted as if she were carved from clay, as she peers over her shoulder at the reader. She is drawing the crude outline of a wolf on the wall, and just above her hand, photographed eyes peer through the cut-out holes of her wolf. This image continues onto the back cover of the book, which depicts Lucy's hair and back, along with several similar drawings of wolves with their mouths open wide, jaws bared, and claws reaching out. This cover art makes explicit the author and illustrator's focus on juxtaposition, layering, and blurring. Lucy as a character seems to be a collage herself. She is solid; her arm is full and shadowed, almost real; her hair is painted in such a way as to suggest movement; and yet her face reads as doll-like. Although she is in the foreground, she is placed on the left-hand side of the cover and her body extends beyond the edge of the frame onto the back cover, again suggesting movement and tension. Central on the cover are the eyes of the wolf peering through the cut-out holes in the wall; these eyes are not painted like Lucy or inked in like the drawings on the wall; they are the most realistically rendered object pictured. The crude, inked-in drawing that outlines these eyes reappears in multiples on the back cover; Lucy's creations take up the majority of the space on the front and back covers. This initial image echoes the deeply ingrained narrative of the wolf that stalks and preys upon the child, but significantly Lucy's agency and ability to see her predator through her art is emphasized.

McKean's blending of visual mediums continues as the reader moves from the paratext to the first two pages of the narrative. In the first full spread of the narrative, the reader is introduced to Lucy and her home. The left page depicts a flower arrangement in a vase. This image is a blend of the photorealistic, the digital, and the painted. The vase, the wall, and the bloom of the flower appear to be realistic photo-renderings, but they are overlaid with a digital effect and brushstrokes are visible. This first image of the narrative conveys a sense of chaos and confusion, and these elements are linked to its pairing with trappings of the domestic space. The large size of the flower arrangement is jarring when compared with the size of the character figured on the facing page. On the right, facing page, the protagonist Lucy is depicted in the center of the page from behind facing away from the reader, her hands clasped behind her back. Beneath her feet, the carpeted floor of her home takes on a quilted, assembled appearance, and the walls leading up the staircase are littered with Lucy's inked drawings of wolves.

This initial spread draws attention to itself as a created, collaged piece of art. The brown, amber, red, and yellow colors repeated throughout the pages convey a sense of warmth and an aged or worn quality. These early depictions in the picturebook create a defamiliarizing experience for the reader, who might expect a picturebook to fall either within the realistic or the fantastic in terms of artistic representation. As Coats emphasizes:

> Collage art in general renders the subject of picturebooks postmodern by revealing the conditions of its construction. Bits of cut paper and found materials . . . were always already something else before they were selected, cut, shaped, and glued to make this new thing. Hence collage art is an apt metaphor for the postmodern vision of the self—as something composed of experience and environment, rather than something organic and integral to itself. ("Postmodern," 85–86)

This is something that a reader of *The Wolves in the Walls* experiences from the paratext and first pages of Gaiman and McKean's work. The representation of collage itself as an artistic practice within *The Wolves in the Walls* calls attention not just to the createdness of the picturebook as an artifact, but also to the cultural construction of childhood, girlhood, and the artist.

(Inter-)Textual Collage: The Cautionary Tale and the Wolf Narrative in Children's Literature

Gaiman and McKean's picturebook goes beyond the use of visual collage in that it employs intertextuality and the pastiche in its representation of its narrative and primary characters. This bridging of both the visual and textual elements of collage is another element that calls for considerable reader participation. As Cherie Allan suggests in her *Playing with Picturebooks: Postmodernism and the Postmodernesque*, the field of children's literature is highly visual, and it is "within this visual culture, [that] available technologies readily allow reproduction and appropriation which, in turn, enable writers and illustrators to draw attention to issues of representation and intertextuality, especially through pastiche and collage" (4). Terry Eagleton has described postmodern art broadly as "eclectic, hybrid, decentered, fluid, discontinuous, pastiche-like" (201), while Linda Hutcheon has pointed out that postmodern texts subvert traditional narrative and interrogate dominant, liberal humanist cultural discourses by working within conventions (4–6). Gaiman and McKean's *The Wolves in the Walls* utilizes intertextuality in its reference not only to contemporary postmodern picturebooks like Scieszka and Smith's, but also in its connection to traditional fairy-tale narratives that feature the well-known wolf antagonist, such as the villain in "Little Red Riding Hood."

In her study *Picturing the Wolf in Children's Literature*, Debra Mitts-Smith expresses that, "No longer bound to the role of villain, the wolf of contemporary fictional picturebooks plays a range of roles" (20), and "the strongest evidence of this transformation is found in the literary relationship of wolves and children . . . wolves and children share a long and complicated history" (22). This is certainly clear in the evolution of the wolf narrative in children's literature, especially in the past fifty years. As Vanessa Joosen argues, today's fairy-tale revisions foreground their own intertextuality and "subsist in the form of 'collage,' which may be defined as 'work which contains a mixture of allusions, references, quotations, and foreign expressions'" (54–55). Just as Coats has argued that "children's Gothic has become prevalent enough as a phenomenon to represent what can be considered a cultural symptom" ("Between Horror" 77), I likewise argue that the use of collage, intertextuality, and a pastiche of old and new source materials to express fairy-tale revision also represents a "cultural symptom" of the changing views about girlhood, agency, and fear.

The connection between Lucy in *The Wolves in the Walls* and Little Red in "Little Red Riding Hood" is apparent through the way in which both narratives set out to describe the relationship between wolves and little girls. "Little Red Riding Hood" features a lone wolf who desires to trick and consume the unsuspecting (or previously warned) protagonist. Lucy, unlike her predecessor, is not warned of the dangers of wolves, but instead senses their presence and the possibility that they might cause her harm. This shift highlights the way in which the narrative scripts of "Little Red Riding Hood" are deeply rooted within cultural ideas of what it means to be a girl. As the moral at the end of Charles Perrault's version of the tale suggests, "Little Red Riding Hood" has always served as a reminder that children (and young girls especially) should be wary of the predators who might be pursuing them, even those who seem harmless. Instead of requiring a mother's prompting to be wary of dangerous individuals who might devour or take advantage of her, Lucy has already internalized this message that wolves may hunt her both in her home and in the streets, and she holds it in her repertoire as an underlying anxiety. Whereas Coats argues that "the anxiety that Lucy is experiencing is a common one for children—what if I lose my home, which represents, for most children, the boundaries of their whole world?" ("Between Horror" 80), I argue that Lucy's anxiety is also about the fear of the wolf and what the wolf represents: danger for a young woman. This is clear from both the illustration and text, which depicts Lucy, eyes wide, in bed with the covers pulled up to her nose: "In the middle of the night when everything was still, she heard clawing and gnawing, nibbling and squabbling. She could hear the wolves in the walls, plotting their wolfish plots, hatching their wolfish schemes" (Gaiman, *Wolves* 8). This fear is emphasized two pages later, when talking to her father about the wolves, Lucy asserts, "It's wolves. . . . I can feel them in my tummy" (10). In these scenes at the beginning of the narrative, it is clear that Lucy is letting her intuition and 'gut feeling' about the wolves drive her expression of fear and anxiety about their presence, and it is Lucy's instincts and awareness of the dangers of wolves to little girls that allow her to perceive the wolves before anyone else in her family. Gaiman appropriates this traditional tale in order to tell a story not just about a child and a wolf, but also about the relationship between a girl and her community, as well as a girl and those who might prey upon her.

While traditional versions of fairy tales themselves include multiple versions of the same tale with slightly different aspects with each author's contribution (for example, compare Perrault's "Little Red Riding Hood" and Jacob and Wilhelm Grimm's "Little Red Cap" to the multiple similar versions of the tale across other cultures), modern-day postmodern retellings also add something new to the way in which the wolf/child relationship is imagined within contemporary culture. Although there are many postmodern picturebooks that explore the wolf narrative, Scieszka and Smith's picturebook is unique in that it casts wolves as disappearing from their narrative. In "Little Red Running Shorts," the recasting of Little Red Riding Hood as Little Red Running Shorts appears to be a progressive move, in that it highlights the possibility that the female protagonist will outrun the wolf and save herself and her grandmother through her athletic abilities (Scieszka & Smith 18–20). Even her depiction as a short-haired, athletic-wear-sporting girl with attitude who points her finger and stomps off the page suggests a shift in the conception of what it means to be a girl in a Little Red Riding Hood narrative. Instead of devoting three pages to the narrative, as Jack the Narrator says he will, he is able to rattle off the story in seven short sentences. The final sentence has Red answering the door to her grandmother's house and addressing the wolf by using the classic refrain from the tale, "My, what slow feet you have" (18). The facing illustrated page depicts blank white holes where the wolf and Red Running Shorts should be (19), while they trudge off the page together. Significantly, the wolf in Scieszka and Smith's picturebook is wearing a suit, bowtie, and reading glasses. This mirrors similar illustrations in *The Wolves in the Walls* where Lucy discovers that the wolves are having a party and sliding down the banisters wearing the family's nicest clothes (34).

The Wolves in the Walls shares many features with other postmodern picturebook narratives that explore traditional fairy tales. Many of the most significant features of postmodernism are present in Gaiman and McKean's piece: it blurs the boundaries between author, narrator, and reader; it subverts traditional generic and literary traditions; its intertextuality is overt and purposeful; it uses pastiche and collage to underscore humor and play; it provides an open-ended resolution that allows for reader involvement; and it draws attention to its own createdness as an artifact (Pantaleo & Sipe 3). As scholars such as Pantaleo, Sipe, and Joosen have pointed out, in many ways one of the most significant features of the postmodern picturebook is its reliance on the interpretive work of the reader.

Collage and Voice: The Portrait of an Artist and Reader Participation

The degree of reader collaboration created through the use of textual and visual collage, as well as the representation of artistic voice and creativity through their female protagonist, marks Gaiman and McKean's *The Wolves in the Walls* as a significant contribution to postmodern visual texts and fairy-tale revisions for young readers. As Panealeo and Sipe note, postmodern picturebooks invite readers to "generate multiple, often contradictory interpretations and to become coauthors in ways that traditional picturebooks do not offer" (4). Thus, the postmodern picturebook as a genre invites readers to participate, and I would argue further that it is specifically the collage aesthetics and assemblage of fragments that require reader participation. This destabilization of reader expectations through both visual and textual form moves the reader to act as "coauthor" and co-creator. In her article, "Towards a Feminist Reading of Gaiman's Picturebooks," Dalmaso similarly emphasizes the ways in which *The Wolves in the Walls* appropriates and subverts traditional narratives and "forces the reader to coauthor the texts as she navigates the different layers of meaning" (30). It is not only through the manipulation and destabilization of traditional narrative and visual structure that *The Wolves in the Walls* calls the reader to active participation, it is also through the way in which the text uses voice and creativity—in addition to the analysis and inquiry of artistic collage and intertextuality—to invite the reader to take up the role of collagist.

When speaking specifically about *The Wolves in the Walls* as a visual artifact, scholars have further underscored this point. As Coats suggests, "The compositions are technically fascinating, impelling readers to a figure-it-out response: How did he create this effect? What are the objects in this collage and why are they here? Which objects are real and what is computer generated?" ("Between Horror" 81-2). Coats goes on to point out that:

> Faces are made of assemblages rather than seamless wholes, TV images are blurs of colour, and jam jars run off the page into infinity,

creating images that are obviously artificial and manufactured and yet as organic and recognizable as dreams; hence we sense that the images are attempts to capture mental states and meanings that require interpretation rather than unthinking absorption. ("Between Horror" 82)

I would push Coats's argument further by extending it to the textual aspects of and the blending of genres in the picturebook as well. Readers likewise are encouraged to try to figure out which wolf narratives from fairy tales and other picturebooks Gaiman is employing in his work. The combination of various aspects of a variety of wolf narratives similarly evokes a dreamlike, fantastic melding together of narratives. This intertextuality and pastiche compels the reader to question the story construction and to consider which elements are from which stories and why the author chose to use these narratives.

The act of invoking the reader as active participant in the text plays a significant role in empowering the young reader. Speaking of the effect of the work on the young reader, Coats argues, "Gaiman's device of treating what could be a horrible situation with a humorous twist is a move that empowers young readers" ("Between Horror" 82), and "McKean's illustrations of Lucy and her family's predicament, for instance, don't just inspire wonder at their virtuosity; they inspire analysis" ("Postmodern" 80). Likewise, in discussing Lucy's agency and power as a protagonist, Danya David points out in her analysis of several of Gaiman and McKean's collaborative works that the author/illustrator team "present their readers with ... wildly courageous, loyal, resourceful, and emotionally strong female protagonists," and David further emphasizes that "Lucy ... glean[s] information from [her] intuition and dreaming, and skillfully manipulate art, language, and narrative, in order to discern, define, and reclaim borders." In addition to presenting young readers with a collage of visual and textual forms, McKean and Gaiman also provide a strong female protagonist with artistic inclinations that the reader might look to as a model.

Lucy as an artist and creator acts not just as a powerful agent of her own story, she also represents a mirror and window for young protagonists through which they might see themselves as creators and agents of their own narratives. Lucy as a character addresses the critical cultural trauma of sexism and lack of representation of active, creative female characters who are the heroes of their own narratives. The formal innovations of the text create room for a narrative that involves the reader as questioner, co-creator, and active participant and takes a decidedly feminist stance. Gaiman and McKean's visual and textual moves promote the writing, activism, and artistry of young women. Lucy is depicted as actively drawing, creating, and acting throughout her narrative. Lucy is also portrayed as the most knowledgeable person in her narrative—as someone who uses her intuition and intelligence to solve problems and save the day—even when those who hold power over her disbelieve or silence her. *The Wolves in the Walls* subverts these narratives and utilizes other various intertextual wolf stories in order to achieve this feminist appropriation; additionally, Lucy's narrative also acts as a feminist *Künstlerroman*.

As Roberta S. Trites indicates in her *Waking Sleeping Beauty: Feminist Voices in Children's Novels*, "the *Künstlerroman* is a novel of development . . . [that] deals specifically with the growth of the artist" and "within the genre of the children's *Künstlerroman* exists a subgenre, the feminist *Künstlerroman*, which demonstrates the growth of a child whose identity is consistently formed by her desire to be a writer [/artist]" (64). Trites further contends "that so many children's novels involve girls learning about the power of language indicates, however, that the genre is a powerful forum for feminist writers [/artist]" (64–65). Thus, it is significant that picturebook narratives that depict girls learning about the power of visual art designate the genre as a powerful forum for feminist artists. In line with Trites' discussion of the protagonists of the feminist *Künstlerroman*, Lucy accepts creative endeavors as "primary to her self-creation" and recognizes the power in her own creative and artistic constructions (65). Citing Hélène Cixous, Trites characterizes the protagonist of the feminist *Künstlerroman* as learning to "'write her self,' to 'put herself into the text—as into the world and into history—by her own movement'" (65). Likewise, Lucy learns to represent her self and her experiences in her art in order to cultivate her voice. The walls of Lucy's home are plastered with her drawings. They are framed, affixed to the walls, and used as wallpaper in certain areas of the dwelling.

Lucy's drawing of herself appears on the thirty-second page of the picturebook. As the family is depicted creeping through the walls of their own home and "peeking out through the eye-holes of paintings," the reader is introduced to Lucy's drawing of herself and her family. On the right side of the page, Lucy and her mother are shown in the wall, and on the left side of the page, Lucy's own drawing appears huge. Lucy's representation of herself is centered in the page with her representation of her mother draping her arm across her shoulder. Lucy's representation of her father to appear as the largest figure is undermined by the fact that he and her representation of her brother (as the smallest figure) are not fully shown on the page. Lucy's drawing is significant in that it depicts a mirrored representation of the characters of Lucy and her mother as they appear on the right-hand side of the page. While Lucy's drawing does feature her entire family, her representation of herself and her mother are central.

Gaiman and McKean's *The Wolves in the Walls* is a work of visual, textual, and theoretical collage that endeavors to create a highly participatory narrative that addresses the cultural and individual traumas of sexism. The use of visual collage defamiliarizes the reader, while the use of textual collage invokes the reader as collaborator. The repeated depiction of Lucy's artwork and the portrayal of Lucy as artist, agent, and activist in her own narrative invite the reader to also take up the role of collagist as they parse Lucy's narrative. *The Wolves in the Walls* as an artifact marks a shift in children's literature toward participation and reader agency.

Works Cited

Allan, Cherie. *Playing with Picturebooks: Postmodernism and the Postmodernesque*. New York: Palgrave Macmillan, 2012. Print.

Coats, Karen. "Between Horror, Humour, and Hope: Neil Gaiman and the Psychic Work of the Gothic." *The Gothic in Children's Literature: Haunting the Borders*. London: Routledge, 2007. 77–92. Print.

_____. "Postmodern Picturebooks and the Transmodern Self." *Postmodern Picturebooks: Play, Parody, and Self-Referentiality*. Ed. Sylvia Pantaleo & Lawrence R. Sipe. New York: Routledge, 2008. 75-88. Print.

Cran, Rona. *Collage in Twentieth-Century Art, Literature, and Culture: Joseph Cornell, William Burroughs, Frank O'Hara, and Bob Dylan*. Farnham, Surrey, UK: Ashgate Publishing Ltd, 2014. Print.

Dalmaso, Renata Lucena. "Towards a Feminist Reading of Gaiman's Picturebooks." *Neil Gaiman in the 21st Century: Essays on the Novels, Children's Stories, Online Writings, Comics and Other Works*. Ed. Tara Prescott. Jefferson, NC: McFarland, 2015. 29–38. Print.

David, Danya. "Extraordinary Navigators: An Examination of Three Heroines in Neil Gaiman and Dave McKean's *Coraline*, *The Wolves in the Walls*, and *MirrorMask*." *Looking Glass: New Perspectives on Children's Literature* 12.1 (2008). Web. 22 Oct. 2016.

Eagleton, Terry. *Criticism and Ideology: A Study in Marxist Literary Theory*. London: Humanities Press, 1996. Print.

Gaiman, Neil. *The Wolves in the Walls*. Illus. Dave McKean. New York: HarperCollins, 2003. Print.

Grimm, Jacob & Wilhelm Grimm. "Little Red Cap." *Household Tales*. Trans. Margaret Hunt. London: George Bell, 1884. Print.

Hutcheon, Linda. *A Poetics of Postmodernism: History, Theory, Fiction*. New York: Routledge, 1988. Print.

Joosen, Vanessa. "Scene 9, Take 45: Collage and the Postmodern Fairy Tale." *The Journal of Children's Literature Studies* 4.2 (2007): 54–76. Print.

McKean, Dave. *Dave McKean: Personal Website*. Dave McKean, n.d. Web. 7 Mar. 2016.

Mitts-Smith, Debra. *Picturing the Wolf in Children's Literature*. New York: Routledge, 2010. Print.

Panaou, Petros & Frixos Michaelides. "Dave McKean's Art: Transcending Limitations of the Graphic Novel Genre." *Bookbird: A Journal of International Children's Literature* 49.4 (2011): 62–67. Print.

Pantaleo, Sylvia & Lawrence R. Sipe, eds. *Postmodern Picturebooks: Play, Parody, and Self-Referentiality*. New York: Routledge, 2008. Print.

Perrault, Charles. "Little Red Riding Hood." *The Blue Fairy Book.* Ed. Andrew Lang. New York: Dover, 1965. Print.

Scieszka, Jon & Lane Smith. *The Stinky Cheese Man and Other Fairly Stupid Tales.* New York: Penguin Books, 1992. Print.

Trites, Roberta S. *Waking Sleeping Beauty: Feminist Voices in Children's Novels.* Iowa City: U of Iowa P, 1997. Print.

Wolfram, Eddie. *History of Collage: An Anthology of Collage, Assemblage and Event Structures.* New York: Macmillan, 1975. Print.

Zipes, Jack. "Why Fantasy Matters Too Much." *The Journal of Aesthetic Education* 43.2 (2009): 77–91. Print.

"What is She?": Neil Gaiman's Intertextual Conversation on Female Artistry in *Coraline* and *The Ocean at the End of the Lane*

Marlyn Thomas

Before 2002, Neil Gaiman was predominantly known for his comics and graphic novels. Through *Coraline* (2002), Gaiman created a story that encompassed the didactic components often found in traditional children's literature but equipped the female protagonist with more agency by allowing her to make intelligent choices and giving her the desire for adventure instead of finding herself in the midst of one. Like many children's literature texts, its reception ranged depending on the age of the reader. Generally, adults believed the novel was too scary for children, while the author reportedly wrote the novel for and read it to his own children, claiming that they did not find the story scary. Gaiman sums up the reception of the work as a story that "children experienced as an adventure, but which gave adults nightmares" ("Why"). Likewise, *The Ocean at the End of the Lane* (2013) features similar elements of adventure and horror through the remembrances of an unnamed adult man, who is visiting his familial home, and the ever-present Hempstock women whose lineage make several appearances in Gaiman's other works.[1] *Ocean* was received as a text marketed to adults but somewhat child-friendly, since most of the book is a remembrance of childhood events. Gaiman opens the story with an epigraph from Maurice Sendak's conversation with Art Spiegelman in which Sendak states, "I remember my own childhood vividly . . . I knew terrible things. But I knew I mustn't let adults know I knew. It would scare them." It's clear that Gaiman addresses childhood and adult fears. This has been stated by various critics.[2] However, the fear of the adult female in these texts has been largely overlooked, further supporting the notion of the innocent girl versus the villainous mature woman formula aptly applied in various ways to many fairy tales and children's literature.

Both texts feature women with supernatural powers who wield influence over their environments and the destinies of other characters. Elizabeth Parsons and company contend that in *Coraline*, the Other Mother is a phallic mother whose dominance must be overcome for the young female protagonist to enter a normative gender role (371). They remark this is the problem with the idea of postfeminism: it overlooks gains made by the demands of feminists while simultaneously indoctrinating younger generations into traditional stagnant gender performance. Laura-Marie von Czarnowsky concludes that "Gaiman seems to advocate a benign and powerful maternalism as ideal femininity" in relation to *Ocean* (19) versus the maternal figure in *Coraline*. The women in both texts have survived centuries of human development; their agelessness is displayed in the Other Mother's title of "beldam" and the clothing of the kidnapped children, whereas the Hempstocks have existed even before "the moon was made" (Gaiman, *Ocean* 33). Their seeming immortality is only one major aspect that these women share. Gaiman's Other Mother, though younger than the Hempstocks, is a precursor to a discussion between the two works on female artistry. The Other Mother creates a home that is the improved version of Coraline's with undeveloped parts that resemble "a blank sheet of paper or an enormous, empty white room" (Gaiman, *Coraline* 71). Coraline also finds a room with crude paintings on the wall and "cardboard boxes filled with mildewed papers" (107). *Ocean*'s Hempstock women are able to read minds, cut and repair time with scissors like the Fates, "do recipes," and perform incantations. Both books focus on women with creative powers, with the Other Mother representing a decidedly more ominous characterization than the Hempstocks. As when Coraline, realizing the Other Mother is not the lovely woman she pretends to be posits, "What is she?" (72), this chapter focuses on this question raised in 2002 about the Other Mother that is answered over a decade later in *Ocean* through mainly the Hempstock women by examining oppression, space, and solicitude in relationship to the female artist. Virginia Woolf's *A Room of One's Own* (1929) is employed to position the Other Mother as the underappreciated and unwelcomed Judith, sister of William Shakespeare as presented in Woolf's text, to further emphasize the overlooked status of female artistry within the text and in discussions about the book and character.

The Cycle of Patriarchal Oppression

Virginia Woolf's *Room* discusses, amongst many things, the female artist's inability to access her potential as directly linked to patriarchal control of funds, inaccessibility to knowledge, and an unsupportive environment. This chapter is predicated on the belief that the Other Mother is the hypothetical Judith,[3] Shakespeare's "sister," an Elizabethan female writer/artist who because of patriarchy is not afforded the agency of her male contemporaries. This belief has its basis in Gaiman's *Coraline*. There are several references to Shakespeare. The Other Mother paraphrases Shakespeare (Gaiman, *Coraline* 75) making it plausible she might have lived during Elizabethan times, a time that Woolf remarks, "scarcely mentions her [the Elizabethan woman]." Miss Forcible is also seen quoting Shakespeare in her conversations (44), while theatre is also present in the other world. Additionally, according to Gaiman ("*Coraline* Q&A" 6), one of the ghost children in the story is, in fact, a fairy, a further nod to Shakespeare, who utilized the belief and disbelief in fairies in many plays; this is also consistent with Gaiman's frequent use of fairy culture in his work. Although the story follows a literary narrative similar to Lewis Carroll's Alice,[4] through the Other Mother, Gaiman develops a character that embodies the sufferings of the female artist in Elizabethan times due specifically to the effects of patriarchy.

Neither *Coraline* nor *Ocean* has many male characters. Those present are fundamentally dependent on female characters for sustenance or support. This fact does not undermine patriarchal rule. As a system, patriarchy does not necessitate a consistent, physical male presence; rather, the presence of male dominance and power as the default norm that governs life through oppressive forms allows patriarchy to thrive without a consistent male presence. In "Understanding Patriarchy," bell hooks writes that, "We need to highlight the role women play in perpetuating and sustaining patriarchal culture so that we will recognize patriarchy as a system women and men support equally, even if men receive more rewards from that system" (24).

The Other Mother as a product of patriarchy is revealed in two distinct ways: her creation of a passive husband and the act of serial kidnapping. In order to exist in the Other Mother's domain, each person is made with or must exchange his/ her eyes for buttons. This is the crucial part of the social contract to exist in her domain. In "'Something Very Old and Very Slow': Coraline, Uncanniness, and Narrative Form," Richard Gooding describes the button eyes as a "constant threat [of] mutilation" (394). However, it is notable that Judith wears the button eyes herself as some artists have been known to excise parts of themselves.[5] The acceptance of the button eyes forms a type of kinship between people and things that are not biologically related to Judith, the ruler of the domain, and further emphasizes an insider/outsider philosophy where those who belong are immediately recognizable. Although she has attempted to build family through a husband, children, and even neighbors, she is content to remain in the other house rather than live in a world outside of her creative abilities. This stance indicates that there is a fundamental difference between her domain and the outside world. The husband she creates is under her rule and is, at times, subjected to severe punishment; he explains to Coraline that "when she gets out of sorts, she takes it out on everybody else. It's her way" (Gaiman, *Coraline* 109). Once the other house begins to disintegrate, the other father becomes no more than a grub-like thing with "almost no features on its face, which had puffed and swollen like risen bread dough" (108). Judith opts to make a husband that can come undone at her will rather than bring one from the real world. While this allows her to work with a blank slate, her escapism from the real world has afforded her the opportunity to become the oppressor instead of the oppressed. Subsequently, she engages in patriarchal behavior by becoming a tool of oppression. This behavior is further seen in the text through the kidnapped children's recollection, "She stole our hearts, and she stole our souls, and she took our lives away, and she left us here, and she forgot about us in the dark" (82). In her desperation to fulfill the gender roles of wife and mother, she subjugates those under her rule, further perpetuating oppressive forms of rule and the real world patriarchy that she may have been subjected.

However, Judith's insulated world is no more counterfeit, in terms of patriarchy and choices for men and women, than the 'real' world in the text. Coraline's father, Mr. Jones, cooks and works from home. When Coraline must strengthen herself to face the Other Mother, it is her father that she thinks of and how he once saved her from bees by allowing himself to be stung. Mrs. Jones also works from home but even in the domestic space pays little attention to Coraline. Coraline feels so neglected, she opts to play in a room where no one goes. Alternately, Judith, Coraline's Other Mother, seems to want nothing more than to do all that Coraline wishes. While it seems Judith is the dark double of a working woman, Mrs. Jones, the Joneses' home as a place absent of patriarchal rule, is a myth. As soon as Coraline asks for a pair of green gloves, her mother purchases clothing in primary colors that will allow her to go unnoticed at school. Mrs. Jones' attitudes and behaviors contradicts her own "freedom" from patriarchy, as while she enjoys the egalitarian mode of life afforded to her, she shows her daughter early on that a girl's best accessory is the ability to blend in and disappear. Woolf recounts the plight of female writers in a time of unacceptance, stating that a writing woman became "a bogey to frighten clever girls with." While such viewpoints deter young girls from pursuing their artistic abilities in a climate where patriarchy permeates every aspect of life, real patriarchy does not have to look like oppression at all. Therefore, Coraline's father can very well protect her and cook for her because Mrs. Jones is dutifully standing by to instruct Coraline on what is proper.

Male characters in *Ocean* are likewise not as knowledgeable or self-sufficient as the female characters. According to Old Mrs. Hempstock, in their family, men are not necessary. She states, "Nothing a man could do around this farm that I can't do twice as fast and five times as well" (Gaiman, *Ocean* 94). Men are transient on the farm, with male relatives seeking adventure and others who come and go. In the text, any male approaching Hempstock land with an air of authority leaves with his mind pushed and memory clipped. When two policemen, the protagonist's father, a plainclothes officer, and the local doctor show up at the Hempstocks' farm, little do they know it is Lettie who has pushed their minds to find the little evidence that would satisfy human curiosity about the coal miner's suicide. Later, when the protagonist's father shows up to make him come home, he ends up confusingly handing him his toothbrush, which Lettie magically transports into his coat pocket. From his first encounter with the Hempstocks, the boy does not want to leave them. The protagonist depends on the Hempstocks for protection and fulfillment in his childhood and looks to them for validation as an adult (although he forgets with each visit). The protagonist's father is blinded by Ursula Monkton—who is actually Skarthach of the Keep, a creature who decides to make Earth-proper her home—largely because of her sex appeal in the wake of his absent working wife, a trope also seen in *Coraline*. Although the Hempstock women seem to have little need for men on their farm and have clearly lived through the same times as Judith, they have not resorted to patriarchy as a form of rule. The male child is neither mistreated nor worshipped; he simply is. Perhaps they do not resort to oppression and dominance because they do not appear threatening or sexual. However, inasmuch as each Hempstock is void of sexuality yet has lived through centuries on Earth, their appearances and behaviors are signifying in that they present themselves as regular working farm women when they are indeed the most powerful women on the Earth. Unlike Judith, who interferes with the lives of children she seeks to love "as a miser loves money, or a dragon loves its gold," (Gaiman, *Coraline* 104) the Hempstocks only interfere with the lives of people to reestablish order, not to disrupt it. It is also rare that they interfere with the world at large seeming to understand in their timelessness that various systems will come and go.

The Importance of Space
Gaiman's texts both stress the importance of a designated space for female artistry. Woolf's famous thesis stresses two distinct things a

woman writer/artist needs: money and a room. In Gaiman's works, along with the need of space (room) is the necessity to express artistry through building and maintaining dominion. The other old man upstairs relays to Coraline that the Other Mother would, "build whole worlds for you to explore, and tear them down every night when you are done. . . . How much better would a world be built just like that, and all for you?" (Gaiman, *Coraline* 117). This incentive to stay in the other house is tempting as Coraline had already run out of places to explore within two weeks of living in the new 'real' neighborhood. While the age of Gaiman's women is hinted at through references, it is even more unclear how old the spaces are that they occupy. Although Judith and the Hempstocks have power to create, they create within existing, magical areas. And although the other house is all that Coraline has ever wanted, she does not decide to stay. She notes several times a presence of something "very old and very slow" (45) something that was "older by far than the [O]ther [M]other. It was deep, and slow, and it knew that she was there" (134). A conversation between Coraline and the cat further reveals information about the space:

> "There's ways in and ways out of places like this that even she doesn't know about."
> "Did she make this place, then?" asked Coraline.
> "Made it, found it—what's the difference?" asked the cat. "Either way, she's had it should be a very long time. . . ." (Gaiman, *Coraline* 73)

Woolf's discussion in Chapter Four of *Room* centers on the commonality that middle-class women writers shared in her time: the common sitting-room. Although not a solitary place and subject to interruption, it was a designated place. Interestingly, the portal to the other house on the Joneses' side is a drawing room filled with furniture left to them after Coraline's grandmother died. Between the Joneses' side and Judith's drawing room is a passageway that takes very little Freudian analysis to see as a recreated birth canal in its walls that "felt warm and yielding . . . as if covered in a fine downy fur" that "moved, as if it were taking a breath" (Gaiman,

Coraline 133). These details mark the space settled by Judith as a feminine space. The only real boy in the other house is one of the ghost children, who had not yet reached a gendered age, as in death, he could not remember if he had been male or female in life. After some questioning, he recollects that "it does seem to me that one day they took my skirts and gave me britches and cut my hair" (82). The insistence that the Other Mother does not know everything about the place and the presence of something older than her suggests Gaiman's Judith has taken a domain for herself that appears to have been a temporary space. This healing space became a place of oppression and forgotten artistry as various arts are found discarded in a cellar and above only places created to lure children.

The Hempstocks' domain is their farm, which they say they have brought with them "from the old country, when we came here" (Gaiman, *Ocean* 40) as far back as the time of William the Conqueror. Although their powers are supernatural, they do not invoke their authority until something does not follow the rules. When Skarthach is awoken by the miner's distress about money and begins giving the local people money that materializes outside of dreams, the Hempstocks decide to intervene. In the initial meeting with Skarthach, Lettie, the youngest of the Hempstocks, attempts to explain to her "You've got nothing to give them that they want. Let them be" (42), showing their intention was not to kill Skarthach only to send her to where she belonged. That they did not create the space they occupy makes it no less theirs. Von Czarnowsky regards the Hempstocks' attachment to the land as an ecofeminist vision and "Lettie's submersion in the pond [in order to heal] is thus the ultimate ecofeminist fusion between women and land" (23). So much are they a part of the land that when they draw power from it, they glow and so does the land. Unlike Judith's healing space turned lair, the Hempstocks have charge of creatures that already live there, such as the kitten that is plucked from the ground. While the area itself contains power, the Hempstocks are able to treat the land with respect without connecting their stewardship with the type of possession governed by the id. This is shown when the protagonist is submerged in Lettie's ocean, and he realizes that he now "knew everything" (Gaiman, *Ocean* 143). Before he can misunderstand that knowing everything is not so much a boast as a burden, Lettie explains "It would destroy you" (145) then softens her speech with "It's nothing special, knowing how things work" (146). The Hempstocks' understanding of human beings and desire allows them to understand what Coraline expresses, "I don't want whatever I want. Nobody does" (Gaiman, *Coraline* 118). Their domain is governed by an intricate set of rules, of which they are stewards. Seemingly, as long as they respect the land, the land respects them in return unlike Judith's domain where the ins and outs have not been revealed to her.

Domestic space, particularly the kitchen, in both texts are revealed as powerful spaces that are both practical and creative. Coraline's father, though male, primarily occupies the kitchen space. Coraline laments his persistence in following recipes in an attempt to make dishes such as chicken that he "did strange things to . . . like stewing it in wine, or stuffing it with prunes, or baking it in pastry" (Gaiman, *Coraline* 27). Disrupting this space is the first line of defense as the Other Mother makes Coraline "the best chicken that [she] had ever eaten" (27). Once Coraline is sure that she does not want to stay in the other house, she is sure to bring her own food from home. When she confronts Judith about her missing parents, she refuses Judith's food and takes a bite from her apple to which "the other father looked disappointed" (59). Throughout the text, there is a theme of eating and devouring. When Coraline asks the cat why the Other Mother wants her to stay, the cat answers, "She wants something to love, I think" and then immediately follows with "She might want something to eat as well. It's hard to tell with creatures like that" (63). This is not farfetched as the ghost children relay, "She kept us, and she fed on us, until now we've nothing left of ourselves, only snakeskins and spider husks" (83). Food operates in the text as a sort of communion. Coraline's refusal to eat the Other Mother's food is a direct insult that communicates she does not wish to be there. In *Ocean*, food is mentioned quite often and in detail. At every turn of events, the Hempstocks offer and encourage the protagonist to eat. Cream and honey, shepherd's pie, toast, and apple pie amongst other foods are served after various episodes. Like Coraline, the protagonist in *Ocean* rejects Ursula's food when he is hungry. Monica Miller states, "The sensory immediacy of the comfort food allows the narrator to ground himself in the present and fully inhabit a sense of safety; the material sustenance reinforces the sense of emotional security" (115). In *Ocean*, there seems to be no separation between what is material and what is immaterial. For every emotion, there is something practical that can be done to combat the immediate sentiment. Woolf states that all too often the details of a luncheon are given with too little attention given to what was eaten. She takes breaks in her work to describe the food and the general environment in the middle of discussing female artistry. In Gaiman's texts, the kitchen is the place of battle where child protagonists and the women they stand against make their stances.

Solitude and the Female Artist

While Woolf stresses a woman's need for a room to have the privacy to honestly hone her craft, she does not liken the room to complete solicitude. As an example, Woolf raises the Brontë sisters as an example of female artists working closely in the creative process. She also relays the countless women who may have been writers but who failed to have validation and training from others. This solicitude is perhaps where Judith as an artist has failed and been driven to madness. Courtney Landis evokes *The Madwoman in the Attic*'s passage about houses as a feminine space reminiscent of the womb (169). However, in *Coraline*, there is a more pervasive idea of the house as a place of entrapment. Coraline's grandmother's furniture and painting is relegated to the drawing room where no one goes because "It was only for best" (Gaiman, *Coraline* 6). Likewise, the Other Mother's admittance that she put her own mother in her grave and "when I found her trying to crawl out, I put her back" (91) stands as testimony of how female ancestors are denied attention, making the project of recovery of female artistry important. As for Judith, this story depicts her occupying a temporal space, where she moves in and resorts to creating people and kidnapping children, resorting to a form of madness that places her artistry on the periphery of her being where she becomes a monstrosity even in literary criticism.

Parsons relays that Coraline is asked to give over her soul for no other reason than the Other Mother's desire to subjugate children (373). While Coraline finds ghost children who have died in Judith's care or lack thereof, it is far more plausible that Judith chooses particular children and specifically chooses Coraline because of their similarities. Woolf says of Judith, "She was . . . adventurous . . . imaginative . . . agog to see the world" (*Room* Chapter 3). Coraline is self-described as an explorer early on in the text. Coraline herself posits that she was chosen because she likes to play "games and challenges" (Gaiman, *Coraline* 84). More pointedly, Coraline is seen writing a story and attempting to draw mist. Judith expresses the desire to "do a little embroidery together, or some watercolor painting" (76) perhaps seeing in Coraline a young artist. Parsons discusses Coraline's several Lacanian moments as such with the mirror in the text and her identity. However, Coraline is not the only female character who has a Lacanian moment. Gaiman presents a mirror in which not only is Coraline presented with an alternate life that would produce a very different reality than at the Joneses', but an opportunity for Judith to see her younger self through Coraline. Coraline's rejection points to more than a choice of feminism between her real mother, Mrs. Jones, and Judith; it is a younger form of Judith rejecting her guidance and artistry, as Coraline concludes the Other Mother "could not truly make anything . . . she could only twist and copy and distort things that already existed " (115-116). In this way, Lacan's mirror stage in Gaiman's *Coraline* makes appearances in several overlapping interpretations.

Judith's solicitude causes her trouble not only in her mental capacity to face oppression but also renders her nonexistent. As Woolf finds in her perusal of the library, there were very few books written on the Elizabethan woman at the time and those that existed either gave her only a passing thought or were written by women who were thought to be either foolish or mad. This trend continues in criticisms of the text as Rachel Martin states in "Speaking the Cacophony of Angels: Gaiman's Women and the Fracturing of

Phallocentric Discourse," "Without the mother, there could be no Other Mother" (25). This reading renders Judith nonexistent because her sole characteristic is in not being a mother. Criticism has forced gender performance on the character even in her negated title of "other" mother. However, Martin does admit:

> When Gaiman pens characters who supposedly breach the gender binary, these characters still act out and are acted upon in very gender specific ways: despite their attempts to transcend the hegemonic roles of masculine *or* feminine, the discourse labels, defines, and limits them nonetheless. (26)

When Judith recoils into the healing space with no intention to resurface, patriarchy eventually wins in the real world by forcing her into solicitude and in her own domain as discussed earlier.

Whereas Judith operates in solitude, the Hempstock women exist in a collective that knows and respects the power of each member. Miller writes, "Art heals all; the act of creation is available to anyone. . . The Hempstocks understand and embrace this philosophy throughout the novel, but particularly through their creativity in the domestic arts" (117). Even their facade of being farm women when they are in fact powerful beings calls for collective cooperation. The reader is eventually confronted with the reality that the Hempstocks are not all powerful and can be harmed, as Lettie is. However, because they have each other, there is a way to right any wrong or correct any misstep. With that truth, the Hempstock women are also not easily concerned about patriarchal viewpoints invading their way of life. When the narrator asks again about the men, Ginnie Hempstock remarks, "We never went in for that sort of thing. You only need men if you want to breed more men" (Gaiman, *Ocean* 167). While they may have endured jeering that, for them, lasted only long enough to blink eyes, Gaiman creates in the Hempstock familial space a female community of artists that juxtaposes the solidarity and rejection of the Other Mother in *Coraline*. While the Hemstocks have the acceptance of the protagonist, it is clear they would continue to create, protect, and generally watch their environment without it. When the protagonist pleads to stay on the

Hempstock farm, he is told "No . . . you get on with your own life" (167). Again, von Czarnowsky explains, "The story is not one of adoption, it is one of a temporary refuge" (23). This key element highlights the use of temporary spaces in Gaiman's work and further supports the idea that not all places are meant to be owned or permanent, which speaks to the madness incurred by Judith in her state of solicitude.

Conclusion

Through *Ocean*, Gaiman offers a glimpse at successful female artistry perhaps as amends for the lack of attention and sometimes sympathy the Other Mother has garnered from critics and readers. Gaiman's works concur with Virginia Woolf's beliefs that a woman writing, creating art, in Elizabethan times must have a place of her own. Gaiman also builds on the idea of a collective group of women artists who successfully live and fight through the same times as Judith without going mad. While the Other Mother in *Coraline* seems to be much more akin to Skarthach of the Keep, who does not understand the guidelines of space and in her ability to create, begins to hurt others and ultimately herself, Gaiman offers sympathy for the Other Mother through *Ocean* in Ginnie's comment about Skarthach, "I don't hate her" (Gaiman, *Ocean* 110), and Lettie later remarks, "She's doing it to make the world into something she'll be happier in. Somewhere more comfortable for her" (116). Here, Gaiman offers a why that is somewhat absent in *Coraline*.

Gaiman's texts also invert the fears associated with feminism and women's apprehension to defy gender performance as assigned to them. In both *Coraline* and *Ocean*, the female characters that both child protagonists fear are those that display traditional elements of femininity, such as sweetness, kindness, and cleanliness. Even after having a decent first visit with the Other Mother, it seems implausible that Coraline will visit again as she "backed away" and "turned and hurried" when the Other Mother tells her they will be waiting for her to come back to be with them "for ever and always" (Gaiman, *Coraline* 44). Likewise, Ursula, who is liked by the entire family except for the protagonist, flirts with the father and eventually engages in sexual intercourse with him. As Danielle Russell states, "In his [Gaiman's] hands, the concept of a 'good' mother becomes more complex" (174).

These texts together provide the lesson that there is danger of solicitude in the face of oppression. The Other Mother's solicitude is perhaps what allows her to become an instrument of patriarchal rule and, therefore, pollute a healing space, since there is no one to honestly collaborate with or communicate. Effectively, she castrates her own ability to create in a positive space. While her insistence on button eyes may have been an attempt to change the perspectives of others, including herself, the domain she occupies becomes a place a horror. Lastly, while the title of the book is *Coraline*, for the sake of marketing to children, the exact text could be marketed to an adult audience with a simple change of title, "Judith," and with this simple alteration, the Other Mother emerges with an identity and backstory that she has previously been denied.

Notes

1. Descendants of the Hempstocks appear in Neil Gaiman's *Stardust* (1999) and *The Graveyard Book* (2008). They are female and as Ginnie Hempstock relays to the protagonist, "There are Hempstock women out there in your world, and I'll wager each of them is a wonder in her own way. But only Gran and me and Lettie are the pure thing." (Gaiman, *Ocean* 167)

2. Childhood anxieties and fear are discussed by many critics including Elizabeth Parsons as well as Danielle Russell in "UnMasking M(other)hood: Third World Mothering in Neil Gaiman's *Coraline* and *MirrorMask*."

3. In Gaiman's text, other mother is not capitalized. The character's original name is never given since "the names are the first things to go" (*Coraline* 81). Since she is given no name in the text, she is alternately called Other Mother or Judith.

4. Various critics have addressed the Carroll-esque aspects of *Coraline*, including Maria Nikolajeva's "Devils, Demon, Familiars, Friends: Toward a Semiotics of Literary Cats."

5. Vincent Van Gogh's ear-cutting incident is famous, although it has been said he may not have cut it himself.

Works Cited

Gaiman, Neil. *Coraline*. 2002. New York: HarperCollins, 2012. Print.

_____. "A Coraline Q&A with Neil Gaiman." *HarperCollins Publishers*. HarperCollins Publishers, 2012. Web. 23 Oct. 2016.

_____. "Why I Wrote *Coraline*." n.p., n.d. Web. 14 Sept. 2016. <http://coraline.bib.bz/why-i-wrote-coraline>.

Gooding, Richard. "'Something Very Old and Very Slow': *Coraline*, Uncanniness, and Narrative Form." *Children's Literature Association Quarterly* 4 (2008) 390-407. Print.

hooks, bell. "Understanding Patriarchy." *The Will to Change: Men, Masculinity, and Love*. New York: Atria Books, 2004. 17-34. Print.

Landis, Courtney. "'The essence of grandmotherliness': Ideal Motherhood and Threatening Female Sexuality." *Neil Gaiman in the 21st Century: Essays on the Novels, Children's Stories, Online Writings, Comics, and Other Works*. Edited by Tara Prescott. Jefferson, NC: McFarland & Co., 2015, 164-178. Print.

Martin, Rachel R. "Speaking the Cacophony of Angel: Gaiman's Women and the Fracturing of Phallocentric Discourse." *Feminism in the Worlds of Neil Gaiman: Essays on the Comics, Poetry, and Prose*. Ed. Tara Prescott & Aaron Drucker. Jefferson, NC: McFarland & Co., 2012. 11-31. Print.

Miller, Monica. "What Neil Gaiman Teaches Us about Survival: Making Good Art and Diving into the Ocean." *Neil Gaiman in the 21st Century: Essays on the Novels, Children's Stories, Online Writings, Comics, and Other Works*. Ed. Tara Prescott. Jefferson, NC: McFarland & Co., 2015. 113-122. Print.

Parsons, Elizabeth, Naarah Sawers, & Kate McInally. "The Other Mother: Neil Gaiman's Postfeminist Fairytales." *Children's Literature Association Quarterly* 4 (2008) 371-389. Print.

Russell, Danielle. "Unmasking M(other)hood: Third-Wave Mothering in Gaiman's *Coraline* and *MirrorMask*." *Feminism in the Worlds of Neil Gaiman: Essays on the Comics, Poetry, and Prose*. Ed. Tara Prescott & Aaron Drucker. Jefferson, NC: McFarland & Co., 2012. 161-176. Print.

Von Czarnowsky, Laura-Marie. "'Power and all its Secrets': Engendering Magic in Neil Gaiman's *The Ocean at the End of the Lane*." *Nordic*

Journal of Science Fiction and Fantasy Research 2 (2015) 18-28. Print.

Woolf, Virginia. *A Room of One's Own*. 1929. The University of Adelaide Library, 27 Mar. 2016. Web. 23 Aug. 2016. <https://ebooks.adelaide.edu.au/w/woolf/virginia/w91r/contents.html>.

"Of viewpoints, of images, of memories and puns and lost hopes": Polyphony and Narrative Braiding in The *Sandman: Worlds' End*

Kyle Eveleth

In his review of *The Sandman Vol: 8: Worlds' End*, Jim Pascoe writes that this "story about a story about stories" has "almost nothing to do with the larger story of the Sandman." It is true that the eponymous prime mover of Neil Gaiman's sweeping comic-art revision of DC/Vertigo's *The Sandman* is almost completely absent from the action, seen only in a memory within a story, let alone from Schrödinger's orator, who may or may not exist. Pascoe, however, misses the overarching importance of this seemingly disconnected collection of metatextual tales about tale-telling: that the whole thing is a kind of wake for the recently-deceased Morpheus. The paradox created by the utter lack of the series' touchstone character combined with his suffocating omnipresence throughout the volume echoes other phantasmal presences in the work: its historical referents, allusions, appropriations, and adaptations, all drawn from the widespread mythological and cultural connotations of dreaming and its embodiment. Lurking in the shadows, present but only sometimes revealed directly, they permeate the work with intertextual cacophony.

The complex interaction of these precursors can be described in part by comics theorist Thierry Groensteen's term *iconic solidarity*. Iconic solidarity, he explains, is the process in comics art by which "the images are visually and semantically over-determined by the fact of their coexistence *in praesentia*" (33). That is to say that the existence of each image in a work, whether in a row, on a page, or in the same binding, resonates with all its brethren to form the narrative matrix in which the story resides. The narrative content is drawn out by a process known as *braiding* (or *tressage*). Braiding is the process by which the narrative thread is discerned by the interrelationship of multiple panels. Interwoven like so many threads (visual and verbal), the interplay of words and images in *Worlds' End* especially is itself braided with not only the other issues that make up Gaiman's *Sandman,* but also the ghosts of its past lives. Pascoe means more than he anticipates when he evokes the "larger story of the Sandman," perhaps unwittingly summoning not merely Gaiman's project at the waning of the twentieth century, but also the Mr. Sandman of mid-century pop singles, the Golden Age comic book ancestor and, far beyond even these, the pre-comics Sandman of myth and bedtime warning. Yet, Gaiman splices all these disparate threads into his cloth: Gaiman's *Sandman* has grand aspirations to braid these various stories together, a design that, in its attempts at universality, has the tendency to violently ablate individual threads. However, ever the partner in far-flung collaborative projects and ever-wary of the limits of the so-called grand narrative, Neil Gaiman leaves open a space for endless continuation. The weave of Sandman's intertextual play resists finalization precisely because of its use of iconic solidarity.

In this chapter, I offer a short history of the Sandman fable as it has been conceptualized through various versions. I do this in order to set all the pieces of *Worlds' End*'s intertextuality out in the open. Then, I analyze how the narrative weave of the story is braided, sometimes to generate meaning and sometimes to divide meaning, offering insights as to the particular form of *Worlds' End*'s iconic solidarity. Finally, I pull back to show the harmony between *Worlds' End*'s structural form and its relationship to the fable in which it participates, demonstrating that just as the visual images are braided in generative and divisive ways, so too are the cultural images that foster its existence, which are woven together in a cohesive pattern. The ultimate goal is to suggest that *Worlds' End* reproduces in microcosm the macrocosmic concerns of collaborative authorship, including ambiguities of ownership and intention and questions of allegiance to canon. By examining the particular relationship between *The Sandman* and the Sandman fable using the particular grammar of comics as a lens, we may draw fruitful conclusions about collaboration in artistic creation, whether between contemporaneous collaborators or spiritual ancestors and new writers.

The Prince of Stories

In their analysis of the interplay between text and image, *How Picturebooks Work* (2006), theorists Maria Nikolajeva and Carole Scott identify the "dynamic interrelationship and creative tension" inherent to visuo-verbal collaborative works (29). This dynamic interrelationship, Nikolajeva and Scott contend, introduces "multiple ownership and multiple intentionality" into the text, which breeds "ambiguity and uncertainty" in the reader (30). For Nikolajeva and Scott, the tension is primarily between the verbal representation of the story and its visualization by a collaborative or adapting artist; the objective is to examine how these competing iterations destabilize or enrich the reading experience. That is, they consider an original text, say Beatrix Potter's *The Tale of Peter Rabbit* (1902), and how it compares to a newly illustrated version, which often signifies differently than the original work.

In prying open the intellectual space of creative collaboration, Nikolajeva and Scott simultaneously open a space between two often-conflated notions: "which version is this?" and "*whose* version is this?" We might think, for example, of Disney's *Sleeping Beauty* versus Charles Perrault's *La Belle au bois dormant* or the Brothers Grimm's *Dornröschen*. Both ask about iterative differences, but the first question absorbs the second by focusing on differences in the story, such as the shift from Sleeping Beauty to Briar Rose, and then drawing conclusions based upon assimilation of the tale across cultures and time periods. However, when we ask *whose* version something is, we implicitly ask about the person themselves as the mediating factor; thus, Disney's version is perceived to have been crafted for a different purpose (entertainment, or perhaps money) than the Brothers Grimm's (preservation of endangered folklore). One seems to be mediated by an entire culture, a belief that suggests the version is more universal, which is appealing given that fairy tales are often understood as universal stories. The other, however, seems idiosyncratic, and sometimes this is true, but it masks the fact that any person is, of course, influenced by the culture and time in which the adaptation occurs. 'Which version' is understood as taking the pulse of a culture, while 'whose version' is an inquiry into the mind of the adaptor and implies ownership of the changes.

With *The Sandman*, Neil Gaiman attempts to destabilize these beliefs even as he destabilizes the relationship between fable and iteration—for, what is a fable but the first (or commonly accepted to be first) iteration of a given tale? To do this, Gaiman draws on both recent comics history and more distant cultural memory. The first of these, perhaps, is the use of the name Morpheus, the Greek god of dreams, to identify Dream of the Endless. But Dream is not merely a representation of the Greek son of Hypnos; he is also referred to as Oneiros—the less-specific term for Morpheus and his ilk, like Phoberos—even as he conflates within himself the countless aspects of the Oneiroi, such as nightmares, lucid dreams, and prophesy. But *The Sandman* is not the story of Morpheus or the Oneiroi, and so Gaiman shifts to European folklore to grant further depth. The Sandman fable has roots in many cultures, but the utterances with which most Western cultures are most familiar before his comics introduction are Prussian romanticist E. T. A. Hoffman's sinister *Der Sandmann* (1816) and Hans Christian Andersen's more lovable prince of stories, *Ole Lukøje* (1842). Hoffmann's Sandman is a vengeful figure in the mold of Krampus or Bloody Mary, who plucks out the eyes of children who refuse to go to bed and feeds them to his children in his abode on the moon. Meanwhile, Andersen's affable character is the safe-keeper of dreams and an accomplished orator. Andersen writes that "[t]here is nobody in the world who knows so many stories as Ole Lukøje, or who can relate them so nicely" (qtd. in Andersen & Paull 65). Andersen's character is not entirely benevolent; a child who is naughty sleeps beneath Ole Lukøje's umbrella and experiences no dreams. These Sandmen reside in the pages of *The Sandman:* Dream often goes by the name "Prince of Stories" and is, from time to time, depicting similarly to other cultural storytellers of myth. He retains the ability to bar people from dreams, or to sentence them to be afflicted with constant nightmares, or worse yet, to be unable to sleep or unable to wake from sleep.

And though he himself plucks no eyeballs, he retains a construct who does, his nightmare-creation The Corinthian.

Gaiman turns from these mythic forms to comics and popular culture of the twentieth century for the bulk of his allusive effluvium. The Sandman enters the American literary canon in 1928 with Susan Horton's short poem, "I'm Looking for the Sandman." Soon after, National Allied Publications writers Gardner Fox and Bert Christman, writing under the singular penname Larry Dean, pitched a gas-masked vigilante hero who, like his creative team and his later iteration through Gaiman, would be saddled with multiple competing and complementary identities. The character was doubly introduced, published nearly simultaneously in both *Action Comics* #40 (July 1939) and *The New York World's Fair Comics* (1939). This Sandman belonged to two quickly-coalescing traditions, bridging the so-called "mystery men" of the pulp detective comics tradition and the nascent superhero tradition, started by Joe Schuster and Jerry Siegel's Superman. Fox and Christman's Sandman had the usual heroic doubling of a normal identity (Wesley Dobbs) and his heroic identity, the two of which were interrelated but incommensurate, but the more personal details of his life are equally dichotomous: the Sandman is born a Jewish-Catholic, travels to the Far East before returning to the West, and, as the Sandman, has rich prophetic dreams that alert him to impending crimes and contrast with an otherwise dull life. But even this Sandman's canonical origin is something of a viewpoint among possible truths. When Fox and Christman revealed themselves as the creators, a second collaborative wrinkle appeared: the role of illustrator Creig Flessel, a staff artist at DC who is credited with creating many covers of early American comic books from 1936 to 1939. Like many artists during the golden age, Flessel's ownership of his art was disputed except where he was credited as author-artist, and he has variously though rarely been credited alongside Fox and Christman as co-creator of *The Sandman*.

Fox, Christman, and Flessel's Sandman, Wesley Dodds, has been an infrequent visitor in other areas of the DC universe since his final mainstream appearance in 1966. In 1941, DC editor Mort Weisinger, most widely known for editing Superman, rebranded the

Dodds Sandman into a kind of pseudo Captain America, switching the gas mask and trenchcoat for purple-and-yellow tights and a sidekick, Sandy the Golden Boy. Superhero writers Joe Simon and Jack Kirby took over writing duties. Their influence on the Sandman canon, however, would prove not to be with Dodds, but with their own creation, Garrett Sanford. The re-imagined Sandman retained his superheroic figure, trading purple for red, but gained the immortality a personification of dreaming deserved. Sanford was a short-lived iteration, revealed to have been an accidental capture into the Dream Dimension from whence sidekicks Brute and Glob originate. Sanford was still not the in-universe, canonical Sandman in 1989, when Gaiman began work on *The Sandman.* That was former Silver-Scarab, Hector Hall.

What is most striking about these tripartite historical Sandmen is that they coexisted within the same universe simultaneously. This has never been a mean feat in comics, particularly with the introduction of the multiverse system of parallel universes. For example, when Gaiman entered talks with Vertigo about reviving the character, Fox/Christman/Flessel's version was slated to undergo a significant revival in the midst of *The Sandman* in the form of *Sandman Mystery Theatre* (1993–1999). But Gaiman's Sandman is not merely another Sandman in the multiverse, as Dodds, Sanford, and Hall are. Rather, Dream of the Endless reveals that he has been all of these individuals in some way, most especially Sanford and Hall. Sanford's creations, the nightmares Brute and Gob, recur throughout *The Sandman.* Their role is especially significant, as they are the creators of the Dream Dimension over which Hall's Sandman lords—and Hall is merely a shell—an echo of the previous Sandmen, a very small part of Dream himself. Despite this parahuman status, Hall nevertheless exerts powerful influence over *The Sandman*'s arc: his son with Hippolyta Hall, conceived and born in the miniature Dream Dimension, supplants Morpheus as Dream of the Endless following the events of *Worlds' End.* Dream's identity, therefore, is dispersed across the multitude of his embodiments. The only way to approach a singular Dream is to juxtapose the Sandmen against one another. Woven into another conceptual framework, finding the meaning in the Sandman is possible only through iconic solidarity: the connections between coeval utterances of Sandmen. The collaborative space between Sandmen—and, by extension, their curators in various media—coagulates into an intricately-braided character, drawn and explicated in Gaiman's offering.

Overlapping Histories: Worlds' End's Structure

In the first issue of *The Sandman*, Gaiman strips away the narrative pasts of his leading entity in an act of knowing unraveling. Dream of the Endless, laid bare in a summoning circle meant for a demon, has lost the symbols of his office: his curiously gas-mask-shaped helmet, his cape, and his amulet. In his absence, the Dreaming itself threatens not to unravel, but to descend into anarchy. The whole scene plays out with heavy-handed irony as it dramatizes both the competing metaphorical understandings on which *The Sandman* rests: first, that The Sandman belongs to himself/selves alone, and second that the Dreaming, as a collection of individual stories coalescing into one realm, can survive (albeit unstably) without Dream. Dream outlasts his mortal captor, as any endless being will, and escapes. But even as he casts off those worldly remnants that shackle him to the Reality Stream, irreducible remnants of past narrative yarns yet linger. "When a world ends," the unnamed Landlady of the Inn of Worlds' End remarks at the end of the volume, "there's always something left over. A story perhaps, or a vision, or a hope" (Gaiman, *Sandman* 56: 3). Even when, in the second volume, Gaiman retroactively continues the Hector Hall *Sandman* by revealing that Hall was merely a fractional avatar of Morpheus, a lesser actor, it does not absolutely remove any of the previous Sandmen from Morpheus' being. Dream was both individuals, both Sandmen, just as the Sandman was both the gas-masked detective, Dodds, and the spandexed superhero, Hall. Because of this, Gaiman's deployment of the most clichéd of letdown endings—Hall's life was literally all just a dream—gains freshness in its multiplicity: Hall was Dream's dream in a dream within the Dreaming. Ultimately, his son Daniel, a remnant of a destroyed world, becomes Dream of the Endless. This supplanting of the main (Morpheus) by remnant (Daniel) is yet another symbolic representation of the work Gaiman does in *The Sandman*, tearing old stories apart to weave them anew.

The Inn at Worlds' End, then, comes to represent the volume in which it appears. Like the book *Worlds' End*, the Inn at Worlds' End expands to encompass the tales told within it, alluding through visuals to the stories the seeing-reader cannot overhear. As a collected edition, that is a bound volume of previously-published serial issues of a comic book, it is curiously part of the whole and yet standalone. Indeed, in the preface to *The Wake,* Gaiman considers them a series of novels in themselves. All, of course, contribute to the larger story of the *Sandman*, even though each is a complete tale of its own. This structure is replicated in the stories. By way of introduction, *Worlds' End* employs one of the oldest frame-narratives in storytelling, the oratory circle, set in perhaps the most iconic of locales, a public house. Like a modern-day *Decameron*, Gaiman's cast of characters relate hard-to-believe tales to one another to pass the time they spend at Worlds' End. Each story correlates with an issue and is marked by a new artist and their stylistic riff on the world of *The Sandman*. In part because of the mechanical limitations of comics production and in part a testament to the solidarity of the enterprise, each story is roughly the same length, suggesting equality amongst the orators. By extension, this grants the artists whose work brings the stories to life an equal share of ownership over the work. "The stories themselves, Gaiman admits, come about in part because of the illustrator he has in mind to collaborate with." ("Acknowledgements"). The Inn's status as symbol of the book is solidified in its description: a refuge for those between worlds and those whose worlds are lost, the Inn is "constantly being created" to suit the needs of the many seeking safe harbor in the reality storm generated by Morpheus' death. In somewhat abstract terms, the constant creation of the Inn mirrors the interpretive work of braiding in comics: it is not a settled function, but rather a dynamic interplay that changes as new images are brought to bear and old ones are shuffled out of memory.

Because braiding is, as Groensteen explains, at once generative and divisive in how it signifies, its core feature is that though it signifies, it is not finalizable (12). That is to say that braiding harnesses multiple messages or narratives because it can at once create and extinguish meaning based upon how elements are woven together into a singular narrative. There are many ways to represent this characteristic in visual media, but an example in *The Sandman* is the frequent use of the unverifiable and the indeterminate. I will focus here, specifically, on Cluracan's story (*The Sandman #52*), and more specifically on a single sequence within it: the dissolution of the Carnifex of Aurelia/Psychopomp of the Plains' power. After being freed by Morpheus, Cluracan must prevent an alliance of power under the Carnifex/Psychopomp by any means necessary. A single page lays out the gradual dissolution of the man's power: the topmost panel, stretching the width of the page and taking up a third of its vertical height, shows a possibly drunken elder priest slandering the leader (Gaiman, "Cluracan's" 20). The middle vertical third is split into two panels, one two-thirds the width of the page and the other one-third, in which the elderly priest's story is continued and people gossip behind him (wider panel) and in which a drunken young noble brags about being hired to remove a problematic heir to a pictured "assemblage of whores." The bottom third is split evenly into three panels, depicting a foreign soldier talking of slavery, the archvicar of western Aurelia confessing forgery, and finally Cluracan, saying "It's amazing how much one can accomplish in an evening, if one is willing to expend a little effort, and to walk briskly" (20).

This sequence allows for at least two possible interpretations: that Cluracan has persuaded these people to spill the truth about the Carnifex/Psychopomp, or that he has impersonated them in order to bring about his end. Both are plausible and, ultimately, supported by the narrative and left indeterminate: the Carnifex/Psychopomp confesses to a disguised Cluracan that all the things mentioned are true. The way the images are laid out also makes both readings viable: one can read the pacing of the panels (one, two, three) as a symbolic quickening of pace to match Cluracan's as he does his work. One can also examine the faces and bodies of the men who give confessions, testing them against one another to see a resemblance or trademark if Cluracan is indeed impersonating them. Finally, this sequence is unique in its pacing, as nowhere else in Cluracan's story is a progressive increase of panels used. This lends credulity to the reading that he has coerced knowing agents into confessing by showing his redoubled efforts, but simultaneously allows one to follow Cluracan as he impersonates important, though nameless, folk.

The endless multiplicity of Cluracan's actions in this sequence is further expanded by his insistences before, during, and after the tale that some of it will be true. Before telling the story, he notes that he has "no facility for fiction" and "lack[s] the ability to embellish" (Gaiman, "Cluracan's" 2). He then mildly dismisses the story as "a dry and unexciting [tale], chiefly dealing with local politics and city history" (2). Throughout the telling of the tale, truth is assured and yet constantly questioned or refuted. Cluracan introduces a moment of possible foretelling by saying that "sometimes we will say true things, and these things we say are neither glamour nor magic, neither prediction nor curse: but sometimes what we say is true. And even if you're a tremendous liar, like myself, well, it's even true for me" (12). Of course, given that the tale being related is (ostensibly) one from Cluracan's personal history, it is impossible to know whether this was a true omen or if it was fixed to match the events of the story. When the tale is finished, the innkeeper asks if it was the truth; Cluracan replies, "all of it except the sword-fight with the palace guard, which I threw in to add verisimilitude, excitement, and local colour to an otherwise bald and insipid narrative" (25). Questioned further about details, he refuses to be pestered further and turns the conversation to the next story. The situation plays a bit like a logic puzzle—which is the lie, and which is the truth? *The Sandman* seems to suggest that this inquiry is out-of-bounds: all fictions are in some way factual and not all facts can be verified.

Further presentations within *Worlds' End* evolve individual and collective meanings by continuing to treat absolute truth as a kind of sacred but malleable thing. The sailor Jim says his/her tale, "Hob's Leviathan," is "true as ever I'm sitting here" (Gaiman, "Hob's" 2), a statement undercut by frequent allusion to adolescent seafaring tales and Ovidian myth. In Petrefax's tale, "Cerements" (#55), the status of truth arises often: with the dangers of telling the story in the first place, for "it is a **true** story, master [Klaproth], and because **you** are in it" (2); next, in the truth of the Necropolis Litharge's creation, for which truth does not matter as truth is meant for teaching and not entertaining (17); in Hermas' tale, relating the dangers of requiring verification for magic (21); and finally in the truth of Hermas'/Petrefax's tale as a whole, which is so true that it must not be spoken (yet has been) (24). The close of the volume reveals that, ultimately, truth is not nearly so important as *belief*: as Hermas explains, that which should not be true, and yet is, becomes true because people "**believe** it should" (Gaiman, "Cerements" 9). Gaiman recycles an earlier idea from the beginning of *The Sandman*, specifically the issue "Dream of a Thousand Cats": enough belief from enough believers has the power to alter reality. Riffing on postmodern theorist Michel Foucault's notion of a "regime of truth," Gaiman reinforces Foucault's primary contention from "The Political Function of the Intellectual" throughout *The Sandman:* namely, that "truth isn't outside power" (Foucault 130). In *The Sandman*, the "general politics of truth," or "the types of discourse [society] harbours and causes to function as true" (130) is articulated by dominance of belief. That is, the collective knowledge and memory of something lends it veracity. It is because Brant holds his memories of the inn close and believes they were real that they remain so, albeit in a shadowy form; only he believes his coworker Charlene ever lived, and so it is only true for him (Gaiman, "The Wake" 21). And so, we must wonder: if Gaiman does not pay homage to these shadowy precursors of his landmark character, did they ever really exist? If the historical Sandmen fade from comic art's collective memory, does Gaiman's Sandman lose his depth? Perhaps most importantly, what happens when the so-called Prince of Stories is no longer a multitude, but a singular?

The structure of *Worlds' End* muses upon this concern as well. Its place in *The Sandman* sequence is odd because it immediately follows the death of its eponymous character and yet heralds the introduction of another version of that character. In fact, it barely features his likeness: appearing twice, once in Cluracan's tale and once in "The Golden Boy," Dream is nevertheless merely an accessory, whose presence enables the main acting character of the story to continue. Dream is reduced to *deus ex machina*. But then, that is kind of Dream's role *throughout The Sandman* run. What initially appears to be tightly-spun arc (*The Sandman* series) is, upon further inspection, rather a loosely-knit compendium of the Endless' adventures in the wake of their brother's accidental entrapment. Dream and his siblings appear both as localized phenomena and as universal beings. The series jumps anachronistically around time and space, across realms and universes, weaving in and out of established canons. Morpheus is not entirely malleable; he is always dark of hair and eye and tall and spindly, even though identifying characteristics shift to match the cultural beliefs of the person to whom he appears. The exceptions to this viewer-specific embodiment are the so-called "Endless" ones, those whose temporalities lie beyond the scope of individual narratives: his sisters, Death, Despair, and Delirium; his brothers, Destiny and Destruction; and his gender-fluid sibling, Desire. Interestingly, the reader is included in this, able to see Dream and his siblings in all their iterations. This places the reader alongside Morpheus, a kind of confidant: both locally important (as reader/meaning-maker) and important on the whole (as interpreter). To re-use the weaving metaphor, Morpheus is, for the reader, not the main thread of the Sandman series, but rather the needle, tying together the disparate weaves of individual stories.

Words about Pictures and Pictures about Words

The seemingly basic authorial and artistic rights of ownership and intentionality have long been a battleground in comic art creation. Including the creation of such now-mainstays as Vertigo, Dark Horse, and IDW, the Bronze Age saw the rise of a wave of rebellious, deeply-talented underground artists and writers, Gaiman among them. And yet, a looming question: in a series wherein Gaiman and his collaborators draw upon the range of cultural and historical Sandmen, to whom does *The Sandman* then belong? Produced in the latter, more postmodern-oriented years of the Bronze Age, *The Sandman* somewhat ironically dwells on questions of ownership, allegiance, duty, and personal liberty in its narration, even as it patches together a pastiche of anachronistic, a-cultural mixed media. Indeed, *The Sandman* furthers two troubling propositions: that a particular *syuzhet* may, in economic terms, belong to one or more entities simultaneously and therefore *none* have sole rights to it and, second, that identification and ownership are merely fleeting claims laid upon notions that transcend historical and cultural moments. The borrowed brothers, Cain and Abel, voice it thusly in issue 71, "In Which a Wake is Held":

> ABEL: Nobody died. How can you kill an idea? How can you kill the personification of an action?
> ENVOY: Then **what** died? **Who** are you mourning?
> CAIN: A **puh-point of view**.

The label on the tin says "Neil Gaiman's *The Sandman*," but the characters and situations appearing within each issue are drawn from the entirety of the *Sandman* mythos. More to the point, they are drawn from the minds and talents of *every* person who touches the thing, whether it is directly via drawing, coloring, wording, or writing, or indirectly as an influence.

The Sandman's meditation upon the nature of ownership is woven into its very being: it is, after all, the product of collaborative interpretation across historical viewpoints, as outlined above, as well as between contemporaneous collaborators who worked on the project. This is par for the course for Gaiman, who often cedes dictatorial intellectual control to more democratic (or at least parliamentarian) methods. This is not to detract from his single-authored works, such as *American Gods*, but rather to suggest that Gaiman is a creator who is profoundly at home in the ambiguity and uncertainty—not to mention the innovations—that legion authorship entails.

It is clear that Gaiman values multimodal collaboration to enhance the end product. Though it would be easy to look at Gaiman's bibliography and conclude that most of the collaborations are Gaiman on text and an illustrator on visualizations of it, this ignores his primarily verbal collaborations (such as *Good Omens*, with the late Terry Pratchett) while also (and more importantly) reducing the role of illustrators to one of reproduction and not interpretation. This reductive stance undermines the importance of work done by Gaiman's collaborators, like frequent co-authors Dave McKean and P. Craig Russell, whose visual additions and adaptations of Gaiman's stories probe the most fundamental question of illustration: how to make visible that which seems only to live in the imagination. At once a literal interpretation of the term "illustrate" ("to light up," or "to bring to light," as to reveal) and a symbolic one (as to illuminate, to clarify or elucidate), Gaiman's collaborators' roles in the production of his comics are not simply to make pictures to match the words. Rather, they offer their own mediations and interpretations, in some cases creating that which was not there before in order to make the image function.

Multiple Personalities and Truth Serums: Unveiling a Masked Hero

We circle back, perhaps inevitably, to the question of why ownership and intent matter when considering comics. To answer it, I will first reconceptualize away from the thread and fabric metaphor I have utilized throughout, shifting instead to a metaphor of viewpoints in the form of windows. The naming of comic book structural elements as "panels" and "gutters" is, perhaps, a tacit resistance to the obvious resemblance the standard comics grid bears to a multipane window. In a comics grid, as in a multipane window, each individual panel is a coalescence of viewpoints: the mediated artist's viewpoint; the stylistic viewpoint; the colorist's viewpoint; the implied viewpoint; and, of course, the reader's viewpoint. But none are situated in a vacuum: rather, they also bear the traces of the viewpoints alongside, nearby, and even far removed from themselves. In much the same fashion as a comic book engenders a constellation of these viewpoints, coagulated for a singular-if-diffuse purpose—to tell a story or make an artistic impression—then Gaiman's *Sandman* offers an even more diverse arrangement of windows. Some are from different artists; some are from the same artist at different times, arguably thus from a different artist. Many include the viewpoints of precursors who built up the Sandman fable over the centuries, and in whose traces are further echoes of the cultures and histories that spawned those viewpoints. But most importantly, these windows are granted equal semiotic footing: they are all integral, via iconic solidarity, to the meaning of the whole. At the same time, however, because of their braided interconnectedness with the others in the volume(s), they retain a central, inalienable selfhood: they are still unique and individual. Gaiman's *Sandman*, in its harmonious relationship between comics grammar and narrative style, foregrounds the interconnectedness and yet individuality of the narrative act.

That we recognize and appraise these contributions is of special importance now, in the early twenty-first century, when American comics still face the problems of readerly representation that Gaiman fought valiantly against in the mid-1990s. *The Sandman* was most widely read by *non-traditional comic book readers*: that is, people—mostly young women—who felt left out of the traditional camp of comics readership. But, just as the success of Gaiman's *Sandman* made the possibility of something better visible to countless readers who had felt ignored by comics, his properties present the ground upon which further progress can be constructed. If we take nothing else away from Gaiman's sweeping retelling of the tale of an Endless entity, then we must, at the very least, value it for its unflinching openness to the unending and the uncategorizable. Gaiman's *Sandman* refers back to and absorbs its precursors and contemporaneous equals as aspects of a multiple and polyphonic Dream of the Endless. Rather than silence those voices in favor of a single idea, Gaiman welcomes the cacophony of competing traditions with open arms, knowing that telling stories about the Sandman actually involves telling stories about humanity. Dream reinforces that message in his ironic final monologue of the series: "I am Prince of Stories . . . ; but I have no story of my own. Nor shall I ever" (Gaiman, *S* 75: 36), and, in so doing, gives over control of the tale to The Bard himself.

Works Cited

Andersen, Hans Christian & Susannah Mary Paull (as Mrs. H. B. Paull). "Ole Lukøje." *Hans Andersen's Fairy Tales: A New Translation.* Trans. Susannah Mary Paull. Chicago: S.A. Maxwell, 1888: 65-75. Web.

Foucault, Michel. "The Political Function of the Intellectual." *Radical Philosophy* 17.13 (1977): 126-133. Print.

Gaiman, Neil. "Cluracan's Tale." *The Sandman* #52. Illus. John Watkiss. New York: Vertigo, Aug. 1993. Print.

—————. "Hob's Leviathan." *The Sandman* #53. Illus. Michael Zulli et al. New York: Vertigo, Sept. 1993. Print.

—————. "Cerements." *The Sandman* #55. Illus. Shea Anton Pensa et al. New York: Vertigo, Nov. 1993. Print.

—————. "Worlds' End." *The Sandman* #56. Illus. Bryan Talbot et al. New York: Vertigo, Dec. 1993. Print.

—————. "The Wake." *The Sandman* #70. Illus. Michael Zulli et al. New York: Vertigo, Sept. 1995. Print.

—————. "In Which a Wake is Held." *The Sandman* #71. Illus. Michael Zulli et al. New York: Vertigo, Sept. 1995. Print.

—————. "The Tempest." *The Sandman* #75. Illus. Charles Vess et al. New York: Vertigo, Mar. 1996. Print.

—————. *The Sandman, Volume 8: Worlds' End: Fully Remastered Edition.* Introduction by Stephen King. Illus. Mike Allred et al. New York: Vertigo, 2012. Print.

—————. *The Sandman, Volume 10: The Wake: Fully Remastered Edition.* Illus. Michael Zulli et al. New York: Vertigo, 2012. Print.

Groensteen, Thierry. *Comics and Narration.* Trans. Ann Miller. Jackson: UP Mississippi, 2013. Print.

—————. *The System of Comics.* Trans. Bart Beaty and Nick Nguyen. Jackson: UP Mississippi, 2007. Print.

Pascoe, Jim. "Amazon Review on *The Sandman* Vol. 8." *The Sandman*, Vol. 8. Amazon.com, n.d. Web. 14 Sept. 2016. <https://www.amazon.com/dp/1563891719?_encoding=UTF8&isInIframe=1&n=283155&ref_=dp_proddesc_0&s=books&showDetailProductDesc=1#iframe-wrapper>.

Nikolajeva, Maria & Carole Scott. *How Picturebooks Work*. New York: Routledge, 2001. Print.

Going Postmodern Gothic: Neil Gaiman's Feminist Fairy Tales

Jill Coste

As a prolific writer of fantasy, Neil Gaiman has mined the dark worlds of urban gothic, plumbed the depths of childhood psyches, and offered dozens of short stories influenced by myths, legends, and fairy tales. While fairy-tale tropes are prominent in much of his work, Gaiman's actual fairy-tale retellings—particularly in short-story form—are few but significant. They do much to reveal his feminist spirit and gothic inclinations; in Gaiman's fairy tales, familiar heroines haunt borders and destabilize narratives. Of special note are Gaiman's revisions of the Snow White story, which offer ruminations on the nature of monstrosity and the endurance of trauma. He uses the gothic in these tales to illuminate the shades of gray that exist between good and evil and to emphasize unexpected paths to individual agency. In his 1994 short story "Snow, Glass, Apples," for instance, the so-called wicked stepmother narrates the action in a confessional format, relaying a chilling tale of a vampiric princess whom the queen desperately tried to kill to protect her people. Nearly twenty years later, Gaiman penned another Snow White retelling, *The Sleeper and the Spindle*. This tale, which brings Sleeping Beauty into the narrative, features a grown Snow White, now queen, setting out to break the spell cast on Sleeping Beauty and save her own kingdom from a creeping plague of sleep. An emphasis on the relationship between mother- and daughter-figures in these tales forces readers to consider fairy-tale villainy in a new light. In both of Gaiman's Snow White revisions, a connection to the stepmother is what ultimately gives the heroines power—the stepmother is not just an evil queen to be defeated; she is an important character, and she lives within and through the presumptive heroine.

Taking a familiar fairy tale and giving it teeth and complexity is a particularly postmodern ambition. The postmodern fairy tale borrows from generic conventions in folklore and the literary fairy tale alike, subverting and twisting and transforming traditional tales. Cristina Bacchilega notes that "postmodern fairy tales reactivate the wonder tale's 'magic' or mythopoeic qualities by providing new readings of it, thereby generating unexploited or forgotten possibilities from its repetition" (*Postmodern* 22). In other words, the postmodern fairy tale relies on foreknowledge of these tales; it relies on cultural recognition and repetition in order to provide new tellings. Gaiman writes a postmodern Snow White tale in "Snow, Glass, Apples" by offering the stepmother's perspective, trusting that readers' familiarity with the original tale will enrich this new point of view. Similarly, by entwining two familiar fairy tales in *The Sleeper and the Spindle* and referring to notable narrative moments within those tales, Gaiman indulges in an intertextual exercise that again relies on readers' knowledge of the source texts in order to then surprise them with a different path.

Furthermore, his focus on the female characters and his attempt to complicate their narratives ranks Gaiman among feminist fairy-tale writers, a complicated, postmodern cohort itself. Fairy-tale revisions that feature clever heroines fighting against patriarchal strictures spring from a contemporary feminist response to the canonized literary fairy tale. While the literary fairy tale has a rich history of female storytellers and gothic proclivities, the standard conception of the fairy tale is one steeped in Disney tradition. In the typical "Disneyfied" tale featuring a female main character, an innocent heroine faces off against a wicked force (often an evil stepmother), transforms through her tribulations, and ends up married off to a prince as part of her happily ever after. Fed up with the simplification of fairy tales and subjugation of female characters, feminist writers in the 1970s began staking claims in fairy-tale territory, offering subversive retellings that allowed the heroines control over their own sexuality and marital choices.

While most of the major authors associated with these fairy-tale revisions are women—Anne Sexton, Angela Carter, Emma Donoghue, Margaret Atwood, among many others—male writers have also contributed to the postmodern, feminist fairy-tale landscape. Robert Coover and Donald Barthelme have, like

Gaiman, provided Snow White revisions that subvert the standard narrative. While we might not classify these male writers as feminist visionaries, their work tackles questions of patriarchy and female agency. Regarding Gaiman's work, Aaron Drucker and Tara Prescott note, in their edited collection *Feminism in the Worlds of Neil Gaiman*, that "we can only speculate on the nature of Gaiman's own feminist convictions" (8), but that "through most of Gaiman's work there remains a surprisingly strong strain of will and agency in the women he creates" (2).

I would argue that the agency Gaiman instills in his female characters is rooted in the way he uses gothic conventions. Instead of an outside force prompting the protagonists to face their inner fears, Gaiman's heroines *already* know what their inner fears are, and the gothic puts those fears into stark relief. With its competitive relationship between stepmother and stepdaughter at the forefront, the Snow White tale is especially primed for revision that explores the complex relationships between women. The gothic in Gaiman's retellings casts light on how the heroines and their enemies are part of a history, a network, and a future of femininity, and the steps to agency for heroines and villains alike are influenced by the women who have come before them. In the introduction to her edited collection *Fairy Tales Reimagined*, Susan Redington Bobby notes that "[f]airy tale revisionists have come into their own by embracing a wide variety of theoretical approaches in their works" (7). She points out that while feminist and social criticism are most common, fairy-tale revisions will benefit from new approaches. The first step to doing that, Bobby posits, will come from examining less canonical revisions. Another way to do that, I propose, is to examine how the gothic functions in fairy-tale retellings, starting here with Gaiman's work. While the gothic leads us back to feminism, it enriches current approaches to feminist fairy tales.

The Gothic Past and Present

The gothic pairs well with fairy tales—both genres rose to publishing prominence in the Victorian era, both are adapted to respond to cultural concerns, and both feature consistent tropes across adaptations.

Of particular note is how both the gothic and the fairy tale remain dynamic, shifting in shape to reflect personal and cultural fears, anxieties, and hopes. As Jerrold Hogle notes in his introduction to the *Cambridge Companion to Gothic Literature*, "[s]ome Gothic tales, such as *Frankenstein* or *Dracula*, have [such] a lasting resonance . . . that we keep telling them over and over again with different elements but certain constant features" (6). Anna Jackson, Karen Coats, and Roderick McGillis, the editors of *The Gothic in Children's Literature: Haunting the Borders*, echo this, noting in their introduction that the gothic genre's "landscapes and conventions change in response to cultural shifts in the fears, values, and technologies that inscribe themselves into our subjectivities" (5). Similarly, fairy tales "are constantly altered, adapted, transformed, and tailored to fit new cultural contexts . . . assimilating new anxieties and desires" (Tatar 11). In other words, both the gothic and the fairy tale work to provide narrative frames for cultural and societal concerns.

On its own, however, the gothic revels in a sense of dread. As McGillis notes, the gothic "deal[s] with the lurid and the taboo. It unearths skeletons from the past and it raises fears for the future" (227). Gothic hauntings take many forms, most notably in the shape of ghosts and monsters, but also in the shape of history and human behavior. The genre first appeared in the eighteenth century with Horace Walpole's *Castle of Otranto* and rose to prominence in the nineteenth century with such landmark gothic texts as Mary Shelley's *Frankenstein* and Bram Stoker's *Dracula*, but it has endured and shifted over the years to cover all manner of Western sins. Fears of industrialization, oppressive patriarchal standards, sexual deviance, and the legacy of slavery are just a few of the cultural concerns addressed in gothic narratives. Furthermore, the gothic is particularly notable for the way it explores the space between binaries. In the gothic, there is no clear good or bad, there is simply a murky space in the middle, a space that sends chills up our spines and makes us question our instincts. In McGillis's succinct words, "[t]he gothic world is decidedly not a pleasant place; it is ambiguous at best" (227).

Gaiman is, intentionally or not, a master of modern gothic. His work hits all the marks of Catherine Spooner and Emma McEvoy's definition of the gothic, which involves "returning to the past . . . dual interest in transgression and decay . . . commitment to exploring the aesthetics of fear . . . and [a] cross-contamination of reality and fantasy" (1). Gaiman's Snow White revisions return to the past by recalling the original tales, and the characters themselves brood over the past; his fairy-tale characters transgress social norms, confront decay, and dwell on what frightens them most; and, though ambiguous in time and place, his fairy tales mix realistic concerns of identity with otherworldly fantasy.

While Gaiman uses numerous gothic tropes in these texts, the ones that work most to subvert conventional fairy-tale narratives are those that link the stepmother and stepdaughter, blurring the lines between them and forcing characters and readers alike to reconsider the relationship. In "Snow, Glass, Apples," gothic imagery connects the queen to the princess and underscores narrative ambiguity, highlighting the fact that in this fairy tale, there is no hero or happy ending. In *The Sleeper and the Spindle*, the queen is now Snow White, but she is haunted by her past, as is the Sleeping Beauty character. Less overtly dark than "Snow, Glass, Apples," the gothic intervenes in this tale in order to illuminate Snow White's ultimate path and release her from her stepmother's legacy.

On the Other Side of the Stepmother's Mirror

In "Snow, Glass, Apples," Gaiman relies on a familiarity with the original Snow White tale, and he follows the same beats, but from the stepmother's perspective. The Snow White story that most modern audiences are familiar with stems from the Grimm brothers' nineteenth-century version, which Disney adapted for its 1937 animated film. In the Grimm tale, which follows the "persecuted innocent heroine" trope, Snow White's mother dies in childbirth, and the wicked stepmother is soon envious of Snow White's goodness and beauty. She tries three times to eliminate her stepdaughter, without success: she commands a huntsman to cut out Snow White's heart, she disguises herself as a peddler and ties

Snow White up in bodice laces to suffocate her, and she brushes the young heroine's hair with a poisoned comb. After the queen finally succeeds in killing Snow White with the infamous poisoned apple, the dwarves grieve, and the prince arrives and awakens the beautiful princess with a kiss. The queen is furious, and she attends the wedding feast and faces a punishment of dancing to death in red-hot iron shoes.

In Gaiman's reimagined version of this tale, the queen states that the story we know and love is not the true tale. She immediately establishes Snow White (whom Gaiman never actually names) as Other: her first line is "I do not know what manner of thing she is" (Gaiman, "Snow, Glass" 324). In the queen's telling, her young stepdaughter is vampiric, a creature who sucks away the lifeblood of her own father, a being that continues to live even after the queen has her huntsman cut the young girl's heart out, even after the queen hangs the heart from the rafters of her chamber, where "it continued to beat and pulse" (329). The queen tells her story as a confessional, and at the end of the tale—after a necrophilic prince, turned off by the queen's sex drive, has encountered the "dead" princess and made an alliance with her—we learn that she is being slowly roasted to death in a closed iron cauldron, in a brutal transformation of the original tale's iron shoes.

In an essay examining the feminist impulse in "Snow, Glass, Apples," Elizabeth Law admires the way the queen "is strength without dominance, power without repression of the feminine" (179). She claims that the queen's feminist power lies in the way "she was not a weakened widow, but instead a wise ruler, both fair and just" (181). In a diametrically different view of the tale, Mathilda Slabbert reads the queen as sexually perverted, with "her own decadent nature" (78). Sándor Klapcsik offers a mediation between the two, reading the queen as an unreliable narrator and asking "can the reader believe the Queen who demonizes Snow White, or, does she just vindicate her case after the death sentence?" (203). These three different readings of Gaiman's queen reveal the postmodern nature of the tale at work—all three scholars pull from previous knowledge of "Snow White and the Seven Dwarves," using their own perspectives to determine the queen's character. What the three readings have in common, though, is the agency they bestow upon the queen and the complexity they note in the narrative. All three also note the connection and mirroring between the queen and the princess, particularly in the way they perform sexuality and resist patriarchal control. Law notes that "[b]oth the queen and her stepdaughter are women who attempt to control their fate in a patriarchal world" (190).

The gothic imagery in "Snow, Glass, Apples" underscores this connection, as it links the princess and the queen as distinctly, powerfully female, emphasizing sexuality and even childbirth. When the child first reveals her vampiric nature to the queen, the queen observes how her stepdaughter "sank her teeth into the base of my thumb, the Mound of Venus" (327). In palmistry, the fleshy part of the palm below the thumb is called the Mound of Venus, and it indicates love and passion. Not surprisingly, the Mound of Venus is also a term for female genitalia. Thus, Gaiman creates a sexual connection between the stepmother and her stepdaughter, but the language is also evocative of a nursing child: "[t]he little princess fastened her mouth to my hand and licked and sucked and drank" (327). Repeated mentions of the queen's Mound of Venus, which throbs whenever she is near the princess, evoke the pain of childbirth. Even the fact that the queen keeps Snow White's heart hung in the rafters of her bedroom is a warped sign of intimate, maternal connection.

Gothic descriptions of nakedness and menstruation also link the queen and the princess in their femininity. When the queen scries into her looking glass (a significant change from the original fairy tale, where the looking glass was a sentient patriarchal influence over the queen), she sees the princess suck the blood of a monk she has tricked in the forest and watches as "a thin blackish liquid began to dribble from between her legs" (332), evoking menstruation. When the queen creates the poison apple, she does so "naked ... and alone in the highest tower of the palace" (332), and when she delivers the apple, she encounters the princess emerging from a cave, also "naked and alone" (334). There is, again, a significant symbolism of birth in this encounter, as the queen notes "The scar on my Mound of Venus throbbed and pulsed as she came toward me, out of the darkness" (334). The princess emerges from a dark cave, symbolic of the vagina, naked and alone and eager to encounter her mother figure. Furthermore, the residue from the queen's witchcraft to conjure the apple is suggestive of the residue between the princess's legs: in a basin where the queen mixed the ingredients to create the poison, "[t]here was nothing left of my blood or of the brown powder . . . nothing save a black residue . . . on the inside" (333).

At the end of her life, the queen is again connected to the princess, this time when she looks at the young girl before the kiln door closes: "She looked at me," the queen notes, "and I saw myself reflected in her eyes" (339). Law and Slabbert offer interpretations of this quote, calling it "a changing of the guard" (Law 190), where a new queen must fight patriarchal dominance, and, in Slabbert's view, envisioning it as an admission that the queen is capable of the same kind of brutality as the princess. Both are fascinating interpretations and note the connection between the two characters, but I'd like to take it further and suggest that the quote is yet another reflection of gothic subversion at work. In addition to illustrating the inextricable link between the queen and the princess, it is also evidence of what Claire Kahane calls the "Gothic mirror," the reflection of child and mother that lies at the heart of gothic anxiety. As Kahane notes,

> the female child, who shares the female body and its symbolic place in our culture, remains locked in a . . . tenuous and fundamentally ambivalent struggle for a separate identity. This ongoing battle with a mirror image who is both self and other is . . . at the center of the Gothic structure, where boundaries break down, where life and death become confused, where images of birth and sexuality proliferate in complex displacements. (337)

Kahane, a feminist-psychoanalytic critic, explores how the female search for Self originates in the womb. The heroine must ultimately confront the mother in order to plumb the mysteries of being female and establish her own narrative. The gothic mirror in "Snow, Glass, Apples" actually subverts our expectations of the fairy tale, as the heroine here—the queen, in this telling—is the mother-figure herself, and she sees her reflection in the daughter-villain. The queen and the princess are *each* both Self and Other, both heroine and villain, reflecting, from a feminist standpoint, a binary cultural perception of women.

Of Spindles and Beauties Sleeping

In Gaiman's *The Sleeper and the Spindle,* the heroine *does* have to separate from her mother figure in order to achieve independence. *The Sleeper and the Spindle* is quite different in tone from "Snow, Glass, Apples," but it is also steeped in gothic elements, which support the subversion of Snow White as a gender-nonconforming heroine and which highlight the importance of the relationship between Snow White and her wicked stepmother. Unlike "Snow, Glass, Apples," which was intimate in its narration and centered on literally retelling a tale, *The Sleeper and the Spindle* features many of the trappings of the traditional literary fairy tale—a kingdom far, far away in a nonspecific time; a journey; a confrontation with something wicked. Gaiman still writes a postmodern fairy tale, though, with the intertextual twining of Snow White's and Sleeping Beauty's stories and unexpected endings to each. Gaiman draws extensively on narrative elements of Charles Perrault's "The Sleeping Beauty in the Wood," with a fairy's curse causing an extended sleep, folkloric rumors about the nature of the sleep and the castle, a battle with briars, and a confrontation with a witch. Yet despite the postmodern mash-up of the narratives, *The Sleeper and the Spindle* is Snow White's story.

The Snow White character in *The Sleeper and the Spindle* is complex and adult, bound by convention yet powerful enough to thwart it. She reads as a queer character, from the illustrations of her tall, angular body to the kiss she ultimately bestows on the sleeping beauty. Gaiman's story is set long after the events of "Snow White and The Seven Dwarves." Snow White is now queen of her own kingdom, and she is preparing to marry. The tale begins shortly before Snow White's wedding date, and the narrative comments on the patriarchal expectations of marriage reveal a cynical perspective. Musing about her impending nuptials, the queen notes "It would be the end of her life . . . if life was a time of choices. In a week from now, she would have no choices" (Gaiman, *Sleeper* 14). While she could die "in childbirth . . . , as an old woman, or in battle," marriage, according to the queen, marks the start of her death (14). As in the female gothic tradition, where marriage signals the woman becoming the property of the man and losing any sense of agency, Gaiman's contemporary retelling equates marriage with the relinquishing of control. Marriage, here, is not the start of a new journey, but rather a path to death, to the slow decay of a life well-lived.

Despite the conventions foisted upon her, Gaiman's young queen has more power than the traditional Snow White, and her power flouts gender norms. When the dwarves seek her counsel about a sleeping sickness that is creeping across kingdoms and causing everyone in its path to fall into a deep unconsciousness, she promptly calls off her wedding and dons her battle gear. As Snow White prepares for her departure, the narration reveals her command and control, repeating at the start of each sentence the phrase "She called for" (21). And when she calls for her fiancé, she "chuck[s] him beneath his pretty chin and kisse[s] him until he smile[s]" (21). The infantilization and feminization of the prince underscore Snow White's queerness, while the emphasis on her control of her kingdom reinforces the subversion of the gender norms that accompany traditional fairy tales. In this version of Snow White, Gaiman takes more of a third-wave girl-power feminist approach, but the gothic elements make this queen complex, connected to the narrative, and haunted by her past.

Indeed, Snow White's past is the reason the dwarves seek her out. "You slept for a year," points out one of the dwarves. "And then you woke again, none of the worse for it. If any of you big people can stay awake there, it's you" (20). Because of her past enchantment, Snow White is the one who might have the power to withstand this new plague. Furthermore, her experience with her wicked stepmother in the past allows her a unique insight into evil, which will come into play later in the story. In short, not just any fairy-tale heroine can complete this quest: it *has* to be Snow White, and it has to be this gothic Snow White.

Chris Riddell's illustrations highlight how very gothic this Snow White is, and how she is connected to the wicked queen who tormented her in the past. In her first illustration, she appears as a sullen young woman awakening in her castle chambers. Her hair is long and black, Morticia-like (if one recalls *The Addams Family*), and her blanket is patterned with skulls. A wooden-carved face with a gaping mouth yawns above her pillow, and thorny vines, suggestive of barbed wire, crawl up one wall. Strange ornaments hang from her bed canopy: pouches and potions and what appears to be an effigy with a ragdoll face. These hanging elements are reminiscent of the queen's chambers in "Snow, Glass, Apples," where the queen hung garlic, dried apples, and, of course, Snow White's bloody heart, inviting further intertextual connections between this new Snow White and the wicked queen.

And yet these gothic elements in Snow White's chambers also invoke a more innocent type of horror, the kind that accompanies Edward Gorey's images, Tim Burton's *The Nightmare Before Christmas*, and the illustrations in Gaiman's *Coraline* (by Riddell). Riddell's rendering of Snow White's wedding dress is adorned with a sharply pointed collar, while bell sleeves end in a ragged hem. The pattern of both the collar and the hem are repeated several pages later in the spider webs that drape the sleeping townsfolk, again connecting marriage to living death. The illustrations also reveal a childlike side to Snow White herself while also showing the first hint of gender reversal: tossed carelessly in the corner is Snow White's armor, boots, and sword (whose handle is topped with another skull). This two-page illustration of Snow White and her living quarters characterizes the heroine, hints at her upcoming journey, and links her to forthcoming events. She is positioned as both strong and vulnerable, characteristics that will be highlighted further when she reaches the tower in which Sleeping Beauty is imprisoned.

Those characteristics are highlighted along her journey, as well. Throughout her trek with the dwarves, Snow White is surrounded by memory, which she must literally push through. In a gothic haunting, the sleepers who populate the towns whisper, creating a ghostly echo chamber of the lines Sleeping Beauty uttered as a child right before she pricked her finger. The sleepers are active, too, turning their heads to follow Snow White and her companions as they move past them, while the language of the text conjures images of slow-moving horror-movie zombies: "They stumble, they stagger, they move . . . like old people whose feet are weighed down by thick, wet mud" (Gaiman, *Sleeper* 35). The zombie-like nature of the sleepers signifies the memories of not only the trapped Sleeping Beauty, but also of Snow White's own history.

As Snow White slogs onward through the fog of sleeping sickness, she is haunted by memories of her stepmother: she walks through a forest, which "was filled with people she knew could not be there. They walked beside her on the path. Sometimes they spoke to her" (41). The stepmother's lines to Snow White and accompanying narration are particularly intertextual, linking her to all wicked stepmothers and to the original Grimm tale:

> "My sisters ruled the world," said her stepmother, dragging her iron shoes along the forest path. They glowed a dull orange, yet none of the dry leaves burned where the shoes touched them. "The mortal folk rose up against us, they cast us down. And so we waited, in crevices, in places where they do not see us. And now, they adore me. Even you, my stepdaughter. Even you adore me." (41)

The "sisters" refer to all wicked stepmothers and evil queens, creating a fairy-tale community of characters, while the glowing-hot shoes that do not smolder evince the gothic fascination with reality mixed with fantasy. The "crevices" even evoke "Snow, Glass, Apples," where the vampiric Snow White took up residence in a cave. And the adoration makes the heroine Snow White complicit in the wicked queen's machinations.

An illustration on the same page reinforces this connection between Snow White and stepmother. The image shows the king, the wicked queen, and Snow White in a vertical arrangement, with the king relegated to the corner, his eyes heavy-lidded, equating him with the zombie-sleepers—he is tangential to the real relationship between Snow White and her stepmother. In the illustration, the queen wears a horned headpiece similar to that of Maleficent in Disney's animated *Sleeping Beauty*, while Snow White wears her armor and skull accoutrements. Again, the skulls connect Snow White to the gothic, but they also connect her to the other wicked woman in this new tale, the witch who enchanted Sleeping Beauty's castle.

The Sleeping Beauty character in Gaiman's tale is a particularly gothic subject, trapped in a tower, but not, as we might expect, the one sleeping. In this story, it's actually the evil witch who sleeps, regenerating her beauty over sixty years, while the original Briar Rose has aged and become decrepit. A skull motif in the illustrations accompanies the unconscious witch, from a skeleton trapped in the vines and thorns around the castle to the ornate headboard of the sleeper's bed, where skulls bloom from more thorny vines. And like Snow White's own bedspread, the sleeper's blanket is patterned with skulls.

Snow White kisses the sleeper awake and quickly grasps the meaning of the dark magic she senses in the room: "The queen looked at the girl, and saw what she was searching for: the same look that she had seen in her stepmother's eyes, and she knew what manner of creature this girl was" (Gaiman, *Sleeper* 54). "What manner of creature" directly echoes the queen's first line in "Snow, Glass, Apples," "I do not know what manner of thing she is" (Gaiman, "Snow, Glass" 325), but this time, the heroine does know because of her own experience with this manner of creature in the past. As the awakened witch tempts Snow White with promises of power in return for adoration, Snow White recalls her stepmother: "Her stepmother had liked to be adored. Learning how to be strong, to feel her own emotions and not another's, had been hard; but once you learned the trick of it, you did not forget" (Gaiman, *Sleeper* 59). Here, the gothic haunting empowers Snow White, allowing her to reject the witch's promises and then empower Briar Rose to destroy the witch.

There is no real happy ending here, though. Briar Rose does not get her youth back. She does get to rest, lying down on her bed, where the skulls have now transformed to roses. That roses accompany Sleeping Beauty and skulls accompany Snow White further reinforces that the connection in this tale lies between mother-figure and daughter-figure, not between fairy tale princesses. And in the last illustration that features Sleeping Beauty, the old woman rests peacefully surrounded by roses, but in the corner, a skull remains, draped in cobwebs, as a gothic reminder of the traumatic past.

Snow White still has one more journey to embark upon, prompted by her experience with the witch. As she burns the witch's remains, she considers her choices, and she decides not to return to her kingdom and to marriage. She abandons her mantle of queen, instead venturing into the unknown with the dwarves by her side. *The Sleeper and the Spindle* ends with the beginning of a new journey, and the last illustration features Snow White and the dwarves in shadow, small against the landscape, weapons drawn. A dragon with a steer in its grip flies overhead, a reminder of the dangers that lie ahead and of the inevitability of death. Now, though, Snow White can choose her own path to death, instead of being locked into marriage, obligation, and tradition.

Conclusions

In her most recent book on fairy tales, Cristina Bacchilega considers how today's fairy-tale revisions provide a space for new transformations, transformations that readers can "anticipate/fear/desire" (*Fairy Tales* 7). Anticipation, fear, and desire are all factors of the gothic, which itself transforms the fairy tale and provides new avenues for contemporary revisions. Fairy-tale adaptations in the twenty-first century are inevitably more complex than ever before, haunted as they are by the numerous adaptations that came before them, by historical context, by the first literary fairy tales, and by centuries of tale-telling. But those hauntings enrich today's fairy tales, and, in the case of Gaiman's Snow White retellings, enrich the heroines themselves. By using the gothic to link familiar heroines and villains and blur the boundaries between them, Gaiman extends traditional literary fairy tales into complicated quests for agency and provocative musings on the nature of truth. Furthermore, the shift in Gaiman's approach to Snow White mirrors a larger cultural transformation that demands increasingly complex narrative roles for women. To suggest a possible answer to a central question in Bacchilega's recent work, "What are the stakes of adapting the fairy tale in the early twenty-first century?" (*Fairy Tales* 7), I look again to the gothic. Just as the gothic dwells on the past in order to parse the present, contemporary fairy tales also have to pull from the past and point to the future, offering new transformations that speak to contemporary concerns. While Gaiman's 1994 Snow White was powerfully villainous and unapologetically grotesque, his 2015 Snow White embodies a post-Katniss feminine essence of toughness coupled with vulnerability. *The Sleeper and the Spindle*, while gothic and subversive, is empowering, revealing to readers that, as Snow White thinks to herself, "There are always choices" (66). Gaiman's twenty-first-century Snow White revision maintains the complicated network between stepmother and stepdaughter that "Snow, Glass, Apples" explores, but it offers the beginning of a new journey instead of the end of one. In the landscape of twenty-first-century fairy tale adaptations, Gaiman's postmodern gothic acknowledges the importance of past iterations of stories and looks to future possibilities.

Works Cited

Bacchilega, Cristina. *Fairy Tales Transformed? Twenty-First-Century Adaptations and the Politics of Wonder.* Detroit, MI: Wayne State UP, 2013. Print.

———. *Postmodern Fairy Tales: Gender and Narrative Strategies.* Philadelphia: U of Pennsylvania P, 1997. Print.

Bobby, Susan Redington. Introduction. *Fairy Tales Reimagined: Essays on New Retellings.* Jefferson, NC: McFarland & Company, Inc., 2009. 5-12. Print.

Gaiman, Neil. "Snow, Glass, Apples." *Smoke and Mirrors*. New York: William Morrow, 1998. Print.

_____. *The Sleeper and the Spindle*. Illus. Chris Riddell. New York: Harper, 2015. Print.

Hogle, Jerrold E. "Introduction: the Gothic in western culture." *The Cambridge Companion to Gothic Fiction*. Ed. Jerrold E. Hogle. Cambridge: Cambridge UP, 2002. 1-20. Cambridge Companions to Literature. Print.

Jackson, Anna, Karen Coats, & Roderick McGillis. Introduction. *The Gothic in Children's Literature: Haunting the Borders*. Ed. Anna Jackson, Karen Coats, & Roderick McGillis. New York: Routledge, 2007. 1-14. Children's Literature and Culture 43. Print.

Kahane, Claire. "The Gothic Mirror." *The (M)Other Tongue: Essays in Feminist Psychoanalytic Interpretation*. Ed. Shirley Nelson Garner, Claire Kahane, & Madelon Sprengnether. Ithaca, NY: Cornell UP, 1985. 334-351. Print.

Klapcsik, Sándor. "The Double-edged Nature of Neil Gaiman's Ironical Perspectives and Liminal Fantasies." *Journal of the Fantastic in the Arts* 20.2 (2009): 193-209. *Gale*. Web. 6 Aug. 2016.

Law, Elizabeth. "The Fairest of All: Snow White and Gendered Power in 'Snow, Glass, Apples.'" *Feminism in the Worlds of Neil Gaiman: Essays on the Comics, Poetry and Prose*. Ed. Tara Prescott & Aaron Drucker. Jefferson, NC: McFarland & Company, Inc., 2012. 1-8. Print.

McGillis, Roderick. "The Night Side of Nature: Gothic Spaces, Fearful Times." *The Gothic in Children's Literature: Haunting the Borders*. Ed. Anna Jackson, Karen Coats, & Roderick McGillis. New York: Routledge, 2007. 227-241. Children's Literature and Culture 43. Print.

Prescott, Tara & Aaron Drucker. Preface and Introduction. *Feminism in the Worlds of Neil Gaiman: Essays on the Comics, Poetry and Prose*. Jefferson, NC: McFarland & Company, Inc., 2012. 1-8. Print.

Slabbert, Mathilda. "Inventions and Transformations: Imagining New Worlds in the Stories of Neil Gaiman." *Fairy Tales Reimagined: Essays on New Retellings*. Jefferson, NC: McFarland & Company, Inc., 2009. 68-83. Print.

Spooner, Catherine & Emma McEvoy. Introduction. *The Routledge Companion to Gothic*. New York: Routledge, 2007. 1-3. Print.

Tatar, Maria. *Secrets beyond the Door*. Princeton, NJ: Princeton UP, 2004. Print.

"Everybody's Here": Radical Reflexivity in the Metafiction of *The Sandman*

Orion Ussner Kidder

There is a moment near the end of Neil Gaiman's *The Sandman* when all the barriers between the world inside the book and the world outside of it completely dissolve, when there is, suddenly and shockingly, no way to say where one ends and the other begins. Two short, simple sentences in the shocking second-person, coupled with a perspective shift between two panels, creates this singular moment of radical metafictional collapse: "Everybody's here. You're here" (Gaiman, *S* 71: 1). To understand that moment, however, critics have to understand it as it occurs within the grand sweep of Gaiman's epic series. It happens near the end of the series, after five years of comics in which the audience has built a long-standing emotional relationship with this imperious, inflexible aspect of Dream called "Morpheus," and it happens immediately after he has died. To understand how the series creates that moment, though, we will first need to understand how metafiction works, so that is where we will start.

Metafiction and Meaning

Metafiction was studied intensely in the 1980s and 1990s, largely in connection to postmodernism and poststructuralism, and this chapter relies on a lot of that research, specifically from the critics Linda Hutcheon, Patricia Waugh, and W. J. T. Mitchell. First, though, M. Thomas Inge's "Form and Function in the Metacomics" offers a very common-sense concept of metafiction, that it "suspend[s] our belief in the reality of the fiction" (1); i.e., it is the *suspension of belief*. Matthew T. Jones defines metafiction using similar terms, claiming that it "thwart[s] the suspension of disbelief by calling attention to the illusion upheld by convention and narrative structure" (284). Suspension of disbelief has become the standard expectation of how fiction is expected to work. It comes from Samuel Taylor Coleridge, who claims that his fantastical poems in the *Lyrical Ballads* are designed to "procure . . . that willing suspension of disbelief for the moment, which constitutes poetic faith" (Ch XIV, para. 3). Metafiction, then, does the opposite. It presumes that suspending disbelief is actually habitual, something we do dozens of times a day without much conscious thought, and provokes poetic skepticism to counteract that habit. That is where Inge and Jones intervene, implying that disbelief, not belief, is what truly requires effort: stopping oneself from believing every little thing one sees or hears out of sheer habit. From this perspective, belief is easy; disbelief is hard.

Most theories of metafiction tend to describe it as 1. self-referential (i.e., the element that provokes skepticism) and 2. reflexive (provoking that skepticism for a specific or determined effect). Reflexivity also contains a double-meaning, referring both to visible reflections and contemplation of oneself. Patricia Waugh's *Metafiction*, for example, claims that metafiction is "[a] self-consciously and systematically draws attention to its status as an artifact in order to [b] posit questions about the relationship between fiction and reality" (2). Linda Hutcheon's *Poetics of Postmodernism* defines historiographic metafiction in terms that are less easy to separate, but the structure is still there: "Fiction and history are narratives distinguished by their frames . . . which [a] historiographic metafiction first establishes and then crosses, [b] positing both the generic contracts of fiction and history" (109-110). W. J. T. Mitchell's *Picture Theory*, which describes metapictures not metafiction, says they "[a] show themselves in order to [b] know themselves: they stage the 'self-knowledge' of pictures" (48). There are others that have the same structure, but these three are the most useful for understanding Gaiman's *Sandman* in terms of metafiction. Self-referentiality, then, is the hand that points to itself, and reflexivity is the meaning that emerges from the gesture. When we look at *Sandman* as metafiction, then, it is vital to have a system to determine what it means just in case it does not mean anything at all because some gestures are meaningless. Waugh, Hutcheon, and Mitchell, between them, constitute that system.

Waugh and Hutcheon both discuss metafiction in terms of literary frames. Within their theories, poetic skepticism is anything that makes readers aware of the frames that surround the text, which is colloquially called *breaking the frame*. Waugh describes frame breaks as "the construction of an illusion through the imperceptibility of the frame and the shattering of [that] illusion through the constant exposure to the frame" (31). In essence, fiction frames are invisible by default but necessary as a way to contain the fiction, so revealing their existence can destroy them, but it does not have to. There is, instead, a spectrum of possibilities. She proposes "two poles of metafiction: one that finally accepts a substantial real world . . . and one that suggests there can never be an escape from the prisonhouse of language" (Waugh 53). The first, structural reflexivity, functions at the level of literary conventions such as genres, modes, and tropes. The second, radical reflexivity, functions at the level of language itself, here understood in semiotic terms as any systematic expression of ideas, which very much includes comics. Structural reflexivity might disrupt one's poetic faith in the *form* of the text whereas the radical might disrupt one's faith in *reality itself* by demonstrating that language is actually meaningless, an epistemic problem at least and possibly even an ontological problem. There are many possibilities within those two extremes, but *The Sandman* uses two specific kinds of effects that Waugh identifies.

In *The Sandman*, structural effects reveal the frame but work very hard to preserve it, and radical effects threaten to destroy the frames that separate stories, but one particular radical moment utterly obliterates the frame between reader and text. Charles Hatfield's *Alternative Comics* identifies a specific kind of structural effect that *Sandman* employs. He calls it "authentication through artifice, or more simply ironic authentication: the implicit reinforcement of truth claims through their explicit rejection" (Hatfield 125). It seems to be a quirk of the human mind that we are often more convinced by something that admits that it is lying than something that insists that it is telling the truth. Radical metafiction, on the other hand, violates, penetrates, or collapses the frame in such a way that the borders between textual worlds disappear, and/or the audience's world no longer holds privileged status as "real" because language has proved to be meaningless. *The Sandman*'s radical effect is what Waugh identifies as a paradox, which "offer[s] a finite statement that only infinity can resolve" (141). The text makes an explicit claim that is true by virtue of being false and false by virtue of being true. Hutcheon, on the other hand, reveals that there is an inherent contradiction within metafiction, and in the process, corroborates Waugh's position.

Hutcheon defines a type of novel called historiographic metafiction, which "both install[s] and then blur[s] the lines [i.e., frames] between fiction and history" (113). What that means is that historiographic metafiction "depends upon and draws its power from that which it contests" (Hutcheon 120). Hutcheon calls this "a strange kind of critique, one bound up, too, with its own complicity" (4). In the case of metafiction, that means that to break a frame, the text has to build one first. To simply *not* build a frame would not be a critique; it would be some other kind of fiction. By this logic, it is the nature of metafiction to be complicit in what it critiques, so we cannot regard complicity as failure. A metafiction that appears to rely, for example, on suspension of disbelief to mount an attack on suspension of disbelief is not automatically disqualified from being metafiction. This commentary demonstrates that destroying the frame—obliterating the separation between fiction and reality—is not the by-definition goal of metafiction but rather one of the many possible outcomes, a principle that will be useful when we look at the specific limits of the commentary offered by *The Sandman*. Waugh and Hutcheon (with help from Inge, Jones, and Hatfield) thus form a basic approach to metafiction, but comics are a combined medium—text and images—so a composite way of looking at metapictures is also necessary.

W. J. T. Mitchell asserts that metapictures are pictures that reveal the nature of pictures. He defines five specific subtypes of metapictures, and two of them are useful for looking at *Sandman*: talking pictures and multistable images. Talking pictures employ combinations of pictures and words that reveal how pictures and words function, sometimes quite differently and sometimes with remarkable parallels. Mitchell's example of a prototypical talking picture is Réné Magritte's "The Treason of Images," which offers a photorealistic image of a smoking pipe with the caption *"ceci n'est pas une pipe"* ("this is not a pipe"). This talking picture demonstrates an image that lies. It pretends to be a pipe when it is really just a drawing of a pipe. Mitchell emphasizes, though, that it is a perfectly coherent drawing of a pipe, so warning the viewer is unnecessary, even pedantic. Ultimately, then, both assertions are true. Yes, of course, it is a pipe. But, of course, it is not actually a pipe. This interaction of word and image to create paradox is exactly what occurs in *The Sandman*, but there is one further kind of metapicture that helps explain it, what Mitchell calls a *multistable image*.

Mitchell's example of multistability is a figure called "the duck-rabbit," a drawing that looks like a rabbit and a duck, depending on what the viewer chooses to see, which is why he calls it is multistable. Again, there is a common conception and a more subtle one, just as with "Treason." The common conception is that a viewer can look at the duck-rabbit as either a duck or a rabbit. Mitchell argues, however, that it is actually a perfectly stable image of a third thing that "looks like nothing else but itself" (52-53): a duck-rabbit. The proof is that not all drawings of ducks look like rabbits, and not all drawings of rabbits look like ducks. The duck-rabbit is a specific entity that lives only on the page. Thus, multistable images reveal that drawings themselves are two-dimensional illusions of three-dimensional reality because in reality, there are ducks and there are rabbits, but only a flat image can be a duck-rabbit. For Mitchell, that lesson is the point of the duck-rabbit, but the concept of multistability is vital to understanding metafiction because, as Hutcheon argues, it has to build its own frames in order to then reveal them or tear them down, so most if not all metafiction is ultimately multistable because it has to start as a stable construction in order to, as Jones put it, thwart suspension of disbelief. That is to say, to reveal its trickery, it first has to trick you. Multistable images, specifically, are visual paradoxes because their stability is the product of their instability and vice-versa, a quality that we will see in *The Sandman*, as well. The series uses talking pictures and multistability in its singular moment of radical reflexivity, but that moment is a product of events that occur earlier in the series, in *The Doll's House* (vol. 2) and of the situation surrounding that singular moment in *The Wake* (vol. 10).

The Doll's House: Structural Metafiction

The events of *The Doll's House* both set up and anticipate many of the larger plot points of the series, including Morpheus' eventual death. However, the important element for my purposes is the fact that Morpheus fights against a radical metafictional collapse, and that in the last few pages of the final issue of the volume, Rose Walker (a human) and Desire (one of Morpheus' immortal siblings) both come very close to seeing the frames that contain them, but then deny that discovery because acknowledging it would compromise their ability to function in their respective contexts. This revelation and then dismissal provokes poetic skepticism and constitutes a structural frame-break.

Rose peers past the surface of her reality when Morpheus mistakes her for a "vortex," which "by its nature, destroys the barriers between dreaming minds . . . Until all the dreams are one. Then the vortex collapses in upon itself. And then it . . . takes the minds of the dreamers with it" (Gaiman, *S* 17: 5). This description strongly resembles Waugh's radical metafiction in which frames collapse and nothing is kept separate, and even by this early point in the series, it has become clear that dreams, in *Sandman*, stand quite directly for stories. Morpheus asserts that "It is one of my functions to prevent this [the results of the vortex] from occurring again" (17: 5), but the only way he knows how to do that is to kill Rose Walker, and both of those story elements are, of course, invented for the sake of plot. However, Unity Kincaid, Rose's grandmother, is the actual vortex, and once she realizes it, she sacrifices herself to save Rose. The climax of the narrative, then, is a brave sacrifice that *prevents* radical metafictional collapse. The frames are made visible, but they remain quite stable. This is quite the opposite of a radical metafiction. Gaiman builds Morpheus' universe, what film criticism calls the *diegesis*, to reflect his character, which in this case means pitting him against a threat that takes the form of what he hates: the absence of structure, of containment, of frames.

Rose experiences Morpheus' threats to kill her and her grandmother's sacrifice as a dream, but a dream that disturbs her sense of reality and that she interprets in metafictional terms. Issue #17, "Calliope," includes excerpts from Rose's diary:

> If my dream was true, then everything we know, everything we think, is a lie . . . we just kid ourselves that we're in control of our lives while a paper's thickness away things that would drive us mad if we thought about them for too long play with us. . . . (Gaiman, *S* 17: 18-19)

Within the story, these "things" are Morpheus and his kind, but in metafictional terms, they refer to both the creators of the series and, implicitly, the readers who are "a paper's thickness away" and delight in her struggle. However, Rose later emphatically rejects the very idea that she is manipulated by outside forces and wills herself to believe in her own agency: "My dream. My weird dream. <u>It was just a dream</u>. / That's all. Just a dream" (Gaiman, *S* 17: 19, underlining in original). She even uses quotation marks within her own statement and speaks of herself in the third person, as if narrating: "'And then she woke up'" (19). She becomes her own storyteller in order retake control of her life, which ironically emphasizes her ontological dilemma of living in a radical universe.

Just a few pages later, in a parallel scene, Morpheus attempts to explain this same awareness to Desire, but in inverted terms. Where Rose perceives herself as a plaything of supernatural/metatextual agents, Morpheus sees himself and his kin, the Endless, as the product of human imagination: "We of the endless . . . exist because they [mortals] know, deep in their hearts, that we exist . . . we do not manipulate them. If anything, they manipulate us. We are their toys" (Gaiman, *S* 17: 23). Morpheus is comfortable with this conception of his diegesis because, as the King of Dreams, his insight extends specifically into the nature of perception, and he quite literally lives in a realm partially ruled by mortal imagination. However, Desire's nature as a manipulator of human agency will not allow him-her to see her-himself as subject to anyone else's will: "Human beings are the creatures of desire. They twist and bend as I require it. If I thought otherwise, I would crack . . . or I would abandon my realm"

(24). Desire cannot conceive of a metafictional universe because Desire could not function in one, psychologically or practically. Therefore, all three of these characters reject radical metafiction, choosing instead stable narrative frames and (the illusion of) self-determination. Rose and Desire willfully ignore the evidence that they live in a radical universe, and Morpheus makes the choice that is required of him to save the Dreaming, the series' most potent, direct representation of storytelling itself. The text reveals the narrative's frames in order to emphasize how vital they are for both sanity and safety. That is structural metafiction, but the very next issue will start to push the series towards the radical.

A Dream of a Thousand Cats: A Radical Universe

Despite how its characters sometimes behave, *Sandman* takes place in a universe that is much closer to the radical end of the spectrum than the structural. Morpheus clearly asserts that mortals define his reality by their collective belief in *The Doll's House*, but the series immediately makes good on that assertion in #18, "A Dream of a Thousand Cats." It demonstrates that the reality in the text can be completely altered based on collective will, so at any given moment, enough people changing their beliefs can change the world around them. The issue plays out this implication when a young house cat seeks out Dream, perceiving him as a great black tom with stars in its eyes, and he explains that there was a time when huge house cats ruled the world, kept humans as servants during the day, and hunted them for pleasure at night. However, enough humans deliberately dreamed of a reality in which they were the dominant species and cats were small that the humans changed reality. Morpheus explains that "They dreamed the world so it *always was* the way it is now, little one. There never *was* a world of high cat-ladies and cat-lords. They changed the universe from the beginning of all things until the end of time" (Gaiman, *S* 18: 19). This effect strongly resembles what is called retroactive continuity, or "retcon," in American superhero comics, which is when a new story retells a previously published story but changes the details and claims it was always that way. It writes over the previous version. What that means is that "A Dream of a Thousand Cats" is, in part, a sly wink at fans who are fully aware of the practice. Of course, it is more than that, too. The cats believes that, through collective action, they might be able to change the world back, but at the end of the story a brown tom laments: "I would like to see *anyone*—prophet, king or *god*—persuade a thousand cats to do *anything* at the same time" (23). This is the punch line of the story, of course, a joke about the solitary and willful nature of cats, but it also voices the very same ontological conundrum that Waugh expresses when she describes radical metafiction.

If reality is a construct of perception (i.e., language), then it is mutable, but to actually manipulate it—to arrange for enough people to alter their perceptions so that they might collectively alter their reality—requires a herculean effort. Shifting the perceptions of an entire culture, for example, is no easy task, and it usually happens only over a great deal of time. In this theory of reality, matter, the world around us, has a direct effect on lived human experience. Mind, the conceptual structures by which we navigate and perceive the material world, is not above or superior to matter. Recognizing their mutual influence reveals how contingent both are and shows us how they are constructed, but it also suspends our ability to conceive of either one as fully stable. Instead, mind and matter are multistable, as in Mitchell's formulation. Alternatively, within Hutcheon's model, metafiction "openly assert[s] that there are only truths in the plural, and never one Truth" (*Poetics* 109-110), so we have matter truths (literal) and mind truths (fictional). Taken together, Mitchell, Hutcheon, and "A Dream of a Thousand Cats," imply that the important question to ask is not *what is true?* but rather *whose truth dominates? Whose truth manages to define reality?* This is a radical metafictional way of looking at the world, specifically *The Sandman's* diegesis, and it prefigures the singular moment that occurs in issue #71, but we need to understand the emotional context of that moment to fully appreciate it.

The Wake: Radical Metafictional Collapse
Gaiman helpfully summarizes the overarching plot of *The Sandman* in the introduction to *Sandman: Endless Nights*, published seven

years later: "The Lord of Dreams learns that one must change or die, and makes his decision" (*Endless Nights* 8). Morpheus, in fact, decides that he must die in order to change. He wants to shed his rigidity, which is very much on display in *The Doll's House*, but that very same rigidity prevents him from changing, so he commits an elaborate form of suicide, at which point he is immediately replaced by another version of himself. This death and rebirth creates a multistable entity. The reborn version asserts "I am Dream of the Endless" (Gaiman, *S* 70:12), and to make the point clear, he even claims rights within a contract signed by Morpheus, but he also asserts that he is "Not Morpheus" and "has no right to that name" (13). He has all of Dream's memories and power, but where Morpheus was dispassionate and rule-bound, he is compassionate and gentle; for example, he returns Abel to life (13). He likewise shifts visually from black-haired and black-garbed with white-on-black speech balloons, to the opposite: white hair and white clothing with black-on-white speech. The other characters in the series know full well that his death is not "real," but they mourn just the same. The audience, which is fully aware that Morpheus is fictional, also mourns the death of a character with whom they have lived for ten volumes of comics and possibly seven years of continuous publication. There is no body to mourn within the text—in an elaborate sequence of panels, they lay a shroud over empty space that takes the shape of a body (Gaiman, *S* 72: 4)—and they cannot lament his actual absence because a version of Dream still lives. The audience has no body to mourn either, except in the metaphorical sense of a body of literature, a corpus. Dream is also still available at any time because that audience can go back and re-read the series, just as in the text, the new Dream is literally a short walk away. Holding a wake makes no practical sense, then, either inside the story or from the audience's perspective. It makes perfect emotional sense, however, because this person that the characters and the audience knows has come to the end of his life. At his wake, Dream becomes demonstrably multistable—dead because he chose to live, alive because he has died; emotionally real because of the impact of his fiction, necessarily fictional for his story to work.

Given that the entity called "Dream" cannot die, as opposed to the specific instance of it called "Morpheus," and has already reappeared by the time of his own funeral, the question is asked at his wake: "*What* died? *Who* are you mourning?" The answer is a "point of view" (Gaiman, *S* 71: 4), which shows exactly the kinds of paradoxically literal explanations that metafiction can sometimes offer. Morpheus is not a person, but instead an "idea [. . .] cloaked in the semblance of flesh" (Gaiman, *S* 21,10), a description that readily applies to fictional characters as well, especially ones depicted visually on a comic-book page. His experiences cannot be directly compared to human experience, of course, because even within the text, he is not exactly real, so Morpheus is doubly fictitious; for the real-world audience, he is a character in a comic book, and in his reality, he is a figment of human imagination. He cannot die, so his funeral is a sham, in a sense. Much like Magritte's "Treason," he is, *of course*, not really dead. But of course, he *is* really dead because despite shifting between many different appearances—pale man in black, African god, black tomcat, and a dozen different artists' interpretations—Morpheus also has a recognizable personality that makes him different than his successor. Within the text, the part of Dream that dies *is* a point of view. Point of view is the sense of identity that arises from experience, from looking at the world from a particular perspective. Thus, any death, of a fictional character or a flesh-and-blood person—or even a fictional personification of the human capacity for imagination—is the loss of a point of view. That is what we mourn at every funeral: a perspective, a subject, a particular articulation of individuality and context. Through metacomic awareness, *The Sandman* offers an extremely literal definition of identity and an explanation of why and what we grieve.

Morpheus' death also parallels the knowledge that *The Sandman* series was coming to an end. At the time of publication, it was known that Gaiman intended to end the series, and the end of a narrative is itself a kind of death, the death of a story, but like Morpheus' death-that-is-not-quite-death, stories cannot die unless they are forgotten. In a literal sense, the story of *Sandman* cannot die even when Morpheus does. It continues for another three issues in which he appears, and DC Comics has published three more volumes of *Sandman* comics written by Gaiman: *Dream Hunters* (1999), *Endless Nights* (2003), and *Overture* (2013–15). From one perspective, these follow-up books might seem like crass attempts to cash in on the immense success of *The Sandman* series, and that profit motive certainly exists—DC Comics would not have produced them without it—but the follow-up books are also consistent with the metacomic nature of the series. Morpheus is a fictional character. He can live and die at the whim of publishers and creators. The audience is, then, reading a simulated wake for a doubly-fictional character who can reappear any time the creator (and publisher) have a mind to do so. The character is, then, multistable in yet another way: finite and infinite. From within this churn of audience emotions and narrative facts, the series contrives a powerfully radical moment.

The Sandman's singular moment of radical metafiction is engineered from a combination of second-person narration, self-reflexive imagery, and panel transition. The first two issues of *The Wake* (#70 and #71) employ highly descriptive, third-person narration. There is, however, an abrupt change at the beginning of #71 that persists until the end of the wake itself. In #70, the audience witnesses Dream's wake in the third-person omniscient mode, jumping from place to place as the attendants gather to mourn, but the opening page of #71 informs the reader that she is, in fact, one of the attendants: "They wait awkwardly, shuffling and making small-talk, in the wasteland that was once the heart of the Dreaming. Everybody's here. You're here" (Gaiman, *S* 71: 1). This "you" means that the reader must be one of the dreamers, and by this point the series has thoroughly associated dreaming, imagining, and storytelling. It is implicitly in the singular, as well, given that comics are experienced in isolation rather than groups, so it is not that "you" are part of an anonymous crowd. "You" are there by "yourself." Zulli's art reproduces this second-person singular effect in a talking-picture effect. The first panel mirrors the third-person narrator voice by showing the visible characters from behind and displaying no awareness of a viewer's presence, but then the second panel reverses perspective and depicts several characters looking directly at the viewer. The symbolism of word and image is inescapable: all of *Sandman* is a dream *and* a story, so of course "You're here." "You" are as "here" as there is a "here" to be in. Morpheus' wake has no other "here" than this dream and this dream has no other "here" than issue #71 of the DC/Vertigo comic-book series called *The Sandman*, as written by Neil Gaiman, illustrated by Michael Zulli, and read by "you." This moment exemplifies Waugh's radical metafiction because the diegesis and the reader's world collapse into each other, but both remain equally viable, equally stable, so it also exemplifies Mitchell's conception of multistability. Understood in these metafictional terms, this use of the shocking second-person displays how representation can be fashioned to express a statement that is both literally true and utterly preposterous: "You're here."

The narrative conceit of the Dreaming, a radical space if there ever was one as well as being the place where the wake occurs, also displays both Hatfield's ironic authentication and Hutcheon's complicit critique. The Dreaming helps the radical moment, "You're here," to take place because it provides a very literal explanation for what would otherwise be only a symbolic assertion. That is to say, it provides the "here." It also accounts for the necessary deletions that any narrative must make in order to move the story along. Exact details of every moment of the wake do not appear in the book because "we need not recount every sermon and eulogy. After all, you were there. You may have forgotten in your waking hours, what you heard that day, but you will remember it, in the soft, lost, slumbering moments between waking and true sleep" (Gaiman, *S* 72: 15). Finally, although *The Wake* continues through issues #73 to #75, which ends the series as a whole, #72 closes the plot with the words "and then . . . you woke up" (24), which emphasizes the idea that the wake itself has been a dream and, by extension, so has the whole series. It is worth noting the obvious parallel between this statement and the final soliloquy of *A Midsummer Nights Dream* in which the audience has "but slumbered here / While these visions did appear" (5.1.16-17), a play that *Sandman* dedicates an entire issue to (#19, "A Midsummer Night's Dream"). Gaiman's gesture is the very same as Shakespeare's, then: gently shaking the audience awake after an extended vision of another world.

This direct assertion that the series has been a dream acts like ironic authentication because anyone who has been paying attention will recognize that it is a cheat, a way of skipping over the boring parts of the story, but as long as the audience is in on the joke, because they have learned the rules of the Dreaming as presented in the story thus far, they are likely to go along with it, even feel charmed by it. The first three issues of *The Wake* thus take on the subjective impression of a dream, and asserting the audience's literal presence within the diegesis as well as the not-totally-knowable nature of the Dreaming renders that diegesis more convincing in the process. It is ironic authentication because it relies on the audience to buy into the fantastical rules of the story to begin with, so the critique—that "here" is a place that exists in the text and nowhere else—is complicit in exactly the kind of narrative rigidity that *Sandman* is speaking against. That is, that the very existence of that "here" is a product of poetic *faith*, not poetic skepticism. Ultimately, *Sandman* never sits still, never settles into a stable diegesis, because it both presents familiar narrative beats—beginning, middle, and end—but also calls into question not only the nature of those beats but the nature of fiction as allegedly not real in comparison to the ostensible reality outside of the text.

Metafiction theory offers a number of ways to understand the complex, reflexive moves that *Sandman* makes. It reveals the frame and breaks it; it is necessarily complicit in its critiques; and it creates multistable effects and conjures paradoxes. Its characters fight for stability, defending the integrity of their narrative frames with their lives even though they demonstrably live in a radical universe, one where the frames are ultimately permeable, capable of disappearing under just the right circumstances. By asserting the simple fact, at a crucial moment, that the reader *is* in the text, *The Sandman* ties the audience's intimate familiarity with a fictional character to their emotional reaction to his death as well as their awareness that the character is not really real even though he is also quite real and not really dead even though he is absolutely dead. The result is, as Waugh defines it, that *Sandman* radically destabilizes the frames that separate narrative and reality, fiction and truth.

Works Cited

Coleridge, Samuel Taylor. *Biographica Literaria*. 1817. *Project Gutenberg*. Jul. 2004. Web. 25 Aug. 2016.

Gaiman, Neil. *Sandman Special: The Song of Orpheus*. Illus. Bryan Talbot, Mark Buckingham, Dave McKean et al. Ed. Karen Berger. New York: Vertigo (DC Comics), March 1999. Print.

_____. *Sandman, The* 1–75. Illus. Alec Stevens, Chris Bachalo et al. Ed. Shelly Roeberg (ed). New York: DC Comics, January 1989–March 1996. Print.

_____. *Sandman, The: Endless Nights*. Illus. Dave McKean et al. Ed. Shelly Bond & Mariah Huehner. New York, NY, USA: Vertigo, 2003. Print.

_____. *Sandman, The: The Dream Hunters*. Illus. Yoshitaka Amano. Ed. Karen Berger, Jennifer Lee. New York: Vertigo, 1999. Print.

Hatfield, Charles. *Alternative Comics: An Emerging Literature*. Jackson: U of Mississippi P, 2005. Print.

Hutcheon, Linda. *A Poetics of Postmodernism: History, Theory, Fiction*. New York: Routledge, 1988. Print.

Hutcheon, Linda. *Politics of Postmodernism, The*. New York: Routledge, 1989. Print.

Inge, M. Thomas. "Form and Function in Metacomics: Self-Reflexivity in the Comic Strips." *Studies in American Culture* 13 (1991): 1-10. Print.

Jones, Matthew T. "Reflexivity in Comic Art." *International Journal of Comic Art* 7 (2005 Spring/Summer): 270-286. Print.

McCloud, Scott. *Understanding Comics: The Invisible Art*. New York: Kitchen Sink Press (for HarperCollins), 1993. Print.

Mitchell, W.J.T. *Picture Theory*. Chicago: U of Chicago P, 1995. Print.

Round, Julia. "Fragmented Identity: The Superhero Condition." *International Journal of Comic Art* 7 (Fall 2005): 358-369. Print.

Waugh, Patricia. *Metafiction: The Theory and Practice of Self-Conscious Fiction*. New York, USA: Methuen, 1984. Print.

The Apocalypse and Other Silly Bits: *Good Omens*, Collaboration, and Authorial One-Upmanship

Laura Nicosia

It has been said that Neil Gaiman and Terry Pratchett's *Good Omens: The Nice and Accurate Prophecies of Agnes Nutter, Witch*, is so entertaining "it feels like it shouldn't exist" (Lough & Britt). Alternatingly irreverent and insightful, the novel appeals to today's war-weary, terrorism-alerted readers as surely as it did to its first generation audience in 1990. Gaiman and Pratchett meld their dry wit, playful sarcasm, slapstick humor, and deadpan observations to create a brazen romp concerning the approaching apocalypse. One of the most successful devices Pratchett and Gaiman use to establish a polyvocality is through the paratextual conversations held at the bottom of the page in the footnotes. These footnotes serve several purposes: direct authorial narration, private jokes, or even direct rhetorical addresses to the readers. When the notes are not adding to the texture of the plot, they break the fourth wall and destabilize the narrative with digressions, inwardly reflective minutiae, and absurdities. Daniel Lüthi asserts that "Pratchett [and Gaiman's] unusual attention to fictionality and the artificiality of a secondary world [as elaborated through his use of footnotes] reveals insights into narrative conventions" and narratology (126). As such, these paratexts affect how the readers relate to both the text and the authors and alter how they travel along the narrative cartography in ways that they could not by following only the primary narrative.

By employing concepts from Gerard Genette's analysis of paratexts, it is possible to explore the vocal layers of *Good Omens*. Commenting on its plural narratives, Gaiman has said, "[It] is not greater than the sum [but] the whole is different than the sum" (qtd. in McCabe). This novel is not simply an accretion of two authors adding chapters sequentially. Gaiman and Pratchett wrote this novel as a bricolage of narratives, notes, direct addresses, and pseudo-intertextual insertions, all blending into a unified articulation of various types of different voices and postmodern pluralistic timelines. Lough and Britt suggest: "The writing styles of the two authors complement each other in ways that enhance their more obscure skills. Gaiman can be very funny, but he's funnier with Pratchett, and Pratchett can be a masterfully loony plotter, but he's a meticulous lunatic with Gaiman." Gaiman explains how their voices mingle in this manner: "collaborations are successful and easy because you're in a room with somebody and you can tell if the joke is funny or not. If the other guy laughs, it stays in. . . . [I]t works because it is not written by two people, it is written by one two-headed person" (qtd. in McCabe). The equation is simple, if mathematically inaccurate: one author plus one author equals a new author. Likewise, one narrator plus one set of paratexts equals one new narrative.

The Winner Gets the Best Gag First

The novel is a re-imagining of the biblical apocalypse and monitors a madcap race for the Armageddon that seems to be careening out of control, rife with misadventures and supernatural gaffes. *Good Omens* is a revisioning where "fairy tales, myths, popular culture and high culture are rearranged and retold in innovative ways" (Lüthi 139). It is chock full of humor at its most silly and intentionally blasphemous. Lüthi insists that this dangerous humor is one of Pratchett's strengths, going back to his *Discworld Series*: "Pratchett began to employ humor not simply to evoke laughter but to address serious issues by ridiculing them" (132). This strength of this kind of sociocultural ridicule allows for "an exhilaratingly chaotic freedom of expression" with "various forms of parody, which mediate comically between an audience and a known prior discourse"—in this case, the *Bible* and the teachings of the Church (Richter 576).

Despite the serious nature of the authors' satire, the main purpose and writing of *Good Omens* was to make each other laugh. In an interview with the BBC, Gaiman reflected on their writing process:

> We wrote the first draft in about nine weeks. Nine weeks of gloriously long phone calls, in which we would read each other what we'd written, and try to make the other one laugh. We'd plot, delightedly, and then hurry off the phone, determined to get to the next good bit before the other one could. We'd rewrite each other, footnote each other's pages, sometimes even footnote each other's footnotes. ("*Good Omens*: How Neil")

There was no outlining, no planning, no editorial proposal. They wrote out of spontaneity and inspiration from each other. When it would have been intrusive to put asides, tangents, and silly bits into the narrative, they used footnotes to introduce punch lines, witty repartee, and conversational banter. The conversations that take place at the bottom of the page create an alternate reading experience for those who choose to read them. They comprise, in essence, a corresponding if supplementary text without "violating the margins of the text, but as expanding the boundaries of the text into the margins of the page" (Effron 201). Indeed, it is possible to read the novel without paying attention to the footnotes at all—or to read them only as one reaches the bottom of the page. Each reading affects the audience's response to the book. Accessing the footnotes "real time," however—as they were entered in the narrative—is to experience how Gaiman and Pratchett engaged in their conversations and narratorial participation.

Genette's concept of paratext identifies eight different categories of notes based upon who is speaking or writing them. These categories are: assumptive authorial, disavowing authorial, authentic allographic, authentic actorial, translations, fictive authorial, fictive allographic, and fictive actorial (Genette 322-323). These categories and their deployment enable conversations about *who* speaks. Tracing *how* these speech-acts *move* and *where* the content leads the reader is also valuable and is what this essay does. Understanding how these categories function and affect the readerly experience may seem secondary to the aesthetic, literary, and narrative experiences of the novel. However, when a reader chooses to engage with the footnotes, complex cognitive gymnastics are undertaken. These narrative calisthenics, resulting from engaging with the novel's collaboratively composed footnotes, provoke different reading experiences. When we consider how footnotes work and why authors (or editors) choose to include footnotes in novels, we gain insights into various authorial manipulations.

The Footnotes: Are You Talking to Me? Or Authorial One-upmanship

Reading *Good Omens* with attention to the footnotes is a byzantine process and requires a willingness to follow convoluted tangents. With the reader's suspension of disbelief, there is the potential for fictive complicity—where the reader chuckles, recognizes logistical absurdities, yet plays along with the illogical happenings. Sándor Klapcsik identifies Gaiman's *oeuvre* as a "liminal fantasy," where the language "is marked by lacks: the lack of the narrator's and/or protagonist's surprise. The fantastic element becomes an essential but apparently ordinary element in these stories." In the case of *Good Omens*, the reader also lacks surprise. She is fully invested in and immersed within the story and laughs along with the authors' joke: "[S]uspension of disbelief is not broken but taken in another direction: an absurdity that nonetheless displays internal consistency and allows readers both to be immersed and learn about the construction of a secondary world" (Lüthi 140). The reader enjoys the process of engaging with the polyvocal story *because of* its absurdities.

This is an apocalyptic romp, after all. Gaiman and Pratchett attract their readers into a sense of acceptance rather than belief, since it is not likely, for instance, that demons from Hell have an affinity for songs on *The Best of Queen*. The reader's subconscious logic may think: "If demons exist, they very well *might* love Freddy Mercury." Acceptance allows for the fictive world to be real during the act of reading. Being in the mind of Gaiman and Pratchett:

> is a delicious and confusing and dangerous place to be—because anything can happen, and probably will. The admission price for this journey is not cheap . . . the steep cost is due entirely to [their] insistence that all riders must surrender their doubts, their cynicism, their pessimism, their bad moods and their slingshots. (Keller)

In total, there are fifty-six footnotes in the American version of the text—all of which were written by Gaiman or Pratchett—or both. Further, the authors' notes are unlike the usual literary footnotes added for factual clarification, scholarly pursuits, or rhetorical persuasion: "a fundamental function of the humanities footnote . . . allows us a means of evaluating the level of scholarship of an essay" (Stevens 211). In no way, therefore, are the footnotes in *Good Omens* meant to reflect authentic scholarly research, empirical data, or theoretical polemics. There are, certainly, occasional footnotes to define a term or to explain the cultural significance of a city or road, for example. But these function as pretense and as such do not acquire complete authenticity.

While it is possible to categorize all of the footnotes in *Good Omens* according to the eight Genettian narrative classifications, this essay explores the novel by illustrating how readers navigate the notes and how the notes affect the entire reading experience. While reading the novel, readers see superscript signs that indicate the insertion of a footnote. How and when they engage with the footnotes affects both the comprehension of the storyline and the experience of fictive immersion. The conversations and explanations that exist below the main text have different purposes. Each may be characterized in any of several narrative movements that affect the reader's immersion within the story arc, but for this essay's purposes, it will focus on four narrative shifts: Simple Explanations and Definitions, Inward Diversions, Outward Diversions, and Direct Addresses to the Readers (Breaking the Fourth Wall).

Footnotes: Simple Explanations and Definitions

The most common kind of footnote is one that defines and offers explanations to content within a main text. While such notes are often encountered in academic discourse, *Good Omens* employs this type infrequently. Such notes are generally brief and do not lend insight into an element of the plot—usually, they clarify an unfamiliar word, place, or name. Notes like these are desirable by reinforcing a sense of factuality. Such footnotes do not need much explanation, but a simple example of the explanatory note is at the beginning of the novel when the narrator enlightens the readers about how God's plan seems like an ineffable game of poker to other "players*" (Pratchett & Gaiman 14). The footnote simply offers "*i.e., everybody" (2). By inserting the footnote, the tone of over-specificity has been struck.

An example of this more traditional footnote is used for the word *houngan* later in the novel. The footnote defines the word: "*magician or priest" (Pratchett & Gaiman 273) and helps the reader to understand the story of the wayward voodoo practitioner. Of course, the authors continue the footnote with, "Voodoo is a very interesting religion for the whole family, even those members of it who are dead" (273). By giving pertinence to the notes, Gaiman and Pratchett establish validity to them. Thus, the reader never knows what she will encounter, which makes the footnote voyage an unpredictable and enjoyable one.

Inward Diversions

Inward diversions may be likened to a writer's creation of a backstory. Often, authors posit complete details about that character's personality, life, family (and so on) even when that character holds a minor place in the text. Such insight into a character's personality and motivation traditionally do not appear in the fiction. However, a writer creates extensive texts about a character to allow him to understand the character intimately, so that when the character is confronted with a new situation, the author genuinely anticipates the character's response. This is what authors mean when they say, "The character tells me what to do." In the case of *Good Omens,* several footnotes act like backstory—with deep internal attention, to the point of digression or diversion. The result, however, is that the reader is brought in, in a more intimate way, to the characters and stories that, in the primary text alone, would not occur. As such, the reader is provided with a sense of privilege and the result is satisfying and amusing.

Despite a feigned factual tone, the specificity of these notes is meant to prompt laughter and provide intimacy at the level of minutiae and the levels of interiority. An example of this happens early in the novel with a footnote that occupies more than half of a page. It contains four paragraphs of explanations and presents plural timelines for the purportedly true story of the fifth-century Saint Beryl Articulatus of Cracow (Pratchett & Gaiman 24). The pseudo-academic tone of the note leads to a sense of authenticity, prompting the reader to believe that Saint Beryl existed. The reader has been lured into believing "in the reality of what is being read" and rather than undercutting the "plausibility of the narrative through attention to creative structure [the footnotes underscore] the implied reality of the story and thus wor[k] as a component of the reality effect" (Effron 204, 207). In the fictive world, while engaged in the reading, Beryl is real. That being said, within the first paragraph, the authors define who the young Beryl was—offering information about her betrothal to a pagan Prince Casimir. It continues with impossibly detailed information about her wedding as she prayed to God to rescue her from marriage. Rather than being liberated, she received "the miraculous ability to chatter continually about whatever was on her mind, however inconsequential, without pause for breath or food" (Pratchett & Gaiman 24).

The footnote continues to present alternate versions of her ascension to sainthood. The first version suggests that Beryl met her demise at the hands of her husband some "three weeks after the wedding, with their marriage still unconsummated. She died a virgin and a martyr, chattering to the end" (Pratchett & Gaiman 24). The second version offers that Casimir purchased earplugs and that decades into their marriage, "she died in bed, with him, at the age of sixty-two" (24).

Finally, the last paragraph of the footnote yanks the reader forward from the fifth century to the twentieth with a deadpan explanation of how the current Chattering Order of Saint Beryl mimics her "at all times except on Tuesday afternoons, for half an hour, when the nuns are permitted to shut up, and, if they wish, to play table tennis" (Pratchett & Gaiman 24). The absurd details of days and times and table tennis are juxtaposed with the note's formal tone and Latinate presentation, the authentic-sounding revelation of alternate versions. Edward Maloney explores the slippery nature of truth or fiction in footnotes by saying that these paratexts "play with the boundaries of fiction and non-fiction [creating] this effect of confusion about the fictional status of the narrative . . . which lends the story a sense of verisimilitude" (qtd. in Effron 202).

That absurd juxtaposition of the sacred and silly provides the reader with a sense that she has been given privileged information inward into the text—while simultaneously being led on a long-winded, wild goose chase; for the moment the reader asks herself, "Is Beryl a real Saint in Roman or Orthodox Catholicism?" the spell has been broken and the veracity of the metafiction has been undercut. There is no Saint Beryl.

Later in the novel, the narrator mentions that Aziraphale (the angelic, book-collecting protagonist) collects erroneous versions of the Holy Bible, "individually named from errors in typesetting" (Pratchett & Gaiman 49). After several textual paragraphs describing the errors found in the inaccurate *Buggre All This Bible* (1651), the footnote provides information that beside the titular error (a complaint by the typesetter working on the Bible), there is another glaring error in the text—the addition of three verses in chapter three of the Book of Genesis, after the expulsion of Adam:

> 25. And the Lord spake until the Angel that guarded the eastern gate, *saying* Where is the flaming sword which was given unto thee?
> 26. And the Angel said, I had it here only a moment ago, I must have put *it* down some where, forget my own head next.
> 27. And the Lord did not ask him again. (Pratchett & Gaiman 50)

After the presentation of the verses, the footnote suggests how the insertions may have occurred. It is offered that common practice for typesetting shops to "hang proof sheets to the wooden beams outside their shops, for the edification of the populace and some free proofreading" (Pratchett & Gaiman 50). A bookshop owner (Mr. A. Ziraphale) with expertise in translations, just happened to be a neighbor to the print shop. He was conveniently never consulted or questioned about the inclusion of these three verses.

The reader recognizes Aziraphale's name of the bookshop owner and feels privileged to be made aware of such inside information:

either Aziraphale inserted the verses himself because they were the true (albeit un-Catholic in tone: the Cherubim guarding the gate was absent-minded at the least, careless at the worst) or some demon wrote them and was never confidently identified. Either way, the footnote takes the reader in hand into a backstory for Aziraphale in a way that would be unknowable otherwise. Again, the reader is brought into the joke and backstory by being proffered this uncanny information.

Footnotes that are Inward Diversions foster in the reader a cognitive movement deeper into the text toward backstory in ways that offer unique privileges to the reader:

> [F]ootnotes call attention to the textuality of the narrative, and in emphasizing the position of text as an object, they also combine the position of the read and the position of the reader within the fictional construct. By highlighting the narrative's textuality, the footnotes identify the physical body of the narrative as a materials item for the reader's consumption. However, these notes also firmly position a reader within the text, especially when they are signed by either the author or a character. In these cases, the notes convey that the body of the text has been read and annotated by the signatory—or, in Genette's terminology, the *sender*—of the note. (Effron 202)

Such fictive elements deployed by the authors, spoken by the narrators, or added by a character, entangle the reader in layers of details that undergird the story and, in this case, do so across timelines.

Outward Diversions

Unlike those footnotes that act as Inward Diversions, some paratexts move the reader's attention to details outside, beyond, or parallel to the text. These are Outward Diversions. With Gaiman and Pratchett launching from the main text with running gags, callbacks, and continuity jokes, they construct narrative paths that entice readers off the page. If this book were a digital text, these footnotes might appear as hyperlinks to divert the reader's attention to sites that relate to the original topic, but swerve to tangents quite absurd.

Such a narrative *non sequitur* is found early in the novel in a description of demonic protagonist Crowley's custom-made watch. The primary text offers: "He glanced at his watch, which was designed for the kind of rich deep-sea diver who likes to know what the time is in twenty-one world capitals while he's down there*" (Pratchett & Gaiman 17). The note adds, "Getting just one chip custom-made is incredibly expensive but he could afford it. *This* watch gave the time in twenty world capitals and in a capital city in Another Place, where it was always one time, and that was Too Late" (17). Such an aside adds nothing to the plot, but prompts the reader to envision where "Another Place" might be—ostensibly, Hell—where it is always too late to be saved. This is a simple example of a diversion of the reader's attention outside the plot—a diversion whose aim is more aimed toward mere humor and supplementary information.

Several instances of these Outward Diversions—perhaps most of the fifty-six footnotes—fall into this category. Sidebar quips and wordplays elicit chortles from the reader, who eventually realizes that the purpose has been distraction in the name of humor. Such a diversionary ramble occurs when the British nanny rings the doorbell only to have a "butler, as they say, of the old school" answer (Pratchett & Gaiman 67). The attached note plays on the use of the word "school" as follows: "A night school just off the Tottenham Court Road, run by an elderly actor who had played butlers and gentlemen's gentlemen in films and television and on the stage since the 1920s" (67). Not only is the digression a tangent to the narrative, it is also a physical diversion to another road in another part of London. It remains apropos to the topic merely by mentioning a butler.

The most tangential Outward Diversion, adding an absurd juxtaposition of class and elegance, occurs when Newt, the private witch-finder, makes himself a cup of coffee in someone else's house: "In the end, as every human being who has ever breakfasted on their own in someone else's kitchen has done since nearly the dawn of time, he made do with unsweetened instant black coffee" (Pratchett & Gaiman 380). The extended footnote is rife with specificities that have nothing to do with the pending Apocalypse—or even Newt's immediate situation:

> Except for Giovanni Jacopo Casanova (1725–1798), famed amourist and litterateur, who revealed in volume 12 of his Memoirs that, as a matter of course, he carried around with him at all times a small valise containing "a loaf of bread, a pot of choice Seville marmalade, a knife, fork, and small spoon for stirring, 2 fresh eggs packed with care in unspun wool, a tomato or love-apple, a small frying pan, a small sauce pan, a spirit burner, a chafing dish, a tin box of salted butter of the Italian type, 2 bone china plates. Also a portion of honey comb, as a sweetener, for my breath and for my coffee. Let my readers understand me when I say to them all: A true gentleman should always be able to break his fast in the manner of a gentleman, wheresoever he may find himself." (380-381)

In this footnote, a list of items builds upon one another in a process of narrative accretion that removes the reader from the main text to another time, another country, another text. The connecting point is breakfast. This footnote succeeds in spiraling the reader's focus out of the novel proper, but not so far that the reader is completely lost in the narrative convolutions. At reaching the end of the footnote, the reader finds herself in vague fugue state—in Italy, but also in London.

The authors employ a different type of Outward Diversion in the last endnotes toward the end of the novel (Pratchett & Gaiman 390). Witch-finder Sergeant Shadwell eats his lunch while reading such works as the infamous *Malleus Maleficarum*, an actual handbook for identifying and fighting witches published in 1487 but condemned by the Vatican in 1490. The treatise includes an endorsement from the Pope: "'A relentlefs blockbufter of a boke; heartily recommended" [*sic*] —Pope Innocent VIII'" (390).

The humor is two-fold in this footnote. First, a Pope of the Roman Catholic Church is ironically endorsing a book eventually banned by the Vatican. Second, if the Pope did endorse any book, he would not use the phrase "relentless blockbuster." While neither silly bit digresses far from the narrative, the layers of humor in such a short statement are easily discernible. However, a curious reader might research the source materials to discover the history and validity of the *Malleus Maleficarum*. Its existence makes the humor that much more hearty. In order to return to the storyline after the footnote, the main text presents "a knock on the door, and Madame Tracy would call out" (Pratchett & Gaiman 390). The knock and call fetch Shadwell out of *his* reverie and transport the *reader* back to the plot of the main text.

Outward Diversions are effective in drawing readers out of the text, sometimes off the current timeline, and occasionally extracted from the geographical the setting. Despite the digression, readers are not so far removed as to lose a sense of the plot, but they do need to be brought back to the primary narrative's timeline.

Direct Authorial Address: Breaking the Fourth Wall, or Wink Wink, Nudge Nudge

Contemporary audiences are more familiar with narrators who breach the traditional bounds of a work and express their own fictionality. When authors break the fourth wall, they are expressing their nature as the creators of a text and contribute to the work's metafictionality:

> This ability of the author and character to converse, albeit in the margins of the text, seems to align the textual and extratextual planes of reality and thus to function as a reality effect. Nevertheless, the ability of the author to engage in a conversation with his character [or his co-author] underscores the metafictionality of the moment, as it highlights the awareness of text as text. (Effron 208).

Often, those direct authorial addresses privilege the audience with secret information and, by doing so, dispense advantageous facts to benefit the reader.

There are numerous examples of the authors addressing their audience with a wry nudge and a chipper wink. Reaching out beyond the page to speak to the reader offers more intimate relationship between author and audience. Readers feel drawn into confidence with the creators and that rapport fosters opportunities for more inside jokes. An early example of such Direct Address occurs when new father Mr. Young (who through a series of gaffes is mistaken for the American Ambassador and mistakenly given the newborn Anti-Christ) suggests that he's tired of British royalty who go "to discos all night long and were sick all over the paparazzi*" (Pratchett & Gaiman 32). The subsequent footnote confirms an acute awareness of its own textuality and pokes fun at the clueless—and innocent—new father: "It is possibly worth mentioning at this point that Mr. Young thought that paparazzi was a kind of Italian linoleum" (32). The snarky statement makes the reader laugh *with* the authors at the expense of a character. By prefacing the footnote with "possibly worth mentioning," the note affirms awareness that *someone* is reading the text and that such a sentience acknowledges the privileged and intimate nature between the author and reader. Similar footnotes serve to reinforce the bond between the two: both parties are analyzing and criticizing together.

Gaiman and Pratchett manage to bring an international audience into their narrative confidence by sharing a joke at their expense. The narrator divulges that Crowley claimed controlling development for Manchester and Glasgow, while angelic protagonist Aziraphale claimed Shropshire and Edinburg. For some reason "neither [spirit] claimed any responsibility for Milton Keynes* but both reported it as a success" (Pratchett & Gaiman 44). Without the note, one would assume that the city could be the product of either spirit; this ambiguity is amusing in its own right. Reading the note, however, veers the reader's attention to a very different point: "Note for Americans and other aliens: Milton Keynes is a new city approximately halfway between London and Birmingham. It was built to be modern, efficient, healthy, and all in all, a pleasant place to live. Many Britons find this amusing" (44).

First, the note is a conscious address to "Americans and other aliens." The American reader would likely feel a sense of disconnect to be categorized an "alien." Nonetheless, the joke is made in good fun. Even if an American were insulted, the last sentence takes a dry-witted jab at the United Kingdom's lifestyle—equal opportunity criticism critiquing both sides of the Atlantic. With each audience getting criticism, so no one party can be affronted. Such humor is an act of irreverence and verbal liberation that holds up the even the audience to criticism. If no one is immune to ridicule, the teasing clears a way for new ideas, social change, and a possible cultural renewal. Gaiman offers:

> One of the great things about humor is, you can slip things past people with humor, you can use it as a sweetener. So you can actually tell them things, give them messages, get terribly, terribly serious and terribly, terribly dark, and because there are jokes in there, they'll go along with you, and they'll travel a lot further along with you than they would otherwise" (LOCUS). *Good Omens* succeeds in focusing the reader's attention to the dark aspects of contemporary life using humor—in both the plot and footnotes. It has been said that "ironic representations [of the apocalypse] can renew the genre" through the use of humor and inversion (Klapcsik).

Perhaps the most pointed direct address from the writer to his audience comes midway through the novel, when witch-finders Shadwell and Newt take stock of their occult-fighting arsenal. Shadwell blindly clings to the past and its traditions. This is apparent when he itemizes the equipment necessary for their quest to find the witch—despite the fact that modern technologies have supplanted old fashioned tools:

> "Ye're all ready. Hae ye got it all?"
> "Yes, sir."
> "Pendulum o' discovery?"
> "Pendulum of discovery, yes."
> "Thumbscrew?"
> Newt swallowed, and patted a pocket.
> "Thumbscrew," he said.
> "Firelighters?"
> "I really think, Sergeant, that—"
> *"Firelighters?"*
> "Firelighters,"* said Newt sadly. "And matches." (Pratchett & Gaiman 195)

The footnote below directly addresses the reader: "Note for Americans and other city-dwelling life-forms. . . ." and continues on for eleven lines of minutiae about central heating, moral fiber, wood, coal, asbestos, open fires, waxy white lumps of incendiary materials, and more. By following the footnote, the reader has been decoyed out of the storyline and brought somewhere else. Ironically, in an oppositional statement, the footnote ends with, "These little white blocks are called firelighters. No one knows why" (Pratchett & Gaiman 195). If no one knows why they are called thus, the entire footnote has just negated itself after an eleven-line tangent. The purpose: a cheap laugh.

The Punch Line, or Fun with a Purpose

The collaborative production of this novel has produced a text that has, at its heart, a polyvocality. With their footnotes, Gaiman and Pratchett utilize the margins of the page to hold sidebar conversations with each other and with their audience. As such, they bring readers into the text more intimately. By talking to and with each other, the authors make their presence known as creators. While neither writer invented the technique, *Good Omens* perfects the process of bringing the reader into confidence by revealing the writing process.

This novel has levels of narration as evidenced by the verbal repartee on the bottom margin of the pages. The footnotes are incidents of authorial discourses intended to provoke laughter and to offer sarcastic critical comments to prompt the reader to reflect on contemporary life. More important, perhaps, is that Gaiman and Pratchett use many of these footnotes to have sidebar conversations between themselves: "The joy of writing *Good Omens* was we were two guys writing it and you knew, if you could make the other one laugh [the humor] worked. It was that simple" (qtd. in McCabe).

Works Cited

Breebart, Leo & Mike Kew. "Words of the Master." *L-Space Web: A Terry Pratchett/Discworld®*, n.d. Web. 21 Jul. 2016. <www.lspace.org/books/apf/words-from-the-master.html>.

"Continuity Nods." *TV Tropes*. TVTropes, n.d. Web. 21 Jul. 2016. <http://tvtropes.org/pmwiki/pmwiki.php/Main/ContinuityNod>.

Effron, Malcah. "On the Borders of the Page, on the Borders of a Genre: Artificial Paratexts in Golden Age Detective Fiction." *Narrative* 18.2 (May 2010): 199-219. Print.

"Gaiman & Pratchett, Together Again . . . Almost." *Locus* 392 (Mar. 1991). Web. 7 January 2016. <www.locusmag.com/2006/Issues/1991_Gaiman_Pratchett.html>.

Genette, Gérard. *Paratexts: Thresholds of Interpretation.* Cambridge, UK: Cambridge UP, 1997.

"*Good Omens:* How Neil Gaiman and Terry Pratchett Wrote a Book." *BBC News Magazine.* BBC, 22 Dec. 2014. Web. 27 Apr. 2016. <www.bbc.com/news/magazine-30512620>.

Jordan, Justine. "*Good Omens* by Terry Pratchett and Neil Gaiman—fun, with footnotes." *Guardian.* The Guardian News and Media Limited, 15 Dec. 2015. Web. 10 January 2016. <www.theguardian.com/books/2015/dec/15/good-omens-by-terry-pratchett-and-neil-gaiman-fun-with-footnotes>.

Keller, Julia. "*Coraline* Author Living His Dream Life." *The Orlando Sentinel.* 31 May 2009. *NewsBank.* Web. 27 Apr. 2016.

Klapcsik, Sandor. "Neil Gaiman's Irony, Liminal Fantasies, and Fairy Tale Adaptations." *Hungarian Journal of English and American Studies.* 14.2 (2008): 317-334. Reprinted in *Children's Literature Review.* Ed. Jelena Krstovic. Detroit, MI: Gale, 2013. 177.

Lough, Chris & Ryan Britt. "Magic & Good Madness: A Neil Gaiman Reread: The Many Bromances of Neil Gaiman." *Tor.com*. Macmillan, 21 May 2013. Web. 15 June 2016. <www.tor.com/2013/05/21/neil-gaiman-bromances/>.

Lüthi, Daniel. "Toying With Fantasy: The Postmodern Playground of Terry Pratchett's Discworld Novels." *Mythlore.* 33.1 (Fall/Winter 2014): 125-142. Print.

Malleus Malleficarum. Wikipedia. Wikipedia, n.d. Web. 30 Jul. 2016. <https://en.wikipedia.org/wiki/Malleus_Maleficarum>.

McCabe, Joseph. "Hanging Out with the Dream King: Neil Gaiman on Comics and Collaborating." *Science Fiction Chronicle* 24.10 (Oct. 2002): 42-46. Reprinted in *Contemporary Literary Criticism.* Ed. Jeffrey Hunter. Vol 195. Detroit, MI: Gale, 2005.

Pratchett, Terry & Neil Gaiman. *Good Omens: The Nice and Accurate Prophecies of Agnes Nutter, Witch.* New York: HarperTorch, 1990. Print.

Richter, David H. "Mikhail Bakhtin: 1895–1975." *The Critical Tradition: Classic Texts and Contemporary Trends.* 3rd ed. Bedford/St. Martin's, 2007. 575-595. Print.

Stevens, Anne H. & Jay Williams. "The Footnote, in Theory." *Critical Inquiry* 32 (Winter 2006): 208-225. Print.

"Spoilers, Sweetie"—A Madman and His Monsters: Neil Gaiman's "The Doctor's Wife"

Kelly J. Murphy

"But you and I both know, don't we, Rose, that the Doctor is worth the monsters," Reinette Poisson, the future Madame de Pompadour, sagely notes to the Doctor's companion Rose Tyler in the *Doctor Who* episode "The Girl in the Fireplace." From Daleks, Weeping Angels, the Ood, minotaurs, werewolves, and beyond, monsters and the monstrous play an ongoing and central role in what fans of the longest running science fiction television program, *Doctor Who*, have come to call the "Whoniverse." Perhaps the prevalence of monsters is not particularly surprising, since the show traces the adventures of a so-called Time Lord from the planet Gallifrey, who travels through space and time in a stolen time machine called the TARDIS (a pleasant acronym for "Time and Relative Dimension in Space"). By his own definition, the Doctor is, accordingly, a "madman with a box" ("The Eleventh Hour"). In any of his (now thirteen) incarnations known to the viewer as regenerations, the Doctor usually travels with a companion, and those companions are almost invariably humans from the planet Earth. So it is often through their eyes that viewers learn about the sometimes-monstrous extra-terrestrial creatures the Doctor encounters. Yet while the Doctor, whose true name remains unknown,[1] looks much like his human companions, he is in fact an alien who, by his nature as an adventurer, encounters many other aliens, some of them entirely monstrous. In short, the Doctor and his monsters go hand-in-hand (or hand-in-tentacle, as the case may be).

It is here where Neil Gaiman—who once claimed, long before he composed his first episode of *Doctor Who*, "The Doctor's Wife" in 2011, that it was "probably a good thing I never actually got my hands on the Doctor. I would have unhappened so much" (*View* 218)—enters our story. When Gaiman finally did get his hands on *Doctor Who*, he both "unhappened" rather large parts of the *Whoniverse*, while also using monsters and the monstrous to illustrate how *Doctor Who* has long wrestled with questions of hope, home, and what it means to be human(y-wumany).

Why Monsters Matter

The monsters and monstrous aliens of *Doctor Who* are entertaining, in varying ways: some are amusing (the Sontarans); some are terrifying (the Weeping Angels); and others are, well, sometimes annoying . . . but very, very deadly (the Daleks). But, as scholars of monsters routinely note, there is more to the things that go bump in the night than their entertainment value. As W. Scott Poole explains:

> The Latin word *monstrum* provides us with our English term *monster*. *Monstrum* is "that which appears" or reveals itself (the English word "demonstrate" is rooted in *monstrum*). *Monstrum* also has a relationship to the Latin word *monere*, meaning "to warn" and relates to the concept of an omen or portent. But in world mythology and religious experience, the monster has done more than represent the hideous and the abnormal. Monsters have been, from ancient times, invested with meanings divine and demonic, theological or fearfully natural. (5)

In short, when monsters appear in the pages of our novels or on our television screens, they often function as warnings or as omens, both representing the world we can know *and* the things about the world we wish we could explain. Invested with meaning, monsters are also "things that should not be, but nevertheless are—and their existence therefore raises vexing questions about humanity's understanding of and place in the universe" (Weinstock 1). Inevitably, stories that feature monsters ask big questions of the viewer: What does it mean to be good or to be evil? What is the purpose of history? What is the place of humans in that history? What does it mean, even, to be human? What separates the humans from the monsters?

Unsurprisingly, *Doctor Who*—with its many monsters—has long asked all these questions and many more. Yet one of the things that render the monsters and the resulting questions in *Doctor Who* different from, say, the monsters and questions of Bram Stoker's

Dracula or Glen Duncan's *The Last Werewolf*, is that many different writers, rather than a sole author, have contributed to the canon of *Doctor Who* since its inception on the British Broadcasting Company in 1963. Here we turn to Gaiman, who is perhaps most famous for his comic book series *The Sandman* or his novel *American Gods*. Gaiman grew up watching episodes of the early *Doctor Who* and was lastingly imprinted by the experience, recalling, "The complaint about *Doctor Who* from adults was always, when I was small, that it was too frightening" (*View* 217). Yet while Gaiman admits that "of course it was frightening," and that he "watched the good bits from behind the sofa," he confesses that the adults should have instead worried about "what it did to the inside of my head. How it painted my interior landscape. When I was three, making Daleks out of the little school milk bottles, with the rest of the kids at Mrs. Pepper's Nursery School, I was in trouble and I didn't know it. The virus was already at work" (217-218). Later, *Doctor Who* producer and writer Steven Moffat would ask Gaiman to write for the series, stating "I just thought 'this guy's a *Doctor Who* fan. I can tell, I can smell it! He loves *Doctor Who*. He's practically writing *Doctor Who* in disguise'" (McAlpine). The *Doctor Who* virus, it seems, really did infect Gaiman.

Gaiman's first script for *Doctor Who*, entitled "The Doctor's Wife," would win the 2011 Ray Bradbury Award for Outstanding Dramatic Presentation as well as the 2012 Hugo Award for Best Dramatic Presentation, Short Form (the first episode of *Who* to win that was not written by one of the showrunners). Unsurprisingly, Gaiman's episode features monsters, the kind of monsters that make viewers watch "the good bits from behind the sofa." In "The Doctor's Wife," the Eleventh Doctor (Matt Smith) and his companions Amy Pond (Karen Gillan) and Rory Williams (Arthur Darvill) find themselves stranded on an asteroid outside the universe after receiving what the Doctor believes to be a distress call from a Time Lord called the Corsair. Of the Corsair, the Doctor notes that he remembered him as a "Fantastic bloke. He had that snake as a tattoo in every regeneration. Didn't feel like himself unless he had the tattoo. Or herself, a couple of times. Oooh, she was a bad girl." Interestingly enough, not even five minutes into the episode, and Gaiman is busy at work "unhappening" previous *Doctor Who* rules, making the possibility of a gender change in a Time Lord regeneration canon. The distress call awakens hope in the Doctor, who believes that all the other Time Lords died at his hands in the Time War.[2] Yet the asteroid, it turns out, is a sentient being called House, who uses energy from Time Lord TARDISes in order to survive and who keeps a strange group of Patchwork People, Auntie, Uncle, Nephew, and Idris, alive on the asteroid to do his bidding. To use TARDIS energy, House must remove the matrices (read: souls) of the TARDISes, placing them within a living body. In "The Doctor's Wife," that body is the woman named Idris (played by Suranne Jones). The resulting episode explores how together the Doctor and the TARDIS-as-Idris save Amy and Rory, defeat House, and return the TARDIS-as-Idris to her home in the famous blue police box the Doctor has long called home. Perhaps most surprising of all the possible spoilers about this episode—and one way that Gaiman "unhappens" the *Doctor Who* canon—is that the Doctor's wife is not the expected River Song, but is, rather, the TARDIS herself. In short, to borrow from Weinstock, when Gaiman gets his hands on the Doctor, he writes an episode filled with "things that should not be," filled with monsters and the monstrous, and thereby "raises vexing questions" about the Doctor's "understanding of and place in the universe" (Weinstock 1).

Hope and Horror: Or, The Patchwork People

Monsters are, notoriously, associated with horror. However, monsters, the monstrous, and all the horror they entail also engender awe and, sometimes, hope. As Timothy Beal writes, "Both religious experience and horror are characterized as encounters with something simultaneously awesome and awful—a feeling captured in the older spelling, 'aweful', which still retrains its sense of awe" (7). Beal continues:

> Whether demonized or deified or something in between, monsters bring on a limit experience that is akin in many respects to religious

experience, an experience of being on the edge of certainty and security, drawn toward and repulsed by a *monstrum tremendum*. The monstrous is an embodiment of overwhelming and chaotic excess, a too-muchness that brings on a vertigo-like sense of fear and desire: standing on the threshold of an unfathomable abyss. (Beal 195)

Beal's *monstrum tremendum* is a play on the theologian Rudolph Otto's idea of the *mysterium tremendum*. For Otto, when we face the "mysterious," we encounter "something inherently 'wholly other', whose kind and character are incommensurable with our own, and before which we therefore recoil in a wonder that strikes us chill and numb" (28). The monstrous, for Otto, is just the "'mysterious' in a gross form" (80). The monstrous, like the *mysterium tremendum*, is something that is equally awful and awe-ful, something that, per Beal, brings on a "vertigo-like sense of fear and desire." Monsters are awful, fearful, horrifying; monsters are awe-ful, wonderful, and (sometimes, strangely) hopeful.

When Gaiman introduces House and his Patchwork People in "The Doctor's Wife," Gaiman also introduces into the story the awful/awe-ful wonder of the *monstrum tremendum* and the horror and the hope that the monstrous entails. In "The Doctor's Wife," the Doctor and his companions are, quite literally, "standing on the threshold of an unfathomable abyss" as they find themselves on an asteroid "outside the universe". The junkyard asteroid is overwhelming and chaotic, and, as it turns out, filled with monsters. The first of the monsters encountered on the asteroid are Auntie, Uncle, Nephew, and Idris, though at first they do not appear to be particularly monstrous. Auntie and Uncle, while somewhat odd, look human, and Nephew, an Ood, is familiar to those well versed in the Doctor's universe (And so the Doctor explains, "It's an Ood. Oods are good. Love an Ood" ["The Doctor's Wife"]). At the start of the episode, these figures represent the Doctor's hope that the Corsair might be alive and that the Doctor might not be the only Time Lord after all.

Yet the Doctor's hopes began to unravel as he tries to speak to the Ood, whose translation sphere is inoperative. As Auntie explains, "Nephew was broken when he came here. Why, he was half-dead. House repaired him. House repaired all of us." When the Doctor repairs the sphere, he hears the voice of the Corsair, "If you are receiving this message, please help me. Send a signal to the High Council of the Time Lords on Gallifrey. Tell them that I am still alive. I don't know where I am. I'm on some rock-like planet." The message is garbled, however, and a number of other voices also speak at the same time. When the Doctor asks who else is on the asteroid, Auntie responds, "Just what you see. Just the four of us, and the House."

Enter the next of Gaiman's monsters: House, a living, sentient asteroid. As Auntie explains, "We walk on his back, breathe his air, eat his food." Next, speaking through Auntie and Uncle as though they were puppets, House addresses the Doctor, saying, "And do my will. You are most welcome, travellers," ominously continuing, "Many travellers have come through the rift, like Auntie and Uncle and Nephew. I repair them when they break." As the Doctor, Amy, and Rory go to "see the sights," the Doctor and his companions have the following exchange:

> RORY: So, as soon as the TARDIS is refueled, we go, yeah?
> DOCTOR: No. There are Time Lords here. I heard them and they need me.
> AMY: You told me about your people, and you told me what you did.
> DOCTOR: Yes, yes, but if they're like the Corsair, they're good ones and I can save them.
> AMY: And then tell them you destroyed the others?
> DOCTOR: I can explain. Tell them why I had to.
> AMY: You want to be forgiven.
> DOCTOR: Don't we all?

The monsters and the monstrous in Gaiman's *Whoniverse* bring on Weinstock's "vertigo-like sense of fear and desire": what if there are other Time Lords, what if the Doctor is not alone, and what if the Doctor can be forgiven for his acts in the Time War? At the heart of the episode—and at the heart of the Doctor's desire—sits the Doctor's hope for forgiveness, the monster chasing him since the end of the Time War.

Yet Gaiman uses his monsters to turn the Doctor's hope to horror: there are no other Time Lords on the asteroid. In a moment of awful realization, the Doctor learns what happened to the Corsair and the other Time Lords when they reached House:

> AUNTIE: House, House is kind and he is wise.
> DOCTOR: House repairs you when you break. Yes, I know. But how does he mend you? You've got the eyes of a twenty year old.
> UNCLE: Thank you.
> DOCTOR: No. Oh, no, I mean it literally. Your eyes are thirty years younger than the rest of you. Your ears don't match, your right arm is two inches longer than your left, and how's your dancing? Because you've got two left feet. Patchwork people. You've been repaired and patched up so often, I doubt there's anything left of what used to be you. I had an umbrella like you once.
> (The Doctor looks down and sees that Auntie's arm has the Corsair's snake tattoo.)
> AUNTIE: Oh, now, it's been a great arm for me, this.
> DOCTOR: Corsair.
> AUNTIE: He was a strapping big bloke, wasn't he, Uncle?
> UNCLE: Big fellow.
> AUNTIE: I got the arm and then Uncle got the spine and the kidneys.
> UNCLE: Kidneys. ("The Doctor's Wife")

Here, the Doctor discovers that Auntie and Uncle are monsters: creatures made up of the body parts of others, including Time Lords like the Corsair. When House and the Patchwork People first appear, they function to reveal and demonstrate the question of hope (and the desire for forgiveness) that underlies the Doctor's story. The Doctor is both drawn toward them in his desire to discover what happened to the Corsair and the other Time Lords and then repulsed by their monstrous form generated out of the bits and pieces of those he sought in the first place.

Moving from hope to horror, Gaiman's *monstrum* also function in the sense of the related Latin root *monere*, "to warn." As Weinstock notes, "the monster tells us what we hope or imagine we are not, as well as what we fear deep down we are or may become" (1). In some ways, Gaiman's House is a monstrous mirror of the Doctor.

For while the Patchwork People believe that House "repairs" them, that House heals them much like a doctor would, in reality House uses the people who land on him and discards them when he is done. The Doctor, of course, needs his companions—but also must inevitably leave them, for the Doctor will invariably outlive his human companions. While Gaiman's Patchwork People reveal the Doctor's greatest hope—a hope for forgiveness from his own people—the true nature of the Patchwork People, and the reality of House who made them so, warns viewers that the Doctor himself can be monstrous. After all, House and the Doctor have something in common: they are each responsible for the deaths of Time Lords. And so upon learning what happened to the previous Time Lords, the Doctor turns to Auntie and Uncle: "You gave me hope, and then you took it away. That's enough to make anyone dangerous. God knows what it will do to me. Basically, run!"

House and Home: Or, The Embodied TARDIS

Of course, while the Doctor tells the Patchwork People and House to "Run!," longtime *Doctor Who* fans realize the irony: the Doctor has been running for hundreds upon hundreds of years. Safe inside his TARDIS, the Doctor has made a career out of running and the TARDIS has become his home. But in Gaiman's episode, the TARDIS is embodied in a human form as Idris and so becomes strange, new, and, perhaps, even monstrous. Weinstock notes how monsters hold a dual threat, for "there is of course the immediate danger to life and limb presented by the prospect of ending up as a snack for a sea monster, dragon, ogre, troll, or blob," (or, perhaps, a sentient asteroid named House), but "beyond this, however, there is the epistemological threat of confronting that which should not be" (2). When the TARDIS becomes embodied, the Doctor must wrestle with something that should not be—a living, breathing, talking TARDIS, who bites the Doctor's ear when she first meets him, claiming, "Biting's excellent. It's like kissing, only there's a winner!" ("The Doctor's Wife"). When the TARDIS' soul is safely ensconced in the blue police box, the TARDIS is the Doctor's home. The embodied TARDIS is, for the Doctor and the audience, an experience of what Sigmund Freud called "the uncanny," *das Unheimliche*, from the German word *Heim*, meaning "home." It is literally the "un-homely," or what Freud calls "the moment when we are faced with something that we have until now considered imaginary" (150). While the TARDIS is the Doctor's home away from Gallifrey, the blue box is the TARDIS' home. As the Doctor notes, House "forced the TARDIS into a body so she'd burn out safely" and "forced her from her home" ("The Doctor's Wife"). By embodying the TARDIS, Gaiman makes the Doctor face that the TARDIS is more than just a box in a moment of uncanny recognition.

This moment, when the TARDIS and the Doctor can talk, creates the experience of the uncanny for the Doctor and the viewer, while also immediately "unhappening" previous *Doctor Who* canon:

> DOCTOR: I don't understand. Who are you?
> IDRIS: Do you not know me? Just because they put me in here?
> DOCTOR: They said you were dangerous.
> IDRIS: Not the cage, stupid. In here. They put me in here. I'm the. Oh, what do you call me? We travel. I go . . . (she makes the TARDIS noise)
> DOCTOR: The TARDIS?
> IDRIS: Time And Relative Dimension In Space. Yes, that's it. Names are funny. It's me. I'm the TARDIS.
> DOCTOR: No, you're not. You're a bite-y, mad lady. The TARDIS is up and downy stuff in a big blue box.
> IDRIS: Yes, that's me. A Type Forty TARDIS. I was already a museum piece when you were young, and the first time you touched my console you said—
> DOCTOR:—I said you were the most beautiful thing I had ever known.
> IDRIS: And then you stole me. And I stole you.
> DOCTOR: I borrowed you.
> IDRIS: Borrowing implies the intention to return the thing that was taken. What makes you think I would ever give you back?

Later, as the Doctor and IDRIS continue to talk, she says:

> IDRIS: Do you ever wonder why I chose you all those years ago?

> DOCTOR: I chose you. You were unlocked.
> IDRIS: Of course I was. I wanted to see the universe, so I stole a Time Lord and I ran away. And you were the only one mad enough.

Now, instead of the Doctor stealing the TARDIS, the TARDIS tells the story from her point of view and reveals that she stole the Doctor (and has no intention of giving him back). What follows is an exploration of the TARDIS and the Doctor's relationship and the resounding reminder, as Amy succinctly notes at the end of the episode: "It's always you and her, isn't it, long after the rest of us have gone. A boy and his box, off to see the universe." ("The Doctor's Wife").

The embodied TARDIS, though hardly monstrous in the sense of the grotesque, nevertheless functions much as other *monstrum* do, by challenging and undoing our (and the Doctor's) understanding of the "way things are" in the *Whoniverse* and of creating a moment of *das Unheimliche*, the "uncanny." Prior to the new series, the TARDIS was largely a thing, occasionally personified as "old girl," but otherwise mostly ignored (Capettini 148). Yet as Emily Capettini notes, "Whereas the TARDIS was often a plot device or set in the classic series, she becomes a character in her own right in the new series" (149). While the TARDIS is not a monster, nevertheless like House and the Doctor, she is an alien (155). And while she is not strictly monstrous, she does, however, challenge the Doctor's worldview (and so writes Capettini, "the TARDIS is talking to the Doctor, which is not something that she has ever been able to do before and is, by this definition and the opinions of the other characters, mad" [151]). The speaking, embodied TARDIS unsettles the Doctor's self-identity. This is especially the case as the Doctor and TARDIS-as-Idris work together to build a makeshift TARDIS console to attempt to rescue Amy and Rory from House:

> DOCTOR: You know, since we're talking with mouths, not really an opportunity that comes along very often, I just want to say, you know, you have never been very reliable.
> IDRIS: And you have?
> DOCTOR: You didn't always take me where I wanted to go.

IDRIS: No, but I always took you where you needed to go.

As many have noted, TARDIS-as-Idris reveals that she has been in charge all along, and so Gaiman uses the TARDIS to "unhappen" all of the stories where the Doctor landed in places he did not plan to land (see Capettini). The Doctor's story is now rewritten, and the TARDIS plays an active role in that rewriting" (Capettini 152).

Of course, while Gaiman's episode establishes the TARDIS as a living entity complete with thoughts, feelings, and emotions, it also reminds viewers that the TARDIS has been the Doctor's home as he travels throughout space and time. While the Doctor might believe he is the last of the Time Lords and his home planet Gallifrey is gone, in some ways, he is nevertheless always home: always with his TARDIS. Accordingly, the TARDIS functions as the opposite of House, a true *monstrum*. House, which provides a place for the Patchwork People to reside, does not provide safety. Rather, they are simply there to do House's will. The difference between the home provided by the TARDIS when it contains its soul and what the TARDIS becomes when House inhabits it is perhaps most evident when Amy and Rory are locked inside as House takes over. Rory notes, "Listen, whatever happens, at least we're together. And we're in the TARDIS, so we're safe" and House responds, "You're half right. I mean, you are in the TARDIS . . . So, Amy, Rory, why shouldn't I just kill you now?" In a later scene, House reflects on his new embodied state in the TARDIS, saying:

> HOUSE: Corridors. I have corridors. So much to learn about my new home. But you haven't answered my question, children.
> RORY: Er, question?
> HOUSE: You remember. Tell me why I shouldn't just kill you both now?
> AMY: Well, because. Rory, why?
> RORY: Because killing us quickly wouldn't be any fun. And you need fun, don't you? That's what Uncle and Auntie were for, wasn't it? Someone to make suffer. I had a PE teacher just like you. You need to be entertained, and killing us quickly wouldn't be entertainment.

HOUSE: So entertain me. Run.

Suddenly, the safety of the TARDIS is threatened as House enters (and, hauntingly, echoes the Doctor's own command, "Run!"). As Beal explains of monsters, they are "paradoxical personifications of *otherness with sameness* . . . They represent the outside that has gotten inside, the beyond-the-pale that, much to our horror, has gotten into the pale" (4). Gaiman uses the monstrous House to show what happens when the outside gets inside, or, put more simply, when a monster takes over the TARDIS. Like other scholars of monsters, Beal also points to Freud, writing:

> One helpful way of thinking about this paradoxical sense of the monster as a horrific figure of otherness within sameness is by way of Sigmund Freud's concept of the *unheimlich*, that is, the "unhomely" or "uncanny." If *Heimlich* refers to that which belongs within the four walls of the house, inspiring feelings of restfulness and security, then *unheimlech* refers to that which threatens one's own sense of "at-homeness," not from the outside but from *within* the house. The *unheimlich* is in some sense what is in the house without belonging there, the outside that is inside. The horror of the unhomely experience, then, involves the awareness that something that should be outside the house is in it. It is an experience of otherness with sameness. (4-5)

While Gaiman's House is, quite literally, taking up residence inside the Doctor's home (read: the TARDIS), for Freud, "home" is usually an "individual human consciousness" (Beal 5). In his discussion of monsters and the *unheimlich,* Beal extends it "to mean anything from self to society to cosmos" (5). In other words, "The *unheimlech* is that which invades one's sense of personal, social or cosmic order and security—the feeling of being at home in oneself, one's society, and one's world" (5). By transposing the TARDIS and House, Gaiman uses monsters and the monstrous to briefly undo the world that the Doctor, Amy, and Rory know and feel comfortable in. In so doing, Gaiman raises questions about what it means to be a home and to have a home, while also demonstrating through House and the embodied TARDIS the ways that monsters and the monstrous challenge our worldview. And monsters, by challenging our worldview, cause us to ask questions about what it means to be human, to be alive—or, in the Doctor's words, what it might mean to be "humany-wumany."

Human(y-Wumany): Or, The Big Word, The Sad Word

When examined, Gaiman's monsters reveal underlying questions about what it means to actually be alive. In a different episode, the Doctor finds himself crying at the end and remarks, "Happy crying. Humany-wumany" ("The Doctor, the Widow, and the Wardrobe"). Accordingly, for the Doctor, being human seems to be more than simply being alive, but encompasses things "humany-wumany," like happy crying. In particular, the monstrous and the monsters in Gaiman's "The Doctor's Wife" warn against seeing the Time Lord as an infallible, unfeeling figure and emphasize that he shares, despite being a Time Lord of Gallifrey, aspects of what it means to be human(y-wumany).

In Gaiman's "The Doctor's Wife," the monsters and the monstrous are omens that warn against too easily interpreting the Doctor as an infallible figure. This is perhaps most clear when the Doctor sends Amy and Rory back to the TARDIS to look for the Doctor's "missing" sonic screwdriver. (The screwdriver is, in fact, in his pocket, and he is simply trying to get them out of the way.) Amy instructs Rory to look after the Doctor, who in turns tells Rory to look after Amy, and so Rory follows Amy away from the Doctor and towards the TARDIS:

> AMY: I told you to look after him.
> RORY: He'll be fine. He's a Time Lord.
> AMY: It's just what they're called. It doesn't mean he actually knows what he's doing.

Here, Amy reminds the viewers that despite the "Lord" in his name, the Doctor is very much fallible—he is not a god, not a Lord in any sense other than a name. Later, after House absconds with the TARDIS while Amy and Rory are inside, the Doctor stops and says, "Okay, right. I don't, I really don't know what to do. That's a new feeling." Gaiman's Doctor, faced against the monstrous House, does not know what to do. The happy look on the Doctor's face as he realizes this seems to emphasize that, for Gaiman, this Time Lord's moment of fallibility, which is ultimately such a human experience, is, in fact, good.

By emphasizing the Doctor's limits, Gaiman's episode explores how the Doctor can be both so Other and alien while also so similar to the humans with whom he travels. Accordingly, "The Doctor's Wife" asks what is perhaps the most fundamentally human question of all: what does it mean to be alive? So when the TARDIS-as-Idris is first locked up by Auntie, Uncle, and Nephew, she laments from inside her cage, "I'm, I'm . . . big word, sad word. What is that word so sad? No. Will be sad. Will be sad." Later, she asks him, "Are all people like this?" and when the Doctor asks for clarification, she replies, "So much bigger on the inside. I'm, oh, what is that word? It's so big, so complicated. It's so sad." Finally, at the end of the episode, as Idris' human body can no longer contain the TARDIS matrix, the Doctor and the TARDIS-as-Idris have the following exchange:

> IDRIS: I've been looking for a word. A big, complicated word, but so sad. I've found it now.
> DOCTOR: What word?
> IDRIS: Alive. I'm alive.
> DOCTOR: Alive isn't sad.
> IDRIS: It's sad when it's over. I'll always be here, but this is when we talked, and now even that has come to an end. There's something I didn't get to say to you.
> DOCTOR: Goodbye?
> IDRIS: No. I just wanted to say hello. Hello, Doctor. It's so very, very nice to meet you.

Gaiman, reflecting on his infection with the *Doctor Who* virus long before he penned "The Doctor's Wife," wrote that another part of the infection included this: "some things are bigger on the inside than they are on the outside. And, perhaps, some people are bigger on the inside than they are on the outside, as well" (18). In "The

Doctor's Wife," Gaiman uses the embodied TARDIS, who like all monsters challenges the way that we view the world, to show that outward appearance is not, in fact, all that matters; House might have been a large, sentient asteroid who could place his consciousness in the TARDIS shell, but the TARDIS, in the form of a dying human woman, could still defeat the bigger, scarier monster. After all, notes Gaiman, some things—and some people—are bigger on the inside than they are on the outside.

Following the TARDIS-as-Idris' dissolution, the Doctor asks Rory if he is okay, and Rory responds, "No. I watched her die. I shouldn't let it get to me, but it still does. I'm a nurse." The Doctor replies, "Letting it get to you. You know what that's called? Being alive. Best thing there is. Being alive right now, that's all that counts." For the Doctor, who cried visible human(y-wumany) tears as the TARDIS-as-Idris slipped back into the blue police box, no longer able to talk with him, "letting it get to you" means being alive, and that is all that counts.

Are You There? Can You Hear Me?

As Gaiman's episode winds down, the Doctor, sitting alone in the control room as he attempts to build a firewall around the TARDIS matrix, asks, "Are you there? Can you hear me?" When there is no response, he says, "Oh, I'm a silly old. Okay. The Eye of Orion, or wherever we need to go." Immediately, the levers of the TARDIS control panel move on their own, and the Doctor cries out, "Haha! Whoo hoo!"

By all accounts (and based on the awards it received), Gaiman's first *Doctor Who* episode, "The Doctor's Wife," was a brilliant success. Dan Martin notes, for example, how "The patchwork people, the talking planet, the steampunk stylings all felt like vintage Gaiman, but the episode was also steeped in *Who*-ness, in a way guest writers don't always manage" (Martin). Steeped in *Who*-ness—in other words, in the pre-existing canon of *Doctor Who*, an officially recognized set of television episodes, movies, and books about the Doctor that has, like most canons, its own rules and axioms. Yet Gaiman's episode managed to reflect his own infection at the hands of the *Doctor Who* virus while "unhappening" and retelling the Doctor's story. But even more than that, Gaiman's "The Doctor's Wife" illustrates how monsters make for good stories, and how, through monsters, good storytellers reveal and wrestle with the vexing questions that make us—and even the Doctor—human(y)-wumany.

Notes

1. Although, the longtime viewer of the program who remembers Tom Baker's Fourth Doctor may remember 1979's "The Armageddon Factor," when the Doctor casually mentions that he went by the name "Theta Sigma." It did not stick and was later retconned into a nickname.
2. The Doctor believes that he killed all of the Time Lords, along with the entire Dalek race, on the final day of the Time War in order to end the possibly universe-destroying battle between the two alien races. However, the Doctor, in fact, did not kill the Time Lords. Rather, Clara Oswald, one of his companions convinced him to instead hide Gallifrey and the Time Lords in time. The Doctor's memories of this have been erased, though, and he wanders through space and time believing he is responsible for deaths of all the Time Lords.

Works Cited

Beal, Timothy K. *Religion and Its Monsters*. New York: Routledge, 2002. Print.

Capettini, Emily. "A boy and his box, off to see the universe: Madness, Power, and Sex in 'The Doctor's Wife.'" *Feminisms in the Worlds of Neil Gaiman: Essays on the Comics, Poetry and Prose*. Ed. Tara Prescott & Aaron Drucker. Jefferson, NC: McFarland and Company, 2012. 148-160.

"The Doctor, the Widow, and the Wardrobe." *Doctor Who*. Writer Steven Moffat. Dir. Farren Blackburn. Perf. Matt Smith, Claire Skinner, & Karen Gillian. BBC Wales, 25 Dec. 2011.

"The Doctor's Wife." *Doctor Who*. Writer Neil Gaiman. Dir. Richard Clark. Perf. Matt Smith, Karen Gillian, & Arthur Darvill. BBC Wales, 14 May 2011.

"The Eleventh Hour." *Doctor Who.* Writer Steven Moffat. Dir. Adam Smith. Perf. Matt Smith, Karen Gillian, & Arthur Darvill. BBC Wales, 3 Apr. 2010.

Freud, Sigmund, David McLintock, & Hugh Haughton. *The Uncanny.* New York: Penguin Books, 2003. Print.

Gaiman, Neil. *The View from the Cheap Seats: Selected Non-Fiction.* London: Headline Publishing, 2016. Print.

"The Girl in the Fireplace." *Doctor Who.* Writer Steven Moffat. Dir. Euros Lynn. Perf. David Tennant, Billie Piper, & Noel Clarke. BBC Wales, 6 May 2006.

Martin, Dan. "Doctor Who: The Doctor's Wife—Series 32, Episode 4." *Guardian TV & Radio Blog.* Guardian News & Media Ltd., 14 May 2011. Web. 13 Sept. 2016. <https://www.theguardian.com/tv-and radio/tvandradioblog/2011/may/14/doctor-who-doctors-wife-gaiman>.

McAlpine, Fraser. "'Doctor Who': Ten Things You May Not Know About 'The Doctor's Wife.'" *BBC America.* New Video Channel America, LLC, 2016. Web. 13 Sept. 2016. <http://www.bbcamerica.com/anglophenia/2015/08/doctor-who-10-things-you-may-not-know-about-the-doctors-wife>.

Otto, Rudolph. *The Idea of the Holy; an Inquiry into the Non-Rational Factor in the Idea of the Divine and Its Relation to the Rational.* Trans. John W. Harvey. New York: Oxford UP, 1958. Print.

Poole, W. S. *Monsters in America: Our Historical Obsession with the Hideous and the Haunting.* Waco, TX: Baylor UP, 2011. Print.

Prescott, Tara & Aaron Drucker, eds. *Feminisms in the Worlds of Neil Gaiman: Essays on the Comics, Poetry and Prose.* Jefferson, NC: McFarland and Company, 2012. Print.

Weinstock, Jeffrey A. *The Ashgate Encyclopedia of Literary and Cinematic Monsters.* Farnham, UK: Ashgate Publishing Group, 2013. Print.

Crafting Advocacy through Intimacy and Empathy: A Rhetorical Analysis of The Reading Agency Lecture[1]

Kristin K.A. McIlhagga

For those unfamiliar with it, The Reading Agency is a British charity whose published mission is "to inspire more people to read more, encourage them to share their enjoyment of reading and celebrate the difference that reading makes to all our lives. We support people at all stages of their reading journey. Because everything changes when we read." Since 2002, when the agency was formed, it has created successful campaigns encouraging children to read more at their libraries, increased reading opportunities in prisons, worked with libraries to add new members, and developed an adult literacy program. On the occasion of their tenth anniversary, The Reading Agency launched the now annual Reading Agency Lecture. According to the Agency, the lecture series "aims to provide a platform for leading writers and thinkers to share original and challenging ideas about reading and libraries as we work out how to create a reading culture in a radically changed 21st century landscape." As such, the lecture has become a platform for celebrity advocacy supporting goals affiliated with the organization.

On October 14, 2013, Neil Gaiman delivered the second annual Reading Agency Lecture. Gaiman's lecture, eventually titled "Why Our Future Depends on Libraries, Reading and Daydreaming," was delivered to a room full of "leading figures from libraries, the arts, education, government and the literary world plus ambassadors and authors championing" the work of The Reading Agency ("Neil Gaiman Delivers"). While this particular speech was delivered in person, it was archived and allowed to be placed on The Reading Agency's website for public dissemination in accordance with Gaiman's wishes. Gaiman stands out as one who is unimaginably accessible to his readers and fans via the internet and social media, especially as it concerns things he can advocate. His outreach via social media is massive. For example, Between May of 2009 and June of 2016, he mentions libraries in nearly 100 different public tweets (not to mention the private ones to personal individuals). Unsurprisingly, one can find *many* videos of Gaiman's readings and lectures online. The Reading Agency lecture has been viewed on YouTube more than 34,000 times (August 30, 2016) and as of June 24, 2015, the text printed in the *Guardian* had been shared more than 400,000 times (Gaiman [@neilhimself]).

When something as innocuous as a lecture given by an author who readily admits he gives far too many lectures goes viral, it begs the question: What about this lecture resonated with so many people to cause it to be seen, read, and shared so many times? I will argue that this lecture is a strong example of how Gaiman creates a sense of intimacy with his audience. By sharing anecdotes from his childhood and from parenting, Gaiman crafts empathy with his audience and then, having bonded, cajoles them to join him in advocacy of libraries and reading in general. He views such advocacy as an obligation and one that demands being fought for by the army of those hearing his words. What follows will be a close rhetorical analysis of the way that Gaiman makes the argument that "everything changes when we read," building empathy through intimacy with the audience, and then move to showcase his call for the preservation of libraries for the betterment of everyone's future ("Neil Gaiman Delivers").

Examining the Rhetoric of The Reading Agency Lecture

In Gaiman's Reading Agency Lecture, he informs the audience that reading and libraries are crucial for children, for individuals, and for a global society. He argues that, "Literacy is more important than it ever was. . . . We need global citizens who can read comfortably, comprehend what they are reading, understand nuance, and make themselves understood" (Gaiman, "Why" 11). He makes his arguments by explaining his perspectives about what reading does and what it is good for, two topics that may seem obvious and self-evident particularly for those who are literate and consider reading a crucial part of their lives (6). In making his points, Gaiman speaks to those in attendance at the lecture that evening in 2013 (who presumably were there because they already believe that reading is important), but, thanks to the archiving of the lecture online, he was also emboldened to speak to anyone watching it via YouTube, reading it in the Guardian, and, eventually, reading it in his own book 2016's *The View from the Cheap Seats*. In other words, Gaiman's digital footprint lead anyone even remotely familiar with him (or who happens to read the *Guardian*) into the lecture hall with him that evening.

Gaiman begins his lecture, which he retitled for *Cheap Seats* as "Why Our Future Depends on Libraries, Reading, and Daydreaming," by stating his goals unequivocally:

> I'm going to be talking to you about reading. I'm going to tell you that libraries are important. I'm going to suggest that reading fiction, that reading for pleasure, is one of the most important things one can do. I'm going to make an impassioned plea for people to understand what libraries and librarians are, and to preserve both of these things. (5)

His language conveys a sense of the imperative with strong structurally-paralleled appeals that what he is stating is "important"; it's an "impassioned plea." He sees himself as championing these appeals as the words he said (and wrote) are emphasized by drawing the agency to himself and starting each sentence from the first-person "I am" (contracted, obviously, to "I'm"). While the fact that these are Gaiman's own ideas is clear, the repetition underscores an emphasis arguing that this is advocacy work that he believes is important (stated *twice*) not to mention extremely personal, as anyone familiar with his biography might know. In this opening passage, he starts from himself and his beliefs and then broadens the scope by explicitly recognizing his own public identities as author, reader, and a citizen that is part of a much larger community. Not unlike a photographer widening and narrowing his lenses, Gaiman zooms in and out, from the personal to the public, by shifting the point of view among first, second, and third person as a method of drawing the audience closer to him *vis-à-vis* their seeing shared experiences. This will inspire the empathy that allows them to bond.

Next, Gaiman acknowledges personal biases that might be seen as getting in the way of his argument (Who really trusts a car salesperson to be unbiased about selling someone a car?), and he instead uses those biases to showcase his authenticity. Gaiman acknowledges this: "I am biased," he says; "enormously and obviously" (5) as an author of fiction and as a writer of all types of books:

> For about thirty years I have been earning my living through my words, mostly by making things up and writing them down. It is obviously in my interest for people to read, for them to read fiction, for libraries and librarians to exist and help foster a love of reading and places in which reading can occur. (5)

Gaiman articulates that, for him, his career isn't *just* about selling books; it is about encouraging people to read any way that they can (and any way that he can get them to). Openly owning his biases at the outset contributes to a sense of intimacy that he continues throughout the lecture by way of his sharing the dirty secret in the room: the author would like you to read books. Go figure. Because people read, he is able to make a livelihood as a writer; yet, openly owning this bias creates a trust with the audience because he isn't pretending they, nor his biases, don't exist. Sharing his biases openly gives him the strength of authenticity because he isn't hiding them or even remotely trying to hide them. As such, he draws the audience in to him by not hiding the part of his identity that is very closely tied to the topic of reading.

He goes on to share the goals of The Reading Agency and articulate again what he is speaking about, and then he pivots unexpectedly to briefly discuss prisons. Prisons? Why prisons? Prior to this lecture, Gaiman attended a talk in New York about the growth industry of private prisons in America. He states: "The prison industry needs to plan for future growth—how many cells are they going to need?" (6). This is a strange topic shift after clearly stating that he would be discussing the importance of reading. The fact that he does not tell the listener until the end of the paragraph why he does so intimates that he wants the audience to openly wonder: "What could prisons possibly have to do with reading?" He mentions that there is an algorithm that can predict to a disturbing degree of accuracy how many prison cells will be needed fifteen years from now "based on asking what percentage of ten- and eleven-year-olds couldn't read" (6). Here, Gaiman shows his cards and creates a sense of urgency, an appeal to our empathy for humankind starting from childhood. The idea of thinking about ten- and eleven-year-olds who don't read as future criminals appeals to the audience's fear for their children and all children (if not for themselves) and a shared hope for decreasing future prison populations. He widens his lenses here to the panoramic perspective, pushing the audience to think outside of just themselves and to think about the greater human society, the children who may one day populate those prisons. Essentially, he argues that in order to have fewer people in prison, we must nurture literacy.

He then goes on to argue that, "Literate people read fiction" and describes what he sees as the two most important uses of fiction; 1. as a gateway drug to reading (6) and 2. as a way to build empathy (8). He says: "The drive to know what happens next, to want to turn the page, the need to keep going, even if it's hard, because someone's in trouble and you have to know how it's all going to end . . . that's a very real drive" (6). He draws out and transforms the otherwise negative analogy of a gateway drug with words like "drive," "want," and "need," feelings associated with the desire by which some drugs make people wish to continue using. But then he transforms his metaphor—it is the desire to keep going and find out more as we read, Gaiman argues, that leads us "to discover that reading per se is pleasurable" (6).

Next, Gaiman brings the audience's focus back to children. Gaiman considers that if literacy rates can predict future jail needs, then those children must be considered now. He states that we must raise literate children by "finding books that they enjoy, giving them access to those books and letting them read them" (7). He then makes an anticipatory gesture: What if the children want to read what some might consider to be "bad" (7)? He addresses that concern quickly. To those who believe there are bad books or bad authors for children he says, "It's tosh. It's snobbery and it's foolishness . . . every child is different, they bring themselves into the story," and "well-meaning adults can easily destroy a child's love of reading" (7). Gaiman appeals to the audience by reminding them that, if they happen to be one of these more small-minded individuals—it's okay—you meant well. However, he pivots, if children are discouraged from reading particular books or authors, how can they ever have experiences with books that are pleasurable? In addition to reminding the audience that each child is different, he also quietly reminds them that "not everyone has the same taste as you" (7). The ways that he speaks about and for children reminds the audience that children are also citizens and what matters most is the fact that children who are readers may become adults who are readers.

He pushes further to say that whatever gets children reading and experiencing pleasure from that reading should be encouraged: "We need our children to get onto the reading ladder: anything that they enjoy reading will move them up, rung by rung, into literacy" (8). Here, he reminds the audience that literacy is the ultimate goal, not critical examinations of the literature. His use of the collective "we" furthers the previous section's direct address and engages the audience as his co-conspirators in supporting a literate society.

Gaiman brings the spectator into his own world with a brief personal vignette from his perspective as a parent, adding to the sense of intimacy he makes with the audience. He notes how he enthusiastically gave his then eleven-year-old daughter a copy of Stephen King's *Carrie* as a follow-up to the books of R. L. Stine. He states that "Holly [had] read nothing but safe stories of settlers on prairies for the rest of her early teenage years" (8). Needless to say, it didn't go as well as Gaiman planned. However, the intimacy of sharing a parenting story of a failure from someone otherwise seen as anything but a failure creates empathy with those who are parents. It gets at the concern many adults have when it comes to nurturing young readers: the fear of doing it wrong. Gaiman's parenting story is a way of acknowledging that while raising literate children may not always go the way we imagine, what matters more is getting children reading despite guilt or failure that may ensue.

Gaiman next reminds the audience what we do as readers when we actually read. In the first paragraph of this section, he addresses the audience as "you" no less than thirteen times. He writes:

> You build up from twenty-six letters and a handful of punctuation marks, and you, and you alone, using your imagination, create a world and people it and look out through other eyes. You get to feel things, visit places and worlds you would never otherwise know. You learn that everyone else out there is a me, as well. You're being someone else, and when you return to your own world you're going to be slightly changed. (8)

Gaiman pulls back the curtain on what we do as readers to make meaning; grow understanding; and, ultimately, create empathy. Here, he reminds those in the audience who are already literate that they need to remember how amazing a thing reading actually can be. Reading allows us to create new worlds and learn about others; how could anyone not want that for others? He articulates *how* reading prose fiction builds empathy by "feeling things, visit[ing] places and worlds you would never otherwise know" (8). When we realize as readers that, "Everyone else out there is a me as well" we are able to empathize, to acknowledge that my experiences are not the same as someone else's experiences.

Gaiman's key questions at the beginning of the lecture were: "What is reading?" and "What is it good for?" He has, thus far, argued that reading is good for building empathy, but that rhetorically begs the question of why building empathy through reading is important in the first place. His answer is that once we visit other worlds and understand the experiences of other people, "you can never be entirely content with the world that you grew up in. And discontent is a good thing: people can modify and improve their worlds, leave them better, leave them different, if they're discontented" (8). Throughout this section, Gaiman uses the second-person 'you'. This direct address of the audience implies that they, too, have had these reader experiences and reminds them that they are literate citizens. In reminding the audience of the ways they build empathy and can use it to change the world, he appeals to their empathy as citizens—and, as such, he crafts them from individuals into a community of readers.

Libraries And Library Advocacy

One of Gaiman's goals that he states clearly at the beginning of the lecture is to "make an impassioned plea for people to understand what libraries and librarians are, and to preserve both of these things" ("Why" 5). Much like he did as he described the ways that reading builds empathy for those who take it for granted, he makes similar moves as he talks about libraries, the places where the books are held, and librarians, the gatekeepers to those books. He does not presume the audience's understanding of why libraries are important or even what they are.

Gaiman returns to first person to zoom in on his own experiences using libraries as a child. Again, this adds weight to his advocacy, if an author who writes and publishes as much as Gaiman does was an avid library user as a child, it must be a good thing. He shares memories of his parents dropping him off at the library on their way to work during summers and his having read his way through the children's section "looking for vampires or detectives or witches or wonders" (9). He describes an idyllic childhood reading experience similar to one recounted earlier in the lecture. The experience of finding the stories he liked and reading them, without judgment that the books he was reading were "wrong." Libraries, so goes the inference, allowed him to have those experiences, to discover himself as a reader.

Gaiman also talks about the librarians. He shows the enormous influence they had on his reading life as a child, not by forcing or withdrawing particular books but through encouragement and respect.

> They were good librarians. They liked books and they liked the books being read. They taught me how to order books from other libraries on interlibrary loans. They had no snobbery about anything I read. They just seemed to like that there was this wide-eyed little boy who loved to read, and they would talk to me about the books I was

reading, they would find me other books in a series, they would help. They treated me as another reader—nothing less, nothing more—which meant they treated me with respect. I was not used to being treated with respect as an eight-year-old. (9-10)

These personal stories from childhood affirm Gaiman's earlier statements about the importance of encouraging children to read. The implicit idea being proffered to those listening to him speak about such things is that the experiences he had at his library and the interactions with librarians who helped him become a literate citizen in addition to an author—wouldn't that be nice if it happened to other children as well? Again, Gaiman's arguments about the importance of reading and libraries aren't just theoretical, they are also personal, adding to the sense of intimacy he creates with his audience by sharing details from his own biography. Gaiman's personal stories serve to showcase the importance of the people who work in the library as well as the institutions themselves by pointing to himself as the result of those experiences.

From this point, Gaiman again zooms out from his personal experiences into a panoramic perspective of libraries. His personal anecdotes help the audience see through his eyes, employing his memories. He then uses that sense of empathy as a comprehensive view of libraries that otherwise might not have been considered. He presents the library not as "a shelf of books" (10) but as a place of freedom and information: "Libraries are about Freedom. Freedom to read, freedom of ideas, freedom of communication. They are about education (which is not a process that finishes the day we leave school or university), about entertainment, about making safe spaces, and about access to information" (10). It is his tacit contention that some like to think of libraries as just "a shelf of books," that libraries seem unnecessary in a time when many books exist digitally. For him, this is anathema: to think that libraries are only books on shelves is to misunderstand what libraries are in the twenty-first century. Gaiman appeals to the audience as citizens of the world. He presumes that they will agree that the these reasons (education, entertainment, safe spaces, and information) are important to have in developing a literate and humane society.

Libraries today, Gaiman argues, are about the nature of information: "For all of human history, we have lived in a time of information scarcity, and having the needed information was always important, and always worth something. . . . Information was a valuable thing, and those who had it or could obtain it could charge for that service" (10). In other words and being far more pragmatic in his approach than earlier: information equals money, security, and power. When information was primarily in books and many people couldn't afford them, libraries were crucial as places to gather information that could only be acquired from within books. Libraries, as such, are repositories for books, and librarians help people sort out what information they need as well as how to find it. Gaiman feels that if the perception is that libraries only hold books, then they do not in fact seem necessary given that most information that was previously only in books is now available on the Internet. He tells the audience that "we've moved from an information-scarce economy to one driven by information-glut" (10). And, with this shift has come a change in the nature of libraries and librarians, he says: now citizens need help sifting through and narrowing down the vast amounts of available information. The repetition of the word "information"—sixteen times—reminds the audience of the importance of understanding this change in information (not to mention the sheer volume of it) and how librarians are trained to help them navigate this ever-expanding sea of it.

Gaiman paints a picture of libraries as a place with free Internet and access to all the information that comes with it. Such information can help people find jobs and apply for them, again mixing ideals with a healthy dose of pragmatism: "A library is a place that is a repository of, and gives every citizen equal access to, information. That includes health information. And mental health information. It's a community space. It's a place of safety, a haven from the world. It's a place with librarians in it" (11). Gaiman speaks about libraries as spaces that will help people imagine a different world, a better world. However, he again pivots to outline the threat to their existence. "Libraries are gates to the future," Gaiman tells us, and yet there are people who are "seizing the opportunity to close libraries as an easy way to save money, without realizing that they are, quite literally, stealing from the future to pay for today" (12). Gaiman recalls his biases as a British citizen when he shares findings from a study that indicates "England is the only country where the oldest age group has higher proficiency in both literacy and numeracy than the youngest group" (12). Remember that he has built his argument on the necessity of raising literate children, and yet, here is a study saying that what is happening is anything but that.

Obligations to the Future (of the Library and Readers)

Recalling the goals stated at the lecture's opening, Gaiman underscores the idea that everyone has a responsibility to help create a literate society, to make the world a better place. Having identified himself as a reader, a writer, and a citizen at the beginning of the lecture, he likens these obligations to the responsibilities of citizenship. By identifying with each of these three roles at the beginning, Gaiman gains some gravitas as he makes his closing argument, as if to say, "I'm doing it, and you can, too." While his audience (whether listening or reading) may not all be writers, or even readers, it can be assumed that all are citizens of some community. And now that Gaiman has built a *shared* community with his audience, he invites them to join him in a call to action. He outlines these actions as obligations and responsibilities we have to the future.

Gaiman closes out the lecture by outlining "responsibilities and obligations to children, to the adults those children will become, to the world they will find themselves inhabiting" ("Why" 12-13). This closing functions as a call to action for anyone listening to or reading the lecture to join Gaiman in fostering a more literate society and, ultimately, making the world a better place. He introduces the section by using first person "*I* believe," making less a claim and more a conjecture, but then brings the audience in with "*we* have responsibilities to the future" (12, emphasis added). He continues to remind the audience of their responsibilities, not only as he describes each of them but also with the repeated use of the collective "we" and "our." In the final fourteen paragraphs of his lecture, he repeats the collective "we" or "our" *fifty* times, stressing the collaborative nature of the call. The repetition of both collective pronouns as well as keywords "read," "readers," "reading," "libraries," and "language" underscores the imperative nature of these obligations.

Gaiman argues that everyone has an obligation to "read for pleasure, in private and in public places. If we read for pleasure, if others see us reading then we learn, we exercise our imaginations. We show others that reading is a good thing" (13). He continues the call to action with repeated use of "we" as he reminds the audience of the importance of nurturing children as literate people: "We have an obligation to read aloud to our children" (13). In using the pronoun "our," he reminds the audience that all children deserve to be read to. He goes on to shift the language slightly as a way of reminding the audience that the goal of reading to children is for them to develop their own love of reading. He says, "To read them things they enjoy. To read to them stories we are already tired of. To do the voices, to make it interesting, and not to stop reading to them just because they learn to read to themselves" (13) Gaiman is reiterating his earlier points about the importance of allowing children to read what they want, to caution that "well-meaning adults can easily destroy a child's love of reading" (7). Raising literate children, he implores, requires that we give them space to find pleasure in reading, and he wants the audience to remember that we must all be part of nurturing young readers.

Gaiman tells the audience that they also need to be thoughtful about language, that they have an obligation to language "to push ourselves: to find out what words mean and how to deploy them, to communicate clearly, to say what we mean" (13). This call to responsibility, in which he includes himself, encompasses the three roles of reader, writer, and citizen. As readers, one needs to push themselves to read beyond what they know, to understand more deeply, and to not allow language to "be a dead thing that must be revered" (13). Writers, he feels, can do this through the language they choose and use in prose, poetry, nonfiction, etc. Readers do this, too, through the texts they select and the way they choose to engage with them. Here, Gaiman even places further burden upon himself and his fellow writers to aid the perspective reader. To his fellow writers, he declares the obligation to write true things and not bore readers. And while it is imperative to write true things, Gaiman, somewhat ironically, cautions authors to avoid preaching, lecturing, and "not to force predigested morals and messages down our readers' throats" (14). He again creates a sense of urgency and imperative, that writers must also be part of the work to improve our future. He sees the stories and worlds that writers create have the potential to "give [readers] weapons and give them armor and pass on whatever wisdom we have gleaned from our short stay on this green world" (14). His language here is reminiscent of the ways he discusses prose fiction as a means for readers to gain windows into other worlds. Gaiman adds a personal appeal regarding the purpose of fiction, which offers readers both weapons and armor; writers must be aware of this immense responsibility. And he adds weightiness to the obligation of those authors who write for children, warning them that "if we mess it up and write dull books that turn children away from reading and from books, we've lessened our own future and diminished theirs" (14). Although he said earlier in the lecture that there are no bad books or bad authors for children, perhaps an author who doesn't take his responsibility seriously might make such a list.

The next obligation begins with another call to arms, "We all—adults and children, writers and readers—have an obligation to daydream. We have an obligation to imagine" (14). While this may, at first, seem to be disconnected from the goal of supporting reading and libraries, Gaiman shows us the connection. It is through daydreaming and imagination that, he says, "individuals change their world over and over, individuals make the future, and they do it by imagining that things can be different" (14). By focusing on the actions of the individual, he reminds the audience that every single person listening or reading this lecture has the capacity to improve the world. He again points out what may seem obvious, but unlike earlier in the lecture he announces it, "I'm going to point out something so obvious that it tends to be forgotten" (14). While earlier in the lecture he articulated obvious aspects of reading, here he is demanding we pay attention to the obvious. Speaking to the audience present that evening, Gaiman asks them to look around the room and consider, "everything you can see, including the walls, was, at some point, imagined. Someone decided it might be easier to sit on a chair than on the ground and imagined the chair" (14). As if anyone could still be sitting at this point.

This obligation, all of these responsibilities Gaiman shares, are not just about reading, but about making a better world *through* reading. He reminds the audience of all of those people who daydreamed and imagined a different way of living: "Political movements, personal movements, all begin with people imagining another way of existing" (15). Gaiman wants the audience to imagine with him the possibility of a better world. The sense of empathy and intimacy he has built brings the audience along with him. If it were in a church, the audience might start yelling 'Amen' as he brings forth the obligation "to make things beautiful, to not leave the world uglier than we found it" (15). As Gaiman used both personal and public approaches throughout his talk, he ultimately built up to these final appeals to the audience's humanity. That their responsibility as human beings is to make decisions, act, and join Gaiman in advocacy to "preserve and protect knowledge and encourage literacy" (15). He closes his lecture by coming back one last time to children as a moment of possibility and potential: "I hope we can give our children a world in which they will read, and be read to, and imagine, and understand" (15). Gaiman underscores the importance of helping children learn to read, harkening back to those ten- and eleven-year-olds who currently don't read and have become little more than future prison statistics before their lives have barely begun.

Note
1. For the purposes of reading this analysis, the full lecture is available for free at: https://readingagency.org.uk.

Works Cited

"Neil Gaiman Delivers Our Second Annual Lecture." *The Reading Agency*. The Reading Agency, 2013. Web. 30 Aug 2016. <https://readingagency.org.uk/news/media/neil-gaiman-delivers-our-second-annual-lecture.html>.

"Neil Gaiman: By the Book." *New York Times Book Review*. The New York Times Company, 3 May 3, 2012. Web. 30 Aug. 2016. <http://nyti.ms/18OC4Zr>.

Gaiman, Neil. "Neil Gaiman: Why Our Future Depends on Libraries, Reading and Daydreaming." *Guardian*. The Guardian News and Media, Ltd., 15 Oct. 2013. Web. 30 Aug. 2016. <https://www.theguardian.com/books/2013/oct/15/neil-gaiman-future-libraries-reading-daydreaming>.

_____. *The View From the Cheap Seats*. New York: Harper Collins, 2016. Print.

_____. "Why Our Future Depends on Libraries, Reading and Daydreaming: The Reading Agency Lecture, 2013." *The View From the Cheap Seats*. New York: Harper Collins, 2016. 5-15. Print.

_____. [@neilhimself]. "Proud & amazed to see my talk about reading & Libraries for The Reading Agency has been shared almost 400,000 times: the guardian.com/books/2013oct..." *Twitter*. Twitter, Inc., 24 June 2015. 4:24 p.m. Web. 30 Aug. 2016. <https://twitter.com/neilhimself/status/613789868292898816>.

"Reading Agency Lecture 2013." *YouTube*. Uploaded by Reading Agency, 22 Oct. 2013. Web. 30 Aug. 2016. <https://youtu.be/yNIUWv9_ZH0>.

The Reading Agency. The Reading Agency, 2016. Web. 30 Aug. 2016. <https://readingagency.org.uk/>.

RESOURCES

Chronology of Neil Gaiman's Life

1960	Neil Richard Gaiman is born on November 10, 1960 to Sheila and David Bernard Gaiman in Portchester, Hampshire, United Kingdom.
1965	The Gaiman family moves to East Grinstead, West Sussex, and Gaiman begins to supplement his reading at the local library with the works of J. R. R. Tolkien, C. S. Lewis, Lewis Carroll, and a bevy of American comic books that he received c. 1967–68.
1970	Begins Ardingly College.
1974	Begins Whitgift School.
1977	After graduating Whitgift, Gaiman becomes a freelance journalist, writing for newspapers and outlets such as *The Sunday Times*, *The Observer*, *Knave*, and *Time Out*.
1983	With Mary McGrath, Gaiman has first child, a son, named Michael Richard.
1984	Gaiman's first professional short story, "Featherquest" is published. Proteus Publishing Company hires him to write a biography of Duran Duran entitled *Duran Duran: The First Four Years of the Fab Five*. He also produces a book of quotations with Kim Newman entitled *Ghastly Beyond Belief*. Rustling through a comics kiosk in Victoria station, Gaiman happens upon an issue of *The Saga of The Swamp Thing* by Alan Moore; this would begin his fascination with the author and his work, and a friendship would ensue. Moore would introduce him to the process of scripting comics in 1985.

1985	Marries Mary McGrath in March. Later that year, Holly Miranda, a daughter, is born to Mary McGrath. Gaiman begins writing further short stories, such as "How to Be a Barbarian" and "How to Spot a Psycho." He also meets Terry Pratchett through an interview for the first time.
1986	Gaiman writes his first comic for *2000 AD* entitled "You're Never Alone with a Phone" and "Conversation Piece." He meets Karen Berger at DC Comics and pitches *Black Orchid* (which would be published between 1988–89); she offers him the opportunity to revive a DC property. This conversation leads to the genesis of *The Sandman*.
1987	Gaiman formally quits his job as a professional journalist. Gaiman meets illustrator Dave McKean in New York City, where the two collaborate on *Violent Cases*. It will be the first of many collaborations between the two.
1988	As an avid fan of Douglas Adams, Gaiman writes *Don't Panic: The Official Hitchhiker's Guide to the Galaxy Companion*. Publishes *Black Orchid*. *The Sandman* #1 is published on November 29 (though it was cover dated January 1989). Gaiman also takes a phone call from author Terry Pratchett to begin a collaborative novel that would become *Good Omens*.
1989	With Mark Buckingham, Gaiman publishes *Total Eclipse*, featuring the character Miracleman; this becomes his first published work with the character.
1990	Publishes *Good Omens* with Terry Pratchett. Picks up and begins writing the comic book *Miracleman* (formerly *Marvelman*) at issue #17 from Alan Moore.

1991	Gaiman wins his first Eisner Awards for *The Sandman* in the categories of Best Continuing Series, Best Graphic Album, and Best Writer. He would win again (in multiple categories) in 1992, 93, 94, 2000, 04, 07, and 09 (More than twenty-six to this date). He would also win Harvey Awards, Hugo Awards et al. in the same year. Perhaps most notably, *The Sandman* #19 "A Midsummer Night's Dream" wins the prestigious World Fantasy Award, the first comic ever to do so.
1992	Gaiman and family move to America near Menomonie, Wisconsin, to be closer to McGrath's family.
1993	Publishes the collection of short stories *Angels and Visitations*. Publishes *Death: The High Cost of Living* with Chris Bachalo.
1994	Madeleine Rose Elvira, a daughter, is born to Mary McGrath in August. Publishes *The Tragical Comedy or Comical Tragedy of Mr. Punch: A Romance* with Dave McKean.
1995	Publishes *Sandman: Midnight Theatre*.
1996	Scripts the television series *Neverwhere* (with Lenny Henry) and, dissatisfied with the BBC treatment, subsequently publishes the work as a novel.
1997	Adapts the English version of the film *Princess Mononoke* from Studio Ghibli. Publishes *The Day I Swapped My Dad for Two Goldfish*.
1998	Publishes the collection of short stories *Smoke and Mirrors*. Writes the screenplay "Day of the Dead" for the television series *Babylon 5*.

1999	Publishes *Stardust*. Publishes *Sandman: The Dream Hunters*.
2001	Publishes *American Gods*. Opens *Neil Gaiman's Journal*, his ongoing blog.
2002	Publishes *Coraline*. For *American Gods*, Gaiman wins the Hugo, the Nebula, the Locus, the Bram Stoker, et al. awards for best novel.
2003	Publishes *The Wolves in the Walls*. Publishes *The Sandman: Endless Nights*. Gaiman wins the Nebula and Hugo awards for *Coraline*.
2004	Publishes *Marvel: 1602*. In *Legends II*, a collection of short stories edited by Robert Silverberg, Gaiman publishes "The Monarch of the Glen," the first official sequel to *American Gods*. "Black Dog," the second sequel," will be later published in *Trigger Warning*.
2005	Writes screenplay for *MirrorMask*. Publishes *Anansi Boys*.
2006	Publishes short story collection *Fragile Things*.
2007	Divorces Mary McGrath. Publishes short story collection *M is for Magic*. Writes the screenplay for *Beowulf*. Gaiman also visits the Republic of China and is inspired by the trip to start a series about a panda named Chu.
2008	Writes *The Graveyard Book* and *Odd and the Frost Giants*. Wins the Newbery and Carnegie Medals for *The Graveyard Book*, becoming the first author to do so for the same work.

2009	Pens the poem "Blueberry Girl" for friend Tori Amos. The poem is later illustrated by Charles Vess and published as *Blueberry Girl*. Gaiman wins the Hugo Award for *The Graveyard Book*.
2010	Publishes the poem "Instructions," with illustrations by Charles Vess, as *Instructions*.
2011	Marries Amanda Palmer. Writes his first episode of long-time BBC series *Doctor Who*, "The Doctor's Wife."
2012	Gaiman is awarded an honorary doctorate and is invited to give the commencement speech at The University of the Arts in Philadelphia. The speech becomes viral online, becoming known as the "Make Good Art" speech published in 2013. Additionally, he forms the nonprofit organization, The Gaiman Foundation, dedicated to supporting free speech.
2013	Publishes *The Ocean at the End of the Lane*, which is voted Book of the Year in the British National Book Awards. Also publishes *Chu's Day*, the first in an ongoing series aimed at younger readers. Publishes *Fortunately, The Milk* with illustrator Skottie Young. Writes first video game, *Wayward Manor*. Writes the screenplay for "Nightmare in Silver" and "Rain Gods" for the television series *Doctor Who*. Gaiman returns to write the prequel to *The Sandman* with J.H. Williams III; entitled *The Sandman: Overture*, it will be published from 2013–15 after numerous delays.
2014	Gaiman is called upon by United Nations High Commission for Refugees to visit Jordan during the Syrian Civil War to recount the tragedies he sees. He makes a short film with the UNHCR and writes a piece for *The Guardian* to account for the trip.

2015	Publishes the collection *Trigger Warnings*. With Amanda Palmer, a son, Anthony, is born in September.
2016	Publishes collection of nonfiction pieces entitled *The View from the Cheap Seats*.
2017	Publishes *Norse Mythology*.

Works by Neil Gaiman

(Edited volumes not listed)

Comics and Graphic Novels

2000 AD:
> "You're Never Alone with a Phone," 1986 (with John Hicklenton in No. 488)
>
> "Conversation Piece," 1986 (with Dave Wyatt, in No. 489)
>
> "I'm a Believer," 1987 (with Massimo Belardinelli, in No. 536)
>
> "What's in a Name?," 1987 (with Steve Yeowell)

Judge Dredd Annual '88: "Judge Hershey: Sweet Justice," 1987 (with Lee Baulch)

Revolver Horror Special: "Feeders and Eaters," 1990 (with Mark Buckingham)

Violent Cases, 1987 (with Dave McKean)

Outrageous Tales from the Old Testament, 1987
> "The Book of Judges" (with Mike Matthews)
>
> "Jael and Sisera" (with Julie Hollings)
>
> "Jephitah and His Daughter" (with Peter Rigg)
>
> "Journey to Bethlehem" (with Steve Gibson)
>
> "The Prophet Who Came to Dinner" (with Dave McKean)
>
> "The Tribe of Benjamin" (with Mike Matthews)

Blaam! #1: "The Great Cool Challenge," *1988* (with Shane Oakley)

Seven Deadly Sins: "Sloth," 1989 (with Bryan Talbot)

AARGH! #1: "From Homogenous to Honey," 1998 (with Bryan Talbot)

Black Orchid, 1988–89 (with Dave McKean)

Redfox #20: "Fragments," 1989 (with SMS)

Signal to Noise, 1989 (with Dave McKean)

Trident #1: "The Light Brigade," 1989 (with Nigel Kitching)

The Sandman, 1989–1996 (with Sam Keith, Mike Dringenberg, Chris Bachalo, Dave McKean et al.)

The Sandman's seventy-five issues have been collected in ten volumes:

Vol. 1 *Preludes and Nocturnes*, 1991
Vol. 2 *The Doll's House*, 1990
Vol. 3 *Dream Country*, 1991
Vol. 4 *Seasons of Mists*, 1992
Vol. 5 *A Game of You*, 1993
Vol. 6 *Fable and Reflections*, 1993
Vol. 7 *Brief Lives*, 1993
Vol. 8 *Worlds' End*, 1994
Vol. 9 *The Kindly Ones*, 1994
Vol. 10 *The Wake*, 1995

The Books of Magic, 1990–91 (with John Bolton, Charlie Vess et al.)

Breakthrough: "Vier Mauern," 1990 (with Dave McKean)

Miracleman, 1990–92 (with Mark Buckingham):

Mister X Archives:

"Mr. X: Heartsprings and Watchstops," 1989 (with Dave McKean)
"Cover Story," 1991 (with Kelley Jones)

Sandman Special, "The Song of Orpheus," 1991 (with Bryan Talbot)

Taboo:

"Babycakes," 1990 (with Michael Zulli, in No. 4, 1990)
"Blood Monster," 1992 (with Nancy O'Connor, in No. 6)
"Sweeney Todd: Prologue," 1992 (with Michael Zulli, in No. 7)

Cerebus #147: "Being an Account of the Life and Death of the Emperor Heliogabolus," 1992 (with Aardvark-Vanaheim)

Vertigo Preview, "Fear of Falling," 1992 (with Kent Williams)

Clive Barker's Hellraiser #20: "Wordsworth," 1993 (with Dave McKean)

Spawn #9, 1993 (with Todd McFarlane)

The Children's Crusade, 1993–94 (with Chris Bachalo et al.)

Vertigo Jam, "The Castle," 1993 (with Kevin Nowlan)

Roarin' Rick's Rare Bit Fiends #2–3: "Celebrity Rare Bit Fiends," 1994 (with Rick Veitch)

Angela, 1994–95 (with Greg Capullo)

The Last Temptation, 1994 (with Michael Zulli)

Negative Burn:
- "We Can Get Them for You Wholesale," 1994 (with Joe Pruett and Ken Meyer Jr.)
- "The Old Warlock's Reverie: A Pantoum," 1998 (with Guy Davis)

Sandman: A Gallery of Dreams, 1994 (various artists)

Spawn #26, 1994 (with Todd McFarlane and Greg Capullo)

The Tragical Comedy or Comical Tragedy of Mr. Punch: A Romance, 1994 (with Dave McKean)

Sandman: Midnight Theatre, 1995 (with Matt Wagner and Teddy Kristiansen)

Batman: Black and White #2, 1996: "A Black and White World" (with Simon Bisley)

Elric: One Life No. 0, 1996 (with P. Craig Russell)

It's Dark in London: "The Court," 1996 (with Warren Pleece)

The Dreaming #8, "Three 'Lost' Pages from 'The Wake'," 1997 (with Michael Zulli)

Neil Gaiman and Charles Vess' Stardust, 1997–98

Cherry Deluxe #1: "The Innkeeper's Soul," 1998 (with Larry Welz)

Frank Frazetta Fantasy Illustrated #3: "The Facts in the Case of the Departure of Miss Finch," 1998 (with Tony Daniel)

Oni Double Feature #6–8: "Only the End of the World Again," 1998 (with P. Craig Russell)

Shoggoth's Old Peculiar (with Jouni Koponen, one-shot, Dream Haven, 1998)

The Spirit: The New Adventures #2: "The Return of the Mink Stole,"1998 (with Eddie Campbell)

Vertigo: Winter's Edge #1, "The Flowers of Romance," 1998 (with John Bolton)

Neil Gaiman's Midnight Days, 1999 (various artists)

Sandman: The Dream Hunters, 1999 (with Yoshitaka Amano)

Vertigo: Winter's Edge #2, "A Winter's Tale," 1999 (with Jeffrey Catherine Jones)

Green Lantern/Superman: Legend of the Green Flame, 2000 (various artists)

Vertigo: Winter's Edge #3, "How They Met Themselves," 2000 (with Michael Zulli)

Harlequin Valentine, 2001 (with John Bolton)

Heroes: "The Song of the Lost," 2001 (with Jae Lee)

Murder Mysteries, 2002 (with P. Craig Russell)

The Extraordinary Works of Alan Moore: "True Things," 2003 (with Mark Buckingham)

Marvel 1602, 2003 (with Andy Kubert)

Creatures of the Night, 2004 (with Michael Zulli)

Melinda, 2005 (with Dagmara Matuszak)

Eternals, 2007 (with John Romita Jr)

John Romita Jr. 30th Anniversary Special: "Romita—Space Knight," 2007 (with Hilary Barta)

Sandman: The Dream Hunters, 2008–09 (with P. Craig Russell)

Batman: Whatever Happened to the Caped Crusader?, 2009 (with Andy Kubert et al.)

CBLDF Presents: Liberty Comics #2: "100 Words," 2009 (with Jim Lee)

The Collected Death, 2009 (with Dave McKean, Chris Bachalo et al.)

Wednesday Comics, 2009 (With Mike Allred)

The Sandman: Overture, 2013–2015 (with JH Williams III)

The Graveyard Book Vol. 1 and 2 (Graphic Novel), 2014 (with P. Craig Russell)

Drama

The Wolves in the Walls, 2005–6

Mr. Punch, 2008

Film (screenwriter)

Princess Mononoke, 1997 (English translation & adaption)

A Short Film About Jon Bolton, 2003

MirrorMask, 2005

Beowulf, 2007

Nonfiction

Duran Duran: The First Four Years of the Fab Five, 1984

Don't Panic: The Official Hitchhiker's Guide to the Galaxy Companion, 1988

Don't Panic: Douglas Adams & The Hitchhiker's Guide to the Galaxy, 1993

Dustcovers: The Collected Sandman Covers 1989–1996, 1997 (with Dave McKean)

Gods & Tulips, 1999

Alchemy of MirrorMask, 2005 (with Dave McKean)

Beowulf: The Script Book, 2007 (with Roger Avary)

Make Good Art, 2013

Dream State: The Collected Dreaming Covers, 2014 (with Dave McKean)

The View from the Cheap Seats: Selected Nonfiction, 2016

Long Fiction

(Note: as Gaiman chooses not to distinguish between "Adult" and "Non-Adult" Fiction, this list does not either.)

Good Omens, 1990 (with Terry Pratchett)

Neverwhere, 1996

The Day I Swapped My Dad for Two Goldfish, 1997 (with Dave McKean)

Stardust, 1999

American Gods, 2001

Coraline, 2002

The Wolves in the Walls, 2003 (with Dave McKean)

Anansi Boys, 2005

MirrorMask: The Illustrated Film Script of the Motion Picture, 2005 (with Dave McKean)
MirrorMask (Children's Edition), 2005
InterWorld, 2007 (with Michael Reaves)
The Dangerous Alphabet, 2008 (with Gris Grimly)
The Graveyard Book, 2008
Odd and the Frost Giants, 2008
Blueberry Girl, 2009 (with Charles Vess)
Crazy Hair, 2009 (with Dave McKean)
Instructions, 2010 (with Charles Vess)
Chu's Day, 2013 (with Adam Rex)
Fortunately, the Milk, 2013 (with Skottie Young)
The Silver Dream, 2013 (with Michael and Mallory Reaves)
The Ocean at the End of the Lane, 2013
Chu's First Day of School, 2014 (with Adam Rex)
Hansel and Gretel, 2014 (with Lorenzo Mattotti)
The Sleeper and the Spindle, 2014 (with Chris Riddell)
The Truth Is a Cave in the Black Mountains, 2014 (with Eddie Campbell)
Eternity's Wheel, 2015 (with Michael and Mallory Reaves)
Norse Mythology, 2017

Short Fiction (Collected)
Angels and Visitations, 1993
Smoke and Mirrors, 1998
Adventures in the Dream Trade, 2002
Fragile Things, 2006
M is For Magic, 2007
Who Killed Amanda Palmer, 2009 (with Kyle Cassidy and Beth Hommel, 2009)
Trigger Warnings, 2015

Short Fiction (Uncollected)

"I, Cthulhu, or, What's a Tentacle-Faced Thing Like Me Doing in a Sunken City Like This (Latitude 47° 9' S, Longitude 126° 43' W)?," 1987

"Culprits Or Where Are They Now?," 1990 (with Kim Newman and Eugene Byrne)

"Now We are Sick," 1991

"An Honest Answer," 1993 (with Bryan Talbot)

"Cinnamon," 1995

"The False Knight on the Road," 1996 (with Charles Vess)

"The Shadow," 2009

"House," 2013

"How the Marquis Got His Coat Back," 2014

"Kissing Song," 2014

Television (screenwriter)

Neverwhere, 1996

Babylon 5, "Day of the Dead," 1998

10 Minute Tales, "Statuesque," 2009

Doctor Who:
    "The Doctor's Wife," 2011
    "Nightmare in Silver," 2013
    "Rain Gods," 2013

Video Game

Wayward Manor, 2013

Bibliography

Abbruscato, Joseph. "Being Nobody: Identity in Neil Gaiman's *The Graveyard Book*." *The Gothic Fairy Tale In Young Adult Literature*. Eds. Joseph Abbruscato & Tanya Jones. McFarland, 2014. 66-82. Print.

Bealer, Tracy L., Rachel Luria, & Wayne Yuen. *Neil Gaiman and Philosophy: Gods Gone Wild!*. Open Court, 2012. Print.

Błaszkiewicz, Maria. "Allegorizing the Fantastic: A Spenserian Reading of Neil Gaiman's *Neverwhere*." *Basic Categories of Fantastic Literature Revisited*. Ed. Andrzej Wicher, Piotr Spyra, & Joanna Matyjaszczyk. Cambridge Scholars, 2014. 127-143. Print.

Brisbin, Ally, and Paul Booth. "The Sand/wo/man: The Unstable Worlds of Gender in Neil Gaiman's *Sandman* Series." *Journal of Popular Culture* 46.1 (2013): 20-37. Print.

Burstyn, Franziska. "Alice and Mowgli Revisited: Neil Gaiman's *Coraline* and *The Graveyard Book*." *Inklings: Jahrbuch für Literatur und Ästhetik* 30 (2012): 72-86. Print.

Campbell, Hayley & Audry Niffenegger. *The Art of Neil Gaiman*. Harper, 2014. Print.

Camus, Cyril. "Fantasy and Landscape: Mountain as Myth in Neil Gaiman's Stories." *Mountains Figured and Disfigured in the English-Speaking World*. Ed. Françoise Besson. Cambridge Scholars, 2010. 379-391. Print.

_____. "Neil Gaiman's *Sandman* as a Gateway from Comic Books to Graphic Novels." *Studies in the Novel* 47.3 (2015): 308-18. Print.

_____. "The 'Outsider': Neil Gaiman and the Old Testament." *Shofar: An Interdisciplinary Journal of Jewish Studies* 29.2 (2011): 77-99. Print.

Cantrell, Sarah. "Feminist Subjectivity in Neil Gaiman's *Black Orchid*." *Feminism in the Worlds of Neil Gaiman*. Ed. Tara Prescott & Aaron Drucker. McFarland, 2012. 102-115. Print.

Carroll, Siobhan. "Imagined Nation: Place and National Identity in Neil Gaiman's *American Gods*." *Extrapolation: A Journal of Science Fiction and Fantasy* 53.3 (2012): 307-26. Print.

Cates, Isaac. "Memory, Signal, and Noise in the Collaborations of Neil Gaiman and Dave McKean." *Drawing From Life*. Ed. Jane Tolmie. UP of Mississippi, 2013. 144-162. Print.

Coats, Karen. "Between Horror, Humour, and Hope: Neil Gaiman and the Psychic Work of the Gothic." *The Gothic in Children's Literature: Haunting the Borders*. Ed. Anna Jackson, Karen Coats, & Roderick McGillis. Routledge, 2008. 77-92. Print.

Collins, Meredith. "Fairy and Faerie: Uses of Victorian in Neil Gaiman's and Charles Vess's *Stardust*." *ImageTexT: Interdisciplinary Comics Studies* 4.1 (2008) Web. 8 Sept. 2016.

Croci, Daniele. "Watching (through) the *Watchmen*: Representation and Deconstruction of the Controlling Gaze in Neil Gaiman's *The Sandman*." *Altre Modernità* 11 (2014): 120-35. Print.

Curry, Alice. "'The Pale Trees Shook, although no Wind Blew, and it Seemed to Tristran that they Shook in Anger': 'Blind Space' and Ecofeminism in a Post-Colonial Reading of Neil Gaiman and Charles Vess's Graphic Novel *Stardust* (1998)." *Barnboken* 33.2 (2010): 19-33. Print.

Czarnowsky, Laura-Marie von. "'Power and all its Secrets': Engendering Magic in Neil Gaiman's *The Ocean at the End of the Lane*." *Fafnir: Nordic Journal of Science Fiction and Fantasy Research* 2.4 (2015): 18-28. Print.

Dalmaso, Renata. "When Superheroes Awaken: The Revisionist Trope in Neil Gaiman's *Marvel 1602*." *Feminism in the Worlds of Neil Gaiman*. Ed. Tara Prescott and Aaron Drucker. McFarland, 2012. 116-130. Print.

David, Danya. "Extraordinary Navigators: An Examination of Three Heroines in Neil Gaiman and Dave McKean's *Coraline, the Wolves in the Walls, MirrorMask*." *Looking Glass: New Perspectives on Children's Literature* 12.1 (2008) Print.

Dean, Tanya. "Piano Guts and Other Mothers: Staging Fantasy in David Greenspan and Stephin Merritt's Musical Adaptation of Neil Gaiman's *Coraline*." *Journal of the Fantastic in the Arts* 24.2 (2013): 264-74. Print.

Drucker, Aaron. "Empowering Voice and Refiguring Retribution: Neil Gaiman's Anti-Feminism Feminist Parable in *The Sandman*." *Feminism in the Worlds of Neil Gaiman*. Ed. Tara Prescott & Aaron Drucker. McFarland, 2012. 81-101. Print.

Evans, Timothy H. "Folklore, Intertextuality, and the Folkloresque in the Works of Neil Gaiman." *The Folkloresque: Reframing Folklore in a Popular Culture World.* Ed. Michael Dylan Foster & Jeffrey A. Tolbert. Utah State UP, 2016. 64-80. Print.

Fleming, James R. "Incommensurable Ontologies and the Return of the Witness in Neil Gaiman's *1602.*" *ImageTexT: Interdisciplinary Comics Studies* 4.1 (2008) Print.

Harris-Fain, Darren. "Putting the Graphic in Graphic Novel: P. Craig Russell's Adaptation of Neil Gaiman's *Coraline.*" *Studies in the Novel* 47.3 (2015): 335-45. Print.

Jahlmar, Joakim. "'Give the devil his due': Freedom, Damnation, and Milton's Paradise Lost in Neil Gaiman's *The Sandman: Season of Mists.*" *Partial Answers: Journal of Literature and the History of Ideas* 13.2 (2015): 267-86. Print.

Jones, Robert William, II. "At Home in the World Tree: A Somaesthetic Reading of the Body at Home in Neil Gaiman's *American Gods.*" *Open Library of Humanities* 1.1 (2015) Print.

Katsiadas, Nick. "Mytho-Auto-Bio: Neil Gaiman's *Sandman*, the Romantics and Shakespeare's 'The Tempest.'" *Studies in Comics* 6.1 (2015): 61-84. Print.

Klapcsik, Sá. "Neil Gaiman's Irony, Liminal Fantasies, and Fairy Tale Adaptations." *Hungarian Journal of English and American Studies* 14.2 (2008): 317-34. Print.

Klapcsik, Sandor. "The Double-Edged Nature of Neil Gaiman's Ironical Perspectives and Liminal Fantasies." *Journal of the Fantastic in the Arts* 20.2 (2009): 193-209.Print.

Kosiba, Sara. "'Flyover Country': Neil Gaiman's Extraordinary Perceptions of the Midwest." *Midwestern Miscellany* 38 (2010): 106-19. Print.

Lancaster, Kurt. "Neil Gaiman's 'A Midsummer Night's Dream': Shakespeare Integrated into Popular Culture." *Journal of American & Comparative Cultures* 23.3 (2000): 69-77. Print.

Llompart Pons, Auba. "Another Turn of the Screw: From Henry James's Gothic Children to Neil Gaiman's Children's Gothic." *Weaving New Perspectives Together: Some Reflections on Literary Studies.* Ed. María Alonso Alonso et al. Cambridge Scholars, 2012. 171-184. Print.

Mellette, Justin. "Serialization and Empire in Neil Gaiman's *The Sandman*." *Studies in the Novel* 47.3 (2015): 319-34. Print.

Miller, Monica. "What Neil Gaiman Teaches Us about Survival: *Making Good Art* and *Diving into the Ocean*." *Neil Gaiman in the 21st Century*. Ed. Tara Prescott. McFarland, 2015. 113-122. Print.

Noone, Kristin. "The Monsters and the Heroes: Neil Gaiman's *Beowulf*." *Weird Fiction Review* 1 (2010): 139-53. Print.

Parsons, Elizabeth, Naarah Sawers, & Kate McInally. "The Other Mother: Neil Gaiman's Postfeminist Fairytales." *Children's Literature Association Quarterly* 33.4 (2008): 371-89. Print.

Porter, Adam. "Neil Gaiman's *Lucifer*: Reconsidering Milton's Satan." *Journal of Religion and Popular Culture* 25.2 (2013): 175-85. Print.

Prescott, Tara. *Neil Gaiman in the 21st Century: Essays on the Novels, Children's Stories, Online Writings, Comics and Other Works*. McFarland, 2015. Print.

Reed, S. A. "Through Every Mirror in the World: Lacan's Mirror Stage as Mutual Reference in the Works of Neil Gaiman and Tori Amos." *ImageTexT: Interdisciplinary Comics Studies* 4.1 (2008) Web. 8 Sept. 2016.

Robertson, Christine. "'I Want to be Like You': Riffs on Kipling in Neil Gaiman's *The Graveyard Book*." *Children's Literature Association Quarterly* 36.2 (2011): 164-89. Print.

Romero Jódar, Andrés. "Paradisical Hells: Subversions of the Mythical Canon in Neil Gaiman's *Neverwhere*." *Cuadernos de Investigación Filológica* 31-32 (2005): 163-95. Print.

Round, Julia. "Transforming Shakespeare: Neil Gaiman and *The Sandman*." *Beyond Adaptation*. Ed. Phyllis Frus & Christy Williams. McFarland, 2010. 95-110. Print.

Rudd, David. "An Eye for an I: Neil Gaiman's *Coraline* and Questions of Identity." *Children's Literature in Education: An International Quarterly* 39.3 (2008): 159-68. Print.

Rusnak, Marcin. "Playing with Death: Humorous Treatment of Death-Related Issues in Terry Pratchett's and Neil Gaiman's Young Adult Fiction." *Fastitocalon: Studies in Fantasticism Ancient to Modern* 2.1-2 (2011): 81-95. Print.

Sanders, Joe. "Of Parents and Children and Dreams in Neil Gaiman's *Mr. Punch* and *The Sandman*." *Foundation: The International Review of Science Fiction* 71 (1997): 18-32.

⎯⎯⎯⎯. *The Sandman Papers*. Ed. Joe Sanders. Fantagraphics, 2006, Print.

⎯⎯⎯⎯. "Tidings of Discomfort and Joy: Neil Gaiman's 'Murder Mysteries'." *New York Review of Science Fiction* 20.11 (2008): 1-6. Print.

Slabbert, Mathilda. "Inventions and Transformations: Imagining New Worlds in the Stories of Neil Gaiman." *Fairy Tales Reimagined*. Ed. Susan Redington Bobby & Kate Bernheimer. McFarland, 2009. 68-83. Print.

Smith, Clay. "Get Gaiman? PolyMorpheus Perversity in Works by and about Neil Gaiman." *ImageTexT: Interdisciplinary Comics Studies* 4.1 (2008) Web. 8 Sept. 2016.

Sung, Eunai. "Neil Gaiman's *Stardust* and the Victorian Fantasy." *British and American Fiction* 20.1 (2013): 81-104. Print.

Tally, Robert T., Jr. "Lost in Grand Central: Dystopia and Transgression in Neil Gaiman's *American Gods*." *Blast, Corrupt, Dismantle, Erase: Contemporary North American Dystopian Literature*. Ed. Brett Josef Grubisic, Gisèle M. Baxter, & Tara Lee. Wilfrid Laurier UP, 2014. 357-371. Print.

Tiffin, Jessica. "Blood on the Snow: Inverting 'Snow White' in the Vampire Tales of Neil Gaiman and Tanith Lee." *Anti-Tales: The Uses of Disenchantment*. Ed. Catriona McAra & David Calvin. Cambridge Scholars, 2011. 220-230. Print.

Wearring, Andrew. "Changing, Out-of-Work, Dead, and Reborn Gods in the Fiction of Neil Gaiman." *Literature and Aesthetics: The Journal of the Sydney Society of Literature and Aesthetics* 19.2 (2009): 236-46. Print.

Wehler, Melissa. "'Be Wise. Be Brave. Be Tricky.': Neil Gaiman's Extraordinarily Ordinary *Coraline*." *A Quest of Her Own*. Ed. Lori M. Campbell. McFarland, 2014. 111-129. Print.

Wilkie-Stibbs, Christine. "Imaging Fear: Inside the Worlds of Neil Gaiman (an Anti-Oedipal Reading)." *The Lion and the Unicorn* 37.1 (2013): 37-53. Print.

About the Editor

Joseph Michael Sommers is a very fortunate dude. He is an Associate Professor of English at Central Michigan University where he teaches courses in children's and young adult literature as well as courses in modern and contemporary Anglophone literature, visual narratives, and popular culture. He publishes work on figures such as Judy Blume; Stan Lee; Robert Kirkman; and, not coincidentally, Neil Gaiman. And he is the husband of Sulynn and the father of Maggie and Gwendolyn, which is fortunate, as without the latter there would be no introduction to this book nor book itself because it never would have occurred to him to construct such a thing otherwise. As such, this book exists primarily due to those two blueberry girls.

Over the past several years, he (who is actually me, but propriety suggests I refer to myself in third person) has brought out academic essays on all manner of things, such as the culture of childhood in nineteenth-century lady's journalism; the maturation of Marvel Comics' characters in the post-9/11 moment; Hellboy amongst the Melungeon people; dialogism in Bradbury's *Fahrenheit 451*; and, of course, *Twilight*. More recently, he has brought out further work on Christopher Nolan's *The Dark Knight*, a revisionary examination of C. S. Lewis' *Narnia*, posthumanism in *The Walking Dead*, and several book-length collections, such as *Sexual Ideology in the Work of Alan Moore* (With Todd Comer), *Game on, Hollywood—Essays on the Intersection of Video Games and Cinema* (with Gretchen Papazian) (both McFarland Press, 2012 and 2013 respectively), *The American Comic Book* (Salem/ Grey House Press, 2014), and the forthcoming *Conversations with Neil Gaiman* (University Press of Mississippi). At present, he is working on new essays examining the intersection of scientific principles in the Marvel Universe, the construction of homegrown zines in *The Adventures of Captain Underpants*, the history of comics presses in America, and still more Neil Gaiman-related projects. He is, indeed, a very lucky, very blessed man, and for that, among many other things, he is very grateful.

Contributors

Kristin Bovaird-Abbo is an Associate Professor of English at the University of Northern Colorado, where she regularly teaches classes on Old English, Middle English, history of the English language, linguistics, the Arthurian Legend (medieval to modern), and medievalism. While her areas of special interest include medieval language and literature, particularly Middle English romance and ecocriticism, she enjoys the chance to explore the use of medieval tropes and themes in modern literature, particularly the works of J.R.R. Tolkien, George R.R. Martin, J.K. Rowling, and Neil Gaiman.

Jill Coste is a PhD candidate at the University of Florida, where she studies fairy tale revisions in contemporary young adult literature. She holds an MA in children's literature from San Diego State University.

Kyle Eveleth is a Ronald E. McNair Postbaccalaureate Fellow and doctoral candidate at the University of Kentucky, where he specializes in twentieth and twenty-first-century American literature, children's/young adult literature, and visual narrative. His dissertation examines the rise of youth culture and young adult literature in America in the early twentieth century. His recent publications have focused on Rutu Modan's *Exit Wounds* in *disClosure: A Journal of Social Theory*, on Alison Bechdel's *Fun Home* in *The South Central Review*, and on the Bronze Age of American superhero comics in *Critical Insights: The American Comic Book*. He is coeditor with Joseph Michael Sommers of the forthcoming collection, *The Comics Work of Neil Gaiman: In Darkness, In Light, and In Shadow*.

Krystal Howard is a doctoral candidate at Western Michigan University, where she teaches children's and young adult literature and writing. She is currently completing her dissertation project, "The Collage Effect and Participatory Reading in Contemporary Children's and Young Adult Literature," which was awarded a 2016–17 Dissertation Completion Fellowship from the Graduate College at Western Michigan University; her essay "The Verse Novel for Young Readers: College, Confession, and

Crisis in Jacqueline Woodson's *Brown Girl Dreaming*" was the winner of the 2016 ChLA PhD Level Graduate Student Essay Award. Her research interests include children's and young adult literature, comics studies, literary theory and criticism, and contemporary poetry; she has published scholarship on the history of the American comic book, gothic comics for young readers, and Neil Gaiman and Dave McKean's picture books. For more information, please visit www.krystalhoward.com.

Orion Ussner Kidder is a comics scholar and adjunct professor at Simon Fraser University. He has published several texts on metacomics by Alan Moore, Warren Ellis, and now Neil Gaiman, and he has been the reviewer for *Year's Work in English Studies*' "American Comics" chapter since 2013. He lives in Vancouver with his wife, their son, and their cat.

Kristin McIlhagga is a lecturer at Wayne State University, where she teaches courses in children's literature, language arts, and English methods. Her research focuses on intersections of children's literature studies across the disciplines of English, education, and library science. Her current work focuses on expanding the ways pre-service teachers conceptualize and enact the role of children's literature in PK-12 classrooms. She has presented her work at the annual conferences of the Children's Literature Association, Modern Languages Association, and National Council of Teachers of English. After completing her dissertation in 2016, she celebrated by getting her first tattoo: a Neil Gaiman quote.

Kelly J. Murphy is an Assistant Professor in the Department of Philosophy and Religion at Central Michigan University, where she teaches classes on the Hebrew Bible and the New Testament. She is the coeditor of a textbook entitled *Apocalypses in Context: Apocalyptic Currents Through History* (Fortress Press, 2016) and is the author of a forthcoming work on masculinity and the Book of Judges (Oxford University Press, 2017). She has also written for the *Fortress Commentary on the Bible: Old Testament and Apocrypha* and the *Women's Bible Commentary, Third Edition*, as well as for publications like *The Washington Post*, *Religion Dispatches*, and *Bible Odyssey*. She serves on the steering committees for the Society of Biblical Literature's Poverty in the Biblical World section and the Ideological Criticism section.

Laura Nicosia is an Associate Professor of English and has served as Director of English Education at Montclair State University for thirteen years. She teaches modern and contemporary American literature and young adult literature, pedagogical methods of teaching English, and educational uses of technology. She is Immediate-Past President of the New Jersey Council of Teachers of English and serves as State Representative to the Assembly on Literature of Adolescents. Along with numerous articles on American literature, she is the author of *Educators Online: Preparing Today's Educators for Tomorrow's Digital Literacies* (Peter Lang, 2013) and is coeditor of the forthcoming *Through a Distorted Lens: Media as Curricula and Pedagogy in the 21st Century*. Her most recent literary publication, "'Blood is not destiny, no matter what others may believe': Bacigalupi's *Ship Breaker* and Complications of the Monster" is included in *Frontiers in American Children's Literature* (Cambridge University Press, 2016).

Julie Perino is a PhD candidate and lecturer in the Department of English at the University of Kansas and studies composition and rhetoric. She has presented on gender representations in film at Northwestern's Queertopia 2.0 and 3.0 conferences, where she delivered papers entitled, "She has the Phallus; He is the Seductress: The Queered Crime World of *Rock N Rolla*" and "Gender and Genre: The More Things Change, the More They Stay the Same." Recently, she has turned her interest in film genres, gender portrayal, and film to adaptations of fairy tales and presented on these topics at the American Culture Association and Popular Culture Association's national joint conference.

Marlyn Thomas is an instructor in the Department of English at Alabama A&M University in Huntsville, Alabama. She teaches composition and humanities courses. Her research interests include spirituality and hybridization in young adult and postcolonial literature. She earned her MA at Kansas State University in children's literature and cultural studies in 2008.

Annette Wannamaker is a Professor of Children's Literature in the Children's Literature Program in the Department of English Language and Literature at Eastern Michigan University, where she teaches courses about illustrated texts, children's and adolescent media, criticism and theory of children's literature and culture, and young adult literature. She is the North American editor-in-chief of *Children's Literature in Education* and has edited several collections of academic essays. She is the author of *Boys in Children's Literature and Popular Culture: Masculinity, Abjection, and the Fictional Child* (Routledge 2008) and of various articles focused on literary and cultural studies. She is an active member of the Children's Literature Association and served as its president from 2015–2016.

Justin Wigard is a PhD candidate in English at Michigan State University, where he was awarded a University Distinguished Fellowship. His most recent academic work, "Harlequin, Nurse, Street Tough: The Visual Evolution from Non-Traditional Harlequin to Sexualized Villain to Subversive Antihero" examines the visual semiotics at play in the evolution of DC Comics' Harley Quinn's costumes as they shift from cartoon to video game to film in order to reveal how these costumes reflect changes in Harley's identity. Wigard wrote his contributions to this volume while listening to Leon Bridges' phenomenal album *Coming Home*, particularly the titular song. In the eighth grade, he sketched his best mental image of *Neverwhere*'s Beast of London and still considers it his best artwork to date.

Index

adaptation vii, xxxiii, 6, 9, 10, 12, 14, 47, 59, 61, 115
adult literature 3, 6, 67, 69, 70, 71, 72, 73, 233, 235, 236, 237, 238
advocacy ix, xiii, xix, xxv, 195, 196, 197, 202, 208
Alexander, William 74
Allan, Cherie 86
Ambrose, Tom 10
Amos, Tori ix, xxi, 30, 217, 230
Andersen, Hans Christian 115
Appelhaus, Christopher 11
Articulatus, Beryl 167
Atwood, Margaret 130
Avary, Roger 10, 223

Babylon 5 11, 215, 225
Bacchilega, Cristina 58, 130, 142
Baker, Tom 193
Bakewell, Gary 49, 63
Balder x, xi, 31, 32, 33, 34, 35, 36, 37, 38, 39, 41, 42, 43, 44, 45
Barker, Clive xxx, 220
Bartam, Jessica 51
Barthelme, Donald 130
Barthes, Roland 74
Bealer, Tracy L. 4
Beal, Timothy 181
Bechdel-Wallace test 48
Beckett, Sandra 72
Bender, Hy 5
Bennet, Hywell 53
Beowulf 10, 11, 15, 16, 216, 223, 230
Berger, Karen xxxi, 160, 214
Bible 162, 168, 236

Bildungsroman 18, 19, 21, 23, 24, 26, 27, 28, 29, 62
Bissette, Stephen R. xxxvi, 4, 16
Black Orchid xxxi, 214, 219, 227
Blake, William 52
Blaschke, Jayme Lynn 3, 16
Bloom, Harold 69
Bobby, Susan Redington 131, 231
Breaking the Fourth Wall 165, 172
bricolage 161
Brontë sisters 105
Brottman, Mikita 68
Brown, Paula 47
Buckley, Chloé Germaine 4
Burton, Tim 139
Byatt, A.S. 69
Byrne, Deirdre 58, 63

Cahill, Susan 59
Cain and Abel 124
Callen, Don 20
Campbell, Hayley 4
Capaldi, Peter 55, 63
Capettini, Emily 187
Carey, Mike 57
Carroll, Lewis xxix, xxxii, 78, 98, 213
Carter, Angela 130
Casanova, Giovanni Jacopo 171
Ceasar, Julius 8
children's literature 3, 4, 6, 14, 67, 70, 71, 72, 79, 81, 82, 86, 87, 93, 96, 235, 236, 237, 238
Christman, Bert 116
Cixous, Hélène 92
Clark, Beverly Lyon 68

239

Clarke, Arthur C. xxx
Clifford, Lucy xxxiii
Cluracan 120, 121, 122, 127
Coats, Karen 83, 84, 132, 144, 228
Coleridge, Samuel Taylor 146
collaboration xi, xii, xxxi, 14, 90, 114, 124
collage xi, 81, 82, 83, 84, 85, 86, 87, 89, 90, 91, 93
Collins, Suzanne 73
comic book viii, xiv, xxx, xxxi, xxxii, 6, 8, 73, 76, 113, 119, 125, 126, 156, 180, 214, 236
Comic Book Legal Defense xxxii, xxxv
Coover, Robert 130
Coulais, Bruno 11
Cran, Rona 81, 82
Crow, Samantha Black 34

Dalmaso, Renata Lucena 83
Dandy, Jack 25
Danes, Claire 59, 63
Darvill, Arthur 180, 193, 194
David, Danya 91
daydreaming 80, 207, 209
DC Comics xxxi, 5, 17, 62, 157, 160, 214, 238
Dean, Larry 116
Delaney, Samuel R. 3
Dery, Mark 73
dialogism 233
Díaz, Junot 13
Dobbs, Wesley 116
Doctor Who ix, xiii, 4, 7, 11, 178, 179, 180, 181, 185, 186, 191, 192, 193, 194, 217, 225

Doll's House, The 4, 151, 153, 155, 220
Donoghue, Emma 130
Drucker, Aaron 4, 110, 131, 144, 193, 194, 227, 228
dual address 71
Duncan, Glen 180
Duran Duran vii, xxx, 213, 223

Ebert, Roger 10
Eisner Awards 7, 215
Eklund, Tof 4, 16, 19, 30
Eliot, T. S. 8
empathy xviii, xxiv, xxv, 196, 197, 199, 200, 201, 202, 203, 208

Fabry, Glenn 57, 62
fairy tales 47, 48, 58, 60, 61, 77, 83, 88, 89, 91, 96, 114, 129, 130, 131, 132, 133, 138, 142, 143, 162, 237
Falconer, Rachel 72
fantasy viii, xv, xx, xxi, xxix, xxxiii, 3, 8, 9, 14, 47, 48, 58, 67, 73, 129, 133, 140, 164
feminist revisions xii, 47, 48, 54, 59, 60, 92, 129, 130, 131, 134, 136, 137, 138
Fetisher, Sam 38
Flessel, Creig 116
folk tales 61, 69, 72
Foucault, Michel 122
Fox, Gardner 116
frame/frame breaks 8, 49, 50, 51, 54, 58, 76, 85, 119, 148, 149, 151, 159
Fraser, Laura 51, 63
Freud, Sigmund 29, 186, 189

Gaiman, Claire xxix
Gaiman, David Bernard xxix, 213
Gaiman, Holly xxx
Gaiman, Lizzy xxix
Gaiman, Maddie xxxiii
Gaiman, Michael xxxiii
Gaiman, Neil xxxii, xxxiv
Gaiman, Sheila xxix
Genette, Gerard 161
Gilbert, Sandra M. 52
Gillan, Karen 180
Golden, Christopher xxxvi, 4, 16
Gooding, Richard 99
Gorey, Edward 139
gothic xii, xxxiii, 12, 129, 130, 131, 132, 133, 135, 136, 137, 138, 139, 140, 141, 142, 143, 236
Graham, Ruth 70
graphic novels xii, 3, 57, 96
Green, John 73
Green, Roger Lancelyn 31
Grimm brothers 133
Grimm, Jacob 88
Grimm, Wilhelm 88, 94
Groensteen, Thierry 112
Gubar, Susan 52, 62

Habermas, Jürgen xviii
Hannabuss, Stuart 77
Hatfield, Charles 148
Hauser, Gerard xviii
healing space 103, 107, 109
Hempstock, Ginnie 107, 109
Hemstock, Lettie 78
Hoffman, E. T. A. 115
Hogle, Jerrold 132
Horton, Susan 116
Howlett, Georgina 70

Hugo Awards 7, 215
Hume, Kathryn 8
Humphreys, Dewi 49
Hutcheon, Linda 86, 146, 147

iconic solidarity 112, 113, 118, 126
identity 18, 19, 22, 23, 31, 52, 56, 78, 81, 92, 106, 109, 116, 117, 133, 136, 156, 187, 198, 238
imagination 83, 125, 152, 156, 201, 207
Inge, M. Thomas 146
intertextuality 81, 82, 83, 86, 87, 89, 90, 91, 113
ironic authentication 148, 158, 159

Jackson, Anna 132, 144, 228
Jones, Matthew T. 146
Jones, Terry xxx
Joosen, Vanessa 87
Joseph, Paterson 55
journalism vii, xx, xxx, 13, 17, 233
Joyce, Lindsey 12
Jungle Book, The x, xxxiii, 17, 22

Kahane, Claire 136, 144
Keynes, Milton 173
Kidd, Kenneth 29
kidnapping 99, 105
King, Stephen 13, 127, 200
Kipling, Rudyard x, xxxiii, 17
Kirby, Jack 117
Klapcsik, Sándor 47, 134, 164
Klaw, Rick 3
Kotzer, Zack 12

Krstovic, Jelena 4, 176
Kwitney, Alisa 5

Lacan, Jacques x, 19, 35, 46
Landis, Courtney 105
Law, Elizabeth 134
Lewis, C. S. viii, xxix, 213, 233
Loki/Low Key Lyesmith 31, 34, 41
Lukøje, Ole 115, 127
Luria, Rachel 4, 227
Lüthi, Daniel 161

magic xxi, xxiv, xxv, xxix, 25, 44, 69, 77, 121, 122, 130, 141
Magritte, Réné 150
Maloney, Edward 167
Manilow, Barry xxx
Marmur, Elizabeth 50
Martin, Dan 192
Martin, George R. R. xxiv
Martin, Rachel 106
mature readers 76
Mayhew, Richard 9, 49
McEvoy, Emma 133, 145
McGillis, Roderick 132, 144, 228
McGrath, Mary xxx, xxxiii, 213, 214, 215, 216
McKean, Dave xi, xxx, 9, 80, 81, 83, 84, 94, 125, 160, 214, 215, 219, 220, 221, 222, 223, 224, 228, 236
media theory viii, ix, x, xi, xix, xxxiv, 3, 14, 48, 50, 72, 82, 83, 118, 120, 124, 195, 196, 209, 238
Melville, Herman 69
Mercury, Freddy 164

metafiction xii, 146, 147, 148, 149, 150, 151, 153, 154, 156, 157, 158, 168
metaphysical empowerment 60
metatextual 112, 152
metonymy 17, 19, 20, 21, 22, 27, 29
Meyer, Stephenie 73
Michaelides, Frixos 83, 94
Michals, Teresa 68
Miller, Monica 105
Milliard, Kenneth 28
MirrorMask 7, 9, 94, 109, 110, 216, 223, 224, 228
Mitchell, W. J. T. 146, 147, 149
Mitts-Smith, Debra 87
Miyazaki, Hayao 9
Moby-Dick 69
Moffat, Steven 180, 193, 194
Monkton, Ursula 101
monster 179, 183, 184, 185, 187, 189, 192
Moore, Alan 8, 213, 214, 222, 233, 236
Morpheus xiv, xv, 112, 115, 117, 118, 119, 120, 123, 146, 151, 152, 153, 155, 156, 157, 158
mothers 52, 140
multistable images 149, 150

narratology 161
Nebula Awards 7
Neverwhere xi, 9, 47, 48, 49, 50, 52, 53, 55, 56, 57, 58, 61, 62, 63, 215, 223, 225, 227, 230, 238
Newbery Medal xxiii, xxvi, xxviii, 6

Newman, Kim xx, 213, 225
Nikolajeva, Maria 109, 114
Norse myth 34

objectification 49, 56, 57, 58, 59
obligation 3, 5, 7, 9, 11, 13, 15, 78, 79, 142, 196, 206, 207, 208
Odin/Mr. Wednesday xxxii, 31, 32, 33, 34, 38, 39, 41
Oswald, Clara 193
Other Mother xxxiii, 19, 30, 75, 97, 98, 99, 100, 102, 103, 104, 105, 106, 107, 108, 109, 110, 230
Otto, Rudolph 182

Palmer, Amanda ix, xxxiv, xxxvi, 217, 218, 224
Panaou, Petros 83
Pantaleo, Sylvia 81, 94
paratexts 161, 162, 168, 169
parody 47, 162
Parsons, Elizabeth 97, 109
participation 82, 86, 90, 93, 163
Pascoe, Jim 112
patriarchy 98, 99, 100, 101, 107, 131
Perrault, Charles 87, 114, 137
picture book xxxiii, 67, 71, 75, 76
poetic skepticism 147, 148, 151, 159
Poisson, Reinette 178
Polunochnaya, Zorya 37, 40, 41, 42, 43
polyphony xii, 112, 113, 115, 117, 119, 121, 123, 125, 127
polyvocality 161, 175
Pond, Amy 180

Poole, W. Scott 179
Poppins, Mary 8
postmodernism 89, 146
Potter, Harry 69, 72, 73, 79
Potter, Mary-Anne 58
Pratchett, Terry xii, xxxi, xxxv, 7, 17, 124, 161, 175, 176, 214, 223, 230
Prescott, Tara 4, 94, 110, 131, 144, 193, 227, 228, 230
Prigmore, Shane 11
prisons 195, 198, 199
psychoanalysis x, 19, 29
Public Sphere Theory xviii, xix
Pullman, Philip 73

rack focus 50
radical metafiction 151, 153, 154, 157, 158
Ragnarok xi, 31, 32, 33, 34, 37, 39, 40, 41, 42, 45
Rauch, Steven 5
Reading Agency Lecture, The xiii, xx, 195, 196, 209
reflexive/self-reflexive xii, 17, 18, 19, 20, 23, 147, 157, 159
remediation xi, 47, 49, 62
Reynolds, Kimberly 83
rhetorical analysis xx, 196
Riddell, Chris 139, 144, 224
Room of One's Own, A 97, 111
Rose, Briar 114, 141, 142
Rowling, J.K. 73, 235
Russell, Clive 53
Russell, Danielle 109
Russell, P. Craig xxxiii, 4, 6, 125, 221, 222, 229

Saklofske, Jon 20

Sanders, Joe 5, 231
Sandifer, Philip 4, 19
Sandman, The vii, xii, xiv, xv, xxviii, xxxi, xxxiii, xxxiv, 3, 4, 5, 6, 7, 8, 9, 14, 17, 19, 29, 112, 113, 115, 116, 117, 118, 119, 120, 121, 122, 123, 124, 126, 127, 146, 148, 149, 150, 154, 156, 157, 158, 159, 180, 214, 215, 216, 217, 219, 220, 222, 228, 229, 230, 231
Sanford, Garrett 117
satire 162
Schuster, Joe 116
Scieszka, Jon 83
Scott, Carole 114, 128
self-reflexivity xxv, 21
Selick, Henry 10
Sendak, Maurice 75, 96
Sexton, Anne 130
Shakespeare, Judith 97, 98
Shakespeare, William 8, 98
Shelley, Mary 132
Siegel, Jerry 116
signifier/signified 23, 24
Silverberg, Bob xxx
Simon, Joe 117
Sipe, Lawrence R. 81, 94
Slabbert, Mathilda 134
Sleeping Beauty xxii, 71, 92, 95, 114, 129, 133, 137, 139, 140, 141, 142
Smith, Clay 20
Smith, Lane 83, 95
Smith, Matt 180, 193, 194
solicitude 97, 105, 106, 107, 108, 109
Spiegelman, Art 96

Spooner, Catherine 133
Staczynski, J. Michael 11
Stardust xi, 7, 10, 17, 29, 47, 48, 49, 55, 56, 58, 59, 60, 61, 62, 63, 109, 216, 221, 223, 228, 231
stepmother 50, 52, 129, 130, 131, 133, 135, 137, 139, 140, 141, 143
Stine, R. L. 200
Stoker, Bram 7, 8, 132, 179, 216
structuralism 146
structural metafiction 153
Sweeney, Mad 34, 40

talking pictures 149, 150
TARDIS 11, 178, 181, 183, 185, 186, 187, 188, 189, 190, 191, 192
Thom, Randy 11
Thorne, Tristran 58
Time Lord 178, 180, 181, 182, 187, 190, 191
Tindle, Shannon 11
Tolkien, J. R. R. viii, xxix, 213
Travers, Peter 10
Trites, Roberta S. 92
Tyler, Rose 178

Uesugi, Tadahiro 11

vampire 25
Van Gogh, Vincent 109
Vaughn, Matthew 10, 59, 63
Vechernyaya, Zorya 34, 37, 41
vertigo 182, 183
Vess, Charles xx, 62, 127, 217, 221, 224, 225, 228

View from the Cheap Seats, The vii, xxviii, xxxvi, 13, 194, 197, 218, 223
Von Czarnowsky, Laura-Marie 97

Wagner, Hank 4
Walker, Rose 151
Walpole, Horace 132
Waugh, Patricia 146, 147
Weisinger, Mort 116
Wilkie-Stibbs, Christine 83
Williams, Christy 54, 230
Williams, Rory 180
William, William Carlos vii
Winnicott, Donald 23

Wolf narrative 82, 87, 89
Wolfram, Eddie 81
Wolves in the Walls, The xi, 81, 82, 83, 84, 86, 87, 89, 90, 92, 93, 94, 216, 222, 223, 228
Woolf, Virginia xii, 97, 98, 108

Yuen, Wayne 4, 227

Zemeckis, Robert 10
Zipes, Jack 83
Zulli, Michael 127, 158, 220, 221, 222